RETURN FROM THE ABYSS

DONALD E. FINK

Print information available on the last page.

Rev. date: 05/30/2015

To order additional copies of this book, contact:
Xlibris
1-888-795-4274
www.Xlibris.com
Orders@Xlibris.com
705582

Dedication

To Carolyn for her love, devoted support, and excellent proof reading; to pilot friend Tom Robbins, for a thorough beta read and suggestions that improved the final manuscript; to Keith Ferris for permission to use his famous painting, *Little Willie Coming Home*, on the cover; to Bob McAuley for his World War 2 aircraft drawings, and to Mark for his excellent work in designing the cover.

Also by the Author:

Escape to the Sky, Xlibris, 2012

Battle not with monsters, lest ye become a monster, and if you gaze into the abyss, the abyss gazes also into you.

—*Friedrich Nietzsche*

Chapter 1

LUCK RUNS OUT — APRIL 1, 1944

Wind whipped across Ben Findlay's face. Flying! He was flying again in the Yellow Peril, ol' Brice's open-cockpit Stearman trainer. What the . . . ? Wait! Was he hanging his head too far out into the slipstream? Ben shook his head, blinked rapidly, and tried to clear his vision. His mind whirled.

Must be in a bad sideslip. Maybe a spin? Hey! *What the . . . ? Gettin' too big a face full of slipstream and prop wash. Am I in a spin? Whoa! What the hell? Way too much wind! What's happenin'?"*

"No! Falling!" he shouted. "Falling?"

Ben fell, arms and legs flailing like a rag doll in a tornado. Why was he *falling*? How long had he been falling? Where from? Air rushed into his mouth and nose, cutting off his breath. His cheeks puffed open, baring his teeth in a ghoulish grimace.

Boeing Pt-17 Stearman Trainer

He gasped. *S'posed to do something . . . What? Parachute? . . . Damn it, did I bail out? Should be in a parachute . . . Yeah! Parachute. Ripcord. Find the damn ripcord!*

He clutched his right arm to his chest. His fingers grasped the chest strap of his parachute harness. He clawed to the left.

D-ring . . . Got it!

He jerked the D-ring, snaking out the parachute release wire with it. *Pop!* The drogue chute opened, streaming folded silk out of his parachute pack. *Boom!* The main chute blossomed full of air and snatched Ben upright. His chin smacked to his chest as the harness leg straps bit into his crotch. His left arm flopped at his side. Ben's ears rang. Shock waves pummeled his body. Thunderous explosions shattered the air. Rapid-fire blasts beat against him as he dangled below his parachute canopy. Heavy cannons belched flames and smoke into the sky around him.

Why can't I open my left eye?

He raised his right hand to his face. The left side felt funny. Like what? Crusty! He touched the leather helmet and goggles he always wore on bombing runs. The helmet was twisted halfway off his head. He couldn't shift it.

What the hell? Feels like it's melted!

He peeled back the helmet and pried open his left eyelid. Everything appeared fuzzy, but he saw he was dropping toward a circle of large antiaircraft guns blasting shells into the sky.

Damn! I'm over a flak nest!

He reached for the parachute riser cords to steer away from the cannons, but he couldn't raise his left arm. As he approached the ground, a wind gust snatched his parachute, pushing him toward a small hill.

"Ground!" he shouted. "Damn it! Gonna hit hard! Can't get the hang of parachuting."

Ben's mind flashed back to his hard landing in 1940 when he bailed out of his flaming Spitfire while flying for the Royal Air Force in the Battle of Britain. That landing had been a bitch and banged him up badly. He tensed for landing as he slammed awkwardly onto the earth. He heard something snap as breath whooshed from his lungs. He slipped over the abyss into the void of unconsciousness. His white parachute fluttered into a snowdrift around him.

USAAF Major Benjamin A. Findlay sprawled on a muddy hillside thirty miles west of Regensburg, Germany. He and nearly two thousand of his fellow airmen from the U.S. Army Air Forces Eighth

Air Force Heavy Bombardment Command had just rained tons of bombs on the Messerschmitt airplane factory near Regensburg. Fierce antiaircraft flak blocked their escape route. Thick ugly clouds of it blackened the sky around his B-17 Flying Fortress bomber *Round Trip* spitting flame and white-hot shrapnel into their path.

Germany's standard antiaircraft weapon was an 88 mm cannon produced by the Krupp heavy industrial group and refined by Rheinmetall into the "eighty-eight Flak gun." Flak was an English abbreviation derived from the German word *Flugzeugabwehrkanon*. Germany deployed the gun in various antitank and antiaircraft versions, and it was feared by opposing armies because of its large caliber shell, high muzzle velocity, and accuracy.

Round Trip had carried Ben, the aircraft commander, and his nine crewmembers home safely from twenty-nine missions against targets across occupied Europe and Germany. Their luck ran out on this mission, their thirtieth, the one that would have completed their combat tour and earned them their tickets home.

Darkness enfolded Ben, but he jarred awake as concussions from the nearby antiaircraft guns shook the ground and pounded his body. He sat up, screamed as pain shot through his left arm and ribs, and flopped back into the dirt. He stared blankly into the smoke-filled sky.

Where the hell am I? How'd I get here, wherever here is?

Gradually his mind cleared, replaying the brilliant flash that had blinded him as he wrestled his B-17 through the flak-infested sky beyond Regensburg. But he couldn't remember what happened then—couldn't organize his thoughts. Ben twisted his head and squinted at several figures running toward him. He strained to focus his eyes and clear his mind.

Shit! Here come more of those damn Brit farmers. Gotta explain again that I'm not a German before they shove another shotgun in my face!

But the men who surrounded Ben this time were not Yorkshire farmers like those who had mistaken him for a German pilot when he bailed out of his Spitfire during the Battle of Britain in 1940. These men wore the field gray uniform of the German Wehrmacht. And what they pointed at Ben were not pitchforks and an ancient blunderbuss shotgun. They pointed Mauser Kar98k German infantry rifles with fixed bayonets. One jabbed his bayonet at Ben's face and yelled, "Achtung! Schwein hund! Bleib unten oder ich werde dich wie eine Wurst aufzuspießen!"

Ben didn't speak German, but he understood the bayonet jab and thought he heard the soldier call him a swine hound and say something about, what, a Wurst . . . a sausage? Curious. He shrank back. His mind began to clear.

Oh yeah, I was flyin' Round Trip. *Everything exploded in my face. Must have taken a direct hit from one of these antiaircraft guns. What happened then?*

An 88 mm shell had exploded under *Round Trip*'s nose with sufficient force to rip open the fuselage. The seconds after *Round Trip* was hit unwound in Ben's mind like a slow-motion movie. He remembered being knocked backward out of his seat. Did his safety harness break? He had tumbled out of the raised flight deck and landed on someone—Sergeant Anderson, his engineer? Ben remembered snapping his parachute harness and . . . *flames!* Everything was on fire.

Boeing B-17F Bomber

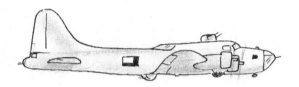

With a grinding shriek, *Round Trip*'s shattered fuselage ripped apart, spitting out Ben like a wad of used chewing gum. Then blackness until he regained consciousness as he hurtled toward the earth and pulled the ripcord. An image of Brice, Ben's old crusty flight instructor back in Michigan flashed into his mind. Ben shook his head. "Oh hell! Brice, I'm in a fix now," he moaned.

His captors continued to shout commands Ben couldn't understand. His mind whirled. He felt giddy and slumped backward. As he again slipped over the abyss into darkness, he chuckled.

Violated a basic rule of air combat, Brice. "Never bail out over a place you just bombed . . ."

But Ben hadn't bailed out. He had been blown clear of his disintegrating bomber at an altitude of twenty thousand feet. He fell thousands of feet before he came to and pulled the ripcord on his parachute. His long free fall had been fortuitous. If he had pulled the ripcord immediately, he would have been exposed to extreme cold and probably suffered from hypoxia while floating through the rarified upper atmosphere. He had landed safely but almost on top of the German gunners who had shot him down.

Ben Findlay's air war was over.

Chapter 2

GERMAN HOSPITAL — 1944

Ben writhed in fevered delirium. His hospital bed sheets tangled into sweat-soaked knots. His German nurse watched with concern, waiting for him to regain consciousness. It had been three days since a stretcher crew carried him in, his tattered uniform singed and bloody. She wondered if he would ever wake again. She didn't like the men who visited him and plied him with questions, but one did not argue with the Gestapo.

While seemingly comatose, Ben's subconscious mind raced. At times, he was talking to someone—several people, it seemed. Who were they? He couldn't see them clearly, thought he was talking, but not sure. He seemed to be telling his whole life story, starting with doing chores on his Michigan farm, hand milking his cows, and squirting milk into the open mouths of the barn cats lined up behind the cows. What brought that to mind?

Then he was sitting on the platform of the farm's windmill, straining to see over the horizon. Suddenly, the round grizzled face of his flight instructor Brice loomed over him, yelling at him to relax and "stop stranglin' the goddamn stick!" Ben reached out to embrace his old mentor and great friend but managed only to twist the sheets into more knots.

His mind flashed images of flying Brice's Stearman bi-plane, his struggling to master overhead circling approaches, and wheel landings. Then he recalled his meeting with Frank Silverman, who was recruiting pilots to fly for the Republican air force in Spain's civil war, training with Silverman, and a group of young pilots. Whom was he telling this to?

In another fevered moment, it was late 1937. He traveled to Barcelona with eleven other American pilots and Silverman on the way to fly Russian Polikarpov I-16 fighters for the Republicans in Spain's bloody civil war. He shuddered as his brain replayed his first aerial kill flying his stubby Russian-made open cockpit fighter. He had lost control while maneuvering to avoid an attacking German Condor Legion Bf 109 fighter, and the confused German pilot had overshot Ben as he floundered around the sky. He ended up sliding ahead of Ben, giving him an easy shot.

Polikarpov I-16 Fighter

Reggie! Where was Reggie, his British flight leader, also flying as a volunteer pilot with the same Russian Squadron? How about Ted, his closest buddy in Spain who flew with a companion Russian Squadron? Ted! Where was Ted? Then the image of Ted being strafed in his parachute swarmed into Ben's mind, causing him to writhe in anger and sorrow. They flew the Russian fighters that Soviet leader Stalin shipped to Spain to counter the fighter and bomber units that Nazi Germany and Fascist Italy sent to support the Nationalist rebels in the civil war. Ben and Reggie were the only non-Russian pilots flying as volunteers in Russian Squadron 27. Ted had been assigned to Squadron 26.

Ben slid back into darkness. Then in a mind-bending swirl, he was talking again. Was he answering more questions? He escaped to England after the defeat of the Spanish Republic in early 1939. He followed Reggie, whose father, an official in the British Air Ministry, helped them enlist in the Royal Air Force on the eve of World War 2. This led to images of flying Spitfires as Reggie's wingman in the Battle of Britain.

Ben tottered along the fringes of consciousness. His overwrought brain continued to grapple with questions someone kept asking. They led him through the early years of the air war over England and to the critical decision he made after America entered the war. Determined to carry the war to Germany's homeland, Ben transferred to the U.S. Army Air Forces and opted to fly Boeing B-17 heavy bombers. After witnessing what Luftwaffe bombers did in Spain and England, Ben vowed to wreak what havoc he could on Germany. He returned to the United States, retrained as a bomber pilot, and joined the 509th Heavy Bombardment Group, flying *Round Trip*, his faithful B-17G. He and his crew returned to England. Someone asked how many B-17 groups were based in England. He didn't know for sure, but probably shouldn't say anyway, he cautioned. They also wanted to know about the Norden bombsight, but Ben didn't know many of the details. Whit, his bombardier, was the fella to ask about that.

Then they asked about D-Day. When was the invasion scheduled and where? Why were they asking him that? He had no idea when or where.

Finally, Ben was flying his thirtieth mission, the last in his combat tour. They had just bombed Regensburg, Germany. As they turned for home, a blinding flash and an explosion consumed his airplane.

He came full circle. *Round Trip* blew up in his face, and he tumbled out. He finally got his parachute open and nearly landed on the antiaircraft battery that had shot him down. His mind whirled.

Where are the fellas I've been tellin' this to? Who the hell are they?

Chapter 3

PRISONER OF WAR

Pain surged through Ben's body, jarring him awake. He groaned, twisted his head to look around.

"Where am I?" he muttered.

Something covered the left side of his face: bandages. His head was wrapped in bandages. He tried to raise his left arm but couldn't move it. Reaching across with his right hand, he felt a thick plaster cast encasing his left arm from his knuckles to over his shoulder. He took stock of his ravaged body, wriggled his toes, and moved his feet. So far, okay. He moved his legs. Both worked. He knew he could move his right arm. How about trying to sit up?

"Sheeit!" he screamed as lightning bolts of pain shot through his left side.

What the hell have I done? Feels like half my ribs are broken.

His scream brought a female figure hurrying to his side. She wore a flowing black gown. Her head was topped with a large white winged hat that reminded Ben of the smoke funnel he had seen in a picture of an Italian cruise ship. A cherubic face encased in a starched white oval that puffed out ample red cheeks loomed over him. Ben realized he must be in a civilian hospital, but he assumed that German soldiers guarded all doors.

"Sie summonded mein, herr?" she asked quietly. "You summoned, sir?"

"Pain!" Ben gasped. "In pain. Got any morphine?"

"Ach, so. You speak English. An Englander."

"I'm American!" Ben grunted, nearly adding that he was from Michigan. He remembered saying that to the Yorkshire farmers nearly four years ago when they threatened to shoot him because they thought he was a German Luftwaffe pilot. They thought he said "Mitchigan," which convinced them he was from somewhere in Germany.

"Why the hell did I say that? Won't make that mistake again," he mumbled. "God, what a mix up that was."

He writhed in pain and gritted his teeth. The nurse swept off to find his doctor.

"Hey, fella," a voice cut through his pain. "You awake? Can we talk?"

Ben twisted carefully and peered at a man lying in the next bed. His left leg, encased in bandages or a cast, was suspended on a rope and pulley rig. He grinned and flipped Ben a salute.

"Uh yeah, I guess I'm awake," Ben grunted. "Mind's a little fuzzy. Not sure . . . Who're you?"

"Anderson, Lieutenant Charlie P.," he said. "B-24 driver 'til we got blasted outta the sky over Regensburg."

"Me too," Ben said. "I mean, blasted outta the sky over Regensburg. Is that where this hospital is?"

"Yeah. Beautiful downtown Regensburg," Anderson said. "But I think we'll be hauled outta here to a POW camp as soon as the docs say we're okay to travel."

"Where'd you come from in a B-24?" Ben asked.

"Not supposed to say, are we?" Anderson responded.

"Yeah, of course. Oh, I'm Findlay. Major Ben Findlay. I lead a B-17 unit. Umm, guess we gotta be careful about saying what we flew or where we came from, eh?"

"Yeah, really. Ya know, name, rank, serial number, and that's it," Anderson said. "But I know all about you. You been blabbing your head off to the Germans . . . like talkin' in your sleep. You gotta watch that."

"Talking in my sleep?" Ben asked.

"Yeah, there's been a couple of German officers in to see you regular like. Gestapo, I think. They put screens around your bed and talked softly, but I could hear most of what they were saying to you and each other. I'm from Milwaukee. Speak pretty good German. The bastards really pressed ya."

Ben groaned. "Omigod, did I reveal any secrets?"

"Not sure, but I think so. They worked you pretty hard. I think they kept you pumped fulla drugs. Not much ya could do, I guess, but ya need to be careful.

"And I heard 'em talking among themselves," Anderson added. "They said they were gonna work you a bit more. They haven't even told the Red Cross that you're a prisoner."

Their conversation was cut short when the nurse returned with a syringe of morphine. She injected it into Ben's right arm, and he slipped back into the black abyss.

Ben recovered slowly. His fractured shoulder and ribs knitted, but the burns on the left side of his face festered with infection. He slept a lot and wasn't sure whether the men who questioned him in his dreams had returned. Was it a dream, or had Anderson been right? Had he really been blabbing his head off to the Germans? And where was Anderson? Did he remember seeing them wheel him out in a wheelchair? The new fella in the next bed looked like a mummy wrapped in thick bandages. Ben couldn't even tell whether he was breathing.

As Ben's physical condition improved, his mental condition deteriorated. He tossed in his bed and sank into deep depression. Getting up the first time and looking at himself in the bathroom mirror didn't help.

"Who the hell are you?" he said to the haggard face that stared back at him. His crew cut had grown long and shaggy and the fresh-faced kid with the winning grin was gone, replaced by a sunken-eyed older fella with an ugly burn scar on the left side of his face.

"You also look crooked," Ben muttered. "Have to work at squaring my shoulders soon as my bones are healed." He straightened his once-six-foot frame, grunted in pain, and shuffled back to bed.

Ben lay on his back and stared at the ceiling, remembering his time in the hospital in Cambridge, England. A Luftwaffe 109 fighter had screamed out of the sun and blasted his RAF Spitfire, forcing him to bail out. He awoke in the hospital. "Gwen! Ah, sweet Gwen." He sighed, staring at the ceiling. "She nursed my wounds but stole my heart."

Gwen was a member of the Women's Auxiliary Air Force Nursing Corps, and Ben had gone to see her after his recuperation leave, and their friendship blossomed into love.

But the ugliness of war intervened. Gwen had been injured when an errant German bomb struck her house, wounding her and killing her mother. Then the Royal Navy informed Gwen that her husband, listed as dead after his ship had been sunk, was alive and in a German POW camp. A sob welled up Ben's throat when he recalled parting with Gwen at the railway station, seeing her off to stay with her aunt while recovering.

Unable to bear the memory of their parting, Ben pushed Gwen to the back of his mind. "Gotta think about somethin' else," he moaned. He began mentally replaying the final mission over Regensburg.

Damn it! Should've known we'd be jinxed bein' stuck with that poor sap Starkey as a substitute copilot. But what could I do? Gordy wasn't fit to fly. I should've insisted on the best copilot outta the reserve pool.

He rubbed his face with his right hand.

Ah hell, can't put the blame on Starkey. He didn't know what was going on. I'm the one who screwed up. Having Anderson's lead group blasted outta the sky in front of us put us in the soup from the beginning. But we regrouped and hit the target. An', an' I should've seen the flak patterns on the way out. If only I had called for a left turn instead of a right. Might have flown outta that flak trap.

Ben rolled onto his right side and pulled up his knees. Lying here, stewing about what could have been wasn't doing any good. It was done. Now he had to make the best of a bad situation.

The local Gestapo Kommandant pressured Ben's doctor, with the unlikely name of Wolfgang Bayerhoff, to release him for transfer to a prisoner-of-war camp for enemy flyers. Dr. Bayerhoff refused to release Ben despite the risk of defying the Gestapo. He wanted to be certain Ben's infected burns were fully healed before releasing him.

Chapter 4

THE GESTAPO

A Gestapo officer flanked by two enlisted soldiers marched up to Ben's bed as he lay on top of the covers dressed in his cleaned and crudely repaired uniform. "Achtung! Holen Sie sich bi's und komm mit uns!" the officer commanded. Ben understood that they had come for him.

"Here we go," he muttered as he stood and faced the trio. *Guess Doc Bayerhoff's finally been overruled. Wonder where they're takin' me?*

One of the soldiers grabbed Ben's wrists, twisted his arms behind his back, and snapped on handcuffs. Ben cursed as pain flashed through his recently healed shoulder. Bastard!

"Easy on the shoulder, Schultz," Ben snapped. "Don't want you breaking it again." This earned him a vicious twist of the arm that forced a grimace and caused his knees to buckle. "Okay, Schultz, made your point," he grunted.

"Mein name ist Braun," the soldier snarled in Ben's ear. He twisted Ben's arm again.

"Okay, Schultz, whatever you say, Schultz," Ben sneered. The soldier reached to give Ben's arm another twist, but the officer stopped him with a curt command.

"You vill do better to mit us cooperate," the officer said to Ben. "Insolence vill only in trouble get you."

"So you speak English," Ben muttered. "That'll make it easier."

They marched Ben out of the hospital and shoved him into the rear seat of a waiting car. The two soldiers jammed in on each side of him and the officer slid into the front passenger seat.

"Goin' for a ride in the country?" Ben asked. He winced as "Schultz" jabbed him in the ribs.

Ouch! I deserved that. But I'm damned if I'm gonna cooperate with these bastards. 'Bout all I can do is make fun of 'em. But maybe that ain't the smartest thing to do, Benjamin.

"Save your humor, Major Findlay," the officer snapped over his shoulder. "You vill later need it."

The staff car wound through Regensburg. Skeletons of bombed-out buildings lined its streets, looming like sightless prehistoric monsters. Huge mounds of bricks, shattered glass, and broken beams lay around them. A musty stench of death hung in the air. Ben peered through the smoky haze that cloaked the city like a dust-laden veil.

Looks like we hit more than Herr Messerschmitt's airplane factory. Wonder if the RAF Bomber Command fellas did a lot of this with their night raids? Hope the bombs we aimed at the factory were more on target.

The staff car slid to a stop in front of a pockmarked building surrounded by thick walls of sandbags. As they marched him inside, Ben caught the word "Gestapo" on a brass plate next to the door. They stopped at a leather-covered door, and the officer stepped inside. He reappeared and signaled the soldiers to march Ben inside. They paused in front of another leather-covered door, then hustled Ben into the inner sanctum.

A bright light shined in Ben's face. A Gestapo officer seated behind a large wooden desk ignored him. Ben squinted past the light and studied the officer's black uniform with the twin lightning flashes on the collar. He couldn't tell his rank. His closely cropped hair, clenched jaw, and black wire-rimmed glasses gave him a formidable look. A small trimmed mustache drew a straight line across his upper lip. Ben began to sag and looked around for a chair.

"Stand at attention, Major Findlay," the officer snapped without looking up.

"Okay," Ben said, straightening his shoulders. "But could you get these cuffs off my wrists? I'm still recovering from a broken shoulder."

The officer raised the phone and shouted a command. Braun hustled into the room and unlocked the handcuffs, taking the opportunity to again twist Ben's left arm.

"Damn it, Schultz," Ben hissed. "Take it easy on the shoulder." Braun sneered at him and exited the room.

"Who is Schultz, please?" the officer said, still not looking up.

"Nobody. My idea of a joke," Ben muttered.

"This is no joke, Major Findlay. And you will address me as oberstleutnant."

"Don't think I can get my farm boy tongue around that. Can I just call you 'sir'?"

The oberstleutnant raised his head and regarded Ben with cold steel-gray eyes. "So you are what in America is called a wise ass, no?"

"Sorry, sir. I'm just a simple country boy."

"I think not," the officer said coldly. "It will go easier for you if you drop this juvenile attempt at deception."

Ben returned the German's steely stare with a blank look. "One thing," he said after a pause. "I'd like to sit down. I'm just out of the hospital, an' . . ."

Messerschmitt Me 109 Fighter

"My name is Findlay, Benjamin A. My rank is major, and my service number is—"

"We know all of that," the Gestapo officer cut in. "And I might add, a good deal more. You were very cooperative with our interrogators while you were recovering in the hospital. But I have a few more questions."

Damn! Guess Anderson was right. What all did I tell those bastards?

Ben stared silently at the German.

"So?" The oberstleutnant frowned at him.

"I have nothing more to add," Ben said. "Name, rank, and serial number. That's all that's required by the Geneva Convention, if you know or care what that is."

"Simple country boy, eh?" the Gestapo officer sneered. "Come now, Major Findlay, let us drop the pretense. We have more questions, and we expect answers."

15

Ben fixed him with a blank stare and struggled to stand erect.

"As you wish, Major Findlay. As you wish. We will give you some time to think about cooperating with us."

He reached for the phone and snapped a command. Braun and another soldier hustled into the room, took Ben by the arms, and frog-marched him downstairs to the cellar. They were joined by two others, who grabbed Ben's wrists and snapped belts fixed to ropes around each. "Schultz" sneered as he pulled the ropes through ceiling pulleys and hoisted Ben's arms over his head. Ben screamed as lightning bolts of pain shot through his barely healed shoulder.

"Mein name ist Braun! Say Braun!" he hissed in Ben's face. "Say *Braun!*"

"Okay, Schultz," Ben choked. "Brown it is, like the color of cow shit."

Braun smashed a vicious backhanded blow across Ben's face, ripping a deep gash with his Gestapo skull-head ring. "I unnerstan English, American pig. Vill teach you not insult me!"

Braun groped in a dark corner of the corridor and grasped an ugly black rubber truncheon. He poked it under Ben's nose and grinned. In a well-practiced move, he spun on his heel and smashed the truncheon across Ben's left kidney. In another deft move, he whirled and whipped the truncheon across Ben's right kidney. Ben howled with pain and fell limp, hanging on his outstretched arms like some wild game animal being gutted in the forest.

Braun ordered one of the soldiers to splash a bucket of cold water on Ben, which shocked him, sputtering back to consciousness. Braun pressed his face close to Ben's. "You like more of dis, American pig?" he snarled. Ben, unable to speak, shook his head.

"Hokay," Braun said with an evil grin. "But for reminder not insult me." He whipped the truncheon into Ben's groin, and Ben passed out again as the blow triggered his bladder, and urine poured down his pant legs.

The four lowered Ben to the floor and released the belts from his wrists. They dragged him into a dank, unlighted cell and slammed the thick steel door. Searing pain in his kidneys and groin jarred Ben awake. He had no idea how long he had lain unconscious in the dark. Struggling to his feet, he stumbled into a hard wooden stool and dropped onto it. As his eyes adjusted to the gloom, he saw that the cell contained a wooden bunk with a lumpy straw-filled mattress and a bucket in the corner.

"Home sweet home it ain't, but better make the best of it," he gasped. "I'll just sit here and fantasize about flyin' *Round Trip.*"

Flashes of pain wracked Ben's body. He finally succumbed to fatigue and stretched out on the bunk. The lumpy mattress stank of stale sweat and urine. *Probably fulla lice and bedbugs.*

He snorted awake and sat up. Dull pain still coursed through his kidneys and groin. The cell was still dark, so he had no way of knowing how long he had slept. His watch had disappeared when he awoke in the hospital, so he had no means of marking time. He flopped back and immediately fell asleep.

Ben awoke again, smacked his dry lips, and tried to clear his parched throat. "Hey!" he shouted into the darkness. "How about something to drink? Uh, wasser. I need wasser!" There was no response. His ears rang in the total silence. "Wasser, you sons of bitches!" he yelled.

He sat fuming in the dark. Hunger pangs clinched his stomach, but his most urgent need was for something to drink—anything. He sucked his swollen tongue. *Bastards! If they think they can break me this way, they're wrong! Man, what I'd give for a beer! No, don't think about that. You'll go nuts.*

The hours dragged by. Ben strained to hear anything—voices, footsteps, coughing, even a fart, or anything that would tell him other humans were around. "To hell with them," he rasped. "I'll talk to myself. Need to hear a human voice, even if it's my own."

Ben struggled to keep his composure. He lost all track of time and began to hallucinate—saw faces loom out of the darkness. Brice, his old flight instructor, thrust out his grizzled jaw and again shouted at him to "relax, let her fly herself!" Ted, his best friend from the Spanish civil war adventure, flicked him a comic salute and faded into the darkness. Gwen smiled her beautiful sweet smile and told him how much she loved him. Silverman appeared too. What was he trying to tell Ben?

Ben slapped himself hard on both cheeks. "Don't drift off," he snarled. "Keep your wits about ya. You're in a Gestapo solitary cell in Germany. Don't let 'em screw up your mind!"

Ben slept fitfully. He had no idea how much time had passed. Then he sat up abruptly, alert and listening hard. *Was that a door opening? Why don't I hear footsteps?*

He sensed that someone had stopped outside his cell. A slot in the bottom of the door scraped open. No light shone through, but a small metal pot with a clamped cover slid into the cell. Whoever delivered the pot closed the slot and apparently moved away. Again, Ben heard no footsteps. He grabbed the pot and unlatched the hinged top. It was filled with a liquid that smelled vaguely like soup."

He raised it to his lips. "Don't care if it's panther piss," he croaked. "It's liquid, and I'm drinkin' it."

The watery lukewarm broth might have had some meat, but the taste had to be imagined. Ben sipped slowly, relishing the feel of the liquid sliding down his throat. He gulped the remainder and immediately doubled over as spasms wracked his shrunken stomach.

"Don't barf it up," he hissed through clenched teeth. He sat upright, clutched his arms across his stomach, and breathed deeply. The spasms passed, and he flopped back on the foul mattress.

The tasteless broth arrived regularly for what Ben thought must be several days. To his delight, one serving had a soggy chunk of black bread floating in it.

The next time Ben heard someone approach the cell, the lock turned, and the door jerked open. A brilliant light stabbed his eyes, causing him to blink and cringe away. Someone yelled, "Achtung! Aufstehen! Komen auf diese Weise!"

Ben understood he was ordered out of the cell. Covering his eyes, he stood and groped for the door. He followed a uniformed guard while another prodded him from behind with a rifle butt.

He stood unsteadily in front of the oberstleutnant's desk, squinting against the bright light directed in his face. "So, Major Findlay," the Gestapo officer said still without looking up. "You have found our accommodations satisfactory, ja?"

"Yeah, it's a swell room," Ben said. "Ya oughta come visit me sometime. I especially like the massage your men gave me. At least I've stopped pissing blood."

"Still playing as the wise ass," the oberstleutnant said evenly. "Is it that you wish to spend more time in solitary with another, as you say, massage?"

"What I wish is to sit down before I fall on my ass!" Ben snarled. "You're violating every code in the Geneva Convention by treating me like this!"

"Ach so, a man of many talents. Now you are an international lawyer," his interrogator mocked. "Answer a few simple questions, and you will be treated with more respect."

"Findlay, Benjamin A., major, U.S. Army Air Forces—"

"*Silence!*" the Gestapo officer shouted, slamming his fist on the desk. "I will not be mocked!"

"Not mocking ya. Name, rank, and service number, that's all I'm required to give."

"But we know all about you, Major," he said menacingly. "Your life on the farm in Michigan, your flight training, your service with leftist loyalists in Spain, your escape to England, and your service in the Royal Air Force. We know of your decision to transfer to the American Army Air Forces to . . . how did you put it? Ah yes, 'to bomb the shit out of Germany.'"

Ben forced his face to hold its blank stare. *Damn! Did I really blab everything? I don't remember any of that.*

"You were on your thirtieth mission in your B-17 with the ridiculous name of *Round Trip*, bombing the Messerschmitt aircraft factory less than four miles from here when our valiant antiaircraft gunners destroyed your bomber. You manage to survive, how? Did you jump out of your bomber before it was blown up? Did you abandon your crew to their fiery death?"

Ben leaned forward, teeth bared in a snarl. "Maybe that's the way your Luftwaffe fellas do it, oberwhateverthehell your rank is, but it's not the way we do it in the U.S. Army Air Forces. I was blown clear. Came to just in time to pop my chute before hittin' the ground. I dunno what happened to my crew, but I wish we'd had a chance to put a bomb or two down your chimney."

The Gestapo officer leaped to his feet and lashed Ben across the face with a riding crop. "Schweine hund!" he shouted. "You will show me respect!" Ben stumbled backward.

You dumb shit, Findlay. Whattaya think you're proving? This fella could make life real unpleasant.

"Sorry, sir," Ben said. "I'm hungry, thirsty, and more than a little light-headed. Could I please sit down?"

"Ach so, much better, Major Findlay," the German said. He pointed to a straight-back chair. "Sit!" He kept the bright light focused on Ben's face.

The interrogation dragged on. The Gestapo officer drummed Ben with questions, returning to demands that Ben give him details of the impending invasion of France. Ben stuck doggedly to name, rank, and serial number, but his interrogator persisted in demanding answers.

Finally, Ben reacted angrily. "Look!" he shouted. "Ya can keep this up as long as ya want, but nothin's gonna change. Name, rank, and serial number—that's all you're gettin' outta me." Ben was exhausted. His speech became sloppy. "Far as the goddamned invasion is concerned,

I don't know anythin' about it. That's it! Only I hope it comes soon, and they blow your Nazi ass outta town!" The Gestapo officer moved quickly from behind his desk. Ben didn't see the blow coming.

Ben awoke slowly. A piercing headache threatened to pop his eyeballs out of their sockets. He could tell by the smell and crunch of the mattress he was back in the solitary cell.

"Oh god," he moaned, trying to sit up. "Not very smart, Benjamin ol' boy. Guess I really pissed off ol' Oberwhatsit. What'd he hit me with?"

Ben slumped dejectedly on his pad. Silence enfolded him again, and he lost track of time. Someone shoved a tin pot of watery broth through the door slot at least four times. Did that mean four more days had passed? Braun and the other three soldiers had come by again and strung him up for another "kidney massage." Ben passed out.

He awoke curled on his lumpy pad when he heard footsteps, voices, and doors clanging. *Uh oh, here we go again.*

The cell door slammed open and a dazzling light blinded him. Whoever was holding the light shouted, "Steh auf! Schnell, auf diese Weise!" Ben understood he was ordered to get up and follow.

Omigod! Are they gonna stand me in front of a firing squad?

Ben, squinting in the bright light, stumbled like a hunchback up the stairs, a following guard again prodding him with a rifle butt. Instead of heading for the oberstleutnant's office, the guards led him down a long hallway that seemed to lead to the back of the building. A small van idled by the curb. They shoved Ben into the back compartment. One of the guards clambered in and sat facing him, rifle held across his chest.

Ben couldn't see outside but could tell from the smell they were driving through Regensburg. The van skidded to a stop, and Ben heard locomotives chuffing and smelled coal smoke. The van door banged open and the guard motioned with his rifle for Ben to get out. Ben stood squinting in the sunshine. He was in a rail yard with a string of boxcars in front of him. The guard prodded him with the rifle, and he stumbled toward one of the open cars. The guard reported to an officer holding a clipboard, and Ben heard his name. "Est is gut," the officer said and nodded toward the boxcar. Two guards grabbed Ben by the arms and heaved him into the car. He landed on a tangle of prone bodies as the boxcar door clanged shut.

"Hey, watch it!" someone yelled. "Get the hell off me! Find you own damn space."

"Sorry, sorry," Ben apologized. "The Krauts just threw me in here like a sack a potatoes." He dragged himself toward a small space in a corner. The pulsing pain in his kidneys made him want to vomit.

"Ya sound like an American. Where ya from? Midwest, I bet. Can hear your accent."

"What accent?" Ben responded. "You're the one with the accent. You from New 'Yawk'?"

"Brooklyn. That bother ya?"

"Not at all," Ben said. His mind flashed back to 1937 and meeting with another fella from Brooklyn, Al Brewster. Al was one of the young pilots who had joined Ben, Silverman, Ted, and the other volunteer pilots in Manhattan before leaving on their grand adventure to fly for the Republican loyalists in Spain.

Seems like a lifetime ago, he mused. *Ted and all the other fellas except Fred killed, and for what? Here we are, still beatin' the hell outta each other. Fred was right, nothin' has changed.*

He turned back to his traveling companions. "Hey look, I'm glad to be back with Americans. Who are you guys, and where're we goin'?"

"We're POWs just like you!" someone else yelled. "Some of the fellas think we're on our way to Stalag Luft III, the prison camp for flyers."

Ben blew a puff of relief. *Hell of a lot better than goin' against a wall facin' a firing squad!*

Chapter 5

OFF TO CAMP

The boxcar reeked. Stifling fumes of urine and stale sweat stung Ben's eyes and nose. Sodden straw covered the floor. Slop buckets sloshed in both ends of the car, but with everyone so tightly packed in, half of them couldn't get to the makeshift toilets. "Reminds me of the Lexington Avenue Express on a Saturday night," the Brooklyn man groused, referring to the subway line that served Brooklyn from Manhattan. "Drunks stumbling home used every corner in the car for a latrine."

"Sounds frightfully uncivilized," someone muttered. Ben cocked his head. *He sounds British.*

"Hey," he called out. "Do we have a Brit on board?"

"I say, Yank, yes," came a reply. "I'm a Brit. As your friend from Brooklyn would say, 'that bother ya?'"

"Not at all." Ben chuckled. "Some of my best friends are Brits." This generated a ripple of guffaws. "Matter of fact," Ben continued, "I flew wing on a Brit in Spain in '38 and '39. We flew Polikarpov I-16s for the Republican air force. Followed him to England after the Republic fell and flew wing on his Spitfire during the Battle of Britain and for another coupla years until America got into the war."

"Do say," the Brit replied. "You might turn out to be a decent fellow. Meet you formally after we arrive at our destination."

"How the hell did you get here?" another voice called out to Ben. "Didn't see you processing through Gulag Luft." Gulag Luft, the Luftwaffe's aircrew interrogation center, was near Frankfurt am Main. The Germans held most captured airmen there in solitary confinement for interrogation and then moved them to a collecting center before shipping them to camps like Stalag Luft III.

"Dunno. After I got shot down, I ended up in the hospital in Regensburg for some time," Ben said. "The Gestapo in Regensburg worked me over pretty hard, then threw me on this train. Dunno know why I didn't go to the Gulag Luft."

Ben paused, picturing the map of Germany in his mind. "But hey, if you fellas left from Frankfurt, why'd the train come this far south to Regensburg?"

"Who knows how the Krauts run their railroads," someone grumbled. Then someone said louder, "Better watch this guy. Easy way to put a stooge in among us."

Ben laughed. "Bullshit! I'm as American as any of you. Raised on a farm in Michigan. Ask me anything you want about livin' in the States."

"What outfit are you in?" another voice asked.

"Not s'posed to talk about that," Ben said. "You know, name, rank, service number . . ."

"Ah, ya don't need to sweat that here, fella," someone called out. "Dunno about the others, but I doubt there's a German spy in this shit hole. 'Sides, our group intelligence officer said the name, rank, and service number routine is a lotta crap. If the Krauts want information, they know how to get answers."

Ben frowned. *Wish I'd known that back in Regensburg.*

"Uh yeah, I guess so," Ben said. "Well, I led a B-17 group out of England. Flew into a flak trap after we bombed the Messerschmitt factory outside of Regensburg. I got blown outta my aircraft, was banged up, and spent several weeks in a civilian hospital, then not sure how much more time as a guest of the Regensburg Gestapo."

"B-17? What the hell were you doin' flying a B-17? You said you were a fighter pilot, didn't ya?"

"Damn!" Ben mumbled. "Here we go again. I'm tired of explaining that." Then he said louder, "I chose to fly B-17s when I transferred from the RAF to the USAAF in early '42. My experience flying RAF fighters helped me coach our gunners on how to track incoming fighters. Told 'em to aim for the engine and traverse to the tail when they rolled and exposed their armored bellies as they broke off.

"Mainly, though, I wanted to take the war to the German homeland, and flying bombers was the only way to do that."

"Well, pal, ya did that all right, and here ya are. How many missions didja fly?"

"I was on my thirtieth, the one that earned my crew their tickets home," Ben said quietly.

"Damn tough luck. What about you, weren't you goin' home too?"

"Naw, I'd been promoted to executive officer of my group. Was gonna take the job when I got back. I planned to stay with the group for the duration."

"What group is that?"

"Umm, guess I can say it here," Ben stammered. "The 509th Heavy Bombardment Group."

"Hey! I know that group," another voice called out. "You're based at Parham. I flew P-51 escorts for you guys. How about that? I mean, meetin' up like this?"

North American P-51K Fighter

"Uh, thanks for all your help," Ben said. "We really appreciated the protection you fellas gave us." Then peering around in the gloom of the boxcar, he said, "Hope we have a chance to get better acquainted when we get to wherever the hell we're goin'."

The boxcar lurched from side to side as the train rumbled into the night. "Anyone know for sure where we're headed?" someone called out. "I mean, which camp?"

"I'm still betting on Stalag Luft III," another voice cut in. "It's in Silesia, the western part of what used to be Poland. Check the sun in the morning. I bet we're traveling northeast."

Ben slept fitfully. The pain in his kidneys was bearable but just. By agreement, those on the floor slept for a few hours, while those standing against the walls tried to stay awake and upright. When it came time to change places so everyone had a chance to lie down, there was much shuffling, grumbling, cursing, and coughing as those on the floor struggled upright and those standing curled up in the filthy straw.

After many hours and a couple of shift changes, the sunrise cast narrow beams of light through cracks in the boxcar walls. Those closest to the walls peeked at the outside world.

"Coming into a station," one called. "I can see a rail yard. Lots of tracks."

"Any station signs?" someone asked. "Give us a clue to where the hell we are."

"Yeah," one of the men peeking out rasped. "Think it says Praha. Is that Prague? Are we in Czechoslovakia? Thought someone said we were going to Poland?"

"We're takin' a shortcut across occupied Czechoslovakia."

Ben fixed the European map in his mind. *That puts us pretty far to the east. Damn hard to get back to England, even if we can escape.*

"Lemmesee," one of the POWs said, struggling to his feet. "If we're stopping in Prague, that's gotta mean we're headed for Stalag Luft III. One of the guys with me in a holding cell said the camp for Allied flyers is near a place called Sagan. Used to be 'Zagan' when it was part of Poland. Krauts now claim it as part of the fatherland."

The train screeched to a stop and the prisoners slammed into each other as the couplings of the trailing boxcars clanged together like a giant accordion. "Jesus!" someone yelled. "What kinda idiot is driving this thing?"

They heard shouted commands in German and the footfalls of many boots. Someone marshaled troops outside. The heavy latch snapped open, and a soldier shoved back the heavy door. Bright sunlight streamed in, temporarily blinding the prisoners.

A German soldier waved a rifle at them. "Raus, schnell! Bilden zwei zeilen!" he yelled.

Confused by the command, no one moved. "He says to get out and form two lines," a lanky prisoner said quietly.

"How come you understand German?" Another prisoner challenged. "You some kinda Gestapo spy?"

"If I was, I'd be a damn fool to admit I speak German," he whispered. "I'm from Lancaster County, Pennsylvania. That's Pennsylvania Dutch country. Everybody there speaks German. But keep it quiet," he hissed. "Don't want the Krauts to know that."

The prisoners tumbled out of the boxcar and formed two ragged ranks. They stared at lines of rifle-bearing soldiers interspersed in machine gun positions.

"Don't anybody do anything stupid!" shouted a USAAF lieutenant colonel. "I'm the ranking officer in this bunch, and I want everyone to stand quietly. That's an order!"

"Ach zo, prisoners," shouted a German officer. Ben couldn't make out his rank. "Ve vill here make a brief stop to feed ze locomotive coal und wasser. You may up and down valk, zo undt zo, and do vhat you must your needs to relieve. Anyone attempting escape vill be shot."

"Do as the man says!" the American officer commanded. Many of the prisoners didn't wait to be told twice, some already relieving themselves under the boxcars.

"Herr Obersleutnant!" the American colonel shouted. "These men need food and clean drinking water."

"Zo it comes," the German officer shouted, indicating prisoners pulling baggage carts along the lines. Some handed out battered tin bowls, chipped enamel cups, and wooden spoons. Others ladled thin soup into the bowls, and another group dipped water out of large cans. Ben stared at the emaciated unshaven men dressed in filthy striped pajamas. *Omigod! I hope we get better treatment than these poor fellas.* Ben didn't know they were Jewish slave laborers from a nearby Nazi concentration camp.

After wolfing the soup and slurping a drink, Ben took a long pee and walked back and forth in front of the boxcars. He flexed his knees and stretched his knotted back muscles, trying to ease the pain in his kidneys.

A short RAF pilot with a thatch of blond hair sticking from under his campaign cap approached Ben, "I say, are you the Yank who said he flew with the RAF?" he asked, extending his right hand. "Saunders, Sandy Saunders. Pleased to meet'cha."

"Findlay, Ben Findlay. Pleased to meet you, Squadron Leader," Ben said, recognizing his rank badges.

"Umm, ah." Saunders hesitated. "Oh, of course, you're familiar with RAF rank badges. "And you're a—"

"Major," Ben interjected.

"So umm, tell me about your RAF service. And Spain before that, flying with the Republicans."

"Long story. I was recruited in '37 with eleven other American pilots to fly for the Republicans. Ended up in a Russian volunteer squadron flying the Polikarpov I-16."

"That's an open-cockpit job, isn't it?" Saunders interjected. "Looks like a bat with long chord wings. Blimey, that musta been bloody exciting."

"It's a swell fighter. Not real fast but very maneuverable. We flew in the Barcelona sector, mostly up against Condor Legion Me 109 fighters. Back then they still called 'em Bf 109s. We could beat 'em at low altitude but couldn't match 'em at higher altitudes. We did raise hell, though, with their bombers and attack aircraft."

"Do tell," Saunders interjected. "What bombers did you face?"

"Heinkle He 111s, Junkers Ju 52s, and the Ju 87 Stuka dive bombers. If we got past the 109s, we had a field day with the bombers, especially the Stukas. Finally settled on a tactic for dealing with the Heinkles and Junkers. We'd sneak out at low altitude, then zoom up and attack them from below. They didn't have many guns that fired down."

"Too right!" Saunders said. "But they'd figured that out by the time they launched the blitzkrieg against England as I'm certain you learned. The new belly turrets put paid to all that."

Heinkel He-111 Bomber

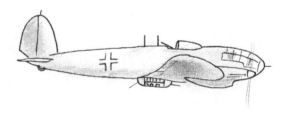

"Yeah, but in the Battle of Britain, the later marks of Spitfires were more than a match for the 109s escorting the bombers," Ben responded. "If we had the altitude advantage, we'd eat 'em up. That cleared the Hurricanes to attack the bombers. Actually, the Hurricane pilots scored the most overall victories in the battle and later come to that. Not sure why the Spitfire got most of the credit."

"Mmm, did indeed," Saunders mused. "But we all had our innings. Showed Herr Goering and his Luftwaffe chaps what for. Those were good times. As Prime Minister Churchill said, 'Never in the field of human conflict has so much been owed by so many to so few.' Damn tough at the height of the battle but good times nonetheless."

"So how'd you end up here with this bunch?" Ben asked.

"Bloody Circus mission over Northern France. Our Spitfire group was escorting a gaggle of Halifax heavy bombers. Usual cockup as most of those missions were."

Ben nodded knowingly, having flown many of those frustrating missions while still with the RAF.

"Jerries bounced us over Rouen, and I tangled with a pair of 109s while trying to protect the bombers," Saunders continued. "I got one of them, and the other got me. And here I am. Simple as that."

Ben grimaced, remembering how he was shot down by a second 109 he didn't see. "Yeah," he muttered. "Happens fast."

"I say, Major," Saunders interjected, "you said you flew wing on a British pilot both in Spain and with the RAF. What's the chap's name?"

"Percy," Ben said, feeling a lump rise in his throat. "Reginald M. Percy. Lately wing commander leading a Spitfire squadron out of RAF Wittering. Shot down and crashed in the channel just before Christmas. Nobody saw him parachute."

"Percy, Percy . . ." Saunders mused. "Reginald Percy. Say, is his old man some kinda maven with the Air Ministry?"

"Yeah, he is," Ben said. "Head of procurement for the RAF. Wonder if he and Lady Percy have gotten over the loss yet?"

"Loss? Ahh, guess you haven't heard the latest news," Saunders interjected. "Jerries picked up a RAF pilot floating in the channel about the time the wing commander was shot down. Been knocked about a bit, unconscious, and had no identity papers . . ."

"Yeah, yeah!" Ben interrupted. "That was a habit from Spain. We didn't carry anything that would identify us. Nationalists didn't like to take prisoners and had a special hate for foreign pilots. Took special pleasure in torturing mercenaries like us before they shot us.

"But hey, you telling me Reggie's alive? A POW!" Ben shouted.

"Only telling you what I heard. Story is he was unconscious for some time. Came to in hospital after several weeks, and the Krauts finally figured out who he was. Yeah, he's now a POW. Bloody hell, he may be in the same camp we're headed to!"

Ben's mind whirled. "Reggie's alive! His folks musta found out 'bout time we were completing our last missions. And then I got shot down over Regensburg. Godamighty!"

Saunders started to reply, but three shrill whistle blasts interrupted him.

"All prisoners to assigned boxcars must return!" the oberstleutnant shouted. "Align for name checking. No one is to be missing."

The prisoners piled back into the boxcar, grumbling and cursing. Ben and Saunders, jammed into a corner by the press of bodies, shrugged rueful smiles. "Pick up where we left off when we get to the bloody camp," Saunders muttered.

Ben closed his eyes. *Do I dare hope Reggie is alive and a prisoner in whatisname Stalag Luft III? What I wouldn't give to see the old bugger again!*

Chapter 6

STALAG LUFT III

Ben leaned against the boxcar wall, struggling to stay awake. He felt like he hadn't slept in days, although he recalled getting a stint on the floor at some point. His chin fell to his chest, and his knees buckled.

"Woof!" he exclaimed and stiffened. "Gotta stay awake 'til my next turn on the floor."

As he sagged again, Ben felt the train slowing. "Hang on!" someone yelled. "If this Kraut engineer slams on the brakes like before, we're about to be squashed like sardines."

The squeal of steel brakes echoed along the line of cars, and the train decelerated to a slow rumble. Steam hissed and the locomotive chuffed repeatedly as the cars clacked across multiple rail switches and came to a smooth stop. "Hey!" someone yelled. "Not bad. Fritz is either learning how to control this thing or we got a new driver at the last stop."

After the train shuddered to a stop, the prisoners heard what sounded like heavy steel gates slide open. The locomotive chuffed, and the train ran a short distance before stopping again.

One of the "peekers" at the wall slits called out, "Looks like we're in some kinda compound. Big open area surrounded by high fences and barbed wire."

"I know where we are," someone called out. "Welcome to Stalag Luft III, gents. Our home away from home for the duration." The prisoners greeted this with a chorus of hoots, raspberries, and curses.

The boxcar door slammed open, and the dazed prisoners stood, blinking like a flock of hoot owls caught in bright sunshine. "Come on!" someone yelled from the back of the car. "Move out. Let's get out of this stinking cesspool!"

"Don't anyone move until we're ordered to!" shouted the colonel who had appointed himself commander of the ragged smelly band. The order came quickly as a loudspeaker commanded, "Abstieg schnell und form in reihen von sechs!"

"The order is to get out quickly and form in ranks of six," the prisoner from Lancaster County, Pennsylvania, whispered to the colonel.

"Right!" the colonel said. Then he shouted, "Everyone move out and form in ranks of six. Keep it orderly!"

Junkers JW-87D Dive Bomber

The prisoners tumbled out of the car and formed ragged ranks. They stood squirming and scratching at the bites of bedbugs and fleas that infested their clothing. Ben looked about, noting the twin rows of fencing topped with barbed wire surrounding the huge compound. The space between the fence lines bristled with waist-high coils of more barbed wire. Tall watchtowers manned by guards with machine guns loomed at fifty-yard intervals along the fence. Ben spotted a shorter fence about ten yards inside the main fence. He would learn later that it marked the dead zone. Anyone stepping into it would be shot.

Ben hopped out of the boxcar first and lined up at the head of the first rank. When all were assembled, a soldier stepped up to him, poked his rifle in his face, and directed him and the five men behind him to stand against a concrete wall around the corner from the assembly area.

Oh god! Here it comes. They hauled me all this way just to face a firing squad.

Instead of turning to face a line of riflemen, Ben and his five companions stared into the lenses of six large cameras mounted on tripods. "You vill stand still for prisoner identity photo," the lead cameraman commanded. Ben slumped in relief, then squared his shoulders and glowered at the camera.

Don't expect me to smile, Kraut. I may be your prisoner for now, but I'm joinin' the first escape bunch I find!

The Germans affixed the photographs to each prisoner's *"personalkarte."* These were used as identity documents to keep records on each prisoner and to track anyone absent from the twice-daily head count or "appel" formations called to reaffirm no one had escaped the camp.

A flurry of activity followed as Ben and his fellow POWs endured buzz haircuts, cold showers, delousing, and cursory physical examinations. They redressed in their ragged patchwork uniforms.

USAAF Colonel Bradford R. Whitney, commander of the American contingent at Stalag Luft III, called them to a briefing in the camp theater built two years earlier by prisoners. He showed them a map delineating the four compounds comprising Stalag Luft III—East, Center, North, and South.

"Each compound has its own Allied commanding officer," he said. "The German officer in overall commander of the camp is Kommandant Friedrich von Striesel. He's an honorable man, speaks excellent English, but will brook no nonsense. Follow the camp rules and you'll not be hassled.

"But," he added with a wink, "that doesn't apply to escape plans."

"There are fifteen huts in each compound," Whitney continued. "Each bunk room holds eighteen prisoners, or 'kriegies' as we call ourselves, in six triple-deck bunks. This makes for tight quarters, so you'll have to work at staying out of each other's way. "Kriegies," by the way, is short for *kriegsgefangenen*, German for prisoner of war.

"The German's completed the first compound East in early 1942. There has been some switching around, but American aircrews have been housed in the Center compound since the end of '42, and in this compound, South, since late '43. Construction has begun on a fifth compound to be designated west.

"The Germans selected the camp's location with care," he added. "First, we're near Sagan, about a hundred miles southeast of Berlin.

That puts us pretty deep in German territory. Supposed to discourage escape attempts. Also, the subsoil is yellow sand, making it difficult to dig and shore up tunnels or to hide the sand, which is a very different color than the black hard-packed dirt of the compound. And the huts sit on posts, so camp guards can look underneath for tunnel entrances. The Germans also have positioned seismograph sensors around the fences to listen for digging.

"However, you're not to sit back complacently and accept your imprisonment. You are to look for any opportunity to escape. There are escape committees mulling new schemes all the time. Anyone interested can see me later."

A murmur of approval surged through the gathered prisoners.

"But a warning: be careful who you associate with," he continued. "Limit your conversations about escape plans to as few individuals as possible and then expand your group carefully. Kriegies staged two escapes from this camp by digging tunnels. You may have heard of them. The Trojan horse escape plan used a kriegie-built gymnastic vaulting horse as cover for the digging and sand disposal. Three prisoners escaped, and two made it back to England.

"In the so-called great escape last March, the Brits dug three tunnels—Tom, Dick, and Harry—from the north compound beneath the wire and out to the surrounding woods. Hundreds of men, led by a contingent of RAF escape specialists, worked on this project. And they succeeded. A total of seventy-six prisoners escaped. Unfortunately, all but three were recaptured. Of those three, two made it back to England via Sweden, and one reached Spain."

Whitney paused. "But be warned, there can be severe consequences. The day after the mass escape, Hitler ordered every recaptured officer shot. He was advised this would prompt severe world reaction but persisted and finally ordered the Gestapo to shoot fifty.

"The camp Kommandant and guards didn't escape punishment. Hitler ordered him shipped to the eastern front to fight the Russians, and several guards were executed," Whitney continued. "Kommandant Von Striesel now has redoubled security.

"He also uses kriegie informers to expose future escape plots before they get organized. So be wary. Anyone caught in an escape conspiracy faces a stretch of solitary confinement, or in extreme cases, transfer to a Nazi concentration camp. He sent several from the great escape group to the Sachsenhausen concentration camp near Berlin."

Noting the looks of disbelief on many of the newcomers faces at the mention of kriegie informers, Whitney snapped, "Don't look shocked that there are betrayers in the camp. Most kriegies can cope with the stress of life as a POW, but some can't. You need to form bonds of friendship and trust. Just do it with care."

He paused and swept the newcomers with a grim look. "Let me add that our camp military justice system will deal with anyone caught informing on fellow kriegies. And our justice will be swift and severe."

He stood on the platform while the newcomers digested his message.

Ben's mind whirled. *Too much to absorb. Throwing a lot at us. I'll worry about escape later. First, I need to find someone who can tell me whether Reggie's here.*

Whitney then explained how the prisoners would be assigned to quarters in "squadrons" of eighteen men to a barracks room. Group commanders would be appointed for each barracks.

He indicated two officers flanking him on the stage. "Lieutenant Colonel Baker on my right is my executive officer and Major Barnett on my left is my adjutant. Anyone with more questions about camp protocol, and you probably have a lot, see them after the briefing.

"Now before I dismiss you, would Major Findlay, Benjamin A. Findlay, please identify himself?" Ben raised his hand.

"Good. Join me by that exit after the briefing." Colonel Baker then called the prisoners to attention and shouted, "Dismissed!"

Ben joined Whitney, snapped to attention, and saluted. "Major Findlay reporting as ordered, sir!"

"Stand at ease, Findlay. Need a chat. My office, Hut 285. Ten minutes. Down the main street to the end, right, and third hut on the right."

"Yessir!" Ben responded. He saluted and stepped out to find Hut 285.

Chapter 7

A Friendly Chat

Ben knocked on the door of Hut 285, and hearing the command, "enter!" stepped inside. Whitney sat behind a table with two majors seated on either side. Ben snapped to attention and raised a salute.

Whitney interrupted him. "You can forgo the formalities, Findlay. We're here for an informal chat. Take a seat," he said, indicating a straight-back chair facing the table. Ben sat and shot the officers a quizzical look.

These other two look like lawyers. Both have command wings, but they still look like lawyers . . .

"I'm sure you're wondering what this is all about," Whitney said without introducing the other officers. "Let me assure you this is not a board of inquiry. We just have some questions. Need some clarification on how you got here."

"Yessir," Ben said, swallowing twice and trying to relax.

"So tell us how you came to be shipped to Stalag Luft III."

"Well, sir, my B-17 got hit over Regensburg after we bombed the Messerschmitt aircraft factory. Flew into a flak trap and took a near direct hit from a German 88 antiaircraft shell. Aircraft began to disintegrate. I got knocked backward out of the flight deck. I vaguely remember checking my parachute harness. We were on fire and, uh, I dunno. Guess I was blown clear. Musta blacked out. I came to after a long free fall and pulled the ripcord."

Ben choked. "Uh, ah, I don't know what happened to my crew . . . Nobody landed near me, so I don't know if anybody else, uh, got out."

Ben hesitated, regaining control. "We were at twenty thousand feet, so I must have fallen about fifteen thousand feet. Looked like

I was at about five thousand feet when the chute opened. My left shoulder was broken, couldn't raise that arm to work the risers, and the left side of my face had been burned. Still see the scars. The other scar on my right cheek is courtesy of the Regensburg Gestapo. Anyway, I landed hard and broke a couple of ribs. I woke up in a German hospital. Don't know how long I was unconscious."

"How long were you in the hospital?" Whitney asked.

"Several weeks. I'm not sure. It was a civilian hospital, but it had a German commander and guards. My doctor Wolfgang Bayerhoff was a civilian doctor. He was concerned about infection in my face burns, so resisted my early release. A Gestapo officer finally came with two soldiers and marched me out. I spent some more time as the guest of the Regensburg Gestapo. Not sure how long. They worked me over pretty good."

"What's your group's designation and base, and on what date were you shot down?" Whitney interrupted.

"Sir, I'm leader of Squadron A of the 509th Heavy Bombardment Group based in Parham, England. Colonel Frank Silverman commanding. Colonel Silverman and I have a long association. Be glad to give you those details, sir. Ah, I was to be promoted to group executive officer effective on my return. It was our thirtieth mission, and the rest of my crewmembers had, uh . . . had earned their tickets home."

"And the date you were shot down?"

"April 1, 1944, sir. April Fools' day."

"You said the Gestapo in Regensburg held you for some time. Why weren't you shipped to the Gulag Luft interrogation center? Everyone who has arrived here since I've been in command went that route."

"No idea, sir. I didn't know about Gulag Luft until after the Gestapo fellas threw me onto the train in Regensburg. Literally, sir, they tossed me into a boxcar like a sack of potatoes. Fellas I landed on weren't too happy."

"How did the Gestapo treat you in Regensburg?"

"Knocked me around some." Ben fingered the scar on his right cheek. "They used a rubber truncheon on my kidneys and threw me into solitary confinement. Let me go hungry and thirsty for several days and then fed me some kinda watery slop once a day for several days. Then two soldiers rousted me out of my cell and marched me upstairs to stand in front of a Gestapo oberstlutsomethinorother. Sorry, just can't get my tongue around that title."

Whitney and his companion officers stifled smiles.

"Anyway, this Gestapo fella tried to give me the treatment, but I insisted on only giving my name, rank, and serial number. He interrogated me several times and had me thrown back into solitary after each session. He hit me two times, once with a riding whip and the second time with something I didn't see coming. He kept a bright light in my eyes, so I only got quick glances at him, not much else."

"And you stuck to name, rank, and serial number?"

"Yessir! But ah, I guess I gave 'em a lot of information when they interrogated me while I was doped up in the hospital."

"They interrogated you while you were drugged?"

"Not sure, sir. I thought I was dreaming—that I was talkin' to at least two fellas. Couldn't be sure because I didn't seem to be able to see them. But when I woke up and needed morphine to knock down the pain, I called a nurse who hustled off to get permission from the doc. Then a fella in the next bed whispered hello. Introduced himself as Lieutenant Anderson, Charlie P. Anderson. He had a broken leg strung up in a traction rig. Said he was from Milwaukee and spoke pretty good German. He said the German officers were pumping me pretty hard while I was still drugged."

"Damn!" Whitney spat out. "Do you remember what you told them?"

"Not really, sir. But it seemed like I shared my whole life's story with them, all the way back to my home on the farm in Michigan. Then if I remember the dreams, I told them everything about flying as a volunteer with the Republican air force in Spain, my service as a volunteer with the RAF from '39 to '42, and why I shifted to bombers when I transferred to the USAAF."

Whitney snorted. "Bastards violated both the spirit and letter of the Geneva Convention!"

"Don't guess they give a damn about that, sir. The Gestapo fella in Regensburg repeated a lot of stuff I had told the fellas in the hospital and laughed when I told him that violated the Geneva Convention."

Ben shifted in his chair. "Sir, I honestly don't know if I gave 'em sensitive information or breached security. Is that why I'm here?"

Whitney frowned and pouched out his lips. "We'll probably never know if you breached security or not. Do you remember if they asked for specifics about the B-17, the Norden bombsight in particular, or where you were based? That sort of thing?"

"Yessir, they did, but I told them I didn't know anything about the bombsight. Told 'em they'd have to ask Whit, uh . . . he was my bombardier." Ben shuddered. "Don't think Whit got out. We took the hit almost directly on the nose."

"Did they ask about D-Day?"

"Oh yeah, numerous times. The Gestapo fella in Regensburg pressed me for details on the invasion. Since I didn't know, I had nothing to tell them."

Ben sat back in his chair and eyed the three officers. "No offense, sir, but this is sounding more like a board of inquiry than an informal chat. Permission to ask a direct question?" Whitney nodded. "Are you looking to press charges against me?"

"No, no! I guess I got a bit intense in my questions, but I repeat, this is not a board of inquiry. We just have to be very careful. As I said in my briefing, we've had prisoners who were turned and cooperated with our captors. We've also had Gestapo officers fluent in English pose as newly arrived prisoners. We're always looking for informers, that sort of thing. And you arrived here in an unusual manner. So we needed to have this chat. Any other questions?"

"Yessir, two. Lieutenant Anderson, my bedmate in the hospital, disappeared while I was drugged with morphine. I have a fuzzy recollection of seeing him wheeled out. He said he flew B24s. Might he be here at Stalag Luft III?"

Whitney had a quiet word with the major on his left. "We'll check the roster. See if Anderson is here. What else?"

"Two more questions, actually, sir. Anderson said he overheard the Gestapo fellas say they weren't going to tell the Red Cross that I was a POW until they were finished grilling me. Can you check if that's true? I'd sure like Colonel Silverman to know I'm alive. And especially my family. I'm sure they've been notified I'm missing in action."

"We'll get on that," Whitney said. "You had one more question?"

"Yessir. In Spain and later when I flew Spitfires as a volunteer with the RAF, I flew wing on an Englishman Reginald M. Percy. Last time I saw him he was a wing commander leading a Spitfire unit at RAF Wittering. He was reported shot down and killed, but another RAF officer I met on the train here said he had heard Wing Commander Percy had survived the crash landing and was fished out of the channel by a German rescue crew. Said he might even be a POW in this camp. Is there a separate British section of the camp? Can I get to it and find out if the wing commander is there?"

"Yes, of course. If he's here, we'll put you together with your British colleague ASAP."

"That'll be swell, sir!" Ben almost shouted. "Reggie and I took turns saving each other's a . . ., uh, saving each other in Spain and during the Battle of Britain. I'd really like to find him here."

"Before we let you go, Major Findlay, tell us a bit about your home. Michigan, right?"

"Yessir. I was raised on a farm near Flint, Michigan." He smiled and almost said "Mitchigan."

"Flint, eh? Is that far from Detroit?"

Ben shook his head. "No. Detroit's about seventy miles south."

"You a sports fan? Professional baseball, football?" Whitney asked.

"Baseball, sir. I played football and baseball—actually, all sports in high school—but pro baseball interests me the most."

"Tell me about your favorite players on the Detroit Lions team," Whitney said casually.

"Uh, wrong cat, Colonel." Ben smiled. "Pro baseball team in Detroit is the Tigers."

"Of course, of course. Who's their star player?"

"Depending how far back you wanna go in history, sir. Way back it was Ty Cobb. Modern times it was Hank Greenberg 'til he got called up. He's in the air force. He was the league home run champion for a couple of years. Played first base."

"Anything special about him other than that he was a star slugger?" Whitney asked.

"Ah, yessir, he, uh, he's Jewish. First Jewish player to star in the majors."

Whitney eyed Ben. "Umm. Good. Now take a few minutes to tell us about your service in Spain and with the RAF. Sounds like you've had some interesting combat experience."

Ben started at the beginning, flying with Brice in Michigan and quickly shifted to his meeting with Silverman serving with him, and Reggie in Spain in 1938 through the fall of the Republic in 1939. He detailed his escape with Reggie to England in time to join the RAF and fight in the Battle of Britain. As he reached his decision in 1942 to transfer to the U.S. Army Air Forces, a lieutenant entered the room and whispered to Colonel Whitney. The colonel raised his hand, interrupting Ben's story.

"We've found Lieutenant Anderson," he said. "He's waiting outside. Let's call him in and ask about meeting you in the hospital."

Anderson limped inside, and Whitney interrupted his formal salute and report. "Lieutenant Anderson, do you recognize this man?"

"Yessir, he was my bedmate in the Regensburg hospital. Said he was Major Benjamin Findlay. From what I overheard when the Gestapo fellas were interrogating him, I think that's who he really is. Hello, Ben, good to see ya. Looks like you recovered okay."

Whitney fired a rapid series of question at Anderson, seemed satisfied he corroborated Ben's story, and dismissed him. Anderson flicked Ben a quick salute. "See ya around the camp, Ben." He smiled as he left.

"Sir, I hope I've convinced you I'm legit," Ben said. "I mean, do I look like a German ringer posing as a POW?"

"We ferreted out a couple of German ringers posing as POWs just a couple of months ago," Whitney said evenly. "At first, they appeared to be at least as 'legit' as you say you are."

The lieutenant returned and handed Whitney a note. "Major Findlay, you'll be happy to learn we've located Wing Commander Percy," Whitney said. "He's in the north compound."

"Hey that's swell!" Ben shouted and raised his right fist in the Spanish Republican salute.

Whitney and the two other officers stood. Ben started to rise, but Whitney motioned him to remain seated. "We'll be back shortly, Major," he said as they walked out.

Ben sat staring at the wall. *Guess I passed muster. Now what?*

The door opened behind him. Ben didn't turn around.

Chapter 8

Reunion

"I say, Benjamin old cock, what the bloody 'ell have you gotten yourself into this time?"

"*Reggie!*" Ben yelled, leaping from his chair and spinning around. "Reggie, my god, am I glad to see you!"

Reggie stood grinning, twirling one end of his rust-red mustache like a gendarme in a French film. His angular face appeared longer and thinner than Ben remembered, and his once straight aquiline nose had obviously been broken and not reset. An ugly red scar slashed across his right cheek from the edge of his mouth to his ear. He stood stoop shouldered, his long lean frame considerably shrunken. But the same amused twinkle sparkled in his hooded gray eyes.

"Hullo," Reggie said. "What's a nice young man like you doing in a place like this?"

The two battle-scarred flyers stepped forward and locked in a bear hug, pounding each other on the back. Reggie stepped back and peered into Ben's face. "Benjamin me lad, 'pears to me that Jerry has bashed you about a bit."

"A bit. Think I can say the same about you," Ben said, tears brimming in his eyes.

"What in hell happened to the left side of your face, Ben? Looks like you've been burned. And if I may ask, old son, why are your shoulders so damn crooked?"

"We can get into the gory details later," Ben said dismissively. "My god, I have so many questions! Where do we begin? We heard you were shot down and killed. Frank and I attended your memorial service at Calvert Hall. Reggie, it was terrible seeing your mom and dad and Elizabeth torn apart with grief."

"Ah yes. Bad show that. But reports of my crossing the Rubicon were a bit premature," Reggie joked. "Anyone say anything nice about me at the service? Mebbe you can fill me in later?"

"Yeah, joke about it all you want," Ben snorted, "but it was bloody tough on all of us, if I may borrow one of your favorite words. Say, have your folks been told you're alive and a prisoner?"

"Yes, yes. Huns finally figured out who I was and eventually informed the Red Cross."

"What took 'em so long?"

RAF Supermarine Spitfire Fighter

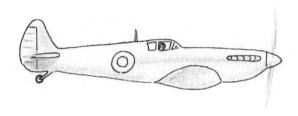

"Well, they found me floating in the channel unconscious and without any identification. Remember, that was a habit we got into in Spain? Was in and out of consciousness for several weeks, well, into the New Year anyway. Don't really remember.

"Took a bit more time to recover from my wounds," he added, fingering the scar on his right cheek. "And apparently, I really bashed the old noggin when I ditched my Spit in the channel. I don't even remember getting out of her before she sank. Anyway, when I was released from hospital, the Gestapo blokes at the Gulag Luft interrogation center worked me over for several weeks. They got bloody nothing out of me and finally tired of trying. Put me in a boxcar with a gaggle of fellow unfortunates and shipped me here.

I couldn't verify that the Boche had reported me to the Red Cross, so I raised the hell of a fuss until they got it done. Must have been sometime in March."

"No wonder I didn't hear," Ben muttered. "We were concentrating on flying our last five missions. Doolittle raised the mission bogey to thirty from twenty-five and, uh, my crew and I on *Round Trip*, uh, we were focused on gettin' them done."

"When and where were you shot down, Ben?" Reggie interjected.

"Leaving Regensburg. We'd bombed the Messerschmitt airplane factory. Got caught in a flak trap and took a direct hit. It was April 1, April Fool's Day."

Reggie guffawed. "Leave it to you to end your tour with a special flourish, old bean. But seriously, what about your crew?"

"Dunno," Ben mumbled. "I, uh . . . I guess I was blown clear when ol' *Round Trip* disintegrated. Nobody else landed near me, and I haven't caught up with any of them since.

"Apparently, I'm the only one who survived," Ben choked.

"Bloody hell! Bum show all around," Reggie said. "So have you been listed as a prisoner of war?"

"Well, that's what's eatin' at me," Ben said. I don't think they've reported me as having survived. I was interrogated by a couple of Germans while I was drugged in the hospital. Fella in the next bed whispered that to me. Then I was questioned by a Gestapo fella, real cold son of a bitch, in Regensburg for a couple of weeks. Later, some soldiers pulled me out of solitary and tossed me into a boxcar on a train that stopped in Regensburg en route to here. Fellas on the train also wondered why I hadn't been processed through Gulag Luft. Thought it was suspicious. Suspected I was a German spy."

"Umm, it was a bit unusual," Reggie said. "But I didn't find that bloody place very enjoyable, so you can be happy you gave it a pass."

"Yeah. I had to convince Colonel Whitney, our commander here, that I wasn't an undercover plant. Think I succeeded, or you wouldn't be here. Now I gotta be certain I'm listed with the Red Cross. Need to get word to my folks and Frank at the 509th an', uh, an' . . ."

"Lady Gwen?" Reggie interrupted. Ben nodded grimly.

Colonel Whitney knocked at the door and entered the room. "Well, have you two war birds brought each other up to date?" he asked. "Wing Commander Percy, I trust you can verify that Major Findlay is who he claims to be?"

"Right-ho, Colonel Whitney," Reggie responded. "This 'ere bloke indeed be who he says he be. Good man, Colonel. Think we can depend on him to help keep this place on an even keel and maybe even help us plan a way out."

"Excellent!" Whitney exclaimed. "Now then, it's coming up on late afternoon appel time. You better get back to the north compound, Wing Commander. And, Major Findlay, we need to join our formation."

"Bloody hell! Where's the time gone? I see it is indeed nearly time for nose counts," Reggie said, looking at his watch. He gave Colonel Whitney a snappy salute, "Good afternoon, Colonel." At the door, he turned and grinned at Ben. "See you around the patch, Sancho. Much to talk about."

"And Sancho would be . . . ?" Whitney asked.

"Long story, sir. Goes back to Battle of Britain days when I was Reggie's wingman. Our squadron code name was La Mancha. Referred back to our days flyin' in Spain. Reggie was Don Quixote, and for obvious reasons, they named me Sancho."

Chapter 9

Life as Kriegies

The days and weeks at Stalag Luft III melded into a boring sameness. Finding enough food to sustain themselves and collectively preparing it became a major preoccupation among the kriegies. Most bordered on malnutrition, and much of the food was bland to the point of tastelessness. But they had clean water and occasional hot showers, luxuries the average citizen across war-torn Germany did not enjoy.

The camp commandant insisted on maintaining high sanitary conditions throughout Stalag Luft III mainly to prevent the spread of diseases, such as cholera, tuberculosis, and malaria rather than to make camp life more comfortable for his prisoners. With eighteen men crammed into each bunk room, highly contagious diseases spread like wildfire.

Slit trench latrines had been dug some distance from the prisoner huts, and the kriegies regularly treated them with lime and eventually covered them with dirt dug from new trenches.

Many kriegies harbored thoughts of escape, but an equal number lost faith in any plans for breaking out. This contributed to tensions in the crowded bunk rooms, which POW group commanders tried to control by keeping the kriegies engaged in a range of camp activities.

The prisoners organized many of the activities themselves. Various sports teams formed, equipped with balls, bats, and even hockey sticks and skates provided by the Red Cross. They further broke the dull routine by staging plays and musical revues in the theater the kriegies had built.

Ben's left shoulder hadn't fully healed, so he didn't join the camp games, and he had absolutely no interest in joining the stage performances. Reggie played a few rounds of cricket with his fellow British prisoners but soon became restive and focused entirely on "finding a way out of this bloody place." He asked Ben if he was interested in joining an escape committee with him. Ben nodded eagerly.

The two high-profile escapes earlier in the year enraged Hitler, and he ordered severe reprisals against the camp commanders, guards, and prisoners. As a result, the guards redoubled their efforts to infiltrate escape committees with suborned kriegies or Gestapo plants. Their efforts produced few arrests but put a damper on escape fever.

Meanwhile, camp life droned on. The kriegies wouldn't have survived on their meager rations without monthly food parcels various national Red Cross organizations sent to many prisoners. These were pooled and shared with all inmates.

Now that the Germans had finally listed Ben as a POW, his family dispatched letters filled with joyous thanks for his survival and parcels filled with homemade goodies and socks knitted by his mother. The American Red Cross handled the deliveries with dispatch. Beyond letters from home, the most treasured items in the Red Cross packages were American cigarettes, Lucky Strikes and Camels. They satisfied many prisoners' well-developed cigarette cravings and also served as valuable barter items for bribing camp guards.

Ben's mother kept a stream of chatty letters coming. Betty, one of his high school friends, was pregnant again, she wrote. Her husband, Roger, a sergeant in the U.S. Army, had been home for a short leave two months ago before being shipped to North Africa. She prattled on about many of Ben's friends, providing details of life on the home front. His father's job had become so demanding she feared he would be "worked to death." Two of his fellow engineers had dropped dead of heart attacks.

Ben reread her latest letter. "Dad sends his regards and hopes they're treating you well. He's spending a lot of time at the Willow Run Proving Grounds near Detroit.

"Food is plentiful, since we live on the farm, and we're awarded special gasoline and tire ration permits because farming is listed as critical to the war effort. So we can get about quite well. We have lots of people coming by to buy our chickens, even before they're fully grown."

She saved the best news for last. Ben's older brother Joe, now a captain in the U.S. Marine Corps, arrived home from the Pacific Theater of Operations two weeks ago for a brief leave.

"He was wounded attacking that awful place they call Kwajalein," she wrote, "but he's doing fine now. I just don't know why they have to fight over all those little specks of islands in that huge ocean. What good can they be to anyone?

"Thankfully, he won't have to go back out there. He's being sent to a big marine base in Southern California, I think it's called Pendleton, to train other marines. This is so confusing. I always thought Pendleton was the company that made those beautiful wool shirts and things for outdoor sports. But I guess they wouldn't be the ones running the marine camp.

"Now I hope they're feeding you well. We'll keep sending food parcels, just in case. Are you getting plenty of exercise? How wonderful it is that your friend Reggie is there with you. It's so good to have friends around. Oh, by the way, your colonel friend sent me such a nice letter. I think that's all I can say about that."

She closed with additional details about Donna, who was driving a big army truck in Alabama. "Oh, I always thought you two would make such a lovely couple. She's engaged to a sergeant, and her mother says he's a very nice man. But he may be shipped overseas, so they'll probably have to wait to get married.

"We love you so much and pray for your safe return home. Mom."

Ben folded the letter with a rueful smile and tucked it away. "Great to stay in touch with the real world," he muttered.

Two days later, the mail clerk called Ben's name. "Two letters, Major," he said, handing Ben the envelopes. A faint scent of lavender wafted from the first envelope addressed in a dainty handwriting. Ben quickly scanned the return address—Gwen Brewster! It was from the beautiful nurse who took care of him in the Cambridge hospital, after he had been shot down in his RAF Spitfire, and became the love of his life. She had returned to Cambridge. Ben winced at the thought of their parting when he put her on a train to her aunt's home after a Luftwaffe bomb destroyed her home, killing her mother.

"Dearest Ben," the letter began. "I am thrilled beyond words that you are alive! Prison camp cannot be very pleasant, but the important thing is you're alive! You no doubt are quite surprised to hear from me. As you can see from the return address, I'm back nursing at the same hospital where we met.

"I was devastated when I contacted your commanding officer shortly after arriving here and learned you had been shot down over Germany. He was so kind and considerate and helped me bear the shock. I wept copious tears and became very depressed."

Ben suppressed a sob as tears welled in his eyes, blurring Gwen's handwriting.

"Imagine my joy when he telephoned and said you had survived and were in a prison camp," her letter continued. "I wept equally copious tears, but this time, they were joyful tears. Thank God, oh, thank God you are alive and safe! I live for the moment when we will see each other again.

"I must say, though, that my joy is tempered with sadness. The Red Cross informed me just before leaving my aunt's home that my husband, Tony, had died in the prison camp where he was taken after the German submarine picked him up in the Atlantic. The wounds he suffered when his destroyer was sunk were so severe he finally succumbed after only a few months in prison. I am emotionally drained after first hearing that he had been killed, then being informed he was alive and a prisoner, and now hearing he had died.

"Oh, when will this terrible war end? How I wish you were here to comfort me!"

Gwen added some news about her work and closed the letter with personal endearments, stressing how much she longed to again hold him in her arms. Ben held the letter in trembling hands for a long moment before quickly reading it again. He then folded it and slipped it into the inner jacket pocket over his heart. He would read and reread it often.

The second letter bore a postmark from an official USAAF address in London. Ben puzzled over its terse confirmation that he had been listed as a POW and his pay, benefits, and time in grade would be maintained. It added that to date, no other member of his crew had been identified as surviving. The air force listed them as KIA, killed in action. It was signed "hasta luego!" ("see you around" in Spanish)

Frank! This has to be a message from Colonel Silverman! Wonderful!

Ben reread the message. The abbreviation "KIA" leaped out at him. Apparently, none of his crewmates had survived. His elation at hearing from Gwen and Silverman spiraled into depression. True to form, Reggie rose to the challenge and tugged, teased, and berated him back from the black abyss.

"Come on, Ben, look lively," he snapped during an afternoon stroll around the camp perimeter. Ben had joined him grudgingly and trudged beside him in a sullen silence. "Damn it, clinging to the past can't help, old bean. You can't change what happened on your last mission. Look, you've heard from Gwen. Dwell on that. Now we must try and do something about getting out of this bloody place."

Ben responded with a muttered curse.

"Okay, Major Findlay, who the hell do you think you're talking to? I'm at the point of telling you to go to blazes! Now pull yourself out of this tail spin or crash and burn!"

Ben tensed and started to snarl at Reggie, then dropped his shoulders and flashed a quick smile. "Okay yourself, you crazy bloody Englishman. I needed that kick in the arse. Let's get back into close formation. You lead."

"Uncommonly civil of you, Sancho. Let's do just that!"

The American camp leaders pulled Ben into the command team for the American compound. They named him group commander of his hut, number 270, and officially appointed him as liaison with the British compound and a member of the British American escape committee. This provided many opportunities for Ben and Reggie to interact. They spent long hours reminiscing about their adventures, including flying with the Russians in support of the Republican loyalists in the Spanish civil war.

"Listen, old bean," Reggie said one afternoon, "never told you this, but back in '38 when you walked into my quarters at Zaragoza Aerodrome, saluted, and announced you'd been assigned as my wingman, I wondered what the bloody hell I had done to warrant having some child from the colonies assigned to protect me from harm. I mean, facing the Nationalist pilots, most of 'em Germans flying for the Condor Legion, was one thing. Dragging you along as well was going to be quite another."

Ben chuckled and started to interrupt, but Reggie cut him off with a wave of his hand.

"You looked exactly like what you were, a fresh-faced hick from the hinterlands of the American West," Reggie continued, "and when you got so wound up telling me about your beloved flight instructor Brice that you fell off your stool and landed on your arse, I thought I was done for."

"But it was an amazing coincidence!" Ben interjected. "I mean, discovering that Brice, who was responsible for getting me ready for Spain, had been your father's wingman in World War 1. No wonder I was excited."

"Do say," Reggie countered coolly. "Suppose you're right. It's what saved the day, my friend. Else I'd have sent you packing and asked our mad Russian commander Colonel Golenkinov to assign some drunken Russian pilot to protect my arse."

"Worked out fine in the end, didn't it?" Ben said quietly. "We did a pretty good job lookin' after each other."

"Indeed we did, old cock. Can't imagine anyone else doing a better job of covering my six o'clock position." Reggie paused and smiled at Ben. "Had some good innings, didn't we?" Ben nodded.

The dull routine of camp life became more oppressive, and Ben felt increasingly restive. More letters from home and highly scented love notes from Gwen considerably raised his spirits. He eagerly joined the combined escape committee's discussions of various escape plans. Pulling Reggie aside after one of their sessions, Ben whispered, "We need to get some more fellas involved with us. I mean, a small group of fellas we can trust."

"Who'd you have in mind?"

"Well, there's this British Spitfire pilot I met on the train. Name's Saunders, Squadron Leader. Sandy Saunders," Ben said. "Know him?"

Reggie nodded. "Good chap. Think he'd be a fine addition to our inner circle. Anybody else?"

"Leave it to you to find another Brit to join us," Ben said. "But I have two Americans to suggest: Captain Archie Banner, the German-speaking fella from Pennsylvania, and Lieutenant Art Kowalski, the one from Brooklyn who was also on the train with me."

"Umm, Kowalski . . ." Reggie mused. "Suppose he speaks Polish? Having chaps who speak both German and Polish would be a big help once we get out."

"Yeah," Ben agreed. "I'll ask Kowalski."

"Capital! I'll also ask Flight Leftenant Duncan Whitford to join us," Reggie said. "Helluva fighter pilot, level headed and a good scout all 'round. Think he played a part in the great escape but didn't get caught. A swell chap," Reggie added, "to use one of your favorite words."

Ben nodded. "Okay. Ah, what'll we call ourselves? Need a unit code name, don't we?"

"Since we'll be sticking our bloody necks out a bloody mile, why not call ourselves the Giraffes?" Reggie joked. Ben flicked him a wry smile, then nodded.

At the first meeting of the Giraffes, Ben surveyed the tiny band. *What a combination of characters. We couldn't be more different if we tried.*

He knew RAF Squadron Leader Saunders from the chat they'd had during the Prague rest stop en route to Stalag Luft III. Sandy flew out of RAF Station Kenley in Surrey before he was shot down. His shock of blond hair had grown in again but still stuck out at odd angles. His wiry frame and darting blue eyes marked him as a fighter pilot. Ben felt certain he relished aerial combat in his Supermarine Spitfire.

RAF Flight Leftenant Whitford, also a fighter pilot, projected an entirely different image. His lanky, loose-jointed frame gave him a long loping stride that made him appear to float more than walk. A large aquiline nose, undergirded by a bushy brown mustache, dominated an otherwise unremarkable face. His dark brown eyes also constantly glanced from side to side, a habit formed by fighter pilots used to scanning the sky around them. He had been shot down while flying a ground attack mission over Germany in a Hawker Typhoon from his base at RAF Manston in Kent.

Archie Banner, the German-speaking USAAF captain from Pennsylvania, had a quiet, confident demeanor. He stood slightly over six feet tall, which predestined him to be a bomber pilot. He commanded a Boeing B-17G on a mission from Wendling Station 118 near East Durham in Norfolk when he was shot down near Frankfurt, Germany. He and Ben shared a common bond in that regard. Banner had a way of pausing before answering questions, fixing one with solemn gray eyes as if seriously considering whether to respond at all much less than what to say. His broad shoulders, long-muscled arms, and powerful hands pointed to years of heavy labor on a farm.

USAAF Lieutenant Kowalski's Brooklyn upbringing gave him a cocky, streetwise attitude. Ben was certain his fluent Polish had a heavy Brooklyn accent and wondered how that sounded to native Polish speakers. Kowalski looked at the world through narrowed brown eyes that seemed to say, "Oh yeah? I'm not so sure, pal. Prove it to me." He had a medium-sized but muscular frame. Ben imagined him flying his North American P-51 fighter like a demon on bomber escort missions. He had been based at RAF Raydon in Suffolk.

Ben pondered the group. *Amazing that all of us from such different backgrounds would end up here in Stalag Luft III plotting escape together.*

"I say, Benjamin me lad, where are you?" Reggie said, breaking into Ben's musing. "Something on your mind?"

"Huh?" Ben grunted. "Ah no, ah, I was just considering our happy band, thinking about how we're gonna work together to break outta this dump.

"I've only been here a short while," he added. "I know some of you've been here a lot longer—some for years. But I can't take much more of this rotten camp life. I'm ready to work on specific ideas for getting out. The cross-channel invasion of France has to be comin' soon. I don't know about the rest of you, but I want to get back in it while there's still a war goin' on."

Chapter 10

GOOD NEWS! – JUNE 6, 1944

Excitement surged through Stalag Luft III as prison couriers sprinted from hut to hut, delivering the latest news. The D-Day invasion had started at 0630 hours that day. Hoots and cheers echoed throughout the camp.

Several shortwave radios had been secreted around Stalag Luft III, some of them built by kriegies from bits and pieces of scavenged material and others smuggled in by German guards bribed with American cigarettes and food. Special crews monitored broadcasts from Western radio stations, primarily the British Broadcasting Corporation (BBC), around the clock. The monitoring crews then briefed the couriers who spread the top news of the day. And on this day, it was of momentous importance.

"Benjamin me lad, this lifts the old spirits I must say," Reggie chortled. "You were bang about wanting to get out of here while there's still a war going on. Just think, Herr Hitler now has a third major front to defend. The Russians are pushing in from the east after their breakout from Stalingrad early last year, the combined American and British armies are slugging up the Italian boot following the invasion of Sicily last fall, and now the Allied invasion force in Normandy is heading toward Germany from the west.

"By god, I wouldn't be in the ol' führer's shoes for anything," Reggie added. "I'm itching to get back to it as well! Let's get to work on some definite escape plans."

The news of the Allies' successes from the east, west, and south encouraged the POWs to believe the tide of the war had truly turned in their favor. By May of 1944, the allies in Italy had liberated Rome, and the majority of the opposing Germany armies retreated to the Gothic Line defenses along Austria's southern border with Italy.

The kriegies rejoiced in the early news of the Normandy landings. The combined Allied sea, air, and land operation, code-named Operation Overlord, ranked as history's largest amphibious invasion, and it had caught the German defenders by surprise partly because the German high command thought current inclement weather would make a cross-channel invasion impossible.

RAF Hawker Hurricane Mk-11B Fighter

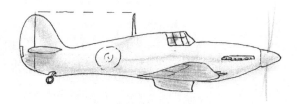

Elaborate deceptions, including leaked disinformation that General George S. Patton would lead the invasion with the fictitious First United States Army Group, convinced Hitler and the German high command that when the main attack came, it would be across the Strait of Dover, which the French call the Pas de Calais. Patton conducted fake maneuvers with a "cardboard army and inflatable rubber tanks" along England's east coast to add credence to the thought that Pas de Calais was the launching point. Even after the Normandy landings began, the German high command kept troops in place to meet a cross-channel attack, believing the Normandy landings were a feint. For the same reason, Hitler also ordered critical Wehrmacht armored units kept in reserve rather than sending them to support the Normandy defenders.

But the Normandy beaches were the targets. The invading forces, under the overall command of General Dwight D. Eisenhower, landed along the coastline of France's Bay of the Seine at the boundary between the Seventh and Fifteenth German Armies. The Allies hoped this would create confusion in command responsibility between the two German armies. American-led forces hit the western beaches, code-named Omaha and Utah; while the British-led forces landed on three eastern beaches, code-named Sword, Juno, and Gold.

The easternmost Sword Beach landings faced the Normandy towns of Ouistreham, Lion, and Luc; while the Sword Beach forces landed at Courseulles with the inland city of Caen as their initial objective. The Gold Beach forces landed between Arromanches and Port-en-Bessin and thrust toward Bayeux. In a twist of history, Bayeux housed the huge Bayeux tapestry, depicting the cross-channel invasion of England by William, duke of Normandy, in 1066. After winning the ensuing battle of Hastings in Southern England, William the Conqueror was crowned king of England.

To the west, forces landing on Omaha Beach faced the heaviest defenses, hitting the coastal towns of Coleville, Vierville, and the Pointe du Hoc. A combination of tides, currents, and winds pushed the Utah-invading fleet farther west than planned, and the landing encountered relatively weak resistance. By the end of D-Day plus 1, secure footholds had been established along all five landing sites.

Allied airborne divisions led by British and American commanders parachuted and landed in gliders on the eastern and western flanks of the main invasion sites and behind German lines to further confuse and divide the defender's forces.

Heavy bomber groups from the Eighth Air Force and RAF Bomber Command also launched raids on the invasion beaches, but a persistently heavy overcast prevented them from attacking reinforced concrete gun emplacements, pillboxes, and command centers close to the beachheads. At the same time, other bomber units flew patterns over the Strait of Dover, dropping tons of radar-reflecting aluminum strips. This "chaff" tricked German radar operators into believing they were seeing a large invasion fleet assembling in the channel.

The Allied armies survived devastating cross fire and bombardment on the five landing sites, overwhelmed the German beach defenses, and pushed inland. Morale soared throughout the prison population as they heard details of the successful thrusts through German lines. The news had the opposite effect on the camp commanders and most guards, who sensed that the invasion represented a critical turning point in the war.

"Benjamin, old man, with Allied spearheads aimed at the fatherland from the south and west and our Russian friends advancing from the east, this gives us three directions to go once we get past the fences of this godforsaken hole," Reggie said.

"Damn right!" Ben exclaimed. "But we need to keep pace with the news and be ready to decide what direction we go when we break out."

Reggie arranged with a friend attached to a radio-monitoring unit to allow them to sit in on a session with the BBC. They hunkered in a darkened room where floorboards had been loosened to make a hiding place for the radio. Two kriegies cranked a makeshift generator to power the radio while two more patrolled outside the hut, ready to whistle warning signals if camp guards approached.

"Does me old heart wonders to listen to the BBC again," Reggie whispered as the English newsreader delivered the latest details of the Normandy action. "Reminds me of gathering around the wireless at Calvert Hall to hear the king's Christmas message."

The scope of the invasion astounded the listeners. The first wave of invaders totaled over 156,000 men from a variety of American, British, colonial, and Allied country units. And thousands more surged toward the beaches in succeeding waves.

Units of the French Resistance, briefed earlier to listen for special code words broadcast by the BBC, sprang into action. They sabotaged rail systems serving Normandy, blew up electrical facilities, and attacked German reinforcing units held in reserve and severed telephone and teleprinter cables. These actions further complicated the German high command's effort to organize its defensive forces. Underground units across Poland, Czechoslovakia, and Yugoslavia also went on full alert, ready to harass German occupation forces headed toward the beaches to reinforce the defender units.

"I can't imagine how the Supreme Allied Command could have involved that many people in the planning and preparation for D-Day and still kept it secret," Ben said marveled. "Think of the thousands who knew, and yet they pulled it off as a total surprise."

"Bloody wonder that," Reggie agreed. "Weather helped, but methinks Herr Hitler probably meddled in the command chain and made things worse by imposing some of his loony ideas on the army commanders. Time will tell what impact that had on the situation."

Good news continued to pour in. The Normandy invading forces broke through on all fronts, isolating and bypassing the heavily defended Cherbourg Peninsula and thrusting eastward across France. Some guards began catering to the kriegies, obviously hoping to be treated well after what many already anticipated as Germany's defeat. Others turned increasingly hostile toward the POWs and meted out unreasonable punishment for the slightest infractions of camp rules.

Chapter 11

CAUGHT IN THE ACT

Several escape committees began planning in earnest. Reggie, Ben, and their four fellow Giraffes discussed a range of schemes, including hiding in large trash containers or laundry trolleys that were hauled daily from the camp. They also studied the undersides of the numerous trucks that passed through the gates to determine whether there was room to cling unseen under the truck beds. Digging yet another tunnel was dismissed because it would require a large escape crew and, more importantly, would take a lot of time. Stealing a German uniform or buying one from a suborned guard were considered but rejected because they feared the guard might betray them.

"Important thing is to keep the ideas coming," Reggie told the group. "Meantime, we need to follow the latest developments on all three fronts so we can choose which direction to head in once we're outside."

One evening, the Giraffes crowded into a clandestine radio room, listening to the BBC. Shrill whistles, pounding boots, and shouted commands reverberated through the hut. Camp guards had ambushed and silenced the kriegies on sentry duty. No warning whistles had alerted the listeners. Guards burst in before they could hide the radio. They sat staring into the muzzles of bayoneted Mauser rifles.

After being marched at bayonet point across the camp, the six Giraffes stood sullenly in front of the Kommandant Von Striesel's desk. Von Striesel, who sat erect and unsmiling, stared coldly at them. "You have violated a basic camp rule," he rasped. "Unsupervised contact with the outside world is verboten—forbidden! We also know you are planning an escape. Have you anything to say?"

No one responded.

"You, ah, Wing Commander Percy," Von Striesel said, consulting a list on his desk, "you are the leader of this escape group, ah, which you call the Giraffes, are you not?"

Reggie stood silently.

"You do not seem surprised that we know all about your activities, Wing Commander, even the ridiculous code name of your group. We have an excellent intelligence system at Stalag Luft III. Little eludes our attention."

Ben stared passively, struggling to show no reaction. *How the hell did they get that information? Can't believe any of our group would betray us.* None of the kriegies knew that Von Striesel had installed an extensive network of hidden listening devices throughout the camp.

"And you, Major Findlay, have you anything to say?"

"No, sir," Ben snapped.

"Kommandant Von Striesel," Reggie said evenly, "we were listening to a BBC broadcast. But surely, you are aware that the entire camp is following recent developments on all three fronts of the war." He put special emphasis on "all three fronts."

Von Striesel stared stone-faced at Reggie. "Of course, Wing Commander, but that does not excuse your infraction of the rules. We will arrest the others as we find their listening sites." He paused.

"Your reference to 'all three fronts' is not lost on me," he added icily. "You and your Allied commanders will make a serious mistake if you think the Wehrmacht and the Luftwaffe are defeated. Plans for counterattacks are in place. The enemy will never reach the fatherland!"

Reggie smiled indulgently but did not respond.

"So we return to the escape plans," Von Striesel hissed. "No one has anything else to say?" The prisoners stood tight lipped.

"Then you give me no alternative. You will be taken to the detention center and locked in solitary cells for ten days. We will see if a little solitude and a diet of bread and water will change your attitudes."

The Giraffes stumbled out of their solitary cells ten days later, pale and thin but resolute. Their parched lips showed the extent of their thirst, and their shrunken stomachs were evidence that the minimal bread portions had barely sustained life. But no one had broken.

The six POWs stood unsteadily in front of the Kommandant's desk. A sumptuous lunch had been laid on a table next to his desk. Von Striesel rose and took a chair at the table. An aide piled food on his plate and poured a chilled Riesling wine in a tall glass. He took a long drink, swirled the wine in his mouth, and turned to the kriegies.

"Are you now ready to tell me about your escape plans?" he asked. Then as if remembering his manners, he said quickly, "Ah, forgive me. Would you like to join me in a bit of food and refreshment?"

Reggie flashed him a crooked grin. "Thank you, Herr Kommandant, but we've already had a hardy lunch. Couldn't eat another bite." The others mumbled their agreement.

Von Striesel carefully placed his wine glass on the table, tucked a linen napkin into his collar, and reached for his knife and fork. "What a pity. Sauerbraten with potato pancakes is one of my chef's specialties."

As he forked portions into his mouth and washed them down with the Riesling, the six POWs stared, their eyes reflecting a mixture of ravenous hunger, thirst, and loathing. No one moved or spoke. Finally, Von Striesel flicked a hand at the guards and snapped, "Nehmen sie die Gefangenen zuruck in ihre quartiere." ("Take the prisoners back to their quarters.")

As soon as the prisoners left, Von Striesel signaled the waiter to clear the table. The Germans also faced short rations. The remainder of the sauerbraten dinner would be divided among his officers.

Word spread that the Giraffes were released. Cheers resounded as fellow kriegies escorted them to a welcome home "banquet" in Ben's hut. As they slaked their thirst on tepid tap water and chewed fried Spam garnished with rehydrated potato flakes, the Giraffes tried to pretend they were dining on succulent sauerbraten and potato pancakes.

Undeterred by their solitary punishment, Reggie and Ben convened the Giraffes in a darkened storeroom. "I'm convinced none of us betrayed our plans to the Germans," Reggie said. "They obviously have a very effective spy network in the camp. Someone must have overheard us. Means we have to be super careful in how, when, and where we talk."

"I agree," Ben chimed in. "Part of their strategy is to spread suspicion among our escape committees—make us feel we can't trust anyone. We've got to keep lookin' for ways outta here. Just need to be more careful how we go about it."

They continued to discuss detailed escape plans and talked to several kriegies with tailoring skills on how to convert uniforms into outfits that would pass for civilian clothing. Despite their precautions, several weeks later, they were rousted out of their bunks and assembled in front of Von Striesel's desk.

He studied a report on his desk without looking up, ignoring the prisoners for several minutes. He slowly raised his head and stared coldly at each of them. "Apparently, you learned nothing from your solitary confinement and my warnings," he snarled. "I have here"—he tapped the papers on his desk—"detailed reports that you are continuing to formulate escape schemes." He read several of their conversations verbatim. "I will not have you exposing me to the führer's wrath by even attempting to escape, verstehst du, do you understand!" he shouted. He obviously did not want to suffer the same fate as his predecessor.

The Giraffes stood mute, staring over Von Striesel's head.

"Gott im Himmel! Was stur schweine du bist!" Von Striesel burst out. "What stubborn pigs you are!"

He signaled the guards to take them away. Then to the prisoners he said, "You will be returned to solitary once more. When you are out, I will put a stop to this impudence!"

As they were led away, Ben whispered to Reggie, "How the hell did they get such details of our plans? I don't think any of the other fellas would rat on us, do you?"

"I really doubt it. Must confess I don't know for sure, Ben. All I can figure is they have listening devices planted all around the camp. They probably watch where we've been gathering and wire them for sound. Guess we haven't been careful enough to keep shifting our meeting places."

When the Giraffes emerged from solitary, they again assembled in front of Von Striesel's desk. He stared silently at them, then "steepled" his fingers under his chin and smiled thinly. "I have a final solution to the problems you have presented me with," he snarled.

Ben jerked involuntarily. *Oh god! Does he mean a firing squad?*

"I could line you up against a wall and have you shot," Von Striesel continued as if reading Ben's thoughts. "But I might have difficulty defending that decision since you have not yet actually implemented any of your misguided escape schemes." He paused. "Instead, I'm going to transfer you to Camp Sachsenhausen near Berlin. We sent several prisoners who had escaped earlier from this camp to Sachsenhausen after we recaptured them. This is a concentration camp and is known for its strict discipline and harsh punishment of any prisoner attempting to escape. You will soon wish you had obeyed the rules and remained here in Stalag Luft III, a place much nicer than the one to which you are going. You will depart by train tonight with several other prisoners who also have challenged my authority."

He signaled the guards to lead them away.

Chapter 12

EXILED!

Camp guards herded the six Giraffes and twenty-four other kriegies exiled from Stalag Luft III into a lone boxcar standing on a siding inside the camp. It was as fetid as the one in which Ben had ridden to Stalag Luft III. Even with fewer prisoners jammed in, it was only marginally more comfortable. The straw covering the floor reeked of urine and human waste from former occupants and housed swarms of fleas, ticks, and lice. But the prisoners were inured to bites of the vermin, which also infested Stalag Luft III.

"Anyone know what we're headed for, Wing Commander?" one of the occupants asked Reggie as they sat in the stifling boxcar.

"Not certain, but Sachsenhausen is a concentration camp, and it probably ain't a happy a place."

"I bribed one of the guards with a pack of Luckies," Banner piped up. "He said they're going to hook us onto the end of an armament train hauling heavy guns, probably antiaircraft 88s, to Berlin. Sachsenhausen is only, what, about twenty kilometers north of Berlin. Guard said the train'll pass near here about midnight. We'll be shunted out and hooked onto it."

Shortly after midnight, the boxcar jolted as what sounded like a rail yard-shunting engine hooked onto it. The kriegies heard the camp gate grind open, and the engine huffed them along the tracks. Following much shunting to and fro, the boxcar's coupling banged into that of another car.

"Feels like we're hooked onto the armament train," Banner said. "Hang on."

As the train rattled into the night, Ben and Reggie lay on piles of sodden straw propped against the front wall of the boxcar. The other occupants sprawled in various positions across the floor. Ben had just nodded off when all were startled awake by muffled explosions somewhere ahead of the train. They tumbled forward as the engineer slammed on the emergency brakes. Steel wheels locked and bit into the rails, flashing streams of sparks visible through cracks in the boxcar walls.

"What the hell!" someone yelled. "Feels like were gonna—"

Thunderous explosions drowned out his voice as their boxcar slammed into the car ahead. The locomotive's steam whistle shrieked like a giant pig being slaughtered. A series of explosions reverberated through the train as the locomotive plunged off the tracks and smashed into trees. Its steam boiler ruptured with a massive whoosh. Trailing cars telescoped into those ahead. Large antiaircraft guns broke loose from their restraining chains and tumbled into the tangled mess. Soldiers screamed as they were hurled into the trees or crushed under heavy cannon mounts.

Ben and Reggie, pinned against the forward wall, raised their arms and legs to ward off the bodies of other prisoners hurtling toward them. The coupling snapped and the boxcar spun sideways, flipped off the tracks, and smashed on its side with a bone-jarring crash. Dirt and tree branches swirled into a giant dust cloud. The impact splintered the boxcar's wooden walls, and pointed shards whistled through the air like a hail of medieval arrows. Several prisoners were impaled.

As the dust cleared, the prisoners lay crumpled and stunned. The spinning train wheels ground to a stop. Then the moans and screams began overlaid with a chorus of curses from some of the German guards. Flashlight beams swept the smoking jumble of railroad cars, and a fusillade of rifle shots cracked and snapped from the forest on both sides of the train. A few rifles returned fire from the train, and a machine gun chattered from one of the cars until a concentrated volley of rifle shots from the surrounding forest silenced them all.

The prisoners coughed and sneezed and added their own litany of cursing to the cacophony of noise surrounding the wrecked train.

"What the hell happened!" someone yelled. "Ah shit! I think my arm's broken."

"Reggie, you okay?" Ben choked.

"Right-ho, Benjamin." He paused to cough and clear his throat. "Bit bashed about but don't think anything's broken. More than I can say for these poor blighters."

Three prisoners from the British compound lay crumpled in a forward corner, their necks twisted at grotesque angles. They had been killed instantly. Ben found a fourth casualty: an American pilot whose skull had been crushed. Reggie ground his fist into his right palm. "Bloody damn shame to die like this."

"Never been in a train wreck before," someone mumbled. "What the hell caused it?"

"Think someone blew up the tracks just as the train was approaching," Reggie said. "Those were the explosions we heard. Okay," he croaked, struggling upright, "let's assess the damage. These four chaps are beyond help. Anyone else hurt?"

"My arm's broken for sure," came one response. "Bent bloody backward. Shoulder might also be broken. At least dislocated." Several others said they were pulling large splinters from arms and legs. No one else responded.

"How about the Giraffes?" Reggie called out. Whitford, Banner, and Kowalski all responded, "Okay." Reggie peered through the dust-filled gloom. "Sandy, how about you?"

Saunders groaned. "Sorry, Reggie. Got a badly busted leg. Double fracture from the looks of it."

"Damn and blast!" Reggie spouted. "Let's have a look."

As they bent examining Saunders's leg, Kowalski shouted, "Quiet! Listen!" Boots crunched on the stones, forming the railway bed. The prisoners heard a murmur of voices interspersed by sharp commands and the crack of pistol shots.

"Sounds like troops are moving through the wreckage and shooting anyone still alive," Reggie hissed. "I think they're headed for our car."

"They're speaking Polish," Kowalski whispered. "Do you think the Polish underground might have launched this attack?"

"Give 'em a yell," Ben urged. "Let's find out.

Chapter 13

Escape!

Kowalski clambered to a split in the boxcar wall and yelled, "Pomoc! Pomoc! Jesteśmy amerykańskich i brytyjskich jeńców wojennych. Prosimy o pomoc!" ("Help! Help! We're American and British prisoners of war. Please help us!") This prompted a flurry of shouts and commands as several individuals milled around outside the car.

A voice called out, "Kim jesteś?" ("Who are you?")

Kowalski sucked in a deep breath. "Jesteśmy sprzymierzone więźniów Stalagu Luft III. Są wysyłane do obozu koncentracyjnego w Sachsenhausen." ("We are Allied prisoners from Stalag Luft III being shipped to Sachsenhausen concentration camp.")

"Mother of god!" the voice boomed back in English. "Your vords I understand, but vere in hell you get dat awful accent?"

Ben choked back a guffaw.

"*Brooklyn!*" Kowalski yelled. "You got a problem with that?"

"Haw, haw, haw!" the voice boomed back. "No problem. I vas in Merchant Marine. Wisited Brooklyn many times but never heared Polish spoken vid such goddamned accent!"

Ben poked Reggie. "I wondered what his Polish sounded like."

"Okay, okay," Kowalski snarled. "You speak English with a goddamned accent, so what! Now get us out of here!"

"Soldier comes vid ax. Ve chop you out real quick."

It only took minutes for the ax wielder to cut holes through the splintered boxcar walls. Flashlights temporarily blinded the prisoners as they squeezed through the ragged openings. They stood shivering in the damp night air, staring at the giant who obviously commanded the partisan band surrounding them.

"Wing Commander Reginald M. Percy," Reggie said, stepping forward and extending his right hand. "Pleased to meet you. Thanks for rescuing us."

"Piotrowski," the giant responded, crushing Reggie's hand in a huge paw. "Commander Polish partisan unit 267. You velcome. Is good to meet you. But ve din' know prisoners of war vere on train."

"We were a last minute addition. Explain later."

Reggie eyed the man looming above him. He was at least six and a half feet tall, and his shoulders appeared to span four feet. A black bushy beard flecked with gray covered most of his face. Equally bushy dark eyebrows helped conceal the rest. His prominent nose protruded from the mass of facial hair like a wild boar peering through a hedge row. Tangles of matted black hair poked out from under a fur-lined leather hat. Multiple layers of outer clothing added to his already massive girth and knee-high leather boots completed the picture. An overwhelming aura of cigarette smoke and body odor wafted from him, convincing Reggie the man had been living rough for quite some time.

"Well then," Reggie began, "jolly good to stand and chat, but we've got four dead chaps inside and these two with broken bones. Can you help us with them? Ah, I suppose we shouldn't stand about too long in case the Germans send someone out to inquire who's mucked up their train."

"Haw! Mucked up deir train. I like dat," Piotrowski boomed. "Ve didn't muck up train. Ve smashed hell out of it and killed plenty Germans in process. But right, must go. Vill bury dead, den get vounded to safe hospital. Now vat in hell we do with rest of you?"

He shot Reggie an amused look. "So, Ving Commander Percy, you vant continue your vay to Sachsenhausen, or maybe ve help you get hell out of here? Back to England, hokay?"

"Hokay, indeed," Reggie said heartily. "Kindly show us the way."

Piotrowski rumbled orders and several partisan soldiers gently lifted the four bodies and carried them into the forest. Others followed with shovels. Two groups lifted Saunders and the other injured pilot onto makeshift stretchers and followed.

"Umm, where do you propose burying our chaps?" Reggie inquired.

"Ve have safe camp some miles in forest in big cave," Piotrowski said. "We go der, do good honors for dead heroes, and get vounded to doctors. You vill see."

"Right, of course," Reggie responded. "Umm, please tell your men I'll need to collect the *personalkartes* and identity discs from our dead colleagues. We'll have to notify their next of kin. Ah, what town or village are we near?"

"Closest town is Lubsko, vest of Bobr River," Piotrowski said. Turning away from the train, he said, "Now for sure get hell avay from train wreck before German patrol finds. Men have stripped all ve need, including strong box of gold, eh? Also fix guns so not verk.

"Hokay, how many men you have ve need help escape?"

"Thirty, uh, sorry, we started with thirty. Now down to twenty-four able to travel. I say, how many men do you have?"

"Fifty but fight like tree hunnerd!" Piotrowski boasted. "Twenty-four, eh? Hmm, makes problem for escape, I tink. First need get to safe camp and make plans. Follow dis vay."

As they trooped after the partisans, Ben looked back from the top of a ridge at the smoking tangled mass of railroad cars and twisted rails. "You sure chose a perfect spot for the ambush. That curve in the tracks and the forest gave excellent cover for your troops. And the narrow cut between those hills where you derailed the train is totally blocked. You've closed the entire right of way."

"Bloody good thing our car was hooked on the end," Reggie said. "Otherwise, we'd have been squashed in the middle of that mess. The Germans will play hell getting that cleaned up anytime soon,"

"Not first time ve attack trains," Piotrowski said, flashing a wolfish grin. "Ve pick spots carefully. Now let's go! Need get to cave hideout soon."

The partisans had a band of horses and pack animals tethered in the forest several miles from the railroad tracks along with several rough farm carts. They loaded the four bodies into one cart and settled Saunders and the other injured pilot in another.

By the time they reached the partisan hideout, Piotrowski's men had dug graves. One silently handed Reggie the *personalkartes* and identity discs, and the others laid the bodies in their final resting places. Reggie ordered his fellow escapees into a burial formation, saluted the graves, and recited what portions of the RAF burial service he could remember. He closed with the Lord's Prayer and quietly ended with, "Burial detail, dismissed!"

Piotrowski stepped forward and with some urgency said everyone needed to get settled in the hiding place. He assured Reggie they would deliver the two injured prisoners to a secret partisan medical facility where they would be given excellent care.

"First, ve get everyone to base camp hiding place. Get settled. Den I go meet partisan chief and figure how we get you and companions de hell out of Poland. Ve got several secret escape routes, like unnerground railroad in America during civil war, you know, but normally, ve only handle small numbers—political prisoners trying escape Nazis, so on. Need figure out how move big numbers."

He paused and scratched his wild thatch of hair. "You stay vid right-hand man Zielinski in camp. I come back in day or two."

Reggie and Ben led the escapees into the partisan camp. A small well-concealed entrance led to a narrow tunnel that opened into the main cave, a huge underground cavern with a vaulted ceiling and several niches the size of small rooms around the perimeter. A large rough fireplace dominated one section of the cave wall in what appeared to be the kitchen. Smoke spiraled up from its chimney, apparently being drawn upward by air rising to a small fissure in the ceiling. Straw-filled sleeping mats lay scattered throughout the cave.

"I say, all the comforts of home." Reggie smiled. "Temperature probably stays at this pleasant level year round."

Zielinski directed them to a pile of straw mats. "Choose mat and find sleeping place."

The escapees busied themselves arranging their sleeping nests. Ben and Reggie directed the partisans carrying Saunders and the other pilot to place them on double piles of straw mats and got them as comfortable as possible. The partisan medical officer fitted crude splints on their broken bones.

"Dis verk 'til ve can get dem to 'ospital," he muttered. "Cook fix breakfast in hour or so. Maybe you get some sleep?"

The five drifted awake to the smell of frying eggs, sausage, and potatoes. Their partisan companions were already hunkered over metal plates, shoveling food into their mouths. The aroma of strong black coffee permeated the air.

"Wow! What a swell way to wake up!" Ben exclaimed. He and his companions scrambled to their feet, did a quick business outside, and headed for a large stone ledge that served as a kitchen counter. Two of the partisans held plates for Saunders and the other pilot as they scooped food into their mouths. Half an hour later, all wiped the grease from their plates with chunks of peasant bread and sat back with satisfied smiles.

"Tell me, Zielinski," Reggie said, "do you chaps eat like this all the time? I mean, we were on pretty thin rations in the Stalag. This was a feast for us."

Zielinski grinned and emptied his coffee cup. "Ve do. Peasants around here good farmers. Dey hide produce from Germans and smuggle food to us. Dis hard vork ve do and need much, how you say, ah, fuel to keep us going. Peasants like verk ve do, fighting Germans."

"Right ho, we can identify with that!" Reggie responded.

The escapees quickly fell into the routine in the partisan's hiding place, helping out with routine tasks of cleaning weapons and relishing what to them was food fit for a king.

Piotrowski returned a day and a half later and sat down with the former prisoners for a discussion of escape options.

"Partisan chief and I agree best plan is to diwide you in four groups and try get you all to Baltic for boat," he said. "Best vay is travel by foot at night. Ve have, uh, arrangements along de vay for hiding places. But better not travel in big numbers. I send guide with each group, and you travel different routes. You Ving Commander go first vid your four odder 'Giraffes' . . . Haw, some crazy code name! Den ve send rest of groups at intervals. Don' vant too many vandering about at same time, eh?"

He stood and beckoned Reggie to a corner. "Means lotta hard walking, but I tink you up to it, eh? But can't take men with broken bones. Slow you down and maybe kill dem."

Reggie nodded glumly. "Of course, of course. Damn and blast! Hate to leave them behind, but you're right. We couldn't manage with them."

He returned to the group. "Okay, we've got our marching orders, so to speak. We five Giraffes will go first. Piotrowski assures me our friends with the broken bones will be well cared for. Everybody ready to take a hike?"

All nodded eagerly. "We're not in the best shape after our time in camp," Ben said, "but I think we're up to it."

"Now you keep uniforms or vant partisan clothes?" Piotrowski asked.

Reggie consulted with the others. "Umm, think we better stay in uniform. If we're caught in civilian clothes, the Germans could accuse us of being spies and put us before a firing squad."

"Haw!" Piotrowski. "Do vat you vant. Ve not let Germans catch you, but if happens, I tink dey shoot you no matter vat you vearing."

"That's as may be," Reggie said. "Have to take our chances. Umm, by the way, when we get out, is there anything we can have sent in for you—guns, ammunition, food, whatever? We can arrange parachute drops if you can establish safe drop zones."

"Tank you wery much, always need for food, guns, ammunition, and medical supplies," Piotrowski said. Then with a leer he said, "Maybe some American cigarettes and English viskey?"

Reggie smiled and nodded. "See what we can do."

"Now I assign Zielinski, to guide you north on escape route to Baltic Sea," Piotrowski said. "You know iss good man. Do as he says and he gets you der. You arrange vid him for safe drop zones. He has some English, eh, but not, how you say, uh, not fluent like me. Haw, haw, haw!"

"In a pinch, I can try to communicate with him in Polish, even with my goddamn accent," Kowalski groused.

The five Giraffes had quiet words with Saunders, wishing him good luck and asking if he had any messages he wanted conveyed to anyone in England. They promised to work on a plan to get him out after his leg healed.

They took Piotrowski's advice and lay down for afternoon naps. They had a long night's trek ahead of them. At 2100 hours, they assembled at the cave entrance, shook hands all around, and thanked Piotrowski again. Zielinski raised a hand signal, and they followed him into the night.

Chapter 14

Journey to Freedom

The five Giraffes struggled to keep pace with Zielinksi who loped through the forest in a hunched half walk and half trot.

"I say, my good man," Reggie called to him, "umm, can we, umm, take a short break to, uh . . . to catch our breath? Some of us have been confined to camp for some time. Not in greatest condition, don'tcha know?"

Zielinski stopped and turned as they straggled forward to join him. "Sorry about pace but dawn coming soon. Ve haf 'nuther fifteen kilometers need go to safe place before daybreak."

"Fifteen kilometers!" Ben exclaimed. "That's over nine miles. How many kilometers have we walked so far?"

"'Bout twenty-five. Dat about what in miles, fifteen? We need do 'bout twenty-five miles a night to keep pace. Iss necessary go on. German patrols come out at dawn searching area around train wreck. Place ve go iss safe hiding spot far enuf away."

"Look, we're in your hands, umm, Zielinski. You're in charge. Just know that we need an occasional stop to catch our breath and have a pee."

Reggie paused and peered into Zielinski's face. "I say, ought to know your rank or better yet, your first name. Can't just call you Zielinski."

"Vladimir. You call me Vlad."

"Okay, Vlad it is," Reggie said. Turning to the others, he asked, "That all right with you gents?" Ben and the other three nodded their approval.

"Ve go now," Vlad said.

For the next three hours, they trooped behind Vlad as he led them through stands of huge oak trees whose trunks disappeared into the darkness above. He skirted brush-clogged areas where the forest thinned to allow enough sunlight during the day to nourish ground cover vegetation.

"Need stay clear of bushes," Vlad cautioned. "Vild boar der. Dangerous beasts."

They crossed several streams that tumbled into gorges on either side of their trail and stopped at the edges of small clearings festooned with waist-high grass. After Vlad determined no German patrols were around, they scooted across to the thick forest on the other side. They encountered few major roadways along the route but paused at the dirt tracks that meandered through the forest to check for German patrols before slipping across.

Finally, they arrived at a large circular clearing in the forest. The sky was lightening, heralding their first full day of freedom. Vlad signaled them to stop. A small lean-to barn stood in the middle of the clearing. A wagon wheel track led to its double door.

"Dis da safe place," Vlad whispered. "Looks like nobody here. Now you go voods and do nature business. No toilet inside but have bucket for emergencies."

After doing their business, the five gathered around Vlad. "Stay here. Let me check all is hokay." He moved forward in a crouch, circled the barn, and scuttled back. "All hokay. Follow me. Show you hidden entrance to safe place unnerneath."

"What kind of hiding place can be 'unnerneath' that?" Ben wondered

"You see," Vlad said. "Wery clever spot. Ve got many along route to the sea." He led them to a small tree stump at a corner of the barn, slid his knife blade under the edge of a concealed trap door, and flipped it up, stump and all. The opening led into a tunnel burrowed under the barn.

"Now that is pretty clever," Ben marveled

Vlad led the way with his flashlight, guiding them into a fifteen-by-fifteen-foot square room under the barn floor. The solid wooden ceiling was supported by side walls of vertical timbers and boards. Packed dirt served as the floor.

"What's up above us?" Ben asked.

"Regular barn. Local farmers store hay and grain der," Vlad said.

"But if German patrols search the barn, won't they look for trapdoors in the floor?" Ben persisted. "Can't they pull up floorboards and expose this room underneath?"

"No. Dat beauty of dis hiding place." Vlad smiled, pointing up. "Dis, uh, double ceiling. On top dis iss layer of dirt packed hard. German's pull floorboards and find dirt. Not find room unnerneath."

"Damn clever." Reggie smiled. "Damn clever."

Vlad lit a candle so he could save the batteries in his flashlight. He rummaged through a heavy wooden box in the corner and pulled out a round loaf of rough peasant bread and a large Polish sausage wrapped in oilcloth. He dropped the cover of the box, pulled out his knife, and cut hunks of bread and sausage for each. "Eat, eat." He grinned. "Not, how you say, gourmet, but keep us going, you bet. Water in porcelain jug der. Iss clean. Drink!"

After "dinner," the five Giraffes flopped onto straw-filled pallets on the floor. They had trekked over twenty-five miles, and they slipped quickly into soft-snoring sleep. Vlad spent a few minutes studying his map by candlelight. He calculated they had covered 40 of the total 240 kilometers (150 miles) to their destination, a small fishing village on the Baltic coast. Several fishing boat captains working with the partisans routinely smuggled people escaping Nazi Germany across to Trelleborg, Sweden, south of Malmo. The RAF and the USAAF had secret agreements with several Swedish shipping companies to take Allied escapees north up the Kattegat Sea between Sweden and German-occupied Denmark, around the northern tip of Denmark, south on the Skagerrak to the North Sea, and then across to Scotland.

The biggest challenge Vlad faced was getting his band of escapees undetected to the Baltic coast. Tonight, they'd have to cover another forty kilometers on foot to reach the next safe spot. That meant a departure no later than 2200 hours. This would get them to the next spot before daybreak.

If all went according to plan, they'd spend the day sleeping in another underground bunker and would be picked up that evening by a farmer driving a truck loaded with large bales of hay. Six of the bottom bales were ventilated boxes just large enough for the escapees to curl into. The sides and ends were covered with glued hay, making them indistinguishable from the real bales. It would make for an uncomfortable ride, but they would cover the one hundred kilometers (about sixty miles) needed to find the third bunker safe spot.

This would leave sixty kilometers (about thirty-eight miles) to cover on the final two nights. Vlad would push them to trek forty kilometers the night after they were dropped off by the truck, leaving an easy twenty kilometers for the final night. They would be smuggled on board a fishing boat with hiding places under large salted fish crates. Satisfied, he had the details in hand. Vlad snuffed out the candle and curled up on a straw pallet.

Vlad shook the others awake at 2030 hours. "Need be ready leave in little over hour," he said. "I hear no noise above, so tink barn not searched. Soon as fully dark, sneak out by twos and do business. Then come back for bread and sausage dinner. We take chunks for night lunch on road."

"Who supplies the food and water and keeps this place cleaned up?" Ben asked. "You must have quite an organization."

"Plenty supporting us partisans," Vlad nodded. "Dey wery careful awoiding Germans ven doing. Ve tankful for help, and dey tankful ve continue fight Germans. Helping you escape vay of fighting back. You get to England, come back, and bomb Germans." He then quickly outlined the travel plans for the next three days.

Pockets bulging with chunks of bread and large slices of sausage, the escapees slipped out through the tunnel and followed Vlad into the forest. They struggled through the night's trek, which crossed rough terrain cut with valleys and small rivers. At least the rivers provided a ready source of drinking water. As they flopped on a hillside for a rest break, Reggie asked the Giraffes how they thought the escape was going.

"Aching from head to foot," Archie Banner said. Reggie noted he hadn't been very vocal so far during the trip. "But I think we're making good time. Frankly, I'm surprised we haven't encountered any German patrols. I guess that's the beauty of Vlad's plan for hoofing it cross-country at night. Have to say, though, I'm lookin' forward to meetin' up with that truck at the next safe house. Give my poor old feet a break."

Duncan Whitford agreed. "Vlad knows what he's doing. Good bloke that. I like the cross-country approach too. The chaps we got out of Stalag Luft III through the tunnel earlier this year got tripped up trying to travel in the open, even though the civilian clothes our tailors made from their uniforms looked quite authentic. But traveling out in the public raised too many chances of being discovered. Think we're better off traveling this way." He slumped back with a frown. "Can't help thinking of poor old Sandy. Hated to leave him behind. Wasn't much else we could do, I suppose. We'd have played hell trying to drag him along."

"Look," Ben said, "I think we can trust Piotrowski to take good care of him. The partisans have one helluva support organization, really impressive. We'll get him out."

Kowalski, who had engaged in quiet conversation with Vlad, trying to improve his "goddamned accent," nodded his approval. "I'm happy with this arrangement. Also lookin' forward to riding awhile in that truck."

The footsore band arrived at the next safe place just before dawn. This barn, nestled in a small grove of pine trees, had a similar concealed entrance and the double ceiling that would fool anyone probing through the floor above. Following the same doing-nature's-business procedure, they settled in for another bread and sausage meal.

"You know, this stuff tastes great," Banner said. "Never turn up my nose to Polish sausage again."

Vlad briefed them on the departure plan for that night. "Truck vill arrive in dusk, and farmer makes look like loading hay. You slip outta bunker and into barn by small back door one by one. Farmer put you in false bales and pile real bales on top. I follow as last. No conwersation. Do as quiet as possible."

The Giraffes slept soundly, not hearing the German patrol that searched the barn overhead.

Chapter 15

MISSION ACCOMPLISHED

Vlad shook them awake at 2000 hours. "Keep wery quiet," he whispered. "German patrol searched barn earlier. Didn't find anyting suspicious. Left after hour or so. Tink dey gone, but need be wery careful. Farmer vill vatch for any Germans hanging around. Not come vid truck if dey still here. He tap signal if all hokay for transfer."

After what seemed an interminable wait, they heard the farmer tap the all-clear signal on one of the barn's beams. He was ready to load them into the truck.

"Hokay, everybody move quickly," Vlad whispered. "Out the tunnel one by one, delay two minutes between, and slip in back door. Farmer vill load you in disguised boxes."

"I say, what's this chap's name?" Reggie asked. "Need to thank him properly."

"No names!" Vlad said. "People helping partisans need hide identity, yust in case . . ."

"Of course, of course," Reggie agreed. "Should've thought of that myself." Turning to Ben, he winked and said, "Just like in Spain, eh?"

As each escapee slipped into the barn, the farmer helped them squeeze into one of the boxes. With all six, including Vlad, snugged into their hiding places, the farmer piled real bales of hay around and on top of them. Ben suffered the onset of claustrophobia but overcame it by sucking slow deep breaths at one of the ventilation holes and forcing his body to relax.

"Reggie," he hissed. "Can you hear me? You getting' enough air?"

"Right-ho," Reggie hissed back. "Not the most comfortable accommodations, but it'll be all right for the couple of hours it takes to make the next safe house."

"Everybody must be quiet," Vlad called out. "No talking. Settle back and enjoy ride. I do dis many times."

Ben smiled. *Good to know our loyal guide is coming with us and not just boxin' us up and sending us into the night.*

The truck jounced along a dirt road so rough it felt like they were running on a railroad bed. Ben dozed and tried to shift his weight to ease cramped muscles. By the end of the trip, he figured he'd need an hour of stretching before he could stand straight.

About two hours into the trip, he tensed as the truck ground to a halt. Ben heard a murmur of voices, sounded like German. Someone shouted a command, and he heard the cab door open and shut. Apparently, the driver had been ordered out. Following what sounded like another command, the tailgate of the truck banged down. At least two men conversing in German seemed to be clambering over the bales, some of which were shifted around. Ben heard a peculiar zipping noise and realized it was the sound of bayonets slicing into the bales. Fortunately, the soldiers did not dig to the bottom layer and shove their bayonets into the false bales.

Finally, they crawled back out of the truck, and after another lengthy conversation in German, the driver got back in the cab, slammed the door, and started the engine. The truck jolted forward, stopped, and then moved ahead as though the driver had been cleared through a checkpoint barrier.

As they rumbled along the road, Ben put his mouth to an air hole and whispered, "Anybody know what that was all about?"

"It was a German checkpoint," Archie Banner whispered back. "They had two soldiers search the bales and then asked the driver why he was transporting hay at this time of night. He kept his nerve and said because there was a lot of military traffic during the day, and he was afraid of the American fighters that came out of nowhere and strafed the columns. Apparently, they believed him 'cause we're on our way again."

"Please to not conwerse," Vlad whispered. "Rest quiet. Ve be at safe place in less than two hours."

The routine at the third safe house was the same as that at the first two, with the exception that after crawling out of the false bales, all spent extra time bending and stretching to relieve muscle cramps they had suffered while lying curled in the hay-covered boxes. Once inside the bunker, Vlad treated them to a special meal—smoked mackerel and bread.

"Now this is eatin' high off the hog." Ben smiled as he munched the fish only recently caught in the Baltic Sea. "Wouldn't a beer or a crisp white wine go well with this?"

"Easy there, old bean," Reggie said. "Don't get the juices flowing for a pint quite yet. I'll stand us all a round or two in the first pub we reach back 'ome."

"Tonight," Vlad interrupted, "ve go on foot once more. Need do 'nuther forty kilometers to next safe place. Iss wery near coast, den mebbe have less than twenty kilometers for last stage to fishing willage. No moon until early morning. Dis help us get der in total dark. Now sleep. Need strength for last big walk."

No one needed further encouragement as the chorus of snores proved.

They were all up and ready to go before Vlad made the rounds to wake them. All slipped out to complete "nature's business," then returned for a quick breakfast of bread and smoked mackerel.

"Ve go," Vlad announced, pushing them to the door. "Must to be wery quiet. Ve getting close to place vhere are many German patrols. I know route like back of hand. Follow closely in single file vid little noise as possible."

Vlad picked his way through the forest so surely he seemed to be following a dotted line on the ground. He halted at several points and signaled everyone to slide into the bushes. The crunch of heavy boots and muffled conversations in German impressed the Giraffes with the nearness of the patrols.

The night trek passed quickly. Either they were getting used to the steady pace Vlad set or the periodic scoots into the bushes broke up the otherwise plodding routine. The fourth safe house lay under a stone toolshed attached to a row of stone buildings. The entrance concealed under a rain barrel let to a small underground chamber also fitted with the double ceiling to fool anyone looking under the floorboards of the building above.

Once they were settled in, Vlad outlined the plan for the coming evening, the last leg of their journey to the sea. "Ve have good darkness tonight, only part moon early in morning. After leave here, I lead you to beach near fishing village. Der ve slip you on fishing boat taking load of smoked mackerel to German detachment on Denmark's Bornholm Island just off coast of Sveden. Before reaching Bornholm, boat from Sveden meet up vid you, and you transfer to it."

Vlad sat back and scratched his head. "Trick vill be to keep touch vid boat from Sveden to make sure you meet hokay. This most dangerous part of trip. Germans haf patrol boats in waters between Bornholm Island and Denmark. But fishing boat captain knows vater wery vell. Should be hokay. Once transfer, Svedish captain maybe take you to Trelleborg, south of Malmo or maybe go out direct to Nordsee. He has all arrangements for getting you to England."

"'Getting you to England!'" Ben exclaimed. "That has a nice ring to it, eh?"

"Indeedy do!" Reggie agreed as Banner, Kowalski, and Whitford grinned their approval.

Reggie and Vlad hunched over a map in the flickering candlelight. Vlad showed Reggie several safe locations for future airdrops of weapons and supplies from England. Reggie noted the latitude and longitude coordinates and worked out the coded messages that would be exchanged with the partisans to schedule the drops.

"Once airdrop set, ve scout area to make sure is safe," Vlad said. "Ve lay out drop-zone banners and flash-code messages vid lamps ven airplanes arrive. Vorks fine. Ah, you not forget brandy, hokay?"

"Right you are, my good man," Reggie said. "Some fine brandy for you and some cigarettes and whisky for Commander Piotrowski. Now let's turn in. I'm really bushed."

Despite his fatigue, Ben couldn't sleep. His mind leaped ahead to England to rejoining the 509th and, especially, to seeing Gwen again. He pulled her letters from his jacket breast pocket. He didn't have enough light to read them, but he savored the faint scent wafting from them. When he finally dozed off, Gwen played a central role in a very pleasant dream.

Vlad roused them by 2100 hours and hustled them through preparations for departure on the final leg of the journey. He seemed unusually tense.

"I say, Vlad old fellow," Reggie said. "You seem to have the wind up. Anything in particular bothering you?"

"Vind up? Vat dis?" Vlad asked. "You talking 'bout veather?"

"No, no." Reggie chuckled. "That's a saying of ours. Means, are you nervous about something?"

"Ah, unnerstan," Vlad responded, although his puzzled expression indicated he really did not. "Oh, ah, I see. You mean me nervous? Some nervous, yes. Dis most tricky, how you say, ah, dangerous part of journey. Must to be wery careful and have good luck, eh?"

Chapter 16

OUT OF ENEMY TERRITORY

Vlad picked his way carefully through the forest as they trekked northeast of Szczecin, a Polish seaport town located at the southern tip of the Szczecin Lagoon. The lagoon, connected to the Baltic Sea via a canal, was fed by the Oder River flowing north along the Polish German border. He headed for their final overland destination, a small fishing village on the Baltic seacoast. They reached it shortly after midnight, and Vlad signaled the others to hide in a wooded area above the sand dunes.

"I go find fishing boat captain. Make certain no German patrols about so he can take you on boat," Vlad whispered. "Stay still and quiet. I back in hour or so. Vill announce vid vhistle signal, one you know," he added as he put his thumbs together vertically and blew softly between his two knuckles.

The Giraffes began to fidget as the wait stretched to two hours. "Reggie, do ya think something might have happened to Vlad?" Ben whispered. "Haven't heard any yelling or shooting. Sure hope he hasn't stumbled into a patrol and been arrested."

"Steady on, Sancho. We'll give Vlad another half hour or so, and then we'll have to find a better hiding place in case he doesn't make it back before daybreak."

A soft whistle wafted through the night air. Vlad slid over a sand dune and sat grinning at them. All five puffed a collective sigh of relief.

"Many German patrols on roads and along beach. Needed hide for some time. Soldiers left, and I contact fishing boat captain. He ready to board you. But please, must to be wery quiet and vatch me. If I signal like dis vid hand, you drop and be still. Hokay?"

They all nodded their understanding and scrambled after Vlad, who led them sliding down dunes toward the beach. He trotted in a crouch toward a cluster of boats pulled up on the sand and peeked out between two of them to ensure there were no patrols in the area. Seeing none, he scuttled out onto a flimsy dock. The five escapees followed and stood nervously, peering down into a large fishing boat loaded with wooden containers. The stench of rotting fish overpowered their senses.

Vlad regarded them with an amused smile. "I say, you got vind up, as Ving Commander says? Nervous, no? Smell not so bad after you get used to it. Now here captain."

A short portly man stepped out of the shadows on the deck. He had to be the captain if for no other reason than the typical sea captain's whiskers that bristled from his ruddy cheeks. He wore a crumpled sea captain's cap perched on a thatch of hair that looked like steel wool, a pea coat that had withstood many years of salt spray, and rubber knee-high boots over corduroy pants. He flashed them a wolfish grin.

"Not have much English," he rumbled, "but velcome on my boat."

"Hey, Kowalski," Ben said, "here's your chance to improve your Polish."

Kowalski pushed forward, removed his cap, and said, "Witam, jestem Kowalski z Chicago. Dziękujemy za poświęcenie nam Na statku. Będę cieszyć się rozmawiając z tobą w swoim ojczystym języku." ("Hello, I am Kowalski of Chicago. Thank you for taking us on your ship. I shall enjoy conversing with you in your native tongue.")

The captain beamed, grabbed Kowalski's hand, and pumping it vigorously said, "Witamy, witamy. Będę cieszyć się naszą rozmowę. Teraz chodź, chodź Na pokładzie! ("Welcome, welcome. I shall enjoy our conversation. Now come, come on board!")

Kowalski turned and embraced Vlad, thanked him for leading them out of Poland, and stepped past the others. "We've been welcomed on board, gents. And didja notice, no rude remarks about my accent?" he sniffed.

Reggie turned to Vlad. "Good man, Vlad." He grinned, shaking hands and patting him on the back. "I say, you've done a magnificent job of getting us here. Don't know how we're ever going to repay you."

"Come back in airplanes and bomb Germans. That good repayment."

Ben grabbed Vlad by the shoulders and looked into his eyes. "Vlad, we couldn't have made it here without you. I'll never forget what you've done for us. I only hope that after this rotten war is over, we can meet again." He crushed Vlad in a bear hug, turned, and climbed down into the boat.

Banner and Whitford embraced Vlad, whispered their thanks, and followed Ben into the boat. Reggie gave Vlad a final tip of his hand. "Sorry we can't prolong our goodbyes, my good man, but it's probably not the best idea to stand here chatting with German patrols prowling around us."

"Good luck, Ving Commander. Fly many missions. Make quick end to var," Vlad said as Reggie hopped into the boat.

The five stood at the railing as the boat's two-cycle engine started with a wheeze and chuffed them away from the dock. As they moved out into the channel, Reggie called them to attention and commanded, "Hand salute!" Vlad raised a solemn return salute, and all held their salutes until Vlad's lonely figure and the rickety dock disappeared into the gloom.

Ben swallowed twice and croaked, "Makes you realize we're fighting this lousy war for a lot of fantastic people. Sure hope the Russians can push the Germans back and liberate Poland soon. Vlad and his people deserve it."

Ben did not realize that Soviet dictator Josef Stalin would manipulate the liberation of Poland, especially Warsaw, for political reasons by delaying the final push against the German occupying troops. This was part of his plan to assure Soviet control of the country after the war. Thousands of Polish patriots, who later might prove troublesome to the Soviets, would rise up against the Germans in anticipation of joining the advancing Soviet forces. But they would be overwhelmed and killed by the Germans while the Soviet Army sat waiting on Poland's eastern border.

The five escapees hunkered in different positions on board the fishing boat as they chugged into the night. "Vlad was wrong about one thing," Whitford grumped. "One does not get used to the rotten fish smell."

"Small price to pay, old boy," Reggie said. "Hopefully, the smell will keep any German patrol blokes from examining the boat too closely should they stop us."

"Captain said if we're stopped by a patrol boat, we're to squeeze under the large boxes," Kowalski said. "They're on raised rails, which allows just enough space for us to scoot under them."

"If there's a god in heaven, let him direct the patrol boats somewhere else," Banner pleaded. "Don't think I'll ever get this smell out of my uniform, much less the rest of me."

"Doubt you'll be keeping that uniform after we get home," Ben said. "It's looking pretty ratty. Think Uncle Sam will buy you another one."

Kowalski, who had been chatting steadily with the captain, said he had made the trip to Bornholm Island many times. "His routine is well known to the German patrol boat crews, so they only stop him occasionally to make it look like they're doing their duty.

"Captain Vlad said the plan is to rendezvous with a light freighter out of Trelleborg, Sweden, at a spot west of Bornholm. The biggest challenge is going to be to find the freighter if the weather is bad. Both ships will steer to a latitude and longitude position just inside Swedish waters," Kowalski continued. "Once we reach the rendezvous point, we'll have to spend time circling to make the actual contact.

"Oh, by the way, the captain says his name also is Vlad. Guess that's like John Smith back home. He has two other crewmen on board, the man at the helm and a deckhand. Didn't offer to introduce either of them."

"Fine by me," Ben said. "If we happened to get caught, I don't want to know any of their real names."

The steady chuff, chuff of the fishing boat's two-cycle engine lulled them to sleep despite their uncomfortably damp and smelly surroundings. All agreed they didn't savor having to slip under the fish crates if they were intercepted by a patrol boat.

They startled awake when the throttle slammed shut and the engine wheezed to a stop. Ben peered over the railing and saw they were drifting in a thick fog. Captain Vlad slipped back to them and whispered to Kowalski.

"He said there's a German patrol boat ahead on the port side. Keep very quiet. Not even a small sound. Listen, you can hear its engine."

All ears strained and picked up the muffled thump of the patrol boat's engine. A searchlight speared a beam into the fog, but a curt command caused it to be switched off. The fog reflected the beam, blinding the observers on the patrol boat.

Ben squeezed his nose to stifle a sneeze. *Damn, that would have given us away!*

The fishing boat bobbed as it drifted quietly with the current. Silence pressed in on them. The patrol boat captain also had switched off his engine. Ben held his breath. Was that water lapping against a boat hull?

Finally, after what seemed an eternity, the patrol boat engine thrummed to life, and the German vessel moved slowly away to the starboard side. Captain Vlad let the fishing boat float on quietly for half an hour before restarting the engine.

"Blood hell," Reggie wheezed. "That was a bit too close for comfort."

Captain Vlad eased back from the forward deck and gave them a thumbs-up signal. "Hokay now. German patrol boat gone. Now we find Svedish freighter."

They eased out of the fog bank into a clear starry night. Captain Vlad quickly used his sextant to catch a star fix and determined they were close to the rendezvous point. As he stowed his sextant, the shifting breeze rolled the fog bank back over them. By previous arrangement, Vlad circled his boat in a spiral to the left. The captain of the Swedish freighter also planned to circle in a left spiral that hopefully would bring the two ships together. A special code would be tolled quietly on the captain's bells on both ships to help guide the helmsmen.

After circling for about half an hour, the muffled tone of a captain's bell penetrated the fog. Ben and his fellow escapees scrambled to the railings and listened intently, barely breathing. The bell tolled the agreed upon Morse code.

"Think it's off to the port side," Banner whispered.

Apparently, the captain agreed, as he ordered the helmsman to tighten the turn to the left. He softly rang out the answering code on his bell. This pas de deux, a sea-going ballet in the fog, continued for another fifteen minutes. The tolling bell from the Swedish freighter eased closer with each turn. Finally, they heard a slight bow wave from a steel hull. A signal light flashed the same Morse code signal, and the ghostly shape of the freighter nosed out of the fog. Both captains jockeyed their vessels into position, and the fishing boat bumped lightly into the freighter's hull. A ship's ladder with a small platform affixed to the bottom dangled from the railing.

"Please to be quick! Climb ladder," Captain Vlad commanded. "No waste time. Patrol boat may have heard bells. Go now!"

The five quickly thanked Captain Vlad for getting them into neutral waters, shook hands, and clambered up the ladder. The fishing boat backed away and disappeared into the fog as Captain Vlad steered a course that would take him back to Bornholm Island.

Chapter 17

Onward to England!

Ben, followed by his four companions, tumbled unceremoniously onto the rolling deck of the Swedish freighter. They scrambled to their feet and stood facing a tall lantern-jawed man with an unruly shock of blond hair escaping from under his seaman's cap. He stood spread-legged in a typical seaman's stance and studied them with piercing blue eyes hooded by overgrown blond eyebrows.

Reggie saluted. "Permission to come aboard, Captain. Umm, I'd like to apologize for our appearance. We've been traveling under some difficult conditions."

"Välkommen ombord på goda skeppet *Striegland!*" the man boomed. "Ah, I mean, velcome on board de good ship *Striegland!*" he added with a broad smile. "I am Captain Nils Sonderby and dis is first officer Lars Pederson." Lars stepped forward and snapped them a curt nod. "Ve don' need introductions to all of rest," Sonderby added. "You now are in neutral Svedish vaters, but ve still be careful."

Ben shivered. *Neutral Swedish waters. Whoeee! Outta German control. Now on to England!*

"I'm Wing Commander Reginald Percy," Reggie said, stepping forward and extending his right hand. "Let me say how grateful we are for your help in getting back to England."

"It is pleasure and honor," Sonderby responded. "Sveden is neutral, ja, but many of us don' like de Germans. Happy to help de Allies."

"Thank you." Reggie smiled. "Let me introduce my colleagues, Major Benjamin Findlay, Flight Leftenant Duncan Whitford, Captain

Archie Banner, and First Lieutenant Art Kowalski. We're a mixed bag. Whitford and I are Brits. These other three are Americans."

"Good to have all on board," Sonderby said, waving his long arms expansively. "Now ve get you below to your quarters. Pedersen vill show da vay."

"Umm, before we go below, Captain, can we discuss the plan of action from here?" Reggie asked. "I mean, are we going to stop in Sweden or work our way directly to England?"

"Go direct to England, I tink. But first you get some sleep," Sonderby said. "Ve discuss details over breakfast."

"Thank you, Captain. Uh, we'll need to shower and try to air out what's left of our uniforms."

"Ja, for shure," Sonderby said. "You been near a lotta fish, I tink. Get outta de uniforms. Ve fix you vid some dungarees and shirts after you vash and smell better. Also, razors for shaving."

They followed Pederson below to double-bunk cabins. All quickly stripped off their bedraggled uniforms and underwear and dumped them outside their cabins as Pedersen instructed. They luxuriated in showers, short and hot in the finest seagoing tradition, and emerged feeling renewed yet bone tired. They found fresh skivvies and clothes folded on each bunk. Ben lurched past Reggie and tumbled into his bunk. The steady thump of the *Striegland*'s engine quickly lulled him to sleep. He snorted awake as Reggie shook his shoulder, feeling like he had slept only a few minutes.

"Rise and shine, old cock," Reggie said. "It's gone past 0630 hours, and I hear movement about. Captain Sonderby said we'd talk over breakfast, and I'm hungry enough to attack the proverbial 'orse. Also anxious to hear the plan of action for gettin' 'ome to England."

"Wuff! Gimme a minute to get the old brain working, Reggie, and I'll be right along," Ben said.

"Right-ho, but don't dally too long making yourself pretty," Reggie said. "Out the door, right along the corridor, umm, what the hell do they call the hallway in the navy?"

"Dunno." Ben yawned. "Hallway works for me."

"Right. Well, turn right and when you get to the stairway thingy, go up one deck. Then follow your nose to breakfast. See you there."

Breakfast was a feast compared to the bread, sausage, and smoked mackerel diet they'd been on for the past week, not to mention the basic subsistent rations in Stalag Luft III. Ben scooped a small mountain of scrambled eggs on his plate, trimmed it with a rasher of bacon and several slices of cheese, added orange juice, freshly baked bread with jam, and headed for the coffee urn. He greeted Captain Sonderby and Lars as he slid in next to Reggie on a bench attached to the table.

"Gud morgon, Major Findlay," Sonderby grinned, his ruddy cheeks filled with food like a giant chipmunk. "You sleep vell?"

"Must have, Captain," Ben responded as he dug into the scrambled eggs. "Don't remember a thing until Reggie shook me awake 'bout half an hour ago. Didn't realize how tired I was."

They ate without conversation for the next fifteen minutes, the silence broken only by the sound of Sonderby slurping coffee from his saucer in finest Scandinavian style. Ben finally leaned back with a satisfied sigh and emptied his cup. Reggie pushed his plate forward and grinned.

"Nothin' like a good cup of coffee in the morning, especially good Swedish coffee," Ben said. "When's the last time we tasted real coffee, Reggie?"

"Months, me lad. Must be months."

The other three escapees stumbled in looking like they had just rolled out of their bunks. After exchanging quick greetings, they turned on the food table with ravenous intentions.

"So, Captain Sonderby, what's the operational plan from here?" Reggie asked. "I take it we indeed are not stopping in Sweden. We'd have been in port by now."

"Correct. Decided not to stop in Trelleborg. Could make complications. Have enough fuel to go direct from here."

He pulled a large chart from a nearby table. "Here, I show you course. Ve now steaming nord along Svedish coast up de Kattegat, staying close in Svedish waters. When pass Goteborg, ve turn sout into Skagerrak to da Nordsee. Den ve sving nord on course dat takes us around tip of Scotland."

Ben strained to follow the captain's sausage-like finger as it traced their route on the chart.

"Manifest says ve carry food to Ireland, vich ve are," Sonderby continued. "Ve cleared for course around nord of Scotland's Shetland Islands and den sout to Galway on west coast of free Ireland."

Reggie stiffened at Sonderby's reference to "free Ireland" but did not challenge him.

Pretending not to notice Reggie's reaction, Sonderby continued, "As ve reach Orkney Islands, ve radio coded signal to identify us as carrying escaped prisoners from Germany. After ve deliver you, navy grant us permission to steam tru Pentland Firth between nord coast of Scotland and Orkneys. Not open to merchant ships in vartime, but exception made 'cause ve bringing you home. Saves a lot of sailing time not having to go nord around Shetlands."

Reggie nodded. "And we thank you again."

"As ve approach Orkneys, Royal Navy vill send military ship, probably destroyer, and fast boat out from Scapa Flow to meet us, and ve transfer you over," Sonderby continued. "Dey takes you to port, and ve continue on to Ireland. Tink it vill vork."

"Indeed it should!" Reggie shouted. "And soon as we land at Scapa Flow, I'll get on the blower to RAF Station Wittering, report in, and ask for air transport. They should be able to lay on a Dakota transport straightaway to fly in and fetch us south.

"I say, Ben, we'll be at RAF Wittering and your Yank base at Parham, before you can say 'Bob's your uncle!'" Turning to the other three, he continued, "As for you chaps, we'll arrange for the Dakota to drop you at your stations along the way. How's that sound?" They pounded their approval on the table.

Chapter 18

HOMECOMING!

The *Striegland* steamed into the North Sea and turned northwest on a heading for the Orkney Islands. As the sun rose behind them and headed toward the noon zenith, lookouts on the *Striegland* scanned the sea for British and German warships, especially submarines. Captain Sonderby had ordered an extra-large Swedish flag flown from the standard on the fantail to ensure that crews on ships of both combatants would recognize them as a neutral ship. Large Swedish insignia also were painted on each side of the *Striegland*'s funnel.

"Dis, how you say is, uh, tricky part," Sonderby said, as he sat sipping coffee in the wardroom with his five passengers. They had just enjoyed what to them was a sumptuous lunch. "Ve steam slowly on zigzag course to be safe from submarines and to make nighttime arrival in Orkney Islands. Vant complete transfer to Royal Navy ship in darkness."

"I can hardly believe we're this close to gettin' back home to England," Ben said. "Say, listen to me. Gettin' back home to England. Interesting, huh? But it does feel like home."

"Not to mention to lovely Gwen Brewster who awaits you with pitter-patter heartbeats," Reggie teased. Turning to the others, he explained, "Nurse Brewster tended to our man Benjamin when a nasty Jerry shot his Spitfire out of the sky during the Battle of Britain. This led to other involvements, eh, Ben?" Then thinking he may have embarrassed Ben, Reggie quickly added, "Seriously, they make a lovely couple."

"You know what?" Kowalski interjected. "Of all the planning and scheming we did about how we were gonna escape, it's kinda funny that it was the Krauts themselves who sprung us. I mean, puttin' us on that train delivered us to the Polish Partisans, so to speak. Gives the story a nice twist, eh?"

Whitford stretched and grunted contentedly. "Speaking of getting home, do I not remember, Wing Commander, that you promised us at least two rounds of our choice at the first pub we encounter? Umm, I can taste the bitter already. Really looking forward to a couple."

"Indeed I did, Whitford. It's a promise I intend to keep as soon as we land at Scapa Flow."

Banner, who had maintained his usual reticence, piped up, "How long do ya reckon it'll take to get us back to our bases? We should be in Scapa Flow by, what, tomorrow sometime? Ya see, I got three more missions to fly to fill my quota, and then I'm off to my real home, the good ol' U.S. of A. I want to get 'em done as soon as possible. That's what I'm looking forward to."

He paused and then looked at Reggie. "Say, do ya think we'll have to go through a big debrief? Will the top brass wanna hear all about our experience as POWs and about how the partisans helped us escape?"

"Most probably, Archie, but I don't honestly know what it might entail. Since we're going to different home stations, I'm not certain how they'll proceed."

"How about this Dakota transport you're gonna lay on for us?" Kowalski asked Reggie. "That's the Brit version of our C-47 Gooney Bird, right?"

"Right, same airplane, different livery. You Yanks gave us a flock of them early in the war. Fantastic transport, not all that different from its civilian forebearer, the famous Douglas DC-3 airliner. They owned the commercial skies in the late thirties, and now dressed in olive drab, they're helping win the war."

"Tell us about Scapa Flow," Ben said. "It's the Royal Navy's main base, isn't it?"

"Actually, it's the main wartime base for the British Home Fleet," Reggie said. "Most of the fleet's ships have been moved up there from their normal ports along the English Channel. That puts the fleet beyond attacks from German airfields in occupied France across the channel. It also positions the fleet to carry out its primary mission, which is to form the North Sea Blockade and deny the German Navy access to the North Atlantic.

Douglas C-47 (DC-3) Transport

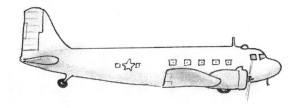

"Scapa Flow, which means bay of the long isthmus, is a large area of water sheltered among five of the Orkneys off the northern tip of Scotland," Reggie continued. "It's not like one of our air stations. Not all contained in a relatively small area. Scapa encompasses over 120 square miles of water, so there's room for a lot of ships. Makes it one of the best natural harbors of the world."

He stepped to a map on the wardroom wall. "Its north and westerly location—here—makes it a relatively safe anchorage as it was in World War 1. It's beyond the range of most Luftwaffe's bombers, except those now stationed in occupied Norway, which is only a couple of hundred miles across the North Sea. The German Navy made one successful submarine attack on Scapa in '39, sinking the HMS Royal Oak at anchorage. There are many channels between the islands that form the Orkneys, but the navy has sealed most with blocking ships, other barriers, and mine fields."

He paused. "Interesting bit of history. Vikings based a fleet there over a thousand years ago, and it has been in use off and on since then."

"All I want is an airfield nearby where your guys can land that Dakota and get us back to our home bases," Kowalski said. "Know anything about that?"

"Ah yes. Actually there are several airfields around Scapa Flow," Reggie said. "I think RAF Station Kirkwall on Mayne Island is the biggest. It has a complicated history. Was originally known as RAF Grimsetter, I believe. Heard it might be transferred to Fleet Air Arm control, so I'm not sure what its current name is. Whatever, it'll be a suitable place for our Dakota to plop down. Then it's 'ome!"

As the *Striegland* steamed toward the Orkneys, all five escapees opted for a little sack time. A solid nap would set them up nicely for the night transfer to the Royal Navy fast boat.

Ben awoke and lay staring at the ceiling, not certain where he was. He felt the rolling motion of the ship and remembered. *We're on the* Striegland *headin' for the Orkneys. Gonna meet with a Royal Navy fast boat, and Reggie will arrange for a Dakota to come for us. Back home in a day or two. Gwen! Gwen! See you soon.*

He rolled off his bunk and noted that Reggie's was empty. "Must be wandering about," Ben muttered. "Wow, smells like dinner!" Again following his nose, Ben hurried up to the wardroom. Captain Sonderby, Lars, and three other ship's officers sat with Reggie, Whitford, Banner, and Kowalski hunched over heaped plates.

"Pardon us for not waiting, old bean." Reggie smiled. "But this succulent repast and our hunger combined to trump good manners. That's a traditional Swedish smorgasbord there on the headboard. Dig in and then join us. Lars will guide you through it."

Ben ogled the smorgasbord table filled with plates of cheeses, something that looked like chunks of fish, meat balls, roasted red potatoes, green beans, and tomatoes. "Tomatoes!" Ben exclaimed. "I haven't seen real tomatoes in years." His cheek muscles ached as his saliva glands kicked into action.

"Ja, yew start smorgasbord here by da sill," Lars said. Seeing Ben didn't know what sill was, he added, "Sill is pickled herring. Here are several kinds, pickled, vid mustard sauce, and smoked. Try dem all vid some hot potatoes. Den take some sharp Swedish cheese on crisp breads. Ja, ja, load up. Dat good for first plate. Now go to table."

Captain Sonderby smiled expansively and signaled Lars. "Now vid all at table, ve have special treat for last dinner on *Striegland*. Traditional smorgasbord always includes aquavit and Swedish beer."

Lars produced a tray loaded with small glasses filled with a clear liquid and several large frosted bottles of beer. "Aquavit like smooth schnapps. Careful, wery strong. De beer is Svedish Jamtlands Pascal, much like English strong ale," he said as he set the small glasses before each diner and filled their beer glasses.

The five pilots sat openmouthed and speechless. They hadn't tasted alcohol in months other than some awful homemade rot gut someone in Stalag Luft III had brewed from raisins and potato peelings. This boggled their minds.

"Now a toast," Sonderby said heartily. "Gud health to you pilots. Velcome home. Make quick finish vid Germans and end de var."

"Hear, hear!" all chorused and tipped their small glasses. Ben felt the strong liquid burn slightly as it slid down his throat. "Wow! This is some swell stuff," he said.

"How you say, uh, ja, chase, be sure to chase aquavit vid de cold beer." Lars grinned. "Makes gud combination. But careful, can make knees go vobbly if drink too much. Eat plenty vid it."

The five had no problem doing just that. Under Lars's direction, they returned to the smorgasbord several times, working their way through several fish dishes, including smoked salmon, before moving on to several salads, egg dishes, and cold cuts of meat.

"Now comes hot dishes," Lars directed. "Swedish meat balls vid lingonberry sauce and Jansson's Temptation. Dis special fixed potato dish like vat yew call scalloped potatoes but vid anchovies."

They topped off the feast with King Oscar's cake, another round of aquavit, and black coffee.

"I have died and gone to heaven," Kowalski sighed, stretching and patting his stomach. "Never had such a fantastic meal! Thank you, Captain Sonderby."

"Indeed, thank you," Reggie chimed in. "A wonderful feast to top off our journey. We're forever indebted to you, Captain Sonderby and Lars, for getting us home and treating us like kings along the way. Right, fellow Giraffes?"

All five responded with table thumping and hearty cheers of, "Hear, hear!"

After dinner, Sonderby gathered them over a nautical chart. "Ve here now," he said, jabbing the chart with his forefinger. "Dat means ve arrive in Orkneys in about three hours, nearly midnight. Vill standoff at entrance to Pentland Firth, off shore from Yohn O'Groats on Scotland's nordern tip. Expect Royal Navy ship, probably destroyer, intercept us der. Ven ve pass inspection, dey signal fast boats come in, first to collect you five and second to lead *Striegland* on path tru minefields protecting Scapa Flow to udder side."

He looked up with a smile. "Your uniforms been cleaned and patched. Maybe better get dressed for transfer to navy boat."

Ben and his companions paced the decks, flopped in and out of chairs in the wardroom, or wandered into the bridge wheelhouse. The three hours passed so slowly it felt like they had dropped into a slow-motion time warp. Ben poked his head into the wheelhouse for the fourth time in fifteen minutes.

"Uh, hello again, Captain Sonderby," he said. "Any contact with the Royal Navy yet? Must be getting' close, aren't we?"

"Jashure, receiving Morse code message from HMS *Scorpion* yust now," Sonderby said. "Standby 'nudder minute."

Ben slipped out of the wheelhouse, cupped his hands, and yelled, "Reggie, pass the word! Message coming in from the destroyer. We're gettin' close to the rendezvous!" The other four scrambled up the stairs to the bridge and crammed into the wheelhouse.

"What's the news?" Reggie asked. "Do you know for sure it's our contact?"

"Jashure," Sonderby said. "Message come from HMS *Scorpion*, Royal Navy S-Class destroyer. Ve rendezvous in fifteen minutes. So get ready."

The five backed out onto the bridge deck and whooped in unison. They grinned and slapped each other on the back. So close to home!

Sonderby ordered the *Striegland*'s engine room to throttle back to "ahead slow" and alerted the lookouts to watch for a Morse code message from an Aldis signal lamp on HMS *Scorpion*. It flashed minutes later with a command to come to a full stop and prepare for inspection. The sleek form of HMS *Scorpion* emerged from the gloom, and a powerful searchlight flashed across the *Striegland*'s deck. Sonderby knew that four 4.5-inch guns and twin Mark IV 40 mm Bofors guns were trained on him in the wheelhouse. He ordered his helmsman to follow the *Scorpion*'s orders precisely.

The destroyer edged close enough to allow communications by a loud hailer. "Order all hands on deck and form at the port railing," a disembodied voice echoed through the damp night air. "Tell your five extra passengers to stand in the bow facing our light."

Ben, Reggie, Archie, Art, and Duncan stood at attention at the bow railing, squinting into the searchlight.

"Who is your leader?" the voice asked. "Stand apart and identify yourself."

Reggie shifted his position and called out, "Wing Commander Reginald M. Percy, Royal Air Force, commanding number 962 Spitfire Wing based at RAF Wittering."

"Identify your companions," the voice called out.

"RAF Flight Leftenant Duncan Whitford, USAAF Major Benjamin D. Findlay, USAAF Captain Archie Banner, and USAAF Lieutenant Arthur Kowalski," Reggie shouted back. "We escaped from a train that was transferring us from the German POW camp Stalag Luft III in occupied Poland to the Sachsenhausen concentration camp near Berlin. We're requesting permission to land at Scapa Flow so we can arrange air transport back to our respective bases in England."

"Standby" came the response. "Meanwhile, we'll dim the light." The searchlight switched off, and softer beams from smaller lights continued to illuminate the wheelhouse.

After another interminable wait, Reggie slipped into the wheelhouse. "I say, Captain Sonderby, what's causing the delay?"

"Imagine dey checking with Royal Air Force and U.S. Army Air Forces to confirm you listed as prisoners of war," he responded. "Hope dis not take so long. Ve'll not be able to transfer in nighttime."

The loud hailer crackled to life again. "All five passengers are listed as German prisoners of war. Now as a double check, we need to verify you are who you say you are. Give us your service numbers, familiar nicknames, names of your commanding officers, and at least two squadron mates."

"Damn and blast! This can take all night and then some," Reggie grumbled. He quickly huddled with the other four, compiled a list of their service numbers and the required names, and handed the list to Sonderby, who ordered his radioman to transmit it to the *Scorpion*.

Three hours later, the *Scorpion's* loud hailer crackled again. "Hallo, *Striegland!* We have confirmed the identities of your passengers. Please follow us toward Pentland Firth."

Captain Sonderby ordered "ahead slow" and told the helmsman to maneuver into a trailing position behind the *Scorpion*. He felt uneasy knowing that the destroyer's aft guns were aimed directly at them.

Finally, the outline of Scotland's northern coast emerged on the port side and the *Scorpion* signaled "dead stop." The voice on the loud hailer called out, "Hallo, *Striegland!* Royal Navy Vosper Motor Torpedo Boats approaching your bow on port and starboard sides. Starboard boat will come alongside and collect your passengers. Portside boat will standby to escort you through Pentland Firth to the North Atlantic."

Ben and his companions gathered at the starboard gate above the ship's ladder, which descended to a ramp affixed to the *Striegland's* starboard side. Ben pumped his fist in the air when they heard the deep-throated rumble of the MTB's three Packard marine engines. The boat slid into view, and the helmsman maneuvered it alongside the ramp. Two crewmen quickly tied up to the ramp. The boat's captain signaled they were ready to transfer the passengers.

"Time to say goodbye, smooth sailing, and heartfelt thanks to Captain Sonderby," Reggie said. "Remember to salute the *Striegland*'s flag as you depart. And before we get on the MTB, ask for permission to board."

Sonderby joined them at gate. "Been pleasure to 'ave yew on board," he said somberly. "Safe trip rest of vay home and good luck helping finish dis damn var."

"Thank you, Captain Sonderby," Reggie said. "Please give us a mailing address so we can keep in touch with you, maybe even meet again after the war." Lars scribbled the address on a scrap of paper and handed it to Reggie.

"We hope we can repay you someday for helping us get back home and treating us so well in the process," Reggie said, stuffing the note in the breast pocket of his tunic. "Good sailing from here." He turned and saluted the captain. "Permission to leave your ship, sir!" Sonderby nodded. Reggie shook his hand, turned to salute the *Striegland*'s flag, and descended the ship's ladder.

Ben and the other three followed Reggie's example and stepped over the side onto the ladder. Reggie ordered the ragged band to give three cheers for Captain Sonderby and the "hip, hip, hurrahs" echoed up from the boat below.

"Ja, ja! Du är välkommen, ah, you are welcome," Sonderby boomed over the railing. "Safe trip from here."

The five were met by Royal Navy Leftenant Commander Albert Watkins, commanding officer of MTB *Victor*. Watkins welcomed them on board and ordered his deck crew to cast off. As they roared into the night headed for Scapa Flow, they watched the *Striegland* get under way and fall in behind the other MTB.

Chapter 19

Heroes Return

"I say, Commander Watkins, jolly good of you to join in this daisy chain to transport us home," Reggie said, dropping into a chair on the bridge. "We're honored that so many people have jumped in to lend a hand along the way."

"We're the ones to feel honored, Wing Commander," Watkins responded. "You chaps will be treated as quite the celebrities—five of you escaping a German POW camp, trekking out through Poland, and hitching boat rides here to Scapa. There's been a great deal of radio chatter about you. Think there'll be jolly good welcome ceremonies at your home stations."

"Umm, could be," Reggie mused. "Actually, there were thirty of us in the boxcar the Germans hooked on the end of an armaments train. Four of our chaps were killed when the Polish partisans blew up the tracks and derailed the train. Sent us arse over tea kettle down the embankment, but most of us survived intact. Two others suffered serious broken bones, so we had to leave them with the partisans. They said they'd get them to a partisan medical facility."

He paused, remembering how difficult it was to leave Sandy behind. "The partisan commander—one helluva man, by the way—split the remaining twenty-four into four groups: the five of us, two teams of six prisoners each, and a final seven-man team. They sent us out with different guides on separate paths to the Baltic. Said smaller groups had a better chance of slipping past any German patrols we might encounter."

Reggie sighed, pushed back in his chair, and rubbed his face with both hands. "Do you know if anyone has heard from the other groups of escapees? There are another nineteen chaps out there trying to get to the Baltic."

Watkins blew a low whistle and shook his head. "We haven't been alerted that any others are on the way. But that doesn't mean they aren't en route. We didn't hear you were arriving until yesterday afternoon, so there's still a chance they've made it too.

"I say, what a hell of a story!" Watkins exclaimed. "The Germans must be sending a lot of prison officials and guards to the wall over this one. Regrettably, probably taking revenge against a few of our prisoners as well. Damn them!"

Watkins turned to speak to the helmsman. "If you'll excuse me, Wing Commander," he said over his shoulder. "I need to check our course. Make certain we follow the proper channel through the minefields."

Reggie stepped back and sat down next to Ben on a munitions case.

"Reggie, I can't believe we've made it," Ben said. "What's the plan from here?"

"Dunno. We'll ask Commander Watkins after he threads us through the minefields."

Dawn broke with a dazzling orange-yellow sunrise over Scapa Flow. Huge mashed potato clouds floated overhead. The five passengers stared in wonder at the vast expanse of gleaming water that formed the anchorage. Lush green grass carpeted the rolling hills on the surrounding islands.

"They sure can get a lotta ships in here like you said, Reggie!" Banner exclaimed. "Makes it possible to spread the ships around, not bunch 'em up like we had to do at Pearl Harbor."

Twenty minutes later, Watkins stepped back to join them. All five crowded around to hear the plan.

"Sorry for the delay," Watkins said. "We've passed the minefields and are running northwest abeam of Widewall Island, that's it off to starboard now. We'll steer westerly and pass between South Walls Island on the port side and Flotta on the starboard side. We're heading for Lyness Royal Navy Base on Hoy Island. Our commander in chief, Admiral Sir Henry Moore, wants to formally welcome you to Scapa Flow and review arrangements for getting you back to your stations."

Ben raised his eyebrows. "Not bad. Welcomed by the admiral himself."

"As I said before, you chaps are quite the celebrities," Watkins chuckled. "I imagine the top brass are eager to exploit your escape for the maximum propaganda value."

"Not particularly interested in the propaganda angle," Reggie grumbled. "Can't see us acting like a bunch of trained bears for whatever propaganda value someone might put on our escape. And we intend to be damned careful about revealing any details that might jeopardize our Polish partisan friends or the Swedish captain who got us here."

"That's a decision that'll be made above my pay level—way above," Watkins said. "My orders are to deliver you to the admiral."

"Another thing," Ben broke in. "We aren't exactly dressed properly for an audience with Admiral Sir Henry Moore."

"Shouldn't worry about that," Watkins said. "First, he's remarkably friendly and approachable. And he knows something about what you chaps have been through to get here. Don't think he'll be stuffy about the condition of your uniforms. You'll still look good in the photos."

Reggie snorted, "Might have known the admiral would want us to pose for photos to support the propaganda campaign." He turned and gazed over the starboard railing.

Sensing Reggie wanted to change the subject, Kowalski asked Watkins about the MTB. "I guess this thing is pretty fast," he said.

"Ah yes. This is a seventy-three foot Vosper Type II boat, the best fast boat the Royal Navy has," Watkins said. "Our three Packards deliver over four thousand horsepower, which gives us a top speed of forty knots. We're very maneuverable like the American PT boats and carry twin eighteen-inch torpedo tubes. Also mount 57 mm cannons, 20 mm Oerlikons, and .303-caliber Vickers machine guns."

"How many in the crew?" Kowalski asked.

"Full complement is thirteen, two officers, and eleven ranks," Watkins said.

He stepped forward to speak to the helmsman and then turned back to his five passengers. "We're passing South Wales Island on our portside and shortly will be approaching Flotta on our starboard," he said. "We'll then have a straight run northwest to Lyness, which'll be on our port side on the island of Hoy. Should deliver you to the admiral's office within the hour."

Reggie nodded. "As much as we're looking forward to meeting Sir Henry, we really want to get to a telephone so we can call our home stations. Let 'em know we're here and arrange for a Dakota to fetch us home."

"I'm certain there'll be plenty of phones in the admiral's offices," Watkins said with a thin smile. "Sir Henry probably has been in contact with both RAF and USAAF headquarters. Would be surprised if they haven't already arranged transport."

"Umm, do hope the admiral doesn't turn our homecoming into a circus," Reggie grumped. "We just want to get home to our stations and back in the saddle while there's still a war going on.

"Speaking of that," he added, "what's the latest news from the front? Or should I say fronts since the Allies are pressing Germany from three directions—west, south, and east. Are Patton and Montgomery making good time across France and the Low Countries after breaking out from Normandy?"

Watkins gave them a fifteen-minute summary of the war news, most of which was positive. "A lot of people are betting it'll be all over early next year," he said.

"All the more reason for us to get back to our home stations," Ben cut in. "Don't know about the rest of you fellas, but I've got a few more licks I wanna get in against the Nazis before Germany crumbles. I only hope there're still solid strategic targets for us to hit and that we won't be tasked to hit civilian centers."

An hour later, Watkins pointed off the port bow. "All right, chaps, we're approaching Lyness," he said. "Sir Henry's aide de camp radioed he'll meet us at the wharf with staff cars to deliver you to the admiral's headquarters."

"So the circus starts," Reggie muttered. "Keep your chins up, lads. The fun is about to begin."

The helmsman maneuvered their boat alongside the wharf, and sailors on the wharf quickly made fast lines thrown to them. A Royal Navy captain sporting the golden epaulette cord of an admiral's aide stood at the entrance to the wharf accompanied by two other officers.

Reggie and his companions lined up, thanked Watkins for the ride, and stepped onto the wharf. As the captain strode toward them, Reggie called the ragged band to attention and saluted. "Sir, Wing Commander Reginald M. Percy requesting permission to come ashore."

"I'm Captain John L. Corfield, Wing Commander Percy," he responded. "Welcome to Lyness. Admiral Sir Henry Moore is anxious to meet you."

Reggie introduced the other four, and they trooped behind the captain to three staff cars idling at the curb. Corfield introduced his companion officers and motioned Reggie to the first staff car. "You ride with me, Wing Commander," he said. Turning to Ben, Whitford, Banner, and Kowalski, he said, "You chaps will follow in the other cars."

The five stood at attention in front of Sir Henry's massive oak desk as Corfield made introductions. "By god, this is a fine day!" Sir Henry boomed. "Good show all 'round. Can't stress how proud we are over your escape—great morale booster for all our men. Proves capture and incarceration are not the end of it. Now stand at ease, gentlemen."

The admiral rose and stepped around his desk to shake hands with each of them. Ben remarked on the man's impressive appearance. His uniform was a dazzling white, and a small field of ribbons decorated the left side of his tunic. *Wings. The admiral is a flyer as well. Impressive.*

Ben estimated Sir Henry was right at six feet tall. His lean muscular frame spoke to an athletic past and a current regime that includes vigorous exercise. He looked younger than Ben had expected, and his full wavy black hair showed only hints of gray. A broad smile played across his face, but his gray-green eyes and full eyebrows formed a deep and penetrating gaze that showed he'd brook no nonsense from anyone.

"Pleased to shake your hand," he said to each of the five. "Three Yanks and two Brits. Now that shows how we Allies work together."

"Thank you, Admiral," Reggie replied. "We're a bit of a mixed bag, but we represent the thirty POWs in our original band. Four were killed in the train crash—"

Reggie was cut off by the admiral's raised eyebrows, which indicated he hadn't heard the details of their escape.

"Umm, pardon me, Admiral, perhaps you haven't heard the full story," Reggie said. He then gave Sir Henry a quick overview of their two solitary confinement punishments for plotting escape plans and their subsequent exile from Stalag Luft III in Poland on a German armaments train bound for Berlin. From there, they were to be transferred to the Sachsenhausen Concentration Camp near Berlin.

As Reggie drew a breath to continue his story, Sir Henry beckoned the five to sit in armchairs while he perched on the edge of his desk. "What an amazing story. Do continue."

Reggie told him that thirty of them were locked in the boxcar at Stalag Luft III and ultimately hooked onto the end of the armaments train headed for Berlin and about the violent train wreck the Polish partisans caused. He led the admiral through their five-day trek to the Baltic Sea, leaving out details of the route and the safe houses along the way.

"We boarded a fishing boat in a small fishing village on the Baltic and sailed into the night to rendezvous with a Swedish freighter out of Trelleborg, Sweden. That's the freighter that brought us across the North Sea to Pentland Firth."

"Well, I'm damned!" Sir Henry exclaimed. "Didn't realize how much was involved. Polish Partisans and a Swedish sea captain, eh? One hell of a story. Pity we can't go public with it. Wouldn't want to jeopardize any of those brave folks who helped you along the way, would we?"

Reggie sat back relieved. "Our sentiments exactly, sir. There still are a lot of prisoners looking for a way out. It's very important that the network be kept secret.

"Umm, speaking of others trying to get out," Reggie continued. "There still are nineteen men from that boxcar who headed for the Baltic in three other small groups. We're anxious to hear how they fared."

"I'll have my intelligence people check on that," Sir Henry said. "Now then, we want to have a few photographs taken of your arrival on home soil. Let's get that done, and then I'll ask you to excuse me. Have a few matters to attend to. But I'd like you to join me for a spot of lunch.

"Captain Corfield will see to your needs until then. Perhaps a bit of rest until lunch? Anything else?"

"That'll be wonderful, Sir Henry," Reggie said. "Two things: we need to get to phones and call our home stations. Let 'em know we're here and arrange a Dakota to fetch us home."

"That's already arranged. Dakota will land at HMS Robin, used to be RAF Kirkland station, tomorrow at 1400 hours. And the second thing?"

"Well, sir, as we were trekking through the Polish outback, existing on peasant bread, Polish sausage, and water, I promised the lads I'd stand them a double round at the first pub we encountered." Reggie grinned. "I'd like to fulfill that promise as soon as possible."

"Done!" the admiral said. "Make your phone calls, and then Captain Corfield will get you transported to the Piper's Arms—best pub in Lyness. I'll need you back here by 1430 hours for a late lunch. Umm, able to stand straight, I presume?"

"Thank you very much, Sir Henry!" Reggie said. "Umm, we're not only short of the king's lolly, sir, we're dead broke. Not a farthing among us. Can we arrange a bit of an advance?"

"Wing Commander, there is no way in hell you will be allowed to pay for a drink at the Piper's Arms or any other pub in Britain, I should think. Word is spreading fast about your escape, and I'm certain there'll be many fighting to stand you chaps a drink." Gesturing to the door, he said, "Now let's get some pictures taken."

Chapter 20

A Rousing Welcome!

The photo session went better than Reggie had imagined. Sir Henry seemed truly concerned about recording their arrival and not "making a circus of it" as Reggie had feared. Fifteen minutes later, Captain Corfield escorted them to the operations center where each was shown into a closed office to make their phone calls in private.

Ben picked up the phone with a trembling hand. An operator came on the line. "Please connect me to USAAF Colonel Frank Silverman at the headquarters of the 509 Heavy Bombardment Wing based at RAF Parham Station," he said.

"It'll take a couple of minutes, sir," the operator said. "Please hang up, and I'll call you when I get through to Parham."

The minutes seemed to stretch to hours as Ben waited with growing impatience for the return call. The double ring jangled his nerves like an electric shock. He grabbed the phone, fumbled the handset off the cradle, and shakily said, "Hello?"

"Ben, is that you?" Frank Silverman's voice boomed into his ear.

"Hello, Frank. Yes, it's me."

"My god! What a relief to hear your voice!" Silverman shouted excitedly. "We learned you were back safely last night when the navy called to verify your identity. I could hardly believe it! Last official word we had was that you were still in Stalag Luft III."

"Yeah, well, I didn't like the food, so I decided to move out," Ben joked. "Look, Frank, it's a long story, and I won't try to give you all the details over the phone, but our initial escape was pure luck. We—that is about thirty POWs the Germans decided were troublemakers—were shoved into a boxcar one night and hooked on the end of a passing armaments train headed for Berlin."

Ben paused to gather his thoughts.

"A band of Polish partisans blew up the tracks, wrecked the train, and killed all the train's crew and guards," he continued. Four of our fellas also were killed in the crash, and two suffered badly broken bones, so we had to leave them behind. The partisans took control and smuggled us to the Baltic coast, and we caught a couple of boats for the trip up here to Scapa Flow."

Ben said, "Helluva lot of details I want to share with you over a beer soon as I get back."

"Ben, I'm nearly speechless," Silverman croaked. "Still find it hard to believe. You know, it took the Germans a long time to verify they held you as a POW. My god, Ben, we all thought you were KIA." Silverman didn't add that he had ordered all of Ben's personal things shipped back home to his mother.

"Yeah, Frank, when I was blown outta *Round Trip*, I ended up in the Regensburg hospital. The Gestapo kept me under wraps for a couple weeks after my recovery so they could interrogate me while I was pumped full of morphine. The commander of the American contingent at Stalag Luft III finally got them to list me as a POW after I got there."

"Damnation!" Frank snapped. "Bastards don't play by the rules, do they?"

"Not by the Geneva Convention rules that's for sure. Say, listen, Frank. How are things going with the 509th?"

"We've taken our licks like everybody else, but we're givin' them more than they're giving us. Weather spoiled our support of the D-Day invasion, which was a big disappointment after all the buildup. But we've been pasting our targets deep in Germany since the breakout from Normandy."

"Great! Ah, Frank, about—"

"Gwen is fine, Ben," Frank interrupted. "I phoned her after we got the word you were headed home soon. She's back working at Addenbrooke's Hospital. Said she was overjoyed and waiting eagerly."

"Yeah, me too! Hopefully I'll see her in a couple of days. Say, speaking of that, what's the latest on sending a transport to pick us up?"

"It's already laid on. Doolittle is sending his personal VC-47. Can you believe that? They'll launch from Doolittle's headquarters tomorrow, but the general needs the airplane until about 1400 hours.

It's at least a four-hour flight to Kirkwall at Scapa Flow, so I expect they'll overnight there and leave early the next morning."

"I see," Ben said, trying not to sound too disappointed. "Just wish we could get away tomorrow morning, but I guess I have to be patient. Ah, what about Reggie and the other three fellas?"

"Doolittle's transport will haul them back to their stations after dropping you off. Reggie, eh? Might have known he'd be involved in all of this. Damn it, Ben, you've got a lot to tell us when you get back."

Ben chuckled. "Yeah, I can't seem to get that crazy Englishman outta my life. He's been a real lifesaver again. Look, Frank, I guess we shouldn't be tying up this line for too long. Gotta lot to talk about, like is the new job still open? I'll see you in a couple of days. So long."

"Of course, the job is open, and it's yours. But it looks like it'll be deputy commander. Tell you all about it when you get back. So long yourself, Ben. Welcome back, welcome back! Oh, by the way, I also cabled the good news to your folks."

All five completed their calls and gathered in the operations center. "Ah, Wing Commander, sir, we haven't forgotten about the pub promise you made back in Poland," Kowalski said with a sly grin. "When can we look forward to collecting on that promise?"

"It's just gone high noon, opening time," Reggie responded. "Let's have Captain Corfield deliver us to the Piper's Arms forthwith. Sir Henry said he doubted anyone there, the landlord, or whatever patrons are about would let us pay for our drinks. Since we haven't a farthing to our names, we'll put that theory to the test. Where's Captain Corfield?"

Corfield confirmed that word of their escape had circulated rapidly throughout Lyness and beyond. He too thought it unlikely they'd be allowed to pay for a drink. "Have a van standing by to get you to the Piper's Arms," he said. "Would like to join you, but the admiral has me jumping through hoops this afternoon."

The van driver pulled up to the curb in front of the pub, hopped out and, slid open the van door. "Wing Commander, let me step inside first and have a word with the landlord. I'm sure he'll be pleased to have you as his guests."

He was right. As soon as the five stepped inside, the landlord rang the bell at the bar and bellowed, "Gents, yer attention please. I am proud to present our five 'eroes what has escaped from captivity in Germany and traveled through many dangers to get 'ome!" He then called for three cheers, which the patrons delivered with gusto.

The five stood grinning just inside the door. Reggie signaled for quiet. "Thank you kindly, landlord. Gentlemen, we appreciate your warm welcome. We just happened to be in the neighborhood en route to our home stations and thought we'd stop in for a pint."

This prompted a roar of approval followed by a scramble for the bar as everyone clamored to buy them a drink. The landlord vigorously rang the bar bell. "Steady on, gents, these 'ere lads be guests o' the house, at least fer the first round. Then yew ken line up proper so and stand 'em a shout as well." Then turning to the five in the doorway, he shouted, "Come in, gents, do come in. Take a seat. What's yer pleasure?"

As they sat, savoring their pints of bitter, Ben smiled at the surrounding circle of grinning red-cheeked faces. *Good solid stock all. Judging from their weathered complexions, they must be herring fishermen.*

Ben stretched and felt the tension drain from his body. It had been building since their escape, and now the anxiety of waiting for the final leg of the journey to Parham. He relaxed as the cozy eighteenth-century pub enveloped him in its warm smoky arms. Massive beams supporting the low-slung ceiling bore the black softness formed by years of smoke from tobacco and the peat fire smoldering in the large open hearth. He inhaled the unique pub smell—a mixture of smoke, beer and scotch fumes, and sweat—pungent and yet somehow pleasing. His eyes drifted to the Snug, the private room behind the bar separated from the noisy common room by a door with a glazed windowpane. It served as a private place for the gentile set and their ladies to enjoy drinks away from the raucous conviviality of the common room. *Sure would like to snug down in there with Gwen and maybe never leave.*

The five could have remained happily drinking on into the night and still not satisfied all of the demands from patrons clamoring to stand them a drink, but Ben remembered they had a luncheon with Admiral Sir Henry. "Reggie," he said, tugging on his sleeve, "much as I'd like to stay here until our VC-47 arrives, we do have a date with Sir Henry at 1430 hours. That's about twenty minutes from now. Better get moving, don't you think?"

"Right you are, Benjamin," Reggie said with exaggerated correctness. "We best say our farewells and summon our driver, what ho?" Ben wasn't sure he had only been drinking bitters.

They arrived back at the admiral's headquarters just in time to be ushered into his dining room. All five moved carefully since the bitters—and in some cases, several whiskies—were beginning to take effect. Sir Henry had ordered an extra special lunch menu and invited several of his staff officers to meet and dine with the heroes of the day.

Following introductions, Sir Henry signaled their glasses to be filled with healthy drams of Springbank, one of Scotland's best single-malt Scotch whiskies and proposed a toast to their bravery, perseverance, and service to their countries. Ben tensed his body and breathed deeply, striving to sit erect and smile politely instead of grinning like a drunken fool.

Ben had a hazy memory of being served an array of delicious dishes, which he washed down with fine wine from a glass that surprisingly never seemed to get empty. Apparently, his four companions were feeling similar effects from the amount of alcohol they had consumed because he noted they all teetered perilously close to raucous behavior. They jockeyed with each other to add their bits to the descriptions of life in Stalag Luft III and their trek across Poland to the Baltic Sea. Sir Henry and his staff officers appeared to be enjoying the show enormously and kept encouraging the five to eat and drink generously. When it came time to pass the port wine, Ben clutched the bottle in a death grip, determined not to pour it into his lap before passing it to the officer on his left.

Sometime in late afternoon, Sir Henry called for "all men to be upstanding" and announced it had been one of the most enjoyable luncheon parties he had ever hosted.

"Now, gentlemen," he said, addressing the five escapees, "we appreciate your agreeing to spend this time with us when we know how anxious you are to get to your home stations. We salute you as true heroes and wish you Godspeed on the rest of your journey." Table thumping followed.

Captain Corfield whispered in the admiral's ear. "Gentlemen," the admiral called out, "Captain Corfield informs me that a van awaits you outside. It'll take you to the wharf where you'll board a fast boat for transport across Scapa Flow to Scapa Landing. You'll then be transported by another van to HMS Robin Station where Captain Arthur Begley is waiting to welcome you and bed you down for the night."

He stood and shook hands with each of the five. "Safe trip from here, right, gentlemen?" All attendees responded with a resounding, "Hear, hear!"

The five snapped to attention, saluted Sir Henry, and walked with exaggerated care to the waiting van.

Chapter 21

Back "Home"

At the wharf, Leftenant Commander Watkins waited at the helm of fast boat *Victor*. They swept away from Lyness, slipped between Fara and Flotta Islands into Scapa Flow, and steered northwest to Scapa Landing. The slight bite Ben felt in the late September afternoon air was softened by a steady autumnal breeze from the south. The temperature hovered in the low fifties, but the angle of the sun as it dipped toward the western horizon indicated they were in the higher latitudes.

"We're between fifty-eight and fifty-nine degrees north latitude and between two and three degrees west longitude," Watkins said in answer to Ben's question. "This temperature is about normal for this time of year as is the breeze. We enjoy light to moderate breezes year round, but in the winter, we're subject to some gales off the North Sea."

Watkins explained that the Orkney Islands have a mild and steady climate, unusual for a northerly latitude, because of the Gulf Stream that runs along the western edge. Temperatures average forty-six degrees Fahrenheit during winter with lows ranging to the high thirties. During the summer, the average is in the midfifties.

"Annual rainfall ranges up to about forty inches," Watkins added. "Winds are a key feature of the climate as I said before. Even in summer, there's always a breeze, and it's only in winter that Scapa can be buffeted by winds up to gale strength."

As they cruised north across Scapa Flow, they gazed off the port side at a glorious sunset. Brilliant yellow and orange shafts pierced

RETURN FROM THE ABYSS

low-flying clouds, sweeping the earth like heavenly spotlights. Others

low-flying clouds, sweeping the earth like heavenly spotlights. Others reflected off the cloud tops, seeming to set the sky on fire. The five were mesmerized by the sight of major Home Fleet ships riding at anchor silhouetted against this vivid backdrop.

"Because we're so far north, we have long summer days—the sun rises around 0300 hours and doesn't set until after 2100 hours," Watkins said. "We're not far enough north to have nearly twenty-four hours of sunlight in the summer or arctic blackness during the winter days. In dead of winter, we have about six hours of daylight."

The setting sun, copious amounts of food and drink, and the steady rumble of the fast boat's three Packard engines combined to lull the five into deep sleep. They lay sprawled in a variety of positions until Watkins gently rousted them as fast boat headed into Scapa Landing.

"We'll be docking in a few minutes," he said. "Commander. Duncan Sanders will meet you at the wharf with a van to transport you to HMS Robin to meet Captain Begley. By the way, they said on the radio they had an updated schedule for your flight back to your home stations."

"Bloody hell!" Reggie exclaimed. "Not another delay!"

"Think it's the opposite," Watkins grinned. "Appears your Dakota will be arriving tomorrow morning, and you'll be flying home that afternoon."

This was greeted with a collective whoop from the five. "Home tomorrow night!" Ben exulted. "Man, that's swell!

Sanders met them at the wharf, bundled them into the van, and slid into the passenger seat. He delivered a mini-travelogue as they left the wharf. "We'll head north on Scapa Road A960 into Kirkwall. Pity it's getting dark, as the town has some fascinating historical sights. Then we'll swing southeast on A960 to the station. The sea on our port side will be the Wide Firth. I'd like to show you more tomorrow, but I suppose you're focused on getting back to your home stations."

Reggie elbowed Ben in the ribs and winked. "Umm, yes, Commander, at this point that indeed is uppermost in our minds. We understand the Dakota is coming in tomorrow morning. Do you have an ETA yet?"

"Last estimated time I heard was 1100 hours," Sanders said. "Allow an hour for refueling, and I should think you'd be on your way right after a spot of lunch with Captain Begley."

Ben mouthed a silent, "Yahoo!" *Can't wait! See you tomorrow night, Gwen!*

"Excellent!" Reggie responded. "We've been gone awhile, some of us a long while, and well, you know . . . mustn't appear we don't appreciate your hospitality and the help the Royal Navy has provided so far."

"Perfectly understandable, Wing Commander," Sander said quickly. "We'll do what we can to expedite the process. Ah, here we are, HMS Robin."

Sanders escorted them into Begley's office. The captain rose from his chair and stepped forward to shake hands with all five. "Welcome to HMS Robin. Can't tell you how proud and pleased we are to have a bit of a hand in getting you chaps home. Sit, sit please."

The five plopped wearily into chairs around the captain's conference table. "Thank you, Captain Begley," Reggie said. "We've had a lot of fine folks helping us along the way. Right now, we're on the other side of bushed, so I hope you'll excuse us if we appear a bit subdued. Also, Sir Henry staged a royal luncheon for us with heaps of wonderful food and not a little to drink."

"Of course, of course," Begley said. "Sir Henry is famous for the 'light luncheons' he hosts."

"The admiral also gave us a couple of hours to visit a local pub Piper's Arms, if I remember," Ben interjected. "The locals lined up and fought to buy us drinks. And we haven't had any real alcohol for many months in the POW camp."

"Right, I understand," Begley smiled. "But I hope you'll do us the honor of joining us for a light supper. I'd like you to meet some of my staff officers, and I promise to make an early night of it."

All five nodded wearily.

The light supper proved a bit heavier than Captain Begley indicated. But all five returnees rallied, fell quickly into the swing of the evening, and soon were eating and drinking to excess. Ben remembered saying a lot of witty things and regaling all assembled with amusing anecdotes about prison life and their escape. He did not remember Reggie dumping him into bed.

"Rise and shine, Sancho!" penetrated his befogged brain. Reggie was sounding reveille. "Sun's risen, and so should we."

"Ooh hell, Reggie." Ben groaned, squeezing his eyes shut and holding his head. "What time is it?"

"The exact time is 0640 hours, and we need to be up and about. We need a good Scottish breakfast and lots of black coffee to get us going. Our Dakota will be here in about four hours."

"What's so special about a Scottish breakfast?" Ben asked. "Please tell me it doesn't include that rotten-smelling stuff that's cooked in a cow's stomach!"

"Haggis!" Reggie laughed. "Not hardly, me lad. That's a pudding made of mixed meats and internal organs from sheep and sometimes cows. It's boiled in a cow's stomach and brought steaming to the table. Takes a strong man not to keel over when the thing is cut open. No, Ben, haggis is best tolerated with a lot of alcohol and friends who'll shame you if you shrink away from it. It's a festive dinner dish and definitely an acquired taste.

"A proper Scottish breakfast is similar to the English breakfast of sausage, bacon and egg, and a grilled tomato," Reggie continued. But the Scots typically add black pudding—blood sausage—and potato scones.

"Oatmeal porridge is usually on the menu as are strong kippers, you know, hot smoked herring," Reggie said. "The Scots also like Arbroath smokies—smoked haddock—which add a special taste. Then they top it off with oatcakes and butteries, a buttery bread like the French croissant."

Ben pondered this. "Oatmeal I know and maybe, what'd you call 'em, butteries. Not sure yet about kippers or smokies, but I'm damn sure I don't wanna try that black pudding.

"And," he added with a wry grin, "I'm real glad it won't involve that stuff that comes in a cow's stomach."

Reggie clapped him on the back. "Right-ho, Sancho. Let's find the mess or whatever our navy friends call the place where food is served. I'm sure we'll find something to suit both of our tastes."

They did, and by the time the other three joined them, Ben was well into a steaming bowl of porridge, several links of sausage, and a small pile of butteries lathered with marmalade. He wrinkled his nose as Reggie addressed his plate of kippers and blood pudding.

After breakfast, they joined Captain Begley in the station operations center, thanked him again for his wonderful hospitality, and stared at the flight line as if willing the Dakota to drone into sight and enter the landing pattern.

As they waited with increasing agitation for their ride home to arrive, Begley tried to distract them with a brief history of HMS Robin. "The station has undergone several changes in name and ownership," he said. "When it first became operational, it belonged to the Royal Air Force and was known as both RAF Grimsetter and RAF Kirkwall. Several squadrons of Spitfires were based here."

He paused. "It was transferred to the Royal Navy in 1943 and renamed RNAS Kirkwall and finally HMS Robin. It serves as a support station like RNAS Hatston, which is located just north and west of Kirkwall. We both provide repair and training services for carrier-based aircraft, but our runways are longer than Hatston's. That's why your Dakota will land here."

Reggie, Ben, and their fellow escapees paced the operations center like caged animals, taking turns to use borrowed binoculars to scan the sky for the Dakota. Reggie called them together. "I say, chaps—fellow Giraffes, if you will—we need write down our particulars. I'm certain we'll meet again in the near future, intelligence briefings and all that. But we need to stay in touch after that, so write down your current unit's address and a home address where we can be reached after this spot of bother is over." He handed out pencils and sheets of paper.

This occupied the five for half an hour. When the five had exchanged addresses, they again took turns scanning the sky for their airplane. Ben felt fatigue sapping his strength and sat, nodding off in a quiet corner. A telephone jangled him awake.

"Gentlemen, you'll be happy to hear your Dakota is inbound," Begley called out. "Pilot estimates they'll be on the ground in fifteen minutes."

Ben grabbed the binoculars and scanned the sky to the south. "There she is!" he yelled. "What a beautiful sight. She's a USAAF C-47 wearing army khaki, but I can make out two stars painted on the nose, so it really is General Doolittle's personal airplane! Guess the designation is VC-47. Do you s'pose it has real airliner seats, not those metal bucket seat butt busters?"

They watched eagerly as the pilot rolled onto a long final leg for a straight-in approach to Runway 32, landing to the northwest into a stiffening wind. The pilot brought the VC-47 down smoothly on the main gear, touched the brakes until the tail dropped to the three-point position, and turned onto the taxiway. Ben hooted and pumped his right fist above his head as the airplane eased to a stop on the ramp. As the propellers clanked to a stop, the ramp crew moved in and placed chocks around the wheels.

The aft fuselage door swung open, and a sergeant appeared with a set of metal stairs, which he snapped into place. A USAAF major stepped out followed by a boyish-looking first lieutenant. The lieutenant began a walk-around inspection of the airplane as the sergeant supervised the refueling crew that swarmed over the VC-47's wings.

The major strode to the operations center door where Captain Begley waited with the five Giraffes. He saluted and addressed Begley, "Good morning, Captain. I'm Major Brad Hutchinson, General Doolittle's personal pilot. Here to pick up some VIP passengers . . ." He paused, looking closely at the shabbily dressed band of five grinning at him.

"Good morning, Major Hutchinson, and welcome to HMS Robin," Begley responded. "Here are your passengers eager, I'm sure, to be on their way." He introduced Reggie, Ben, Duncan, Archie, and Art.

"Pleased to meet you," Reggie said, extending his right hand. "Sorry we look a bit ragged and travel weary, but that's exactly what we are. Had a bit of an adventure getting here, don'tcha know? Get us some new uniforms and a haircut, and we'll turn out much smarter."

Ben pushed forward. "Ben Findlay, B-17 driver based at Parham," he said. "Damned happy to see you, Major Hutchinson. The other three crowded around for formal handshakes. Hutchinson regarded each with obvious curiosity. "You're the guys who busted outta that POW Camp in Germany, right? I'm honored to meet ya. We'll have a lotta time to gab on the way home."

Turning to Begley, Hutchinson said, "Captain, I don't wanna be rude, but we can't stay long. There's a doozy of a storm headin' this way off the North Sea, and we really need to haul ass outta here before the front arrives. Our weather guys said we shouldn't spend more'n an hour here, or we might get caught in it. That could ground us here for several days."

Ben tensed and started to interject. Reggie touched his elbow. "Steady on, Sancho," he whispered. "Let them work it out."

"I know, Major. Our meteorologist has told us the same thing. We're used to tracking storms up here, especially the nor'westers. They can roll in here and stay for days." He paused, "Umm, I had hoped that despite that you might be able to join us for a quick lunch—cold lunch, nothing fancy. But I see we need to get you chaps on your way as quickly as possible."

Begley turned to Commander Sanders. "Duncan, ring up the mess and tell them our guests can't stay for lunch. Have them pack up three picnic hampers, all the fixings. Can't send our guests away hungry. Tell them double time. Need them here in half an hour."

"Thank you, Captain," Hutchinson said. "That'll get us on the way in fairly good time. We'll have to push the old girl, go balls to the wall, and try to stay ahead of the front."

"Balls to the wall? Curious phrase," Begley said.

113

"Huh?" Hutchinson asked. "Oh, balls to the wall. Flyers' slang, Captain. In the old days, the throttle levers had big yellow knobs, you know, balls. When you needed to go fast, you'd shove the balls to the wall, uh . . . throttles full forward to the firewall."

"Like our 'buster, buster, buster,' command telling our fighter pilots to get to the intercept posthaste," Reggie said.

"Ah, of course," Begley said. "Thank you for explaining it. Balls to the wall, eh? I shall use that, if I may, next time I want something done at double time."

Hutchinson walked back out to the VC-47 to check on the refueling. A small Morris van screeched to a stop outside the operations center, and a red-faced petty officer struggled through the door and placed two large picnic hampers on the floor. He turned, gave Begley a crisp salute, and announced he had "one more amper for your guests, Captain."

"I say, Captain," Reggie said, eyeing the hampers, "these would do Fortnum and Mason proud, sir. We'll certainly enjoy them during the ride home."

"You're welcome," Wing Commander Percy said. "Damn sorry you can't stay for lunch, but I understand the need for haste. Umm, you'll find a little libation among the sandwiches and meat pies," he added with a sly smile.

All three hampers were hustled on board as Major Hutchinson strode back through the door. "We're ready to roll, gents."

Ben and the three others joined Reggie in shaking hands and saluting Captain Begley before exiting and hurrying to the waiting airplane. Hutchinson gave Begley a quick salute and turned to follow his passengers. He turned and smiled. "Sorry we have to rush, Captain. Maybe next time we're in the neighborhood, we'll have time for a nice long lunch."

On board, he introduced them to his copilot Lieutenant Baxter and the flight engineer Sergeant Carson.

Chapter 22

RETURN TO THE FOLD

As promised, Hutchinson kept the VC-47's throttles "balls to the wall." Aided by a gusting tail wind preceding the approaching front, the airplane was cruising at 200 mph, just shy of its certified maximum speed of 224 mph. Ben, who had enjoyed the comfort of the VC-47's airliner seats, became restless and wandered up to the flight deck. Hutchinson jerked a thumb at Baxter, who vacated the copilot's seat and eased back to the cabin to join the others for lunch.

"Join me, Major Findlay," Hutchinson said, waving Ben to the copilot's seat. "Ever flown a Gooney Bird?" he asked, using the affectionate nickname for the venerable C-47.

"No, I haven't. Looks pretty straightforward. And call me Ben."

"Sure, Ben," Hutchinson grinned. "I'm Brad. Got her on autopilot now, but if you want to hand fly, there's the switch. As you can feel, we're picking up some turbulence from the front's bow wave, so you might have to wrestle her a bit."

Ben eagerly grasped the control yoke, switched off the autopilot, and savored the rapid response of the airplane as he trimmed the controls for the turbulence. He quickly developed a feel for the airplane and remarked how much more responsive it was to control inputs than the B-17. No surprise, the C-47 was smaller and a lot lighter than the Flying Fortress.

"How long have you been on Forts?" Hutchinson asked.

"'Bout two years now," Ben said. "I'm a squadron commander for the 509th Heavy Bombardment Group. We've been based at Parham since early '43."

"How'd you get captured?"

"Shot down after hitting the Messerschmitt Factory in Regensburg. Ran into a flak trap on the way out and took an antiaircraft hit nearly on the nose. All hell broke loose. Just as I buckled my parachute harness, our bomber exploded, and I was blown clear. That was the last time I saw old *Round Trip*, ah, that was the name of our bomber and my crew." Ben paused and clenched his jaw. "Uh, still haven't heard if anyone else survived."

"Damn tough luck," Hutchinson said. "Maybe you can track 'em now that you're back. How many missions had you flown?"

"That was number thirty. End of mission commitment. My crew was goin' home. I'd been offered a new job at the 509th, so I opted to stay for another tour. Hope the job is still open."

"Wow, really tough luck. Sure hope you'll catch up with some of your crew."

"How about you?" Ben asked. "I can see by your command wings and a couple of rows of ribbons that you haven't just been a C-47 driver."

"Naw, I did a tour in B-25s in North Africa, then moved up to the B-24 for a second tour. Big ugly flying you-know-whats, but they took one helluva beating and kept flying. We carried quite a load. Flew with the Seventeenth Air Force outta Benghazi."

"Were you on the raid that hit the Ploesti oil fields in Romania?"

"Yeah, and damned lucky to survive that screwed up mission. It's a wonder anyone did. You probably know the details. We bombed from less than a thousand feet, so low our gunners had direct shoot-outs with the antiaircraft gunners in the flak towers like a big ass gunfight at O.K. Corral. Command and control collapsed, so we had groups comin' at the target from every major point on the compass. It's a wonder we didn't lose more bombers in midair collisions. I had more near misses on that one mission than I've had in my entire flying career."

"How'd you get this job flying Doolittle around?" Ben asked.

"I got to know the general in North Africa," Hutchinson said. "Got along with him pretty well. When I finished my second combat tour, he asked me to join his planning staff and act as his personal pilot. It's a good job."

Ben nodded and settled back to concentrate on flying the C-47. He liked its solid feel. He remembered watching the DC-3 airliners, civilian versions of the C-47, pass through Baker Field back home in Michigan when he was training with Brice. *After the war, there'll be a lot of these available to the airlines. Might be something worth looking into. Used to wonder what it'd be like to fly for the airlines.*

"So what's the word on your escape from the POW camp?" Hutchinson asked, breaking Ben's reverie. "Can you talk about it? Don't imagine life in a camp was all that pleasant."

"Nope, it wasn't. Thankfully I was only there about four months. Some of the guys, who're still there, and some of my fellow escapees spent years behind the barbed wire. It was no picnic, but the Germans treated us a lot better than what I hear the Japs are doing to POWs in the Pacific."

"Yeah, I hear being captured out there is bad news," Hutchinson responded. "But how'd you guys escape?"

"Long story," Ben said. Then he launched into an abbreviated version of their activities as escape planners in Stalag Luft III, their times in solitary, their banishment to the Sachsenhausen concentration camp, and their escape from the train wreck. He shared some highlights of their trek out of Poland but omitted many details that might endanger those who helped them.

"Holy cow! Quite a story," Hutchinson said. "Say, you want me to get Baxter back up here to relieve you?"

"Actually, no. I'm enjoying flying this thing," Ben said. "How about you goin' back and joining the picnickers? Captain Begley's kitchen crew packed a swell lunch. If I need help or get tired, I'll yell for you or Baxter."

Hutchinson smiled his thanks and ducked back into the aft cabin. Ben sat gazing out over the C-47's nose. They had crossed Scotland's Moray Firth and made landfall on the south side between Inverness on the right and Banff on the left. Edinburgh was the next major waypoint followed by Newcastle, York, and points south. Ben checked the map and was dismayed at the distance left to cover before they reached Cambridge and Parham. Despite the strong tailwind, their progress seemed snail-like to him.

"Maybe I can push the balls a little closer to the wall," he muttered. "Naw, on second thought, I don't wanna overboost the general's engines. He might not take that too well." Ben knew any recorded overboost required a mandatory oil analysis for metal chips in the engine crankcase, which often resulted in an engine change for safety of flight purposes.

They droned south, passing Edinburgh and heading for Newcastle. The radio crackled repeatedly as air traffic controllers coordinated the flight paths for a variety of departing and arriving combat air fleets. Ben switched on the autopilot so he could concentrate more fully on monitoring the increasing radio traffic.

Baxter stuck his head through the cockpit door. "Man, what a feast!" he marveled. "The captain even included several of bottles of chilled champagne." He grinned and feigned a loud belch. "Of course, I only had a sip or two. Say, you need any help? Wanna take a break?"

"Actually, I do," Ben said. "I've been at this for over an hour. Let's get Major Hutchinson up here, and you two can drive while I go back and sip champagne."

After more than a sip or two to wash down a tasty sandwich and a meat pie, Ben pushed back in his seat. His chin dropped to his chest. He must have slept soundly because when he woke with a snort and when he smacked his dry lips, he noticed golden shafts of the setting sun streaming through the windows on the right side.

"Hey, somebody!" he called out. "Where are we? Gettin' close to home?"

"Actually, old cock, we're about twenty minutes out of Parham," Reggie said. "Have a nice nap, did we, with the captain's fine champagne lulling you to sleep?"

Ben snapped upright and peered out the window, instantly recognizing prominent landmarks around Framlingham, Sussex, where his Parham home base was located. He stepped to the tiny head in the rear of the airplane, had a long pee, and splashed cold water on his face. "Not much of an improvement," he mused at his reflection in the small mirror. "But I hope I look a little less like a ragged bum."

The VC-47 droned into the downwind leg of Parham airfield's traffic pattern, turned ninety degrees onto the base leg, and finally turned again onto the final approach. Ben felt like they had slipped into another slow-motion time warp. Did it always take this long to fly the pattern? He realized he was over anxious. In truth, the VC-47's time in the pattern was pretty much the same as the B-17s'.

As the main wheels screeched onto the runway, Ben gawked at the Parham control tower. It looked like a giant anthill. Airmen crowded the balcony surrounding the control cab, the outside stairway was thronged, and what looked like the rest of the base personnel milled around on the parking ramp. A huge "Welcome Home, Major Findlay" banner stretched across the balcony railing.

"Hey, Ben, lookit this!" Art Kowalski yelled. "They got a brass band as part of the welcome party."

Ben stared in disbelief. Colonel Frank Silverman had indeed formed the 509th marching band in front of the control tower. "I'll be damned," Ben croaked. "Ol' Frank has pulled out all the stops, makin' me out to be some kinda hero."

Major Hutchinson pivoted the VC-47 into a parking spot with the door on the left rear of the fuselage facing the crowd. He cut the engines, completed the shutdown checklist, and waited for the ground crew to wedge the chocks against the wheels. Sergeant Carson popped open the rear door and snapped the metal steps in place. The assembled crowd roared, "Welcome home!" Flashbulbs popped, and Sergeant Carson mugged the cameras and waved.

"Okay, Sancho, your public awaits," Reggie teased. "You first."

"Before I go, Reggie, a private thanks and goodbye," Ben said, wrapping his friend in a bear hug. "See you again soon at the briefing." He turned and hugged the other three. "Us Giraffes gotta stick together. See ya later." He turned and thanked Hutchinson and Baxter for the ride home.

Silverman arrived at the bottom of the aircraft stairs. "You got a Major Benjamin Findlay in there?" he called out. "Want him front and center right now!"

Ben hopped down the stairs, saluted, and wrapped Silverman in a back-thumping hug. "Hello, Frank, can't tell you how swell it is to see you." Then as the band struck up the USAAF anthem, Ben yelled, "And thanks for the welcome ceremony. Kinda overwhelming." He waved to the cheering crowd.

"Let's get Reggie and the others out here as well," Silverman said. Reggie, Duncan, Archie, and Art hopped down the steps, saluted Silverman and waved to the crowd.

"Trust my lot will be as happy to see me back home as your people are to see Ben," Reggie said.

"Not to worry," Silverman said. "You'll find welcome ceremonies at each of your stations."

"Speaking of that, Frank, I hope you excuse us for not staying for your festivities," Reggie said. "We're all anxious to get on 'ome as well."

"Certainly, certainly. Great seeing you again, Reggie. And good meeting you," he said to the other three. "Safe trip." The four shook hands all around and clambered back on board. The VC-47 soon roared down the Parham runway and headed south.

"Now let the fun begin," Frank called out. "We're on stand-down for two days while our aircraft are equipped with updated navigational equipment. So we're gonna have a party." He turned to the crowd and bellowed, "Officers and enlisted clubs open at 1800 hours. Drinks are on the house!" That prompted an even louder cheer.

"Come on, Ben," Silverman said. "That'll give you time to get shaved and showered and into a new uniform. You look a little ratty, not that it's surprising knowing what you've been through. Then I want Doc Samuelson to give you a quick check." He walked Ben to his quarters. It was slow going since old friends and new arrivals alike lined the path to welcome Ben with handshakes and backslaps.

"Frank, I see a lotta new faces and don't see as many familiar faces. You been taking heavy losses?"

"We've had our share, Ben. Not like the bad old days in '43, but a combination of losses and crews rotating back to the States makes for quite a turnover."

They reached Ben's quarters, and Frank stopped outside the door. "Uh, Ben, you'll see that I had your personal stuff shipped back home. Waited as long as I thought I could, then when we didn't hear anything about your status, I had it packed up and shipped out. Can we arrange to have any of it shipped back?"

He added quickly, "That is, if you're still planning to extend your tour and take the deputy commander's job. Larry Coleman has been promoted to full colonel and will take command of the 328th the first of next month. I hope you'll consider . . ."

"I want to ship over, Frank, and I'll take the job. We'll worry about my stuff later. Many thanks."

"Great! Ben, that's fantastic news. Now I'm sure you'll want to make a phone call before you join the celebration tonight. I'll leave you to have a nice chat with Gwen. Ah, she's on duty at Addenbrooke's. I put the number next to the phone. Then get cleaned up and stretch out for a little rest. I'll have Samuelson come by in an hour and give you a quick once-over in your quarters."

As he turned to go, Silverman took Ben by the shoulder. "Ben, I'd send you off to see Gwen tonight, but I think it's important that you join our celebration. We'll get you over to see her tomorrow."

"Of course, Frank," I understand. *But what I really wanna do is get over there tonight and grab that beautiful woman in my arms.*

"Thanks, Ben. I knew you'd understand. See you in a couple of hours." Frank shook his hand and retreated down the hallway.

Ben called after him, "Ah, Frank, one more thing. Where's my ol' copilot Gordy? The Regensburg mission also would have been his thirtieth, earning him his ticket home. Fortunately, he missed it because of that sinus infection. What happened after he got out of the hospital?"

"Gordy flew his thirtieth with us and was offered a B-29 copilot's slot. He's back in the States, MacDill, I think. I'll dig out his records. Get you his current address."

Ben nodded his thanks and stepped into his quarters. It was like coming home even without his personal gear. A new precisely pressed uniform lay spread out on his bunk. Ben stepped forward to look at it and did a double take. "What the . . .," he said, eyeing the lieutenant colonel's silver oak leaf insignia on the shoulders. "Frank, you sly old fox. Nice surprise."

Ben spent over half an hour on the phone with Gwen. She was on duty, and they were swamped with patients from the emergency surgery. Hearing her bell-like laugh intermixed with sobs of joy sent hot flashes of desire through him.

"Gwen, I, uh, I have to take part in Frank's party tonight, but I have the day off tomorrow. Even if you're on duty, I want to drive over to be with you . . ."

"Oh, Ben, dear Ben, I'm on duty tonight, so it wouldn't be convenient to see you now anyway. But I'm off tomorrow! We can have the whole day together, and . . ."

"And what?" Ben asked slyly.

"I'm sure we can work something out." She giggled. "Now look, love, I must get back to my duties. Can't wait to hold you in my arms! What time shall I expect you?"

"I'll try to get an early start." *Gotta make damn sure I'm not hungover.* "I'll call you when I'm ready to leave. Oh, by the way, I need your address and directions." Gwen gave him her address and home phone number, which he scribbled on the back of an envelope.

"Bye, my love," she breathed into the phone. "I can hardly wait." This left him a little unsteady and breathing heavily.

Chapter 23

Back to the Business of War

As Ben and Frank walked across the base to the Officers Club, the din from the combined welcome home and promotion party reverberated through the scrub pines. "We could find this place blindfolded just by following the noise." Ben chuckled. He waved a hand over his new uniform and insignia. "Uh, Frank, I really appreciate this, both the uniform and the promotion."

"You've earned them," Silverman said. "Just like you deserved the Distinguished Service Cross for salvaging the Regensburg mission. Haven't had a chance to tell you yet, but post mission recon photos showed you guys really beat up the Messerschmitt aircraft factory. We haven't had to go back since. But our intelligence guys are hinting there's some kind of new secret activity starting there. Might call for a revisit."

Ben pondered Silverman's comments as they stopped before reaching the Officers Club. "I should be ready to lead missions soon, Frank. Samuelson said I'm in pretty good condition considering what I've been through. Says I'm about thirty pounds underweight. But that can be fixed. Says my shoulder still needs some attention, but it's healing nicely." He looked directly at Frank. "You haven't asked about the scars on my face."

"Didn't want to until you were ready to talk about it."

"Yeah, thanks. I'll be ready in a few days. Give you a full briefing from when we took the direct hit over Regensburg, my time in Stalag Luft III, and our escape. Now let's join the party."

The party was rolling in high gear when Ben and Frank walked into the Officers Club. A whoop of cheers greeted them, and fellow pilots elbowed their way into the melee surrounding them, demanding to buy Ben a drink. The fact that the drinks were free did nothing to detract from their gestures.

Ben tried desperately to sip his way through the evening, determined not to let his boisterous friends get him knee-walking drunk. He wanted to greet Gwen the next day with a clear head, not peering through the fog of a roaring hangover. Silverman signaled him out on the club's porch.

"I'm letting them loose tonight," he said, staring across the base. "They deserve it. We've pushed them to the limit to support the Allied drive across Europe, and this'll help relieve the tension. Also, it's a way to keep them on the base. We'll go operational again as soon as our navigational system upgrade is completed."

German Fieseler Fi 103R V-1 Weapo

He turned to Ben. "We're going into a critical period, Ben. The top brass is pressuring us to knock out Germany's petroleum industry, beat back the Luftwaffe, and clear an invasion path across Europe all at the same time. Then there's those damn V-2 rocket weapons the Germans have developed. They build them in underground hardened factories and launch them from mobile sites. Hard nuts to crack.

"What I'm leading up to is that I'm going to need a strong right-hand man. As my deputy, I'm going to call on you to carry a big part of the mission planning and operations management burdens. I think you're up to it."

"Thanks, Frank, I'll do my best to earn your trust," Ben replied, "but I hope this won't be only a desk job. I'd like to lead my share of missions."

"In time, Ben, in time. First we have to get you cleared by Doc Samuelson to return to flight status. Might even have you fly a few practice missions to prove you still know how to handle a B-17," he added with a sly grin.

Ben bit back an intemperate response, then said, "No worries about that, Frank."

"Also, I'm getting signals that my time in the European theater may be limited," Frank said. Waving off Ben's objections, he continued, "Word is we're forming two new heavy bombardment wings equipped with Boeing's newest B-29s, which'll be deployed to the Pacific. The marines are getting closer to mainland Japan with their island-hopping invasions. We'll soon have several bases close enough to launch major B-29 raids as far as Tokyo with round-trip fighter protection by long-range P-51s and P-38s."

"Wow! That's impressive," Ben said. "How does it affect you?"

"I'm also getting signals I might get one of the wings. It'll mean promotion to brigadier general and a return to the States for retraining. Nothing official, but it's in the wind, so I have to prepare a replacement for me here."

"And that might be me?"

"I sure hope so. But look, let's get back to the party. We can go into all of this in a few days."

"Okay, Frank, but I'm gonna ask you to help me stay sober. I don't want to meet Gwen tomorrow with a hangover." Silverman nodded and grinned.

When they walked back inside, Ben was swarmed by a boisterous crowd eager to share a drink with him who demanded war stories about how he was shot down, his life in the Stalag Luft III camp, and his escape. He reminded himself to be careful, to keep moving, taking a sip here and there, and trying to leave nearly full glasses behind.

By midnight, the few revelers left standing were not alert enough to notice Ben's subterfuge. When Silverman finally escorted Ben back to his quarters, he felt more than a little unsteady on his feet but reasoned it was due more to fatigue than excessive alcohol consumption.

He slipped into a deep sleep, aching to hold Gwen.

Chapter 24

Reunited!

Ben woke at 0600 hours, hopped out of bed, and did a quick cycle of wake-up stretching exercises. He followed this with a steaming hot shower and an icy cold rinse down. He shaved carefully and peered into the mirror. The face that peered back looked thin and a little beaten up, but the scar on the left side had faded considerably. More importantly, his eyes were clear, not bloodshot reminders of a night of reckless drinking.

"Guess this is the best I can do," he muttered to his reflection. "Hang on, Gwen, I'll be there soon."

Ben ate a quick breakfast in the Officer's Club, ignoring the baleful stare of the lone bleary-eyed mess sergeant who hadn't expected to see anyone alive and walking about before noon. He slipped into the vacant operations office and dialed Gwen's number.

Her cheerful, "Good morning, love," sent shivers down his spine. "Hello, Gwen. Ready for a visitor?" Her reply left him in stunned silence. "Swell!" was all he could croak. "Uh, I mean, wonderful! I'll get a jeep from the motor pool and be there in a little over an hour."

"I'll be anxiously waiting," she trilled, causing him to almost drop the phone. "Drive carefully."

Ben fidgeted while the gate guards checked his twenty-four hour pass. Then ignoring Gwen's caution to drive carefully, he roared out onto the A1120 highway, linked up with the A45 westbound, and careened through Bury Saint Edmonds. Having avoided running over anyone, he thundered on toward Cambridge. He nearly lost control when he rounded a curve and screeched to a halt face-to-face with a cow standing in the middle of the road, placidly chewing her cud. After a brief blank-eyed staring match, punctuated with blasts from the jeep's horn and shouts from Ben, the cow shook her head, snorted, and ambled back to her pasture. The jeep's rear wheels left dual tracks of smoking rubber on the roadway as Ben accelerated away.

When he determined he was a few blocks from her apartment in Cambridge, Ben pulled over to the curb and shut off the engine. He leaned his forehead on the steering wheel and took several deep breaths. "Gotta get settled down before I see her," he muttered. "Wouldn't look good to hyperventilate and fall on my face at her feet. Man, I don't get this nervous before takeoff on a mission!"

He collected himself and drove to her address. After pulling to the curb, he shut off the engine and hopped out of the jeep. He wiped his sweaty palms on his pant legs as he climbed the stairs and pushed the doorbell button. Footsteps echoed down the hallway, and his heart skipped two beats. The door opened, and his jaw dropped. There she stood more radiant and beautiful than he remembered still dressed in her bathrobe.

"Hullo, love." She beamed through a smile framed with tears. "Welcome home."

Ben gulped and reached for her, then stopped short. "Hello yourself, you beautiful thing. But hey, am I early? I thought I said I'd be here in a little more than an hour."

She leaped into his arms, pressing herself against him, and smothered him with kisses. She stepped back to catch her breath. "No, silly, you're not early, you're just in time." She grabbed his arm. "Come in, love, so I can get a proper hold on you."

He stepped through the door and kicked it shut behind him. She was in his arms again, kissing and squeezing the breath out of him. When she released him, he stumbled back and grinned. "I guess this means you're happy to see me."

"Happy to see you! I'm delirious!"

Ben grabbed her and gave her a long breathless kiss. "Guess that makes us even. But hey, you're not ready yet. I thought we were going out?"

She stepped back, hands on her hips, and her chin thrust out. "Major Findlay," she said with an exaggerated pout, "how long is your leave?"

He started to point out he was now Lieutenant Colonel Findlay but thought better. "Uh, ma'am, I have twenty-four hours before—"

She cut him off with a sly grin. "And you want to do what, take a tourist walk through Cambridge, stroll along the River Cam, go on a picnic, or visit some of our fine churches?"

Ben mentally smacked himself on the forehead. He didn't have his brain turned on. "Ah no . . .," he stammered. "That can wait until later. Say, is that bathrobe all you have on?"

She giggled and hopped back as he reached for her. Then she ran down the hallway, paused to flip off the bathrobe, and ducked into her bedroom.

Ben charged after her like an enraged bull, shedding his uniform as he ran. He didn't remember taking off his shoes or pants but arrived breathless at her bedside clad only in his shorts. She lay under the covers, clutching the bedspread under her chin in mock alarm. "Why, sir! You're in my boudoir in a state of near total undress! And"—she choked—"you're blushing bright red."

Ben stopped and blinked. *Blushing? I'm so up for this there's barely enough blood to run my heart much less blush!*

"Well, pardon me, ma'am, but I sorta got the impression this is what you had in mind."

Gwen flipped back the covers, and Ben dived for her, somehow shedding his shorts before they entwined in a joyous naked embrace. Their first lovemaking was frantic, almost animalistic, as they relieved months of longing with uninhibited sex. At last, Ben lay sprawled on top of her, trying to catch his breath.

"Uh, Gwen, Gwen, that was fantastic," he murmured. She nodded and snuggled her nose in his ear. "Say, am I squashing you?" he asked.

"No, Ben, I love to feel your weight on me."

They lay dozing for some time when Ben snorted awake and realized he was fully aroused again. He raised himself on his elbows and looked into her clear blue eyes. "'Scuse me, ma'am, but could we—" She shushed him with a luscious kiss.

They made love again, this time slowly and with deeply felt passion, both writhing to gain the maximum sensual pleasure from their joining. When Ben awoke a second time, he lay sprawled openmouthed on his back. Gwen slept beside him, a sweet smile on her lips. He smacked his dry lips, swallowed, and gazed at her, marveling at how lucky he was to be in love with such a beautiful woman who apparently was equally in love with him.

"Back from the abyss to total bliss," he whispered, chuckling at his clumsy attempt at poetry.

Gwen awoke, smiled at him, and grabbed him in a fierce embrace. "Hello, Major Findlay," she whispered, smothering him in kisses. "Ever so lovely to have you home."

"Ever so lovely to be here, ma'am. Thanks for the warm welcome. Uh, by the way, it's no longer 'Major' Findlay," he said, indicating his uniform blouse lying on the floor near the door. "Those are silver oak leaf clusters on the epaulettes. It's Lieutenant Colonel Findlay now."

"Oh, Ben, congratulations! Just think, Colonel Findlay now. When did this happen?"

"Found out last night when Frank had a new uniform fixed up for me before the party. Said it was a reward for saving the Regensburg mission." He shivered at the thought of that last mission and what had transpired since getting shot down. Gwen clutched him and wept.

"Hey, Gwen," he whispered. "It's okay. I'm here now."

"Tears of joy, Ben. Tears of joy."

They lounged in bed for another hour, content to hold each other in a warm embrace. Finally, Gwen stirred. "Umm, Colonel Findlay, perhaps we should be up and about."

He muttered something unintelligible and squeezed his eyes shut.

"Come on, love. Let's take a shower together."

"Shower?" he asked, now interested. "Does this flat have a shower?"

"Well, it's sort of jury rigged. A previous tenant rigged a rubber hose with a shower head to the bathtub spigot. It works quite nicely."

It did work quite nicely, and Ben could have spent the next hour or so fondling Gwen's soft body under the warm spray. She finally turned up the cold water tap and that ended that.

As they dressed, Gwen turned to Ben, clasped his face in both hands, and looked deeply into his eyes. "Ben, you do know I love you more than I can say, don't you?" Ben grinned and nodded. "Is it time for me to ask what happened to this side of your face," she whispered, "or would you rather not talk about it?"

Ben pulled back. "Uh, I'll tell you all about it, the last mission, my capture, and escape, Gwen, but not just yet, if you don't mind . . ."

"I don't mind, love. Take your time. We can deal with all of that later," she added, kissing him passionately.

"Woof!" he said, pulling her close. "You keep that up an' I won't wanna go anywhere but back there," he said, indicating the bed.

"All right, Colonel, that's enough," she said, pulling away, adding with a giggle, "For now, anyway."

After a quick lunch, they emerged into a bright blustery afternoon and walked hand in hand toward the River Cam. They strolled in silence, content to be together but alone in their thoughts. Gwen nudged Ben. "I mentioned earlier a tourist walk through Cambridge.

I was joking, but would you like me to give you a guided tour, show you the major sights you probably didn't get to before?"

Ben shrugged. "How long is the tour? I still don't have my full strength back."

Gwen smiled mischievously. "Oh really? I hadn't noticed."

Ben squeezed her arm. "Okay, Miss Smarty Pants. I just hope it's not as long as some of the historical tours Reggie took me on back in my RAF days. We had to visit every cathedral we passed as we were moving from base to base in those early days. He also spent a couple of days showing me every important historical site in London. That was in '39, just before war broke out. Said he wanted to show me what I was gonna be fighting for." Ben smiled. "And you know, it really meant a lot to me when the going got tough during the Battle of Britain."

"All right, love, then I'll show you what you're fighting for in Cambridge," she said. "We'll only go as far as you feel able. Let's begin here at Addenbrooke's Hospital."

They strolled up Trumpington Street past Pembroke College to Silver Street, one of the main launching places along the River Cam for Cambridge's famous punts, the flat bottom boats that were propelled by one person standing on a rear platform and pushing against the river bottom with a long pole. They reminded Ben of pictures he'd seen of gondoliers plying the canals of Venice in their elaborate gondolas.

"That's Queen's College over there," Gwen said, pointing across the River Cam. "Right here is St. Catherine's College and across the street is Corpus Christi College."

"Sure are a lotta colleges in this town," Ben said, marveling at the beautiful buildings and manicured lawns. "I didn't go to college, you know. Joined up with Colonel Silverman to go to Spain soon's I graduated from high school in '36."

"We haven't even started looking at colleges," Gwen smiled. "Up next on the left is King's College and beyond that is Trinity. Over there is St. John's College and on around the curving streets up ahead are Jesus College, Sidney Sussex College, Christ's College, Emmanuel College, and back to Downing College near the hospital. And there are many smaller colleges all around Cambridge."

Ben looked puzzled. "Why're there so many? Couldn't they have just combined 'em all into one big college or university instead?"

"Actually, they are all part of Cambridge University," Gwen said. "The colleges are just spread around through Cambridge. The

129

university was founded in the early 1200s, which makes it the second oldest university after Oxford . . ."

"The 1200s!" Ben exclaimed. "This really takes me back to Reggie's famous historical tours. He crammed my head fulla all kinds of stories about what happened in England's wonderful past." He turned to Gwen with a grin and said, "Say, speaking of historical spots, didn't we have a historical moment or two in some bushes along here last time I visited?"

It was Gwen's turn to blush as she recalled them snuggling under the bushes and making passionate love. "That's quite enough, Benjamin," she sniffed. "I won't have you mocking what was a beautiful moment in our relationship."

Ben sniggered an apology.

About two hours into their walking tour, Ben spotted the King's Arms pub and turned to Gwen. "Say, love, I'm runnin' low on energy. How about a pint of Cambridge's best?"

"A pint for you, Ben," she said, snuggling against him. "A half for me."

They settled contentedly in the pub's snuggery and sipped their bitters. Afternoon shadows were lengthening when the landlord called, "Time, gentlemen!" Ben finished his second pint and Gwen sipped the last of her second half. "Wonderful places these pubs," Ben said. "Wish we had them at home. We have bars and in the Midwest, taverns, but they aren't the same. These are real family-gathering places."

They strolled hand in hand back to Gwen's apartment, savoring their closeness in silence, neither wanting to break the spell with talking. As they reached her apartment, Gwen pulled Ben into a fierce embrace. "Oh, Ben, I hate the thought of you leaving tomorrow morning. Must you go back to it so soon? I mean, back to the war? You don't have to resume combat operations right away, do you? Isn't your new assignment one that involves mission planning and such, not flying more missions? After all, you completed your mission quota with the, umm, with the Regensburg mission."

Ben started to reply, but she silenced him by pressing her index finger on his lips. Tears welled in her eyes, and she struggled to control her emotions. "Ben, umm, let me finish, please. I know how much your group and your fellow fliers mean to you. And . . . how anxious you are to see this war through to the end. I don't mean to diminish the importance of any of that . . ."

She closed her eyes and suppressed a sob but kept her finger on his lips. "You've been through so much," she whispered, stroking the scarred left side of his face. "Can't you take a recuperation leave like you did when you were shot down flying the Spitfire? Doesn't the American Army have such places, and haven't you earned some time in one?"

She laid her head on his chest and wept quietly. "Sorry, love," she murmured. "I feel such a ninny."

Ben hugged her tightly. "That's enough, Gwen. You're no ninny, and I won't let anyone, even you, say you are. I'm not sure how to put this, but when the war broke out after Reggie and I escaped here from Spain in '39, I made a commitment to see this thing through. Not sure I, or anybody else for that matter, really knew what that meant, but I feel deeply that I have to honor that commitment."

He held her out at arm's length and looked deeply into her soft blue eyes. "Now I've made a new commitment, and I think you have too and that is to us being together for the rest of our lives. And God willing, we're going to do just that."

She blinked the tears from her eyes and looked at him with raised eyebrows. "Why, Ben!" she exclaimed. "That's the first time I've ever heard you mention God."

"Well, yeah," he said, looking slightly embarrassed. "Up 'til now 'God' has pretty much been part of my swearing vocabulary. Church wasn't important when I was growing up. Mom tried to get us to church regularly, but the old man never cooperated, so my brother and I didn't either."

He paused and blinked rapidly. "'Course I regret that now, but what's past is past. Hey, look, if I keep ramblin' on like this, I'm the one who's gonna sound like a ninny."

Gwen started to protest, but he continued, "My turn to talk, love. What I was trying to say before we got sidetracked is that I now have a special reason to do what I can to end this dam—uh, this awful war. And by the way, survive it in the process. You mean that much to me, Gwen. Thinking about you while I was in the POW camp and during our escape really kept me going.

"And now that I'm back, I have both commitments to honor—to do what is needed to help end the war and my responsibility to you. Probably doesn't do much good to tell you to relax and not worry, Gwen, but I'm gonna survive this war, and then we're gonna plan how we're to live with each other for the rest of our days."

As Gwen wept against his chest, he stroked her hair and continued. "When I go back to the 509th, I'll be the deputy commander. Frank's getting signals he's in line for promotion to brigadier general and reassignment as commander of a new B-29 wing that'll be forming soon in the States. He's hoping I'll replace him as commander of the 509th.

"So in addition to running the group, handling all the duties of mission planning and so on, I'll also have to lead missions. I won't be flying as many as before, and I won't have a mission quota, but I will be flying."

Ben held her tightly as he felt her beginning to relax and control her weeping. "All right, Colonel," she whispered, "we'll see this through together. But be warned, as soon as you complete your first commitment to the war, I shall expect you to honor the second commitment you just made." Ben laughed and pulled her face to his, smiling as he kissed away her tears.

They ate a cold supper that evening, and heeding Ben's reminder that he had to leave at "half past dark" the next morning to return to Parham, they undressed and fell into bed in a passionate embrace. Their lovemaking that night reflected their long-term mutual commitment to each other, and they fell into a deep contended sleep.

Ben rose at 0330 hours the next day, washed, and dressed as quietly as possible and turned to the bed where Gwen lay watching him. "Hey, beautiful," he said. "Sorry I woke you, but I have to get goin' soon to make it back to base before my twenty-four-hour leave is up."

"Not before you've had a proper English breakfast," Gwen said as she slipped out of bed and donned her bathrobe. He started to protest, but she silenced him with a kiss and scooted into the kitchen. Twenty minutes later, she sipped a cup of coffee as he wolfed the remainder of his breakfast.

They lingered by the front door for another embrace and a long loving kiss. Ben opened the door, stepped outside, and grinned back at her. "It's been a wonderful twenty-four hours, ma'am," he said, saucily tipping his hat. "We must do this again sometime." He laughed when she replied, "Make it soon, Colonel." He hopped into his jeep, and she blew him a kiss.

Gwen watched, clutching her bathrobe around her neck and suppressing sobs as he gave her a jaunty wave and sped around the corner.

Chapter 25

BACK ON OPERATIONS

Parham station buzzed with activity as Ben zipped through the main gate at 0600 hours and headed for the base headquarters building. The 509th obviously had been alerted for a mission, and it looked like it was an emergency. Their three-day stand-down for upgrades to the navigation systems either had been completed early or cut short, for Ben counted the group's full complement of twenty-one B-17 bombers positioned on their remote parking pads. Ground maintenance crews swarmed over the airplanes, servicing their four Wright engines and topping off the fuel and oil tanks, while armors threaded belts of .50-caliber ammunition into each plane's arsenal of thirteen machine guns. The bombs would be hoisted into the bomb bays as soon as the mission field order confirmed the target and attack profile.

Silverman juggled two telephones as Ben knocked on his office door and stepped inside. "You need to decide damn soon which we're carrying—500-pounders or 750s!" Silverman yelled. "I have the bomb depot holding on the other line," he said, brandishing the other phone as if the party he was talking could see it. "They can't sit on their asses until the last minute!"

He paused, and Ben heard an angry voice on the other end of the line. "Hell no!" Silverman snarled. "If we're going to make a 1200-hours takeoff, we need to know now! No damn it! We can't wait for the field order! What? Well, go in and ask them. Call me back in five minutes!" he snapped and slammed down the phone.

Silverman waved Ben toward the chair in front of his desk and shouted into the second phone, "Harvey, you'll have to wait another five minutes! I know, I know! Look, there's some kind of a row going on at Pine Tree." The USAAF Eighth Air Force Bomber headquarters located at High Wycombe air station northeast of London bore the code name Pine Tree. "Some infantry fool is arguing with the mission planners. He wants us to drop 500-pounders to give maximum spread along the front, and our guys want at least 750-pounders to increase our chances of penetrating the hardened bunkers the Germans built along the line."

Silverman shook his head and waved his free hand in frustration. "You don't have to tell *me* that, Harvey! I know how long it takes. You want to take this to the next level? Fine, call Pine Tree yourself! What? Yeah, you're right there, friend. That would not be a good move."

Silverman pounded his desk and snorted in frustration. "Look, I'll get back to you as soon as I hear. Okay, take ten deep breaths and get your blood pressure under control, Harvey." He slammed the handset in its cradle.

"Welcome back, Ben," he said with a wry smile. "As you can see, our war effort is proceeding smoothly as ever. How was your leave? Ah, never mind, your satisfied grin tells me everything."

"It was great, Frank. Can't thank you enough. I know you bent the rules letting me off the base like that. Gwen and I really appreciate it."

"And how is the sweet lady?"

"Fantastic! We really had a great time. Even strolled around Cambridge a bit," he added with a sly grin. "But hey, what's goin' on here? What's the target, and why the rush? Did I hear you say a 1200-hours takeoff, and they haven't loaded the bombs yet?"

Silverman gave Ben a pained look. "Don't know who dreamed this one up, but it seems Doolittle has been forced into assigning us to another tactical interdiction mission. The combined Allied armies have hit a brick wall all across the front. Germans are digging in for a last ditch fight to prevent us from crossing the Rhine into Germany. They've launched several major counter attacks that have the Allies stalled from the Netherlands and Belgium all the way down to the southern French border. Our troops also have run into some heavily fortified defensive lines. Where the Germans found time to build this line of pillboxes and other concrete fortifications is beyond me, but there they are."

"You mean we're expected to attack tactical targets all along the front?" Ben asked. "We're equipped and trained to hit large targets with concentrated bombing!"

"Yeah, tell that to the top brass," Silverman snorted. "Eisenhower and Montgomery don't seem inclined to listen. They want us to blast a path through the German defensive lines and trigger a breakthrough."

"With what kind of an attack formation, and more importantly, from what altitude?" Ben asked.

"Fortunately, Doolittle prevailed. They wanted us to bomb from ten thousand feet, reasoning there wouldn't be much flak. Doolittle insisted on twenty thousand feet minimum and won the argument. We'll fly looser formations than normal and attack specific points far enough behind the battle lines to make sure we don't drop on our own troops.

"I guess we can be effective against rail centers and highways, but I'm not optimistic we'll be very good at knocking out fortified defenses or troop concentrations," Silverman added. The phone jangled, interrupting him.

"Silverman!" he growled. "Yeah, yeah, okay—750s it is. Of course. What? Not now. We can go into that later. Look, I need to get back to the bomb depot," he snapped, hanging up the phone. His call to the bomb depot was brief and to the point. "Harvey, 750s. Roll 'em. We're damn tight on time."

Preparations for the mission shifted into high gear. Silverman told Colonel Coleman, who would lead the mission, to call the flight crews to the premission briefing at 0830 and prepare for takeoff at 1200. "Ben, I want you to attend the briefing and sit in the front row. I'll announce you as the 509th's new deputy commander."

Silverman stepped onto the raised briefing platform, ordered the assembled flight crews, "At ease," and presented the outline of the mission for the day.

"Those of you who were with us on D-Day will recognize this as another battlefield interdiction mission. We may well be flying more of these as we enter the final phase of the campaign to defeat Germany," he said "This'll give us more valuable experience in operating close to the front lines, so pay particular attention to Colonel Coleman as he lays out the details of the operation. By the way, Colonel Coleman will lead this mission, probably his last since he's soon to be promoted to full colonel and given command of the 328th Heavy Bombardment Group. More on this in a moment.

"Essentially, we're being tasked to blast open paths for our combined Allied ground armies to break through extremely tough resistance by the Wehrmacht as we push them closer to Germany's borders. We'll bomb from twenty thousand feet with a mix of 750-pound general-purpose and antipersonnel bombs. We anticipate relatively strong fighter opposition en route to the targets and on the return, but we expect minimal flak." This generated a murmur of approval.

"Now before I hand the detailed briefing over to Colonel Coleman, I have an announcement," Silverman continued. "As you know, we've welcomed recently promoted Colonel Ben Findlay back to our group following his escape from a German POW camp."

Silverman paused and noted a positive reaction from the assembled airmen. "With Colonel Coleman's scheduled departure, I'm pleased to announce that Colonel Findlay has been promoted to group deputy commander to replace Larry." The pilots responded with sustained applause. Larry had been a popular leader, and Ben was welcomed as a hero having recently returned from the abyss. They also were happy this mission looked like a milk run.

"My sentiments exactly." Silverman grinned. "Larry has performed superbly as my deputy, and we'll miss him. His excellent service with the 509th is why he's been given his own group. Larry, thank you for a great job. We all wish you the best in your new assignment. And, Ben, at the same time, let me welcome you as the 509th's new deputy commander. Okay, Larry, carry on with the briefing."

Ben stood next to Frank on the control tower balcony as the four powerful radial engines on twenty-one B-17s roared to life, belching clouds of smoke that roiled across the airfield. "Wow!" Ben exclaimed. "First time seeing this from up here is pretty impressive."

"Also sobering when you send the boys out like this and wonder how many of them will be coming back," Frank said, puffing intently on a cigarette.

Focke-Wulf FW 190D Fighter

As the B-17s waddled in line to the runway, Ben imagined what the ten men were doing in each bomber—pilots and copilots in the cockpits jockeying the controls and working the brakes, flight engineers kneeling over the throttle quadrants checking engine instruments, bombardiers settling into the glass noses stowing equipment around their Norden bombsights, navigators arranging their maps and charts, radio operators adjusting their equipment and rechecking frequencies, and gunners all the way back to the tail swiveling their weapons, stowing their heated flight suits and trying not to look nervous.

"Did this over a hundred times," Ben mused. "Thirty times actually goin' off to war. Damn, I wish I was in that first ship for this mission."

"The war isn't over, Ben," Silverman said quietly. "There'll be more chances to do just that."

Major Joe Atkinson, the group operations officer, stepped out on the balcony, raised a Very pistol, and fired a green flare into the air, signaling the pilots to start their sequenced takeoffs. Coleman, in the lead bomber already on the runway, ran up the aircraft's engines holding the brakes, then released them and roared down the runway. Ship number 2 taxied into place and thundered after it. This procedure continued until all twenty-one bombers circled overhead in loose formation before heading southeast to rendezvous with the other groups forming the day's battle fleet.

Ben watched them disappear into the distance. "Two plus hours there, time over targets, and two plus back," he muttered. "Should see 'em back around 1730 hours."

Frank nodded. "Let's go to my, uh, our office. Got some things to discuss," he said. Ben followed him into his staff car for the short ride to the headquarters building.

Both men sat relaxed around Frank's desk, nursing cups of steaming coffee. "Wanted to show you what the new job will entail," Frank said, "but before we get into that, I'd like to hear details of how you were shot down, your treatment as a prisoner of war, and especially, your escape."

Ben blew a long puff, shifted back in his chair, and looked past Frank's shoulder toward the flight line. "Yeah, I need to get this off my chest. Probably good practice for when we go before the joint services review board.

"Guess I'll start with the departure on our last mission, big Three O, the one that was gonna complete our tour and get my crew their tickets home. You saw us off. That part went well. But the mission was jinxed from the start. When Anderson's 328th lead group had problems launching and then got shredded on the way in, I had to shift the 509th into lead position at the last minute. But we salvaged the mission."

Ben shifted in his chair. "Everything looked good until, uh, I misread the flak patterns on the way out. Should've led them out with a left turn 'stead of to the right. Never know, of course, but turning right took us into a huge flak trap—"

Frank interrupted. "Ben, you can't dwell on that. Regensburg was ringed with some of the toughest flak defenses in Germany. There was no guarantee turning to the left would have been any safer."

"Yeah, I keep telling myself that, Frank, but I'm still second guessing that decision. Anyway, as I rolled out from that turn, a huge flash and explosion nearly blinded me and . . ."

Ben hesitated, continuing to look with unfocused eyes out the window. He continued, struggling to keep his voice steady. "I dunno for sure what happened, but we must have taken a direct hit under the nose from a German 88. I have a vague memory of being blown backward outta my seat and landing on someone. In the process, I guess I had my parachute snapped on."

Ben coughed, swallowed twice, and cleared his throat.

"*Round Trip* started to disintegrate. When she blew up, I must have been knocked unconscious and either fell out or was blown clear. When I came to, I was free-falling. Thought I was flying ol' Brice's open-cockpit Stearman and getting a face full of wind in a bad sideslip. Fortunately, I woke up in time to pull the ripcord. My helmet was half melted to my head, and the left side of my face was pretty badly burned."

Ben set his jaw and took a couple of minutes to get his emotions under control. He resumed his narrative with a steady voice and spent the next hour leading Frank through the odyssey of his capture, hospitalization, interrogation by the Regensburg Gestapo, and finally, his incarceration in Stalag Luft III. Frank guffawed when Ben described meeting Reggie again at the camp.

"Ben, let's take a break before you complete your story," Frank said. "I need to stretch my legs and have a pee."

When Ben resumed, he briefly described life in the camp and picked up with their bizarre escape after the train wreck. Frank sat openmouthed as Ben detailed how the Polish underground took charge, smuggled them north to the Baltic, and put them on the fishing boat that rendezvoused with the Swedish freighter. Ben named those who had helped the escapees along the way, and said that in return, they had promised to get supplies to the Polish underground via airdrops.

"The Swedish captain turned us over to the Royal Navy at Scapa Flow, and you know the rest of the story from there," Ben said quietly. "We owe these people a big debt and have to make sure we keep their identities secret." Frank nodded his agreement.

Ben shifted in his chair. "By the way, Frank, any word yet about the other three groups the underground was trying to get to the Baltic?"

Frank shook his head. "Need to pursue that," he said. He then pushed back in his chair and squinted at Ben. "One hell of a tale, Ben. Maybe you'll write a book about it someday. I'll be interested in hearing the reaction after you brief the joint services board—"

The phone interrupted. Frank listened intently and hung up. "Tower. Coleman and the boys have radioed they're inbound. Let's get down there."

Chapter 26

THE AIR WAR CONTINUES

Frank and Ben stood at the control tower railing, taking turns scanning the sky to the south with a single pair of binoculars. Major Atkinson stepped out and handed Frank a second pair. "Larry just radioed they're inbound from Dover. Said the mission looked like a big success."

"Did he say how many ships he's bringing back?" Frank asked.

"No. Want me to call him back?"

"Let it go. He's busy setting up the formation for the approach. We'll be able to count 'em soon."

They heard the distant thrumming of B-17 engines well before they could spot the inbound bombers through the channel mist. The noise was mesmerizing, like an oncoming swarm of giant bees.

"There they are, about thirty degrees to the right!" someone yelled. "Lookin' pretty solid. Let's get the count!"

Ben and Frank focused their binoculars on Larry's lead ship. It looked undamaged, and all four propellers were turning. Scanning along the line of returning bombers, Ben spotted one with its Number 1, left outboard prop feathered, and another with a smoking Number 3 engine. "No problem," he muttered. "The fort can fly on two engines, not well, but it'll get ya home." Otherwise, the fleet looked relatively unscathed.

As Larry led the bomber over the field and circled into the landing pattern, Ben felt a surge of excitement. *Can't wait to get back into the cockpit. Gonna have to press Frank about putting me back on flight status.*

All twenty-one B-17s landed smoothly and taxied to their parking pads. "Let's take the staff car and drive down to meet Larry," Frank said. As they pulled up to the nose of his aircraft, Larry dropped out of the forward nose hatch. He grinned and gave them a quick thumbs-up signal. Obviously, the mission had been successful.

This was confirmed at the post mission briefing. The 509th had rendezvoused with five other groups over Southend-on-Sea and headed southeast, crossing the channel from Dover. Four other combined bomber fleets had simultaneously headed for the extended front stretching from Holland to Southeastern France. This had put tremendous pressure on the Luftwaffe's depleted air defense fighter forces, and most Eighth Air Force groups faced minimal fighter attacks, some encountered no fighters at all.

"There wasn't any flak, but we had a lot of unorganized ground fire aimed as us," Larry said. "It wasn't very effective. We got jumped by Luftwaffe fighters on the way out, but again, it wasn't anything like we've faced in recent months.

"That doesn't mean the Luftwaffe is defeated," he added. "I think the German High Command is holding them back to concentrate on protecting high-value targets. We'll face some pretty stiff resistance when we go after certain targets deep in Germany, especially their petroleum industry or the places where they're building those damn terror weapons."

"How effective were you in hitting the tactical targets?" Frank asked. "Were you able to bomb fairly close to the front lines?"

"Frank, I think we really blasted some breakout holes all along the line," Larry said. "The tail gunner in our trailing ship said he saw our tanks and infantry already beginning the move forward under cover of the fire and smoke along the line. It'll be interesting to see whether the Intel folks confirm this."

Subsequent intelligence reports showed Allied ground forces had broken through in several points and that the Germans were shifting armored and reserve units in a desperate attempt to close the gaps.

"That's great, Larry. Now maybe we can get back to our primary targets. Okay, Ben, back to headquarters."

Ben settled again in the chair in front of Frank's desk. "I think I pretty much covered my experiences getting blasted outta the sky and making the trek home," he said. "Any questions, Frank?"

Frank shook his head. "None at the moment, but I'll want to go over some details later, like how do we track the other three escapee groups, and how do we help in the airdrops to the Polish underground?"

Ben looked steadily at Frank. "Good, then I have a question for you: How soon can I get back on operations?"

Frank pursed his lips. "If it were up to me, it'd be next week, Ben, but there are some hoops you have to jump through first. Doc Samuelson has to give you a thorough going over, a top-to-bottom physical, and if he thinks it necessary, a trip up to the hospital at Pine Tree. He may want X-rays of that shoulder. That's the same one you injured when you bailed out of your Spitfire back in '40. You're still standing crooked and obviously protecting it. He needs to verify that it's fully functional. If you lose an engine or two on a mission, you know how much rudder and aileron you have to hold to maintain level flight. Question is, can you do that without further therapy or a rehab leave?"

"Frank, I started doing strengthening exercises as soon as I got outta the Kraut hospital," Ben interrupted. "I know I'm not 100 percent, but I'm gettin' damn close."

"We'll let the docs determine that, Ben. I'm not about to send you back out on ops until I get their clearance. I don't have to spell out the possible consequences if you have a wounded or dead copilot and have to wrestle a damaged ship home."

"Frank, I know the risks involved!" Ben exclaimed. "And I know what it takes to fly a B-17 whether it's been damaged or not! Besides, now that we have the new C-1 autopilots, we don't have to hand fly all the way to the target and back home!" Ben shifted back, hoping he hadn't gone too far with his commanding officer.

"Okay, cool down," Frank snapped. "I know all that, but I'm going by the book. You get you're medical clearance, and then we'll go fly a couple of test hops, and you show me you can handle all emergency situations."

"Test hops?" Ben asked. "Were you serious when you mentioned this before? You mean, I have to prove to you that I can still fly a B-17? Sorry, Frank. I don't want to sound insubordinate, but do you seriously think I might not be able to handle a Fort?"

Frank gave Ben a hard look. "Yeah, Ben, that's exactly what I mean. I'm not questioning your flying skills. But I need to be certain you've regained enough physical strength to cope with whatever emergency situation you might encounter. Now we'll drop the subject until you've had your physical."

As he rose from his chair, Frank turned to Ben. "And by the way, Ben, you'll be restricted from flying over Germany or

German-occupied territory until the Russians liberate Poland." Ben gave him a quizzical look.

"That's right, and there's a good reason. If you got shot down and captured again, the Gestapo would damn well discover who helped you and your companions escape the last time. Could jeopardize the whole Polish underground. So you'll have to wait until all these conditions are met."

Ben started to reply but bit back his words.

"Okay, now let me show you some of the pain-in-the-ass paperwork you'll handle in your new job," Frank said, relieved to be changing the subject.

Ben fidgeted through an hour of explanations of forms, charts, and reports. "Frank, doesn't Sergeant Crawford handle all this administrative stuff? He is the group clerk isn't he?"

"Of course, and he generates much of this bureaucratic paperwork crap," Frank said. "But you'll be putting your signature on them, and you damn well better know what you're signing."

Ben groaned inwardly and tried to look interested as Frank shuffled through the pile. *Know this is part of the deputy's job, but I really want to be able to fly as well. But ya have to suck it up, Benjamin, old lad. If you're going to command the 509ᵗʰ one day, you better put the group's interests first.*

When they had finished, Ben rubbed his eyes and stretched. "Thanks, Frank. Not the most exciting part of the deputy's job, but I know the paperwork has to be done. I can handle it and anything else you want me to take on." Frank gave Ben another look and nodded.

"And now, can you bring me up to date?" Ben asked. "What's happened around here since I left on my one-way mission in April?"

Frank pushed back in his chair. "Take me a minute to think about that, Ben." He lit a cigarette and blew a cloud of smoke toward the ceiling. "We've flown so many missions since then. They've all begun to run together. As you remember, after Doolittle took command of the renamed Eighth Air Force, we joined with the RAF in February for a series of coordinated attacks against Germany's aircraft industry. That was Operation Argument Big Week. You flew in the thousand-plane mission against Leipzig in mid-February."

Ben grunted, "Yeah, and we had over eight hundred escort fighters. The Luftwaffe didn't know what the hell hit them."

These massed raids continued through the third week of February as RAF Bomber Command pummeled the targets by night with its Lancaster heavy bombers, and the Eighth Air Force sent fleets of B-17s and B-24s, numbering eight hundred to nine hundred each, to hit many of the same targets by day. Messerschmitt, Focke-Wulf, and Heinkel aircraft factories were flattened in areas ranging from Leipzig, Oschersleben, Rostock, Bernburg, Braunschweig, and Gotha. Huge fleets of bombers also attacked the ball-bearing production plants in Schweinfurt on the Baltic coast. Those who flew the Schweinfurt raids and survived would never forget the terrible losses they suffered before the Eighth Air Force received its first long-range P-51 and P-38escort fighters with sufficient range to protect the bomber fleets all the way to targets deep in Germany and back home.

Frank pulled a mission log from the bottom drawer of his desk. "Highly successful effort, but we paid one helluva price," he said, scanning the report. "Lost over eight hundred bombers. That's eight thousand men, for god's sake! Unbelievable when you look back on it. Sure, we broke the back of the German fighter aircraft industry and inflicted heavy losses on Luftwaffe fighter command, but when you look at the cost in human lives, you have to wonder."

Lockheed P-38 Lightning Fighter

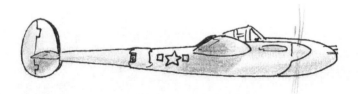

"Frank, you aren't having second thoughts about daylight bombing and the part we're playing in war effort?" Ben asked.

"No, Ben. We're playing a leading role in winning this rotten war, but I can't help thinking about our casualties, about all the young men who've made the supreme sacrifice for all of this."

Frank pushed back in his chair, blinked, and rubbed his face with both hands. "Can't really talk like this with the other officers, Ben. But I know you'll understand and keep your counsel. This is something you're going to face as soon as you assume command of the 509th."

"Already faced it, Frank. I still don't know if anyone else from my *Round Trip* crew survived."

"Yeah, but you have to move on, Ben. I don't expect you to ever forget the bonds you formed with that crew or to stop wondering why you're the only one who seems to have survived. That's fate, or whatever you want to call it. Point is, you did survive, and now you're back to continue the fight."

Ben pursed his lips and gave Frank a long hard look. "Ain't gonna be easy, but you're right. Have to press on."

"Damn right! Look, within a week after sustaining those terrible losses, we launched mass raids into the belly of the beast Berlin. Herr Goering had pledged to Adolf that would never happen. But we continued to hit Berlin, even in lousy weather, thanks to the pathfinder bombers from the 536th and their new H2X radars. Caught the Luftwaffe sitting smugly on their asses under the thick cloud cover, convinced we couldn't attack because of the weather."

Frank smacked his hand on the desktop, sending pencils and papers flying. "Point is, Ben, we took a beating during Big Week and lost a lot of fine men and machines. But we didn't sit around and moan about it. We pressed on to the next mission."

"I get your point, Frank. Thanks."

"You missed the main attacks we launched against the Luftwaffe's airfields in Northern France and Belgium and the transportation infrastructure along the Normandy coast during the buildup for D-Day," Frank continued. "Different kind of missions, but kept the Germans from moving reserve forces into the Normandy landing areas. A big help to the invading troops."

Ben sat forward. "Let me tell you, Frank, when we got the news in Stalag Luft III that the allies had successful landed in Normandy, the camp went nuts. Really boosted our morale and made us even more determined to escape that rotten place."

"I'm sure of that," Frank said. "Once the Normandy invaders broke out and pushed east, we were ordered to concentrate again on Germany's oil industry, but we can expect more missions to support the Allied armies headed for Germany. So that pretty much brings you up to date, Ben. We go on from here."

Frank grumbled and began picking up the paper and pencils he had strewn around the office by banging on the desk. "Essential tools of war," he muttered. "No job is done until the paperwork is completed."

"Speaking of paperwork," Ben chimed, "I need to get back to my quarters and write my folks. Got a lot of catching up to do." Ben spent nearly two hours writing the letter. He wanted to give them as many details as he thought the censor would pass and yet wanted to spare them the worst of what he had endured. He knew his mother would read between the lines anyway.

Chapter 27

AIRBORNE AGAIN

Doc Samuelson gave Ben a thorough physical examination and ordered him to demonstrate the strength of his shoulder with a series of pushups and chinning exercises. Ben gritted his teeth and tried to mask the pain by maintaining a stoic expression. He didn't fool Samuelson.

"Ben, you've regained a lot of strength in your left shoulder, but I can see how much pain you're feeling when you really stress it," he said. "Everything else checks out amazingly well, but Frank asked me to pay particular attention to the shoulder. Wanted me to guarantee him it would take the stress of wrestling a B-17 around in an engine-out situation."

Ben frowned. "Doc, I can't tell you how important it is to get back on flying status. I want to lead the 509th from out front, and that means taking my share of missions. Besides, how can Frank expect you to guarantee I can handle a situation that might not happen? And I'm gonna keep doin' my therapy exercises, feel like I'm gettin' stronger every day."

"Okay, Ben. Everything else checks out. I don't think you need to go to Pine Tree for X-rays or any other tests. I'll tell Frank I rotated both shoulders and didn't find any lasting damage in the left. Far as I'm concerned, you're cleared to fly ops missions."

"That's swell!" Ben exclaimed. "Thanks a lot."

He sat in front of Frank's desk while the group commander reviewed the flight surgeon's report. "Ben, this report looks great. If I were short of pilots, I'd get you back on ops right away. But I said

I wanted to take you on a couple of test flights, and that's what I'm damned well going to do."

Ben leaned forward. "Okay, Frank. I understand. I just want to tell you what I told Doc Samuelson. I want to lead from out front, and to me, that means taking my share of missions." Frank grunted his agreement.

"When can we schedule some test flights?" Ben asked. "We're off the mission board tomorrow. How about an early local hop? Then if I don't pass muster, we can fly again in the afternoon."

Frank gave Ben a tight smile. "Yeah, let's do that. I'll lay on a B-17. Takeoff will be 0730 hours."

Ben jumped to his feet, hit a brace, and saluted. "Yes, sir! Thank you, sir!" He grinned, turned on his heel, and lively stepped out of Frank's office. *Get outta here before he changes his mind.*

Ben was in the cockpit of *Buxom Baby* by 0630 hours. His spine tingled as he inhaled the combined smells of aviation gasoline, oil, stale sweat, and worn leather that permeated the cockpit. He spent part of the hour running through the engine start procedures, locating by touch the myriad switches and controls, and reviewing the critical airspeeds in the B-17 operator's manual. He then "ground flew" the bomber, moving the flight controls and imagining the aircraft's responses. When he felt confident he was ready to fly the ship, he pushed back in his seat and gazed about the cockpit, savoring the thrill of being back in the "office" again.

When Frank swung up through the nose hatch and slipped into the copilot's seat, Ben felt well prepared and ready to go. A sergeant flight engineer joined them in the cockpit.

"Ready to fly?" Frank asked. Ben nodded, and the three of them set about completing the prestart and start checklists with props set for full rpm and mixtures rich. Following the normal engine start sequence, Ben started with engine Number 2 inboard on the left wing. This one had the heavy-duty electrical generators, which helped power the starters on the remaining engines. Ben looked out to the left to ensure ground personnel were clear of the props, and called, "Engine 2 clear, start 2." The flight engineer engaged the starter and its distinctive whine coursed through the cockpit

"Rotation!" Ben shouted as the propeller began to turn. After several turns, the Wright R-1820-97 Cyclone engine coughed and belched smoke. It then caught when fuel ignited in the cylinders. More coughs and gray smoke followed as the propeller continued to turn and the engine caught again. The rpm needle fluctuated and smoothed out at idle rpm.

Ben felt a familiar tremor of excitement run through his body as the engine settled into a steady rumble. Frank looked out the right cockpit window at the inboard engine and shouted, "Number 3 clear, start 3!" Next came engine Number 4 outboard on the right wing and finally Number 1 on the left. The start sequence was used because engines 2 and 3 carry the heaviest generator loads, and starting them first powered up the aircraft electrical systems sooner.

When all four engines were running smoothly, Ben and Frank completed the pretaxi checklist, and the flight engineer gave a thumbs-up, confirming all four were operating normally. "Ready to go, Colonel," he said. Frank radioed the tower for taxi clearance to the engine run-up area, and Ben signaled the ground crewman to pull the wheel chocks. He taxied to the run-up area, turned into the wind, and set the brakes. Two other B-17s were in the landing pattern. Ben and the flight engineer ran each engine and prop through their paces under Frank's watchful eye. That completed and turbochargers checked, Frank radioed for taxi and takeoff clearance. Ben swung the B-17 onto the runway, told Frank to lock the tail wheel in takeoff position, and held the brakes. After a quick scan of the instruments, Ben pushed the two sets of dual throttle levers forward. The roar of the four Wright Cyclone engines rattled "Buxom Baby."

Frank positioned his hands behind to throttles as Ben gripped the control wheel, released the brakes, and used the rudder pedals to keep *Buxom Baby* aligned with the runway centerline. With a partial fuel load and no bombs in the bomb bay, *Buxom Baby* accelerated quickly down the runway. Ben held the bomber in the tail dragger position until it flew off the runway. He called for gear up and banked into a left turn, automatically looking left into the turn to clear any traffic.

Suddenly, the Number 1 outboard engine on the left wing sputtered and lost power. Frank had retarded the throttle to simulate an engine failure.

Ben rolled the control wheel right to level the airplane and pushed right rudder to compensate for the asymmetrical thrust from the two right-wing engines that were overpowering the single inboard engine on the left wing. He grimaced. *Damn it, Frank, don't do me any favors!* This maneuver put special strain on Ben's left shoulder as he struggled to hold the control wheel to the right and pushed right rudder to keep the bomber tracking straight ahead.

"You can give me the engine back anytime you'd like," Ben grunted. "Or you can get on the controls and help me a bit."

"Sorry, Ben. I've been wounded, incapacitated. You'll have to do it alone."

"Okay, but I sure as hell ain't enjoying this," Ben snarled.

"This would be about the worst emergency situation you could encounter," Frank said quietly. "If we had maximum fuel, full crew and armament, and a typical bomb load, you'd have one helluva job maintaining control. I need to make sure you can."

Ben gritted his teeth. Sweat bathed his face and trickled down his spine as he struggled to hold the controls to the right. His arm and muscles ached and trembled, but he kept the bomber on course. As it accelerated, the flight control surfaces became more responsive, and the pressure needed to hold them lessened.

After what felt like an eternity to Ben, Frank relented and reached for the Number 1 throttle. "Okay, I'll give you back your engine just to prove what a nice guy I am." He grinned. "Good job in handling that emergency. Hope you can see why I had to spring it on you."

Ben smiled back with what looked more like a grimace and concentrated on easing the muscle spasms in his arms and right leg.

"Climb out over the practice area and let's do some air work," Frank said. He throttled back engines during several maneuvers to simulate various engine-out situations, and Ben handled them all. After two hours, Frank signaled over his shoulder with his thumb. "Let's go home and do a little pattern work."

He told Ben to fly the traffic pattern at Parham for two touch-and-go landings and a final full-stop landing. Ben smiled when he "greased" the bomber onto the runway each time. As they taxied back to the parking pad, Ben felt exhausted but exhilarated, certain he had passed the flight check. He shut down the engines, completed the final checklist, and followed Frank through the hatch in the lower nose section.

Seated again in Frank's office, cradling steaming cups of coffee enhanced with brandy, Frank asked Ben to review the flight. "Uh, I thought I did okay." Ben ventured. "I recognized all of the emergency situations you threw at me and reacted correctly in all cases. My air work showed I hadn't lost any of my flying skills, and my landings were pretty smooth. Most importantly, I showed I could find my way back home." He grinned.

"I agree with you on all points," Frank said, taking a sip of coffee and watching Ben over the rim of his cup. "My only concern, and it's not a minor one, is whether you've regained the stamina you'll need to fly a long-range mission."

He raised his left hand like a policeman directing traffic when he sensed Ben was about to protest. "Let me finish. I have no doubts about your flying skills or your ability to handle emergency situations. But you know as well as I do how exhausting a long mission can be. I have to be concerned whether you're ready at this point to handle that, even with a good copilot assisting you. So I want you to be patient for another couple of weeks. Work on getting your strength back, get past the interservice review of your escape—that should happen in the next three to four weeks—and I guarantee you'll get to lead the first mission after they're through."

Frank sat back and waited while Ben sat jaw clinched and silent, obviously mulling his response.

"Okay, Frank," he said flatly. "I agree that's a reasonable approach. I'll press on with my strengthening exercises and get past the review board. I know you'll honor your guarantee that I'll lead the next mission." He rose and reached across the desk to shake Frank's hand. "Thanks. Sorry I've been such a pain in the ass, Frank, but you know how eager I am to get back into action."

"Not a problem, Ben. I wish all our pilots were as motivated as you."

Ben bore down on his fitness exercises, focusing on shoulder strengthening routines, and tried not to count the days, which crept by with agonizing slowness. He immersed himself in mastering the details of his new group deputy commander assignment and watched from the tower balcony with increasing frustration each time the 509th bombers flew off to war. He called Reggie at RAF Wittering and was told the wing commander was on recuperation leave. Ben left a message saying he'd call back in a week or so.

Sensing his restiveness, Frank granted him a three-day pass in London, telling him to take it when Gwen could arrange a free weekend to join him. On that happy day, Ben met Gwen at the Cambridge train station, and the two headed for three days of bliss in a small hotel in London's Mayfair district.

A somber mood hung over London, but to Ben, it seemed to sparkle with Gwen at his side. She helped brighten the days. The Luftwaffe's bomber blitz had abated, but Germany maintained pressure on London's population with frequent attacks by V-1 buzz bombs and now the new V-2 rocket-based terror weapons. Despite this, they spent two blissful days making passionate love, occasionally emerging to stroll through Mayfair or join the raucous nightlife in the nearby Soho District. On their last night, Ben reached across the table as they dined in a small pub, grasped both of Gwen's hands, and looked deeply into her soft blue eyes.

"Uh, Gwen, this has been a fantastic weekend for me, and I hope the same for you," he said quietly. She nodded and squeezed his hands. "An' well, I'm not all that good with words, but well, umm, I want to, uh, ask you something, you know, uh, to confirm that you feel, uh, about me like I feel about you." Gwen smiled as he groped for words, swallowing, grinning, and blushing like the Michigan farm boy he no longer was. "Uh, maybe you could help me here? Ah, what I want to ask is—"

"The answer is yes, Ben," she interrupted. "*Yes, yes, yes!*"

"Wow, I haven't formally asked you yet." He gulped. "I have to do that, don't I? Uh, do I need to get down on my knee?"

"You can do it standing on your head, if you want." Gwen giggled. "Umm, you *were* going to ask me to marry you, weren't you?"

"Uh yeah. Of course! Dunno why it was so hard to get the words out, but here goes. Gwen, will you marry me?"

"The answer still is *yes!*" she said, leaning across the table, pulling his face to hers, and giving him a long luscious kiss.

They rode the train home to Cambridge, holding hands and grinning like teenagers smitten by first love. They discussed their wedding plans, which Ben said probably involved miles of red tape and all kinds of delays. "We might even have to wait until the war is over," Ben said.

"I can wait, love," Gwen said, choking back a sob as she thought of the bombing missions Ben would have to fly until then. "I'll just focus on the good times we'll have together until this awful war is really over."

Back in Cambridge, Ben collected his jeep from the car park, buzzed Gwen home, and after a prolonged goodbye, roared off to Parham. He zipped up to the gate with minutes to spare on his three-day pass.

Frank had left a message at the gate telling Ben to come directly to headquarters. He strode into Frank's office, trying to suppress a wide grin. "Again, it seems your time spent with Miss Gwen went well," Frank observed dryly.

"Sure did, Frank," Ben said, letting the grin blossom in full. "I have an announcement to make . . ."

"I can't imagine what it might involve," Frank said. "Sit down. I'll make my announcement first." Ben slipped into the chair and looked expectantly at Frank.

"The interservice review board has set a date to debrief you and your four fellow escapees. Next Thursday. Doolittle's headquarters at Pine Tree at 0730 hours. Full dress uniform. Your four buddies have been notified and will join you at Doolittle's headquarters. There'll be a C-47 waiting for you on the ramp. Takeoff will be 0615."

"Hey, Frank, that's fantastic, even swell!" Ben exclaimed. "I'm really improving the shoulder with my exercises. Once I get the review behind me, I'm in line to lead the next mission!"

"And when Russia retakes Poland, which looks like soon. That's the deal," Frank said. "Now what's your news as if I didn't already know?"

"I proposed to Gwen last night, and she accepted!" Ben exulted. "We don't know what's involved, probably a lotta red tape, but we're willing to wait."

"Congratulations!" Frank said, reaching across the desk to shake Ben's hand. "There will indeed be a lot of bureaucratic crap you'll have to clear, but it's been done before, and we'll see that it gets done this time. Best wishes for a long and happy life together."

He paused and gave Ben a hard look. "In the meantime, we still have a war to win. I assume you're prepared to wait until we finish that business before you proceed?" Ben nodded his agreement.

Ben telephoned Reggie again. "Wing Commander Percy," was the brisk reply.

"Reggie, you old scoundrel!" Ben shouted. "It's Ben and—"

"Sancho! How goes it, old bean?" Reggie broke in. "Trust you're phoning about the debrief next Thursday. I say, I'm damned anxious to get it over with so I can concentrate on fighting the Hun again. How about you? How's the shoulder?"

"Shoulder's coming along fine, thanks. I'm doing daily exercises, and they're really working. I'm not back on operations yet, but Doc Samuelson says I'm ready. Have a deal with Frank to get back in the cockpit as soon as we're finished with the debriefing. I can't wait."

"Know what you mean, old cock. Since I'm in charge here, I can put myself back on ops whenever I think I'm ready. Still have a bit of weight to regain, and I'm also doing exercises to get my strength back. I expect I'll also be back on ops as soon as we finish with the review board."

"Uh, Reggie, I also have some other news to share with you." Ben ventured.

"Does it involve the beautiful lady Gwen?" Reggie chuckled.

"How the hell do you know about that? You been talking to Frank? Seems like everybody knew about this before I did."

"Didn't take a wizard to see where this relationship was going, Sancho. Don't suppose you've set a date?"

"No, we haven't. We expect it'll involve a ton of red tape and administrative crap before we can. An' we've agreed to wait 'til the war is over. By the look of it, that could be some time next year."

"Well, whatever, old bean, heartiest congratulations," Reggie said. "You two make a handsome couple, and I wish you all the best in a long life together. Only wish you were still flying on my wing so I could watch over your farm boy arse 'til this is over."

"Thanks for the thought, Reggie. I've had my fill of gettin' shot outta the sky. Say look, I'm to report directly to Doolittle's headquarters at 0730 hours, so I won't see you until we gather in the hallway outside the briefing room. What say we five Giraffes gather for our own review session in a local pub afterward? Might even get what you Brits call squiffy. Yanks have another 'S' word for it, of course."

They chatted about the war, weather, and whatnot for another ten minutes, then rang off.

Chapter 28

THE HEARING

A sergeant driver waited on the High Wycombe ramp as Ben's C-47 rolled to a stop. He delivered Ben to the Pine Tree briefing room at 0715 hours where he found Reggie and Flight Leftenant Whitford waiting. Captain Banner and Lieutenant Kowalski strode in minutes later. All five gave each other hail-fellow-well-met bear hugs and backslaps, and all asked at the same time how the others were doing. Whitford stepped back and surveyed his four companions. "Only thing that would make this reunion perfect would be to have Sandy here with us," he said quietly. "Wonder how the poor bloke is doing? I trust our partisan friends have gotten him properly taken care of."

"That'll be a question we'll put to the board in there," Reggie said pointing his thumb at the briefing room door. "If we're given the opportunity, I intend to ask them for any news on Sandy and the other nineteen who set out for the Baltic with us."

The door opened, and a USAAF colonel stepped out to greet them. "I'm Colonel Thompson, Eighth Air Force Intelligence," he said, shaking hands all around. "You'll be briefing USAAF General Arnold Combs, RAF Air Vice Marshal Richard Wellington-Thaxby, USAAF Colonel George Deacon, and RAF Wing Commander Robert Willoby. Obviously, we're all involved with intelligence in some way or other. Oh, I'll introduce you so you won't have to formally report in."

The five marched into the room, saluted, and stood at attention while Thompson made the introductions. General Combs ordered them, "At ease," and indicated the five chairs lined up in front of the board.

"Gentlemen, welcome," he began. "We're pleased to have you here today, thank you. This will be an informal hearing, and we'd like you to relax and share with us everything you think is important. You've had some interesting experiences, including being shot down over Germany and imprisoned in one of the Luftwaffe primary prisoner-of-war camps. But of particular interest is your unusual escape and your trek to the Baltic Sea with your Polish partisan guide. Some of the members of this board were instrumental in setting up that escape route, including the link up with passing Swedish freighters. They are particularly interested in learning how well it worked."

He paused and studied the five sitting bolt upright before him. "Gentlemen," he said with a smile, "I told you to be at ease. Forget about the rank you see at this table. We're here to get information. So sit back, relax, and give us each of your stories in your own words. Wing Commander Percy, you first."

Reggie leaned forward and launched into a detailed recitation of being shot down in his Spitfire, of crash landing in the channel, and waking up in a German hospital. He spent the next thirty-five minutes describing how he ended up in Stalag Luft III, his unexpected reunion with Ben, and their involvement in an escape-planning group.

With the unusual code name Giraffes, Air Vice Marshal Wellington-Thaxby broke in, peering over his half-rim glasses, "Whose idea was that?"

"Afraid it was mine, Air Vice Marshal," Reggie said sheepishly. "At the time, it seemed appropriate, seeing that we were sticking our necks out so far. As it was, we were clapped in their miserable solitary cells a couple of times when they learned of our escape discussions. I can provide more insights on that if you'd like."

"Do proceed," General Combs commanded.

Reggie gave the board an account of their treatment at Stalag Luft III, including the camp's excellent security system that apparently allowed the camp commandant to eavesdrop on their private conversations at various locations around the camp. The previous officers in charge of the camp when the great escape was accomplished apparently had been dealt with severely—many probably executed—and extensive security systems had been installed to prevent future breakouts. When their clandestine escape plans were monitored, the current camp commandant Von Striesel ordered the Giraffes imprisoned in solitary cells and fed only bread and water. After their second infraction and stay in solitary, Von Striesel ordered them loaded on a passing armaments train to be transferred to the Sachsenhausen concentration camp near Berlin. The Polish partisans wrecked the train, and thus began their trek north through Poland to the Baltic Sea rendezvous with the Polish fishing boat and ultimately transfer to the Swedish freighter.

"Which delivered us to Scapa Flow where we were collected by a crew flying General Doolittle's VC-47," Reggie concluded. "We were treated exceptionally well by the Royal Navy and RAF in Scapa. Now perhaps it's time for the others to add their comments."

Ben started by describing his humane treatment in the Regensburg hospital and contrasted that with the unpleasant encounter with the local Gestapo commander. He added that he spent much less time in Stalag Luft III than the others and focused instead on explaining how the Polish partisans operated what they called their underground railroad. "The safe houses they established along the route to the Baltic Sea were cleverly designed."

Kowalski talked about the partisans, expressing gratitude for the help they provided in the escape. "Several of them spoke good English, but fortunately, I speak Polish, and Captain Banner speaks German, so we had no problem communicating."

Ben stifled a snigger when he heard Kowalski say he spoke Polish. *That isn't what partisan commander Piotrowski called it.*

When it came Captain Banner's time to speak, he emphasized the number of people who put their lives on the line to help the escapees. "They accepted our thanks but said they owed us for what we were doing to defeat Germany," he said. "They have a fantastic organization and kept saying the way we could pay them back was to win the war and end their occupation. I have great admiration for their skill and courage." He continued for another fifteen minutes, lavishing praise on the partisans for their highly successful underground campaign against the German occupiers. Reggie noted how much Banner contributed to the session. He had been the least vocal during their escape.

Flight Leftenant Whitford said he had little to add to what had already been covered but said how difficult it had been to leave the partisan hideout without Squadron Leader Saunders, who had suffered a badly broken leg in the train wreck. "Sandy is a good friend and a great chap all 'round," he said. "Umm, we couldn't have taken him with us. Would have slowed us down, and lugging him along might have killed him. Partisan commander Piotrowski assured us they'd get him medical care at one of their secret hospitals. If it's possible to get any information on his status, we would really appreciate hearing."

"Well, this has been extremely interesting, gentlemen," General Combs said. "We'll run a check on Squadron Leader Saunders. Let you know when we hear anything. Now does anyone have anything to add before we get to our questions?"

"General, I have a comment and a question," Reggie said. "First, I want to second everything my fellow escapees had to say about the Polish partisans. They are hardened guerilla fighters who give no quarter to the German occupiers, and they are very effective in disrupting German operations throughout Poland. The train wreck was beautifully planned and executed. Tied up that section of railroad for a good bit of time, I should think."

Reggie paused. "I had asked Commander Piotrowski how we could help them, and he asked for airdrops of food, ammunition, and other supplies. Umm, and he added that some fine Scotch whiskey and American cigarettes would be appreciated. I worked out a detailed plan with our guide before we parted company on the Baltic coast. I passed the plan forward and would like to know if any progress had been made in implementing it."

General Combs conferred quietly with his fellow board members and turned back to Reggie. "I'm told your plan has been adopted, the airdrop coordinates have been set, and coded messages will be exchanged with your partisan friends when we're ready to schedule the actual drops."

"General, that's fantastic," Reggie said. "Now, sir, if I may ask one more question, have any messages come through from the three other groups of escapees who set out on different routes for the trek to the Baltic?"

"Wing Commander, we've heard that two of the groups made it to the Baltic connection and rendezvoused with a Swedish freighter. But German patrol boats intercepted them, and they had to run back to the Swedish port of Malmo. The two groups of escapees are currently interred in Sweden. We're working to get them released. No word, I'm afraid, on the third group. Apparently, they didn't make it to the Baltic rendezvous."

General Combs checked his watch. "Gentlemen, we've been at this nearly two hours, and I'm certain that I speak for all of us on the board that so far, we've gained some valuable information. Let's take a fifteen-minute break so we can visit the head, stretch our legs, and have a coffee. We'll reconvene at 0945 hours."

General Combs reopened the briefing by asking the escapees a series of detailed questions about the Luftwaffe's fighter defenses and how they have evolved in the interim between now and the times when each of the escapees had been shot down. "We're trying to determine the state of the German fighter threat, especially with the advent of the Luftwaffe's new Messerschmitt Me 262 twin-jet fighter. Luftwaffe calls it the *Schwalbe*, 'swallow' in English. Don't know if any of you have encountered these high-performance fighters, but you may soon."

Messerschmitt Me-262A 2A Jet Fighter

The 262 was a unique design the Germans started work on in early 1939, General Combs added, "It's based on a jet engine invented by Hans Joachim Pabst Ohain in 1938. Frank Whittle designed his first jet engine here in England a bit before that. It was evaluated on ground-test stands at Royal Aircraft Establishment, but it wasn't flown until very late in the war in a test bed that led to development of the Meteor fighter.

"I emphasize *jet engines*, gentlemen. These produce hot thrust gases to propel the airplane, no reciprocating engines driving propellers. There's disagreement over whether Whittle or Ohain ran their engine first, but we won't go into that," Combs said. "Important fact is the Germans developed an operational jet engine first and proved it on a Heinkel test bed airplane. This paved the way for Messerschmitt to develop the 262."

Combs continued his description, "The fighter features a long-nosed, aerodynamically sleek airframe with a complex wing design—some sections are swept back for high-speed flight—and two Junkers Jumo 004 turbojet engines, one slung under each wing. It has four 30 mm cannons in the nose—there's no propeller, which clears the nose for mounting guns—and has a top speed of over 550 mph, well above our fastest fighter.

"The 262 originally was a tail dragger, but the jet blasts combined with the airflow over the wing adversely affected the tail," Combs continued. "They've now changed the CG on the airplane and added a nose wheel to raise the tail on a tricycle landing gear.

"If they are able to deploy significant numbers of this exceptionally fast interceptor or any of the other advanced jet fighter designs we're getting reports on, our bomber forces will become extremely vulnerable, even with long-range P-51 and P-38 escort fighters. We need to disrupt its production or develop operational tactics to counter it."

Reggie conferred quietly with his four comrades, then turned to the board. "General, we're just getting back on operational service, so we haven't seen this fighter. Heard about it and understand it has amazing capabilities—high speed, incredible climb rate, and heavy armament."

"Right on all accounts. There are reports of other jet-powered designs, and even what appear to be small, delta wing rocket-powered interceptors being fielded," Combs said. "Nasty little things that look like bats and fly like bats out of hell. Could prove to be formidable weapons against our bombers. But this is off the main subject. Let's get back to your escape."

All five board members spent the next hour peppering the escapees with questions pertaining to their particular area of interest. At the end of the four-hour session, Ben and his companions wilted with fatigue. Combs raised his hand, "Gentlemen, I think we've exhausted the topic at hand and our five witnesses as well. Does anyone else on the board have any further questions or points before we release these young officers?"

Air Vice Marshal Wellington-Thaxby raised his hand, and the five escapees shifted in their seats and groaned inwardly. "General Combs, I have a brief closing comment. I'd like to commend these gentlemen for their bravery and dedication to duty. After they were shot down in the line of duty, they steadfastly refused to accept capture as the end of their war against the enemy as their escape

160

proved. I want to personally congratulate them on behalf of His Majesty's Government, the Royal Air Force, and if I may presume, General, on behalf of the U.S. Army Air Forces as well."

The board members responded with applause and table thumping.

"Thank you, Air Vice Marshal," Reggie said. "I don't think any of us considers ourselves heroes. Just did what we were trained to do. But if our examples can inspire others, so much the better."

"In that regard," General Combs said, "we'd like you to keep a low profile until we've made and distributed our final report. At that point, we'll decide how best to share the lessons you men learned the hard way. Of course, we'll have to take care to protect the identities of the Polish partisans and anyone else who helped you escape. Once we have the official sanitized version completed, we'll be calling on each of you to make presentations to your commands and local units. Put you on the regular dog-and-pony show circuit."

All five grimaced at the thought of making the rounds and delivering lectures on escape and evasion.

"I say, it won't be all that bad," Air Vice Marshal Wellington-Thaxby said, noting their expressions. "Just relax and enjoy your moments in the spotlight."

"Now, gentlemen," General Combs concluded, "you've been a big help to us. It's past 1130 hours, so we've been pumping you for going on four hours. We'd like to share lunch with you, but we need at least another hour to resolve details of our preliminary report, so we won't keep you any longer."

He paused. "And frankly, we'd just as soon not send you over to the officer's mess for lunch. Rather not have you besieged by a lot of well-meaning fellow officers wanting to hear all about your experiences. Would you take a rain check from us regarding lunch? We'll call your drivers and have you transported directly back to your duty stations."

Ben started to comment, but Reggie cut him off. "General, we understand the need for continued precautions. We'll accept that rain check and ask if it's all right for us to stop in a nearby pub for lunch and a pint? We've a bit of catching up, if that's permissible."

"Of course, of course," Combs replied. "So if there is nothing else, you are dismissed."

The five snapped to attention, saluted, and marched out of the room.

Outside, Reggie gathered the five drivers. "Gents, we've finished here and are in need of a pint or two and a good pub lunch. Is there a nearby establishment you'd recommend?"

"Wing Commander, I ken recommend the 'Orse and 'Ound, 'bout five mile from 'ere," Reggie's driver piped up. "Best bitters in these parts an' the prettiest barmaids."

"Capital!" Reggie expounded. "That sound like a good reference to you gentlemen?" he said to the Giraffes.

"What kind of food do they serve?" Ben asked. "None of that steak-and-liver combination, I hope. Or the other stuff that comes in a cow's stomach."

Reggie's driver eyed Ben curiously. "Could do a fine steak and kidney pud I suppose, sir. But I doubt ye could find a haggis there."

"Pay no mind to our friend from the colonies," Reggie said. "He hasn't developed a taste for the best of English cuisine, even though he's been with us since '39. And, Ben, I'll tell you for the last time, it is steak and *kidney* pudding, not steak and liver."

"I'll settle for a scotch egg or two," Ben muttered.

"Right ho! Let's get under way."

They soon settled at a table in the Horse and Hound near the fireplace, quaffing their pints. Their drivers sat happily ensconced at a nearby table doing the same. They were in no hurry to return to their duty stations.

"Ben, I trust you aren't offended that I interrupted you when the general released us to return directly to our duty stations. I could just see you agreeing to that in a fit of patriotic fervor, anxious to get back to the war, and all that. We need this pub stop, my good man. You said so yourself."

"Naw, no problem, Reggie. This is a swell idea. But the 509th flew a mission today, and I am anxious to hear how it went. And you know the deal I have with Frank. I've passed my flight physical, and completing this briefing was the last hurdle I had to clear before returning to flight status. I get to lead the next mission."

This prompted a spirited discussion about getting back into the war and speculation on how much longer the Germans would be able to holdout against the combined Allied land, air, and sea assaults.

Three delightful hours passed while the five Giraffes exchanged numerous toasts and reinforced the friendships they forged during their escape. All pledged to gather for regular reunions in the coming months. As they rose a bit unsteadily and headed for the door, they signaled their drivers, who teetered behind them on the verge of being squiffy themselves. Somehow they found the proper staff cars and departed for their respective home stations.

Ben paused outside Frank's door and adjusted his uniform before knocking and entering. Frank smiled inwardly at Ben's formal greeting and the careful way in which he took his seat in front of the desk.

"So how'd the briefing go?" he asked.

"Jus' swell, Frank. Took more'n four hours. Knocked their socks off. We stopped at a pub for a Giraffe's reunion lunch."

"I noticed."

"Hey, Frank. How'd today's mission go?"

"Smooth. Launched twenty and got twenty back. Encountered no fighters on the way in and only one half-assed attack on the way out. Minimal flak over the rail center, so everyone got back with no damage and no casualties."

"Thas' great," Ben said, clearing his throat, painfully aware he was slurring his words. "We alerted again?"

"Yes, day after tomorrow. We'll join in an eight hundred aircraft flotilla. This'll be a big one, and the 509th will lead."

"Fantastic!" Ben nearly yelled. "My first mission since getting back, and it'll be a biggie."

"Uh yeah, Ben, it'll be a biggie, and I have to talk to you about leading it," Frank said. He pressed on as Ben started to protest. "Hang on. You don't have to remind me of the deal. I'm not reneging on that . . ."

"But, Frank!" Ben said, almost pleading. "Why's there any question about it? I'm ready. Poland's under Russian control, and I've cleared all the other hurdles!"

"Hold it, Ben! Hear me out. I've got good reasons to discuss it with you."

"What's the target, Frank?"

"Regensburg."

Chapter 29

BACK TO THE ABYSS

Ben blinked twice and sat back in his chair, his mind suddenly swept clear of any residual effects of the alcohol.

"Uh, umm, Regensburg, eh. Ah okay, Frank, how does this change anything? A mission is a mission. I'd still like to lead it."

"Not so fast, Ben. We need to talk this through," Silverman snapped. "I'm still commander of the 509th, and I decide who leads the group's missions—"

"Frank," Ben interrupted, "I know that, and I don't want to sound like some insubordinate junior officer challenging your authority. You know I have too much respect for you. And uh, and we go back too far for me to ever knowingly cause you trouble."

Ben shifted forward in his chair and grabbed the edge of Frank's desk. "Frank, look at this from my point of view. If I duck this mission because of my bad experience over Regensburg, that shoots my confidence. I need prove to myself that I can lead this mission successfully."

He slumped back in the chair and locked eyes with Silverman. "Frank, please let me lead this one."

Silverman rubbed his chin, shot Ben a grimace, and spoke softly, "Ben, I know how important this mission is to you, maybe now even more than ever before. But this puts me in a tight spot. Doolittle and team are concerned about the new Messerschmitt Me 262 jet fighter. And it's being assembled at Regensburg. That's the target.

"Hell, we're all worried about a fighter that can fly straight and level faster than our prop jobs can dive. If Herr Goering gets enough of them, they can put us out of business until we develop new fighters that can counter them. According to the intel guys, the Germans rebuilt Messerschmitt's Regensburg factory faster than expected and concealed the 262 assembly area in the ruins of the factory you and your buddies flattened last April.

"Our number 1 priority is to blast it again, and . . ." Frank threw up his hands. "Okay, okay. You know how important it is. Ben, I know you can lead the mission and lead it well. I still have reservations about sending you back there so soon, but let's put those worries aside and get to the mission details. This one's going to be a bit complicated."

They stepped to a large map of Europe mounted on the office wall and spent two hours reviewing the mission plan. The 509th would launch twenty B-17s loaded with 750-pound high-explosive bombs at 0730 hours. Ben would form the group over Parham and lead them to a rendezvous over Southeast England with four hundred B-17s from USAAF bases along the channel coast northeast of London. Ten other Eighth Air Force groups would add two hundred B-24s to the flotilla, forming a bomber string fifty miles long. This massive wave of bombers plus several other formations simultaneously attacking targets north and south of the main Regensburg target would stretch the Luftwaffe's depleted fighter groups to their limits.

It also would stretch the Eighth Air Force's ability to launch bomber groups and fleets of fighter escorts from widely spread air bases across Southeastern England, assemble them into increasingly larger formations, and finally integrate them into a massive bomber/ fighter string heading across the channel to Germany. Everyone in the intricate process, from ground-based air traffic controllers to pilots and observers in the circling bombers and leaders of protective fighter squadrons have special see-and-avoid responsibilities in this massed aerial ballet. The procedures had been carefully worked out and perfected on numerous combat missions, and the incidence of midair collisions was remarkably small.

"We can't predict whether the Luftwaffe will concentrate its fighters on one of the attack fleets or try to fend off all three," Frank said. "The north fleet will head for Berlin, which Herr Goering may consider the highest priority target to protect, and the south fleet will attack the industrial and rail centers around Stuttgart. So you shouldn't encounter concentrated fighter attacks until you reach Nuremburg."

Frank stepped back from the map and locked eyes with Ben. "Of course, you can expect heavy flak as you approach Regensburg. Intel hasn't reported that any special fighter units have been moved into the area, but tell your gunners to be especially alert on the way in and back. As to the escape route, you'll have to read the flak patterns over the target and decide which way to lead the fleet."

Frank cleared his throat. "That's the basic plan. We'll leave the details to the individual crew briefings. We'll assemble the pilots' briefing at 0500 hours. Any questions?"

"Ah no, it's all pretty clear, Frank. Which airplane do I get? *Round Trip*, as you know, is history."

"I'll assign you *Buxom Baby*, which you've already flown. Captain Bennett is due some leave. He's flown twenty-seven missions, some of them tough ones. He lost several crew members and needs a rest. Has a crackerjack copilot named Evans, Lieutenant Charles Evans—big broad-shouldered kid from Wyoming. Navigator and bombardier also are top-notch. They'll serve you well."

"Swell. Sounds like we've covered all the bases. I'll go find the crew and get acquainted. Can't thank you enough for your confidence, Frank."

Ben gathered Evans; Lieutenant Bobby Holmes, the navigator; and Captain Sam Anderson, the bombardier, in a corner of the Officer's Club. "Fellas, my name's Ben Findlay."

"Colonel, we know who you are. You're pretty famous around here," Evans interrupted. "Understand we're going to be flyin' with you day after tomorrow, sir."

"Hmm, I see word still travels fast around here," Ben said. "You're right. We'll be leading the raid tomorrow, and I wanted to tell you what to expect and what I'll need from you." The young officers leaned forward expectantly. They'd find out at the next day's briefing that the mission was to Regensburg, their longest mission into Southeastern Germany.

They discussed a range of operational procedures for another half an hour, and then Ben excused himself, saying he had some other task to complete before bedtime.

Back in headquarters, Ben telephoned Gwen at a prearranged time that coincided with her night-shift tea break at the Cambridge hospital. "Hello, beautiful lady," he quipped when she picked up the phone. "Anything interesting happening?"

"Not until now, love." She chuckled. "How are you, Ben? Did the briefing go well?"

He gave her a quick synopsis of the meeting with the senior intelligence officers, adding that they seemed satisfied with the information he and his fellow Giraffes had provided. "The important thing is, Gwen, this clears me to get back on operations. Frank has stuck with the bargain we made. Doc Samuelson says I'm fully healed, and now we've given the intelligence boffins, as Reggie calls them, their briefing. I'll be cleared for operations." Ben paused as he heard a stifled sob from Gwen. "Hey, Gwen, are you okay, love?"

"Umm, yes . . ." Gwen said softly. "I, umm, I'm all right. It's just that, umm. No, Ben, I'm not all right! I'm so worried about you having to go back to war. Oh, Ben, please forgive me, my darling. I shouldn't be this way, but I worry that you won't return safely whenever you fly your missions. I'm such a ninny." She broke into quiet sobs.

Ben sat, clamping the phone to his ear. "Gwen, honey, please, don't get yourself all worked up over this. I'm going to be okay. Sure, there'll still be risks. We both know that. But you have to believe I'm going to be okay."

"Ben, I'm so sorry. I just can't deal with this right now." Gwen choked. I do have to get back to my duties. We're unusually pressed tonight and we're shorthanded . . . Look, love, I *am* such a ninny. Where's my stiff upper lip? I really must ring off. Might you call me at home tomorrow sometime?" She sobbed again.

Ben tried to soothe her, but it was apparent he could only do that in person. "Gwen, I have a very busy day tomorrow." *And the next day, but I can't tell her why.* "But I'll make time to phone you. What would be the best time?" They agreed on a time and after exchanging endearments, rang off. Ben heard Gwen sniffling as the line went dead. He sat several minutes holding the dead phone before hanging up.

"Now gotta get those letters written home," he muttered. "I'll include a note to Joe. Mom can forward it to him."

Ben spent a fitful night. Sleep eluded him as his mind replayed the preparations for the Regensburg mission and dredged up details of the previous doomed mission that ended with him being shot down. He also agonized over Gwen's fear for his safety. He must have dozed off at some point, for he awoke shortly before sunrise, feeling fuzzy headed and not refreshed.

"Better get cracking." He yawned. "Got a ton of stuff to do before tomorrow's mission. Need to write myself a note so I don't forget to call Gwen."

Ben had to step lively to keep out of the way as Parham's ground and service teams completed preparations for the next day's mission. Major Fred Irving, 509th maintenance officer, reported that all twenty-one B-17s were ready for tomorrow. Fueling teams topped off gas and oil tanks, and the armors filled shell magazines for each bomber's arsenal of thirteen .50-caliber machine guns. The bombs would be loaded that evening.

"Looks like it's going smoothly as usual," Frank commented as he and Ben reviewed the reports associated with the mission. "Weather looks good. Marginal here, but overcast across Europe, which should dissipate by the time you approach Regensburg."

"Good and bad," Ben responded. "I'd like solid overcast all the way to minimize the fighter attacks. But can't have everything."

Silverman eyed Ben closely. "How're you doing? You look a little ragged. Have a bad night?"

"Yeah, had a lot on my mind, not just the mission. Gwen's upset that I'm going back on operations. I have to push that aside and focus on what needs to be done tomorrow."

"Right. Best thing for you is to make it an early night. Get some solid shut-eye. Wake-up call will be at 0400 hours."

Ben had another restless night and was awake long before the sergeant knocked on his door at 0400. He spent a brief time in the bathroom, dressed, and headed for the mess hall. He forced himself to eat a hearty breakfast of fried eggs, bacon, and hashed brown potatoes, topped off with jam toast and several cups of coffee. He knew he needed a solid meal of carbs and protein to fuel his body for a long day's work.

Silverman convened the briefing. He frowned at the wave of mumbled curses that swept through the assembled flight crews when Ben pulled back the curtain, revealing the target. "Yes, Regensburg," he said. "More precisely, the Messerschmitt factory on the outskirts. The Germans partially rebuilt the factory the 509th plastered earlier this year and have opened a new Me 262 jet fighter assembly facility cleverly camouflaged in the ruins."

He swept the gathered airmen with a stern look. "I won't try to fool you. This is a bitch of a mission. But we all know what a threat the 262 will pose if they succeed in building and fielding enough of these fighters. We must knock out this factory. Now I'll turn the briefing over to Colonel Findlay who'll lead the mission."

The last phrase prompted a collective gasp of amazement. They knew Ben's history with Regensburg.

Ignoring their reaction, Ben took charge of the briefing. He ran through the mission details: takeoff at 0730 hours, the track to their rendezvous with the other groups, their route to the target, and estimated time over target.

"Two other Eighth Air Force combined groups will launch simultaneous missions against targets north and south of our track, aiming for Berlin and Stuttgart," Ben said. "The intent is to force the Luftwaffe to spread its fighter forces along a broad front. We'll encounter fighters, especially as we get closer to Regensburg, but this tactic should reduce the pressure on us.

"Need to remember to keep the formations tight, don't leave gaps that allow the fighters to get in among us. Keep 'em on the outside. And when they slice by, they'll roll to expose the armored bellies of their aircraft to our gunners, so have them try to aim for the engine and empennage."

Ben cleared his throat. "As to the flak defenses, Regensburg has some of the heaviest concentrations in Germany. And they may have been improved to offer increased protection to the 262 factory. We'll have to read the flak patterns when we arrive over the target and respond accordingly." He then gave them the IP (initial point) from which they would turn onto the final track to the target and the estimated time for the turn. Raising his wrist, he called out a time hack to synchronize everyone's watches.

Ben then told the pilots and copilots, navigators, and bombardiers to meet for their individual briefings. "Man your airplanes at your discretion," he said. "Engine start is 0700 hours. Expect taxi instructions by 0715 and takeoffs will begin at 0730. Form up as usual over the field radio beacon for departure to the rendezvous point by 0800."

Ben called the group to attention and followed Frank out the briefing room door. Colonel Coleman ordered them, "At ease," and the room echoed with a cacophony of jabbering, shouts, and curses about the target.

Frank sat sipping coffee with Ben in the base operations center. "They aren't exactly happy with the mission, but these come with the territory, so I expect they'll rise to the challenge," he said. "Now why don't you put your feet up and relax. I'll meet you here and drive you out to your airplane a bit before 0700."

Ben grunted his thanks and headed for a cot in a back file room. He awoke with a start and looked at his watch. It was 0630. "Woof!" he snorted. "Wouldn't have thought I could sleep." He got up, visited the head, and was waiting with his flight bag when Silverman's staff car pulled up. They had little to say until the driver pulled up in front of *Buxom Baby*, its four engines idling smoothly.

"Not much to say other than good luck and smooth sailing," Frank said, shaking Ben's hand. "See you back here this afternoon."

Ben nodded, grabbed his flight bag, and ducked under the nose of *Buxom Baby*, avoiding the turning propellers. He paused and flipped Frank a salute before swinging up through the nose hatch. On board, he greeted Lieutenant Evans and strapped into the left seat. His adrenaline was pumping in response to the noise, smells, and premission tension, so he kept his hands moving to hide any shaking that might alarm the crew. Evans pretended not to notice. Ben conducted a final communications check with the crew and asked Holmes, the navigator, if he was ready to go. Receiving an affirmative, Ben grasped the control column and signaled the ground crew to remove the wheel chocks. He eased the four throttles forward as Sergeant Howard, the flight engineer, crouched over the engine controls quadrant.

Ben stretched and yawned, trying to find a comfortable position in the lumpy seat as they taxied to the runway. Final instrument checks completed, he maneuvered into takeoff position and told Evans to lock the tail wheel. When the green flare arched away from the control tower balcony, Ben held the brakes and eased the throttles forward. At brake release, *Buxom Baby* groaned, and Ben pushed the throttles to full boost takeoff power. The four propellers bit into the air and pulled her forward. Their slow acceleration confirmed they were hauling a full load of fuel and bombs. Ben concentrated on keeping the bomber on the runway centerline as Evans called out the airspeeds. Finally, almost reluctantly, *Buxom Baby* lifted off and climbed steadily into the English morning mist. Ben signaled Evans to raise the landing gear.

The group formed in an orderly manner over Parham, and Ben led them to the rendezvous point. This was the critical moment in massed formation raids. The chance of midair collisions was high, especially when hundreds of large bombers jockeyed for space in a loose formation. Marginal visibility at the bottom edge of the overcast layer didn't help. But the rendezvous proceeded smoothly, and Ben turned onto a southeasterly course at the head of a fleet of six hundred B-17s and two hundred P-51 escort fighters. He assumed the two hundred B-24s and their escort fighters would successfully tag onto the end of the bomber string.

Ben performed the initial mission tasks automatically, ordering the gunners to test their weapons over the English Channel, reminding them to don oxygen masks as they climbed through an altitude of ten thousand feet and double checking their course with Holmes. He then turned to Evans and signaled him to monitor the autopilot keeping them on course.

Ben sat staring through the windshield as a jumble of memories and emotions tumbled through his mind. He saw his old B-17 *Round Trip* while the faces of his previous crewmen paraded past his subconscious. "Everyone but Gordy gone," he mumbled. "Damn, what a waste!"

"Over France and approaching the front lines, Colonel," Evans called out, breaking Ben's reverie. "Should I switch off the autopilot and alert the gunners to watch for fighters?"

"Huh?" Ben said. "Uh yeah. Your airplane while I tell 'em." He picked up the microphone and switched to the broadcast channel. "All bombers approaching German airspace, time to tuck 'em in. Close formations and tighten those defensive boxes. Remember, don't give the Kraut fighters room to get in between us."

He switched to the intercom channel and told everyone manning guns on *Buxom Baby* to watch for fighters, especially high-speed interceptors diving in from the rear quadrants. "The Luftwaffe has a small number of their new Me 262 jets operational, and we may see some today," he said. "They'll likely attack from the rear, dive through our fighter cover like bats outta hell, pull up to fire short bursts, and roll away into high-speed dives. You'll get only a second or two to aim and fire. Give 'em a long lead as you fire. They'll be traveling faster than anything you've seen before."

The cloud layer below them thinned and finally dissipated. As they flew into bright sunshine beyond Wurzburg, Ben assumed Luftwaffe fighter command had deduced their target was Regensburg. This meant concentrated fighter attacks. He grasped the wheel and signaled Evans that he was taking control. Sweat soaked the lining of Ben's leather flight helmet, beaded on his forehead, and ran in rivulets down his spine. His hands felt clammy in his gloves as he twisted his head, scanning the sky for fighters.

Get a hold of yourself! Don't let the crew see you're nervous.

"All gunners," he called over the intercom, "sing out when you spot bogeys—altitude, heading, and numbers."

171

Sergeant Howard, who had shifted up to his gunner's position in the top turret, made the first call. "Fifteen, no, twenty at one o'clock high! P-51s engaging. Look like 109s. Might be settin' up for a head-on attack."

Ben ducked forward and craned his neck to the right, scanning the portion of sky Howard indicated. In the process, he pushed the yoke forward, and the nose abruptly dipped. He snapped back and adjusted the yoke. "Stop acting like a damn rookie on your first combat mission," he snarled into his oxygen mask. He glanced at Evans, who again pretended not to notice Ben's discomfort.

A second alert sounded on the intercom. "Second buncha bogeys at ten o'clock high! 'Bout a dozen 109s. Also maneuvering for head-on attack from the left."

As the gunners swung their weapons forward to meet the attacks, Sergeant Jefferson called from his tail-gunner position. "Fast fliers punching through our fighter cover. Probably 262s. Here they come! Godamighty! They fired and blasted past before I could even get 'em in my sights! More on the way! Gimme some help back here!"

Me 262 jet fighters slashed through the bomber formations in rolling dives as all rearward facing guns blazed away. *Buxom Baby*'s gunners cursed as their tracer rounds swept fiery arcs well behind the attackers. Gunners in the other B-17s in their immediate defensive box also watched their tracer rounds punch holes in the sky well behind the jets.

"Head-on attack coming!" Captain Anderson yelled from his bombardier position in the Plexiglas nose. "109s comin' from both left and right." All guns with forward-firing arcs swung again to meet the frontal attacks. They were more successful. Several 109s were hit with concentrated .50-caliber fire. Two exploded, and a third rolled into a smoking dive.

"Helluva lot easier to hit these prop jobs, even at closing speeds," someone shouted into the intercom. Jefferson interrupted from the tail-gunner position. "More fast fliers coming at us again! Son of a bitch, they're fast! Gotta lead the bastards. Get at least a piece of one."

Slugs from the 262's four 30 mm nose cannons hammered *Buxom Baby* with deafening blows, blasting pieces off the vertical tail section. In the cockpit, the rudder pedals slapped Ben's feet, indicating the rudder had been hit. He quickly worked the pedals. They were still connected. The seemingly indestructible B-17 absorbed the hits from the large 30 mm rounds and kept flying.

The coordinated head-on and tail attacks continued despite the intervention of their escort fighters. The bomber crews saw several fighters, 109s and P-51s, tumble in smoke and flames from the dogfights raging around them. So far, the lightning-fast 262s eluded both the American fighter pilots and the B-17 gunners. *Buxom Baby*'s two waist gunners cursed in frustration as the attacking fighters swept in, fired, and rolled away at angles beyond the effective firing arcs of their guns.

"Can't get a bead on any of the bastards from here!" one gunner yelled. Nevertheless, they banged away as the enemy fighters rolled into high-speed escape dives.

Ben clutched the control wheel and concentrated on holding *Buxom Baby* on course. In the heat of the battle, a steely calmness came over him. Strong cordite fumes swept through the cockpit, and *Buxom Baby*'s arsenal of .50-caliber guns thundered and rattled the bomber. Enemy rounds punched through the airplane's aluminum skin adding to the din. He stopped sweating, but his clammy undershirt and uniform blouse clung to his skin. "Commander to navigator, how're we doing?" he called on the intercom.

"On track, skipper. Another fifty miles to the IP."

"Commander to tail, how's the formation holding?"

"Pretty busy right now, skipper." The staccato chopping of Jefferson's twin machine guns blasted over the intercom. "Shit! Can't keep these bastards in my sights. Uh, sorry, skipper. Umm, formation's holding tight. Everybody's banging away at these damn 262s, but nobody's hit one that I can see . . . Look out, here comes another pair!"

The running battle lasted another half an hour as Luftwaffe fighters swarmed in to attack the bomber string. The intercom blasted a cacophony of shouts and curses as gunners struggled to ward off the attackers. The escort fighters scored many kills against the German propeller-driven Me 109s and Fw 190s, but they couldn't stop the 262 jets.

"Who the hell said the Luftwaffe was done for!" someone yelled.

Two B-17s in their defensive box formation bucked and rolled as enemy crossfire raked their wings and fuselage. One burst into flames and spun smoking out of the formation. Engines exploded on another, and it dropped out of formation as the pilots struggled to maintain control.

"Two forts hit. Dropping out of formation," one of the waist gunners called out.

"Whose ships?" Ben asked.

"Think the one that spun in was Captain Watkins's *Alabama Baby*, skipper. Not sure about the other."

"It's *Flying High*, Lieutenant Jones," Jefferson called from the tail gunner's position. "Driftin' way outta formation."

Enemy fighters pounced on the lone damaged bomber. Jefferson saw six parachutes blossom from the airplane before it exploded and rained debris earthward. Farther back in the bomber string, several B-17s pressed on, trailing smoke from damaged engines. Another exploded, and its flaming pieces traced fiery arcs toward the ground. Suddenly, the enemy fighters broke off their attacks and rolled away. This meant only one thing: they were approaching Regensburg's antiaircraft flak defenses.

Ben radioed, "All bombers. Fighters breaking off. Means we're about to hit the flak belt. Adjust your formations. Look sharp. Try to figure out the flak patterns. IP coming up soon." The gunners shifted away from their machine guns, and some piled flak jackets on the floor around them. All hated sitting defenseless as exploding 88 mm shells spit white-hot shrapnel into their path.

Ben clenched the control wheel. Sweat drenched him again. His jaws ached as he gritted his teeth. His body began to twitch. "Damn! This is where we got it last time," he snarled to himself. "Hate sittin' here watching those damn flak shells explode. Can't see a pattern to the flak yet."

"Three minutes to IP," Lieutenant Holmes called out.

Ben called the bombardier, "Sam, you ready to take control inbound to the target?"

"On it, skipper. I'll take it soon as we make the turn."

"Give you a hand, skipper?" Evans yelled from his copilot's seat.

"Roger that, Charlie. Get on the controls and help with the turn." Hot pain flashed through Ben's left shoulder. "Handle the throttles and call out course corrections."

As they rolled onto the final track of 120 degrees to the target, the German antiaircraft gunners zeroed in on *Buxom Baby* with a concentrated barrage. A shell exploded nearby, punching holes in the underside of the left wing and the Number 1 engine nacelle. Ben and Charlie wrestled the control columns, keeping the bomber upright and on course.

"Left waist to skipper, liquid streaming outta Number 1 engine. Looks like oil."

Evans scanned the engine instruments. "Losing oil pressure on Number 1."

Sergeant Howard dropped down from the top turret. "Let's feather Number 1!" Ben yelled. "Still running okay, but it'll burn up without oil. Let's cage it and maybe save some oil. That engine might come in handy later."

"Good idea, skipper!" Howard yelled.

Ben turned to Evans. "Feather it, Charlie." Both pilots cranked in trim control and held right rudder and aileron to compensate for the asymmetrical thrust from the two engines on the right wing.

"Approaching target. Need to take control," Anderson called from his bombardier position in the nose.

"Your airplane," Ben responded, releasing his grip on the control wheel and signaling Evans to do the same. Anderson hunched over his Norden bombsight. He used trim nobs to input final course adjustments that kept the sight's crosshairs on the target.

"This is the hardest part, sittin' here and waitin' for bomb release!" Ben yelled to Evans, trying to look relaxed. "After bomb release, we'll—"

A brilliant flash and explosion cut him off. Another 88 mm shell exploded under the left wing, rolling *Buxom Baby* to the right. "*Goddamn it!*" Ben yelled. He and Charlie wrestled *Buxom Baby* upright and steered her back on course.

"What the hell's happening?" Anderson called from the bombardier's position. "I'm on the target run!"

"Steady on," Ben radioed. "We got her stabilized." They had *Buxom Baby* under control, but as they scanned the instruments, the tachometer on engine Number 2 wound down. It had been seriously damaged, and to prevent fire, they quickly shut it down and feathered the propeller. Both pilots rolled the control wheels farther right and pushed harder on their right rudder pedals to overcome the increased asymmetrical thrust that rolled *Buxom Baby* left toward the two feathered engines.

"We're off course!" Anderson yelled. "Steer back to one twenty, or we're gonna miss the aim point!"

"Getting back to one twenty," Ben snarled through gritted teeth. "We've lost both left engines, and she's a bitch to handle. Hang on."

"Back on course," Evans called out.

"Sam, can you reacquire the target?" Ben asked. "Think we can hold what we have."

"Hope so. Hold it. Think I can make it work . . . Okay, hold it. Bomb bay doors open. Steady, steady. *Bombs away!* Your airplane, skipper." *Buxom Baby* surged upward as the released bombs quickly lightened her load.

North American B-25 Bomber

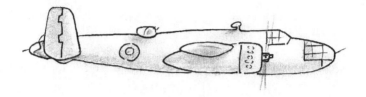

"Got it!" Ben yelled. "Okay, Charlie, let's get the hell outta here. Have to turn right. Can't turn into the two dead engines." Ben's shoulders and right leg burned as muscle spasms coursed through his limbs. *Yeah, Frank, wouldn't you know, the worst possible engine-out situation. Thank God I've got Evans in the right seat.*

As they rolled out on the escape heading, Jefferson radioed from the tail gunner's position that it looked like most of the remaining 509th bombers made it past the target and were joining them on the escape heading. "Think we only lost the two on the way in and one over the target, skipper. Everybody looks beat up but still flyin'. Lotta smoke and flames below. Think we clobbered the target."

"Great!" Ben grunted. *Don't wanna come back to this rotten goddamned place again. Wonder if we put any bombs down the Gestapo's chimney. Here's to you, oberwurstwhateverthehell, you rotten bastard. Wish I had signed one of the bombs for ya.*

As Ben and Evans struggled to keep *Buxom Baby* upright and headed home, the antiaircraft gunners beyond Regensburg continued to pound away at them, determined to destroy as many of the retreating airplanes as possible. The sky blossomed with ugly black clouds sprouting white-hot tendrils of shrapnel. Pieces slammed into *Buxom Baby*, sounding like large hail hitting a tin roof. The 509th cleared the flak belt, and Ben radioed the crew, "Heads up all gunners. Back in fighter country. Call 'em out as you see 'em."

Luftwaffe fighters staged several small-scale attacks, but the main defensive force, including several pairs of the high-speed 262s, concentrated on the tail end of the attack fleet, still approaching

Regensburg. "Wish 'em luck, fellas," Ben called on the intercom. "They're gonna catch hell over Regensburg."

Ben pushed back in his seat as they passed the ground battle line into airspace over the liberated part of France. He tried to flex his tortured left shoulder and right leg muscles but needed to stay on the controls to help Evans maintain the desired course. Compensating for the engine-out condition was beyond the capabilities of the autopilot. "Can you hold her for a few minutes, Charlie?" he yelled. "I need to stretch."

Charlie grunted, "Okay, I got it," and tightened his grip on the control wheel. Ben unstrapped and stood up, stumbling as his right leg buckled. He grimaced, hunched his shoulders, and rotated the left one to work out a muscle knot. He exhaled. "Aw, the hell with it. Better sit back down. You need a stretch, Charlie?" Evans shook his head. "I'm okay, Ben. I can hold out for a while."

Ben bent over, then stepped in place while flexing his shoulders. This eased the main aches and pains. "Okay, lemme sit back down and give you a hand," he said. Together, they held *Buxom Baby* on course as they limped across the English Channel. But they had difficulty holding altitude. "Gonna be tight gettin' home," Evans said as they slid over the White Cliffs of Dover.

"Let's fire up Number 1," Ben said. "See how long it lasts. It'll buy us some time."

"Good idea, skipper," Sergeant Howard said as he bent over the throttles. "There could be enough oil left to keep it running until we reach Parham. And if it craps out, we're no worse off than we are now."

Just as he said that, Number 4 engine out on the right wing coughed and backfired, spewing a cloud of black smoke. "What was that!" Ben shouted.

Howard scanned the engine gauges. "Dunno, skipper. Cylinder temps are high. Maybe it's the higher power setting that's causing some stress. Can we back off on it and still maintain altitude?"

"Let's try it," Evans said as he reduced the manifold pressure on Number 4. *Buxom Baby* wallowed homeward. Restarting the Number 1 engine had helped, although its oil pressure wavered near the red line. They'd have to shut it down again soon.

Ben scanned the instrument panel. "Okay, we're stabilized, but she doesn't like flying with all this aileron and rudder input," he said. "Causes too damn much drag."

He keyed the intercom. "Skipper to radio, we're nearing home. Call Parham and tell the tower we're gonna be down to two sick engines and need a straight-in approach to Runway 34. Not able to make a pattern approach."

Ben radioed the remaining 509th bombers trailing them. "All bombers, we've got engine problems. We'll make a straight-in approach to Runway 34. Anyone else who needs the same, inform the tower. Rest of you, stay clear and follow usual pattern approach."

As they descended on the final approach leg, Number 1 engine surged just as Ben called for approach flaps and the landing gear. The oil warning light illuminated and the tachometer needle dropped toward zero. "Cage it, Charlie!" Ben shouted. Charlie quickly feathered the engine while Ben concentrated on flying a two-engine approach. He flared and touched down on the main gear for a smooth wheel landing, and Number 4 engine belched smoke, backfired, and quit. Both pilots wrestled their control wheels as *Buxom Baby* dropped onto a tail-dragger position. They mashed the brakes as *Buxom Baby* fishtailed down the runway. They slowed the bomber to taxi speed near the far end of the runway and turned off onto the outer taxiway. As they braked to a stop, Number 3 engine on the inboard right wing, their last engine, backfired and clanked to a stop.

Ben sat staring openmouthed through the cracked, smoke-streaked windshield. If the final engine failures had happened barely minutes earlier, they wouldn't have made it to the runway. Ben slumped in his seat. "Godamighty, that's cutin' it too close," he croaked. Charlie sat mute, unable to speak.

An eerie silence descended on the airplane. Finally, someone yelled, "Hot damn, skipper, nice piece of flyin'!" A chorus of cheers echoed through the airplane. Suddenly, everyone was jabbering at the same time. "When I get out of this bucket of bolts, I'm gonna kiss the ground!" Jefferson shouted.

All of the gunners tumbled out of the aft hatch on the right side of the fuselage, whooping and pounding each other on the back. Jefferson dropped on his knees and kissed the tarmac. "*Sweet Je-a-sus!*" another yelled. "Look at that hole in the vertical tail! Damn lucky whatever hit it didn't blow the rudder clean off. We'd been done for then."

"You think that's bad," Jefferson called from the left side of *Buxom Baby*, "come take a look at our left wing. Looks like a big ol' hound dog chewed hell outta it."

As they gathered to gape at the ragged holes in the wing and engine nacelles, Ben roused himself from his stupor. "Better get everything shut down, Charlie. Good job. Thanks for your help." They began cycling the B-17's maze of switches. There was no need to shut down the engines, but they cut off the fuel lines and closed the master switches.

Silverman's staff car screeched to a stop in front of the left wing as fire engines converged on *Buxom Baby*. He hopped out and banged on the forward nose hatch. "Open up! How're you doing in there?" Holmes slid out of his navigator's station and unlatched the hatch. "Everyone okay in there?" Silverman called. Holmes nodded and jerked a thumb up to the flight deck. "Yes, sir. They're just securing everything, Colonel. Be down in a minute."

Anderson crawled white-faced from the bombardier's position in the nose, greeted Silverman, and swung down out of the hatch. "Hello, Colonel. Had a bitch of a time over Regensburg. Fighters, especially the new 262s, beat us up on the way in, and then we ran into the heaviest flak I've ever seen. All you need to do is take a look at *Buxom Baby* to see that." He shuffled off to a waiting crew truck for the ride back to base ops.

Ben rose shakily from his seat and nearly fell into Charlie's lap. "Sorry," he mumbled. "Need to get my legs working. You go first, Charlie."

Evans grunted thanks and squeezed past him. "Mine aren't workin' so well either." He dropped through the hatch and greeted Silverman. "Ben's coming, Colonel. He's working out a few kinks." He stood, surveying the damage to *Buxom Baby*. "Man, oh man, the Krauts sure beat the shit out of us this time, Colonel." He paused and nodded up to the cockpit. "Uh, by the way, Colonel, I wanna tell you that I'll fly anywhere, anytime, and in any airplane with that guy up there. He's one helluva pilot."

Ben appeared in the hatch and dropped to the ground. His right leg buckled, and he struggled to keep his balance. "Woof! Uh hullo, Frank. Sorry we busted up another airplane. Bennett ain't gonna be happy when he sees what's left of *Buxom Baby*."

Silverman stepped forward and shook Ben's hand. "Looks like you salvaged another Regensburg mission, Ben. Well done to both of you," he added, turning the Evans. "Okay, get in my staff car. We'll drop you at base ops, Charlie. You can handle the post mission debrief. I'm taking Ben to the hospital for a quick check by Doc Samuelson." Ben began to protest, but Silverman silenced him with a wave of his hand. "That's that. Let's get moving."

"Pretty significant muscle strain in both shoulders and some in your right leg, Ben," Samuelson muttered. "When I cleared you for flight ops, I didn't anticipate you'd face this on your first mission. Did you guys fly all the way home on two engines?" Ben nodded, grimacing as Samuelson rotated his left shoulder. "So how's Lieutenant Evans doing?" the flight surgeon asked.

"Evans is a strong young kid," Silverman chimed in. "He's at base ops conducting the debrief. Looks okay, but I'll tell him to stop by to see you afterward."

"Ben, I'm going to give you a shot to lessen the pain, and then I'm ordering you to bed," Samuelson said. "I'll give you a pill to help you sleep." Ben started to protest again but nodded resignedly when both Silverman and Samuelson stared him into silence.

Back at his quarters, Silverman steered Ben to his room. "Get in there and hit the sack," he snapped. "I'll catch up with Evans at the briefing. Hard to believe your crew escaped without a scratch from the pounding your airplane took."

"Yeah, damn lucky," Ben muttered, removing his boots and shedding his flight suit. He had a long pee and dropped onto his bunk, peering at Silverman through bloodshot eyes. "Sorry I only brought eighteen home, Frank. Damn! I hate to lose any crews at this point in the war." Silverman dismissed his apology with a wave of his hand. "We got good protection from our fighter escorts on the way to the target and back home," Ben continued, "but the flak over the target was something else. Dunno how any of us got through."

"Well, you did, and initial reports from trailing groups indicate you plastered the 262 assembly facility pretty good."

"Anybody else come home in bad shape?" Ben asked. "I know several came outta the target area with engines caged."

"Yeah, seems everyone took hits, but none as bad as *Buxom Baby*."

Ben flopped back on his cot. He didn't feel Silverman cover him with a blanket or hear him leave the room.

Chapter 30

BACK TO ROUTINE OPERATIONS

A yellow beam of sunlight streamed through a hole in the shade covering Ben's window and danced across his eyelids. His lids fluttered then opened. He blinked, squinting in the bright shaft of light. *Must be after sunrise. Dunno when I've slept this late. Usually up by half past dark.*

Ben sat up fully awake. "Wait a minute," he mumbled, "my window faces west. West? What the hell? I'm lookin' at the sunset. Did I sleep all through the day?" He squinted at his watch. It read 1730 hours.

He hopped out of bed, did his morning business, even though it was late afternoon, and hurriedly dressed. Twenty minutes later, he strode into Silverman's office. "Hullo, Frank. Have you any idea what kinda sleeping pill Samuelson gave me last night?"

"Morning, Ben," Silverman said with a sly grin. "Not sure exactly, but I know it was a powerful one. I told him I wanted you to get a good long rest. Guess he took me literally."

"But damn it, Frank, how does that make the members of my crew, an', an' the other 509th crews feel? I get preferential treatment and they don't?"

"Actually, everybody got the day off, Ben. You all got pretty badly mauled yesterday, so I took the 509th off the duty roster and told all crews to sleep in. Besides, you brought back some beaten up old birds. Our maintenance crews have been working all night to get them airworthy. Uh, by the way, *Buxom Baby* won't be one of them. She sustained some fatal damage—wing spar, engines, tail spar, etc.— that our crews won't be able to repair. Don't know how you and Evans kept her in the air long enough to get home."

Ben winced. "Have you told Bennett yet?"

"He gets back from leave tonight. We're promised three new B-17Gs. Be delivered tomorrow. He'll get the first one. That ought to help soften the blow."

"How about me, Frank?" Ben joked. "I need to replace ol' *Round Trip*, ya know."

Frank glared at him. "Nice try, Ben, but you know you aren't getting your own airplane. Won't be flying enough missions to warrant that. You'll take someone else's airplane like I do."

Ben grinned and shrugged. "Okay, okay. Poor joke on my part. So what do the post mission photos show? We gonna have to go back to Regensburg again?"

"Not for a while, maybe never," Silverman said. "Our bombardiers did a damn good job of sorting through the camouflage, and you destroyed a major portion of the 262 final assembly operation. Intel estimates it could take three to four months to clear the new wreckage and get the line going again. And they may not have the material or man power to accomplish that."

Silverman rummaged in the pile of papers on his desk and produced a document. "I've put you in for another Distinguished Service Cross—you'll get a bar on the one you were awarded for the first Regensburg mission. Good job, Ben," he said, reaching across the desk to shake Ben's hand. "I've requested a special presentation ceremony with Doolittle at Pine Tree."

"Just doin' my duty, Frank. Please don't make a big deal of the medal thing. I'll accept it gratefully, but only in the name of my crew. And I hope you put them all in for an Air Medal."

Ben called Gwen that night and had a long heartfelt talk. He told her about the second Regensburg mission, leaving out the uglier details. Gwen wept tears of relief throughout their conversation, repeatedly telling him how thankful she was that he had survived without injury. He spent much of the time reassuring her that he was well and emphasizing that he would not be flying a lot of missions.

The 509th returned to operational status three days later and was listed on the mission-ready ledger. The massive destruction they had wreaked on the 262 assembly plant meant limited numbers of the hot jet fighters would be available to replace combat losses. Meanwhile, Allied fighter commanders devised tactics to counter the aircraft, which severely outmatched their best propeller-driven fighters. One of the most effective tactics involved Allied fighters orbiting near the Luftwaffe's 262 home bases and attacking the jets as they returned for refueling, catching them when they were low and slow in the landing pattern. Eighth Air Force bombers also increased attacks on German oil facilities at Zeitz and the Leuna synthetic oil refineries at Merseburg, further crippling 262 units that required specially processed fuels.

Ben made peace with Bennett, who named his new B-17G *Buxom Baby Two.* He thanked Ben for bringing his crew back safely. "We joined the 509th as a full crew a year and a half ago, delivering a new B-17. We've flown twenty-seven missions, lost two of our original crew, but your mission makes it twenty-eight for them. I'm determined to keep 'em alive 'til they do their thirty and get their tickets home."

"Way to go. May your future be filled with only milk runs," Ben responded with a grin.

The 509th was alerted two days later for a tactical mission against a major rail center in Germany east of the main battle line. Ben conducted the premission briefing. It looked like a relatively easy mission with minimal fighter or flak defenses anticipated. Ben watched from the control tower balcony as nineteen of the group's B-17s thundered off to the southeast. He then returned to his office and settled into the routine of sweating out their return.

He pulled out and reread his mother's latest letter, smiling at all the news from the home front. His father was still totally immersed in his job, which had him working almost full time at the Willow Run plant. Joe was settled in his training job at the marine's Camp Pendleton base in California and enjoying it very much. This didn't jibe with Joe's letters to Ben in which he said was about to go nuts with the boring training job and was pestering headquarters for another combat assignment.

The phone rang. "Tower, Colonel. Today's mission inbound from Dover." Ben thanked the caller and said he'd be right down. He stopped by Frank's office. "They're inbound, Frank. I'm headed for the tower. Wanna join me?"

Five minutes later, they gathered with several other officers on the tower balcony. "Any word on the numbers?" Frank asked. "Think eighteen, Colonel." All eyes strained upward as the first B-17 droned into view and the count began. "I get eighteen," Silverman said quietly. Several others agreed.

"Who didn't make it?" Ben asked.

"Uh, Bennett, sir. *Buxom Baby Two.*"

Ben clutched the balcony railing, then hammered it with his fist.

Chapter 31

FORTUNES OF WAR

Ben drummed his fingers on the table in the ops center briefing room. He never liked these post mission review sessions, always in a smoke-filled room. The review of his recent brutal mission over Regensburg had dragged on for nearly two hours. *Too much Monday morning quarterbacking. Should have done this, should have done that. Boils down to one thing, you hadda be there and face it real time.*

"What it looks like is that Captain Bennett and *Buxom Baby Two* took some serious hits from fighters on the way into the target," Captain Jones, the 509th intelligence officer, said. "According to several gunners' accounts, at least one engine was hit and maybe some controls were damaged. Whatever, they drifted out of the right-rear corner of the defensive box. Luftwaffe fighters jumped them beyond the effective range of the guns from the remaining B-17s in the formation box. Several gunners said Me 262 jet fighters may have been involved in the final attack. They hit the right-wing root with concentrated fire, the wing folded, and *Buxom Baby Two* spun into the overcast and disappeared. No one saw any chutes."

A pencil snapped like a rifle shot. Ben was shocked to see two halves of a pencil in his hands. He quickly dropped the pieces and pushed them away.

"Damn shame," someone mumbled. "Crew gets a brand new B-17G, and we lose 'em on its first mission."

"You sound like you're more worried about losing a brand new B-17G!" Ben shouted. "That's utter bullshit! The goddamn airplane can be replaced without a problem. This was a crew of ten fine men. Ten men who were on their twenty-ninth mission. One more, and they'd have been outta this rotten war and on their way home! Another goddamned waste!"

Ben abruptly pushed back his chair and strode out of the room.

Silverman adjourned the meeting and followed Ben to his office. "What the hell was that all about?" he demanded.

"Sorry, Frank. I shouldn't have blown my stack like that."

"You're right about that, Colonel," Frank snapped. "You also owe an apology to Olsen and the rest of the officers in that room. You know he was concerned about losing that crew! You're going to be their commander shortly, and you can't lose your temper and stalk out of the room anytime they give you bad news. What the hell got into you?"

"Frank, I am truly sorry. It was a dumb reaction. I'll apologize to them soon as we're done here. And I assure you, it won't happen again."

"I'm banking on that," Frank snapped.

"Not trying to excuse my behavior, but Bennett's crew performed over and above on our last trip to Regensburg. Saved my ass, if you really wanna know. I had a long heart-to-heart with Bennett afterward, and he thanked me for bringing them back under some tough circumstances. Hell, it was the other way around. They brought me back!"

Ben stood and paced the room. "It was what I took as an off-the-cuff remark about losing a brand new B-17G that set me off. Those guys were almost as close to going home heroes as my crew was. It's . . . it's just so goddamned unfair to have them get it that close to completing their tour."

"It's too easy for me to pass it off with some trite phrase like, 'Nobody said it was going to be fair,'" Frank said quietly. "In retrospect, I should have held firm and not let you fly that damn Regensburg mission. Piled too much on you too soon after you returned. And the last twist of fate with the loss of *Buxom Baby Two* was the final straw."

"I should have been able to handle it, Frank. Gonna have to work that out before you leave, or I won't be fit to lead the 509th. Now if you'll excuse me, I gotta find the rest of the fellas involved in the briefing and personally apologize."

"That's a swell idea, to borrow one of your favorite words," Silverman agreed. "But do it as their future commander. Don't grovel."

Ben mended fences with his headquarters colleagues and set about learning how to effectively manage the 509th. The weather

185

had soured into a colder-and-drearier-than-usual English winter. An extended soggy cold front descended all across England and most of the European continent and lingered. Leaden skies and thick fog blanketed the entire region, and snow accumulated on the hills and mountains. When the weather cleared sufficiently at Eighth Air Force bases across England to permit takeoffs, the 509th joined other groups on missions led by Pathfinder B-17s that used H2X radars to find the targets through the clouds.

These missions were unopposed by Luftwaffe fighters grounded by the weather, and German antiaircraft units were equally hampered by the thick drizzling overcast. But the capricious weather patterns in England posed risks to the returning bomber groups. Often, they found the weather had deteriorated behind them, closing their home bases and forcing them to flail about, looking for emergency strips on which to land. Several serious midair collisions prompted Pine Tree to suspend further missions until the weather cleared.

Frank and Ben took advantage of the groundings to issue numerous two- and three-day passes to 509th personnel. Initially, this helped boost the group's flagging morale. But more than a few airmen, bent on venting their frustrations with boisterous drinking matches and drunken fistfights, created a swath of badly damaged bars and pubs stretching from Parham to London.

"I don't begrudge them having a good time, blowing off some steam. That's necessary," Frank fumed, "but this has gone too damn far. We're going to lose some good people to 'noncombat' injuries if we don't rein them in. And I'm about out of ideas for hiding pub repair costs in our maintenance budget."

"Should I cancel all further passes and leave?" Ben asked.

"Let's move slowly. Cut back on the number we're issuing and hope this rotten weather improves so we can focus their anger and frustration on the enemy."

Ben grunted his approval and began riffling through the pass files.

"Speaking of frustrations, Ben, we haven't let you off the leash for a while," Frank said. "It's about time we got you over to Cambridge to visit Lady Gwen, as Reggie calls her. What's her schedule? She have some time off due her?"

"Been meaning to talk to you about that," Ben said. "Talked to her last night, and she has next weekend off. Thought maybe I'd ask for a two-day pass and spend it with her."

"Yours for the asking," Frank responded. "Set it up and, uh, good luck," he added with a grin.

"Thanks, Frank. Uh, now how about you? You haven't had a break since I got back. Haven't you got someplace to go? And maybe somebody to go with?"

Frank flashed him a thin smile. "Wish I did on both counts."

"You know, Frank," Ben said, "long as I've known you, I don't know anything about your personal life. Hope I'm not prying, but do you have a lady friend anywhere?"

"I do, Ben, and you aren't prying. Lady's name is Rachel. She's a lieutenant in the Women's Army Corp, serving with the Fifteenth Air Force. She's an air traffic controller. Was based in Benghazi, Libya, but now she's in Italy. Haven't seen her since we left the States. We write regularly and talk once in a while on the radio phone, but as you know, it ain't the same."

"Can't you come up for some excuse to make a flying visit to Fifteenth headquarters?" Ben asked. "And hey, what about getting involved in those shuttle missions where we hit targets deep in Southern Germany and then fly on to bases in Italy for refueling and rearming?"

"I'm working on it." Frank grinned.

Ben fidgeted through another wet gloomy week until Friday when he commandeered a jeep from the motor pool and headed for Cambridge. He whistled happily as cold rain swirled around the jeep's flimsy side curtains. The weather failed to dampen his spirits. He'd soon be warmed by Gwen. She answered his knock, leapt into his arms, and clung to him as he carried her into the bedroom.

Chapter 32

THE WAR DRAGS ON – DECEMBER, 1944

As the year wound to a close, deteriorating weather drove morale throughout the Eighth Air Force to a low ebb. The Luftwaffe had been beaten on all fronts. Allied air forces owned the skies over most of Europe, including Germany, and Axis ground troops suffered merciless poundings from the air. Massive day raids by Eighth and Fifteenth Air Force bombers, matched by RAF Bomber Command's night raids, wreaked devastation on Germany's cities and industrial infrastructures. The Luftwaffe also lost hundreds of irreplaceable fighters and experienced pilots in the swirling aerial battles. But just as the Allied air forces prepared to deliver the coup de grâce, leaden weather closed the skies across Europe, giving the Luftwaffe badly needed time to regroup and reequip.

Republic P-47D Fighter

It also gave Germany's oil industry time to repair their badly pummeled production facilities. Allied bombers persistently attacked the more than ninety oil refineries dispersed across Germany and in occupied territories, seriously damaging two-thirds of them and leaving only three fully functioning. Those supplying the special synthetic fuel needed by the Me 262 jet fighters were especially hit hard, further limiting the effectiveness of this advanced aircraft that posed such a serious threat to Allied bombers.

"Damn it!" Frank exploded at a meeting with his staff. "Just as we were about to drive a stake through the Luftwaffe's heart, the weather closes in and gives them time to lick their wounds. We might not get another chance like this until spring."

As usual, Reggie hove onto the scene and provided some badly needed distraction. Ben answered his phone, which had not rung for two days.

"Top o' the morning, old bean," Reggie chortled. "Can I interest you in a little diversion? Like a reunion of the Giraffes in Olde Londontowne?" Reggie said he had been talking with the three other members of their escapee band and discovered that both Captain Banner and Lieutenant Kowalski were scheduled to return to the United States for upgrade training. Banner was moving up to the B-29, and Kowalski from the P-51 to the P-38 twin-engine fighter.

"Assume both'll be reassigned to the Pacific Theater," Reggie said. "Your marines have captured islands close enough to the Jap's main island to permit regular bombing attacks as far north as Tokyo with B-29s escorted by the long-range P-38s. Not sure I'd like that mission. Too damn much overwater flying to suit me."

Ben cleared his throat. "Me either. I really wanna finish the war here against Germany. Hope I can stay put until then. Maybe even extend to help wrap things up after we get ridda Hitler and his buncha bandits."

"Would Lady Gwen be a factor in your decision?" Reggie asked.

"Damn right! I aim to marry that lady and take her home with me, if that's all right with you."

"Couldn't be happier for both of you, Sancho. Now then, concerning our last reunion before the Giraffes scatter, newly promoted Squadron Leader Whitford also is eager to join us. Nobody's doing much flying, what with the wretched weather, so what the hell, time to have a bit of fun. Any of these dates look good for you?"

189

Reggie offered several dates on which he and the other three could get three-day passes. Ben said he could match one, and they agreed on a hotel. "Save one evening for a proper 'Hinglish' dinner at Simpson's-in-the-Strand, London's world-famous restaurant," Reggie said. "Been serving the best beef known to mankind since 1828. Bit pricey, but as I told the other lads, this'll be my shout. My way of saying thanks for putting your lives on the line to help save Merry Olde England."

"Reggie, that's very generous," Ben said, "but you don't have to do that. I can pay my own way. Don't have anything else to spend my puny army pay on except a few beers at the Officer's Club and my dates with Gwen."

"My treat, me boy, and there's an end to it."

The Giraffes staged a raucous reunion in the lobby of London's Wellington Hotel and after a round of handshakes and backslapping, adjourned to the bar. The volume reached a crescendo after five rounds in the drinking marathon as the Giraffes vied to be first in relating their experiences since returning to operations.

"Lissen up, you buncha yahoos!" Ben finally bellowed. "I have the story that'll top all your exaggerations and lies! Let's have a little quiet."

"Ah, Sir Benjamin bids us harken to him," Reggie mocked. "Do tell, sire. We humble bastards are at your service."

"That's more like it," Ben sniffed. "You know what mission got me blown outta the sky and landed me in the Kraut cage with you miserable curs, right?"

"*Regensburg!*" they shouted in unison.

"Right! And when I got back 'ome, as knave Reginald would say, I worked very hard to get back in shape. Then made Silverman promise after we completed the intel briefing, I could lead the next mission. He said I'd have to wait 'til the Russians liberated Poland so as not to expose the Polish underground if I was shot down again and interrogated by the Gestapo."

"Liberated!" Reggie yelled. "Wrong word, Sancho. Bloody Russians already are occupying much of Poland and treating the Poles worse than the Krauts."

"Okay, okay," Ben said. "Point is, if I got shot down and interrogated, the Germans would be able to retaliate against our friends in the Polish underground. Anyway, Frank was reluctant to even discuss when I could get back on operations, but I insisted we keep it open.

So soon as we returned from the intel briefing, I reported in ready for duty. All requirements had been met. Russians controlled Poland, so I was clear. Came on a bit strong, but remember, we'd had a long liquid lunch after telling our escape stories to the brass, so I was a bit fulla myself."

Ben steadied himself by holding on to the bar. "Well, sirs, the 509th was alerted the day I got back to Parham. Was a biggie. So I said to Frank, 'Great, perfect timing.' I'm ready to lead it. He began hemmin' and hawin', so I said I was damn well holding him to his promise. Now that I think about it, I was more than bordering on insubordination. Dumb-ass mistake. Still need to apologize to Frank for that set to. But great gent that he is, Frank overlooked that and relented. So I asked what the target was." Ben convulsed in laughter.

"Frank gave me a sad hound dog look and said, *"Regensburg!"* I nearly pissed my pants, but a deal is a deal. So two days later, I led the 509th back to Regensburg." His four companions roared with laughter.

Kowalski shouted. "Didja make it home this time?"

"I'm here, ain't I?" Ben said. "Flew a borrowed airplane *Buxom Baby* and brought it back as fulla holes as a Swiss cheese. But we made it with the help of a great copilot. Nobody wounded. And we left Willie Messerschmitt's 262 factory a smokin' pile of rubble!"

This prompted a round of cheers. Ben signaled for silence. "But lemme tell ya the kicker." He launched into a blow-by-blow account of the entire trip, capping it with a graphic description of losing two flak-damaged engines over the target.

"We were limpin' home on two engines when a third one started crapping out," Ben continued. "Our flight engineer, damn fine fella, nursed it along, and we made it to Parham for a straight-in landing approach. On touchdown, the third engine packed it in, and damned if the last one didn't backfire and quit as we rolled off the runway onto the taxiway."

Ben blinked and swallowed hard. "After we stopped, my copilot and I sat starin' through the windshield. Couldn't get outta our seats. *Buxom Baby* was so beat up, they scrapped it."

"I say, Sancho, that was cutting it damn close," Reggie said seriously. "You okay now?"

"Oh yeah, I'm fine. Had a great crew. Uh, they, uh, saved my ass with great teamwork, especially the gunners. They had two more missions to go to get their tickets home." He turned to the bar and reached for his drink, deciding not to tell them what happened to the crew on their next-to-last mission flying in *Buxom Baby Two*, their replacement bomber.

The other four Giraffes clamored to tell their stories.

"Can't say as I can top that, Benjamin old lad," Whitford chimed in, "but when I went operational again on my Typhoon, I was restricted to flying over the battle line. Same restriction as yours, Ben. We pretty much had control of the skies over much of Europe. Had the hell of a time attacking the Wehrmacht's ground troops and Panzer divisions all along the line. Felt good being able to concentrate on the ground targets without having to look over my shoulder for Jerries. We really gave 'em what for."

Designed in 1938, the single-seat Typhoon, nicknamed Tiffy in the RAF, was first deployed as a fighter. It was soon outclassed by Germany's front line Me 109 and Fw 190 fighters, and British Air Ministry officials considered scrapping the fighter. But they reevaluated its heavy payload capability and changed its mission to ground attack. The full armament load included four 20 mm cannons, two five-hundred-pound bombs, and eight wing-mounted RP-3 rockets with sixty-pound warheads. By late 1944, the Typhoon had become one of the most effective ground attack aircraft in World War 2.

"On my second mission, we joined a gaggle of Tiffys patrolling the main battle line and raised holy hell with the Jerries on the ground," Whitford continued. "We had RT contact with our ground troops, and they called us in for close air support where they needed it."

He began waving his hands as he described their latest attack. "We came in hot and low, using hilly terrain to mask our approach, and popped up at the last minute. Caught a line of Panzer Krauts with their knickers down. They were maneuvering behind the lines and about to launch an armored spearhead attack on our troops. They scrambled to set up their defenses, but they didn't see or hear us coming until too late. We knocked out at least ten tanks. Like you blokes from the colonies say, shootin' fish in a barrel."

Not to be outdone, Kowalski said how much he enjoyed getting back into his P-51 saddle. "While I was away at camp," he said with a sly grin, "my group reequipped with the B model powered by the Packard V-1650-3 version of the Brits' Rolls Royce Merlin engine swinging a four-bladed prop. Man, what an improvement over the P-51A! By the time I got back, the Luftwaffe's fighter command had been pretty much knocked on its collective ass. But I still got in some good licks. Bomber escort sure got a lot easier. Then Doolittle released us to attack ground targets at will on our homeward flights. That's been a blast. I nailed two trains last week. Sorry ass of a squadron commander wouldn't let me paint locomotives on the fuselage next to my aerial kills. Now I'm looking forward to transitioning into the P-38 . . ."

He held up his hand, sipped his drink, and continued, "P-38's a big twin-engine bastard, but I'm told it's a sweet handling machine and fast. Probably headed for the Pacific after training. Not sure I look forward to all that overwater flying, but it'll be a new experience escorting B-29s."

He peered into his drink. "Wonder how the Jap pilots will compare with the Kraut flyers we've been facing?"

Banner, the least vocal of the five, stared silently into the distance.

"I say, Archie, are you with us or somewhere else?" Reggie asked.

"Huh? Oh, not much excitement for me," Banner muttered. "Not like Ben's experience at Regensburg. Most recent missions have been against rail yards, but we've made a couple of attacks against oil refineries. Went after the Merseburg refinery complex in Leuna last week. Didn't face much from the Luftwaffe, and the flak was really light. Made us think the Krauts might be runnin' outta gas and ammunition." He scratched his head. "Guess my mind's on gettin' back to the States. Have a gal in St. Louis I'm anxious to see. Hope I get some leave before startin' B-29 school."

"All well and good," Reggie said. "Afraid I haven't anything exciting to share. I've been flying a bloody desk more than my Spit. Have a lot of new blokes coming in, and I'm spending an inordinate amount of time babysitting them. Would you believe this late in the war, we're still getting young lads with minimal time in Spits, some as little as twenty hours and absolutely no combat training or experience?" He shook his head. "We faced that in '40 and '41 during the height of the Battle of Britain when we suffered significant losses from our small band of pilots, but I don't understand why we have such a pilot shortage now."

They drank in silence until Ben turned to the group. "Dunno about you fellas, but I'm bushed and probably had too much to drink. I'm for calling it a night and ordering a sandwich in my room. We can carouse some more tomorrow and then cap it off with Reggie's dinner at Simpson's."

Everyone agreed to meet for a late breakfast at 0700 hours, a welcome respite from their customary 0400 hours.

The repast presented in the Wellington breakfast room was overwhelming. Too many choices! All five Giraffes looked like they had slept well, but there were subtle hints they all had drunk too much the night before. Ben whispered a warning to the other two Americans about the dried fish kipper thing and the blood sausage. But he highly recommended everything else.

After they pushed back from the table and sipped their coffee, Reggie addressed the group. "All right, gents, what's your pleasure? Anyone interested in a quick tour of central Londontowne?"

"I could do with a nice long nap," Kowalski grunted as he stretched and yawned. "Haven't relaxed like this in a long time."

"Come now, this may be your last time in London," Reggie insisted. "Must see the major sights, or at least what's left of some of them."

Ben, remembering the whirlwind London tours Reggie had led him on just before war was declared in 1939, said he was game to revisit Parliament, Westminster, Buckingham Palace, the Horse Guards, and maybe St. Paul's. "But let's not try to cover the whole damn town in one day."

"Right ho!" Reggie exclaimed, smacking his palm on the table. "Might point out that your list of stops still is a bit ambitious. However, let's make it a mini-tour of the high spots. Then we catch a quick pub lunch, so Ben can have his favorite Scotch egg, and get back here for a nap before we head to Simpson's. Table is booked for 2030 hours."

Ben was struck by how bedraggled London looked. When he arrived late the night before, he hadn't noticed the dull gray bleakness of the sections the Luftwaffe bombers had devastated in their nightly attacks. Now that the blitz had shifted into a new phase, Hitler's latest terror weapons, the V-1 buzz bombs and the V-2 ballistic missiles, struck London in daylight. It was relatively easy to detect the V-1 subsonic flying bombs and antiaircraft gunners and RAF fighters successfully shot many down.

But the V-2s, Hitler's second-generation terror weapons, posed a new threat against which there was no defense. These forty-six-foot-tall guided missiles, powered by a single-rocket engine burning a mixture of ethanol and water for fuel and liquid oxygen as the oxidizer, weighed 28,000 pounds and carried 2,200-pound warheads of high-explosive Amatol. They lofted the warheads to an altitude of sixty miles and onto suborbital trajectories that sent the missiles crashing into central London and later the Dutch port city of Antwerp. They streaked in at supersonic speeds of over 1,800 miles per hour, blasting whole neighborhoods before they were seen or heard.

Despite the depressing atmosphere the five encountered in many areas, Reggie rallied the group on a tour of London's major points, stopping for a passable pub lunch and concluding with a visit to St. Paul's Cathedral. "Amazing thing about St. Paul's is how it escaped major damage while entire neighborhoods around it were blasted into smoldering rubble," he said. "The photographs of the cathedral's magnificent dome standing defiantly amid a sea of smoke and flame lifted the spirits of the citizens of this fair land. Rallied many others throughout the free world, I shouldn't think. Gave us all hope we'd indeed prevail."

The other four nodded thoughtfully.

"Right then," Reggie said. "Let's head back to the Wellington for a pint and put our feet up for a bit. Meet in the lobby at 2000 hours."

Reggie led the group into Simpson's elegant, oak-paneled dining room and fussed with the maître d' over the table selection. Once settled, he announced he would take charge of menu. "You lot are to just sit there and savor some of England's finest cuisine," he announced. "Dunno how they do it, but somehow, Simpson's maintains its standards despite the shortages and rationing."

Turning to the headwaiter, he detailed the menu. "We'll begin with your famous London Particular ham and split pea soup followed by roast rib of Scottish beef with accompanying roasted potatoes, cabbage, Yorkshire pudding, and generous dollops of the finest English horseradish. Umm, let's add a side dish of honey roasted parsnips."

In an aside to the other four, he explained that, "Simpson's Scottish beef is guaranteed to be aged for twenty-eight days, has been in war and peace since the early 1800s. It will be carved at table on one of their antique silver-domed trollies, so you can select your particular cut."

Again, addressing the headwaiter, Reggie continued, "We'll need an English garden salad with an assortment of breads and then top it off with Simpson's English pudding sampler." Glancing at Ben, he muttered, "No, Ben, it isn't anything like a steak and kidney pudding."

Reggie continued, "We'll also have your British farmhouse cheese platter. Now as to the wines, we'll start with two well-chilled bottles of Andre Dezat Loire Sancerre to accompany the starter, then two bottles of Marquis de Bellefont Bordeaux, at least to begin with to support the beef, and a Chateauneuf du Pape to wash down the cheese."

Reggie paused and pursed his lips as he continued to study the wine list. "And let's cap the feast with a fine cognac. Umm, Courvoisier Cognac Napoleon should do nicely. And strong black coffee. I should think that'll keep us occupied for the evening."

The headwaiter, who had been scribbling furiously, raised his eyebrows, bowed to Reggie, and glided away. The four Giraffes sat openmouthed.

"Is all this just for us?" Kowalski blurted. "Or will there be a bunch of banquet guests joining us?"

"Steady on." Reggie chuckled. "This is my gift to you lads for your loyal service to God, England, and the free world. We'll take our time with each course, and you'll be surprised how well it'll all go down."

A muted Westminster clock chimed 11:30 p.m.—2330 hours. They had been at it for three hours. The five breathed a collective satiated sigh and dropped their napkins beside their coffee cups.

"Hope they'll have somebody ready to carry me outta here," Banner muttered. "Mind if I have a smoke? I mean, is it allowed in these august surroundings?" Reggie nodded.

"S'pose we could now retire for another cognac and cigars in the lounge," Whitford joked. "Truth to be told, I'd probably set myself on fire. Do believe I'll need someone to carry me 'ome as well."

"Never had a feast like this and don't expect I ever will again," Ben said. "Reggie, I can't thank you enough for an unbelievable meal." The four responded with halfhearted "hear, hears" and thumped the table.

Their taxi rides back to the Wellington passed in a blur.

Reality reared its ugly head when the five gathered in the breakfast room the next morning. Banner and Kowalski were short-timers due to ship out to the States in the next week or so. The odyssey they had shared was about to end. After a relatively light breakfast, the five gathered in the lobby, paid their bills, and stood looking at each other like tongue-tied school boys.

Reggie broke the silence. "Gents, we've been through a great deal together, and I shan't forget any of you. I wish you all Godspeed and good luck as we see this bloody war through to a finish. We all have each other's mailing addresses. Let's bloody well use them."

He then shook hands with Banner and Kowalski and wished them well in their new assignments. All shared bear hugs and muttered good lucks and turned to go their separate ways. As Ben headed for the door, Reggie called out. "Umm, Ben, can I see you for a moment?"

He pulled Ben aside. "I say, old bean, could you and the Lady Gwen manage to join us at Calvert Hall for Christmas? Might be a bit thin what with all the rationing, but I think Mum can manage something nice with cook."

"Reggie, I'd really like that," Ben said. "Can't speak for Gwen, but I'm sure I can get a three-day pass. I'll ask her soon as I get back to Parham." He paused. "Uh, s'pose this'll be a dressy affair, and uh, I dunno if Gwen has any formal gowns . . ."

"Don't give it another thought, Sancho. We're at war, doncha know? Her nurse's dress uniform will do just fine. Same goes for you. Class A uniform. No need to get all gussied up in a penguin suit." Reggie paused. "I say, what about Frank? Could you both get off station at the same time? Would love to have him join us. Meet the family. Relax a bit."

"Not sure about that, Reggie. I dunno whether Frank celebrates Christmas. He's Jewish, you know. Anyway, I have a feeling he's gonna be transferred out soon. Could well be before Christmas."

"I know Frank's Jewish, Ben. Still, thought he might join us for the secular part of the celebration.

"Pity we'll be losing him. He's become a wonderful friend. But then that makes you the top honcho, right? Nice way to cap you war, eh? Commander of the 509th Heavy Bombardment Group that helped 'bomb the shit out of Germany,' as you said you wanted to do some years ago."

"Yeah, not proud of expressin' it quite like that, but I guess you're right. I'm ready to take command, and I think I can do a good job of carryin' on in Frank's place."

Ben blinked. "But I'm damn sure gonna miss flying with Frank. We go back a long ways, you know."

"Do, indeed, Ben, do, indeed," Reggie said. He clapped Ben on the back, and they parted.

Chapter 33

DISASTER LOOMS

Fog blanketed Parham when Ben's driver maneuvered his jeep through the front gate. "Welcome home, Colonel," the driver said. "Not much action around here while you were gone. Wonder if we'll ever see the sun again?"

"Hope so and soon," Ben replied. "We've got some unfinished business with Germany."

Frank was at his desk when Ben walked into the 509th headquarters building. "Welcome home, wanderer," Frank said, gesturing Ben to a chair. "Cut a wide swath through London with your Giraffe band? You don't look any the worse for wear."

"Hello, Frank. Yeah, it was a great reunion. Thank you for letting me take some more time off to join the fellas."

"No problem, nothing doing here," Frank said, rising from his chair and grunting as he stretched his back muscles. "I've been sitting here doing paperwork for so long I'm getting a hump like the Hunchback of Notre-Dame."

"Well, now that I'm back, I can take some of that burden off of you," Ben said."

"Good," Frank said, turning to peer at the gray mist swirling past the window. "You're soon going to take on the full load, Ben. I got my orders. I'm to wrap up things here in ten days and head back home. The assignment to lead the new B-29 wing has come through along with the promotion to BG."

"Congratulations, Frank!" Ben shouted and rose to shake Silverman's hand. "Well deserved new assignment and promotion.

Damn, now that you're a general, does that mean I hafta show you more respect?"

"No more than you have so far." Frank laughed. "And by the way, this means you're promoted to full colonel and named commander of the 509th. Congratulations all around. Change of command ceremony is next week."

"Hot damn!" Ben said. "I'm ready." He frowned. "But this means you can't join us for Christmas at Calvert Hall, umm, that is, I mean, uh, do you celebrate Christmas?" Ben stammered.

"I celebrate the secular part of the holiday," Frank said. "'Bout as much as anyone does these days, I suppose."

Ben squirmed and looked uncomfortable. "Well, you see, Reggie invited Gwen and me to join his family at Calvert Hall and then said he wondered if both of us—you and me—could get off the base at the same time so you could join the party an' . . ."

"I appreciate the invitation, and I'll tell Reggie so," Frank said. "But I'll be out of here before Christmas. Meanwhile, I'd like to get a few more licks in against Germany before I leave. Weatherman says this stalled front may move on possibly by tomorrow."

He waved his arm around the office. "So now this will soon be all yours, Colonel. Get to it. Let's discuss your replacement as deputy commander." Frank heartily endorsed Ben's choice of Major Joe Atkins, 509th Operations Officer.

Business finished, Ben turned to Frank. "Can I buy you a drink at the Officer's Club? I want to toast your new promotion and ask you about something I've been pondering for some time." Frank nodded and rose from his desk.

On his second beer, Ben cleared his throat. "Frank, I've been thinking about our enemy the German pilots we've been flying against since Spain and now in the big war."

"Yeah, what about them?"

"Well, a lot of us, should say most of us, call 'em a lotta names—bastards, Krauts, Nazis, stuff like that. But I've been wondering what they're really like. I mean, they go out every day and fight like they're ordered to do same as us. Most of 'em are pretty good pilots. I can verify that from my Battle of Britain experience and later."

Ben sipped his beer. "You know, I've been thinking about the 109 pilot who shot me down during the Battle of Britain. I bailed outta my Spitfire and was dangling in my chute when he came zooming back toward me. I thought, Damn, is he gonna strafe me? You know, like what happened to Ted in Spain. But he circled around me and tossed me a salute. I was pretty pissed off and gave him this return salute." Ben raised the single digit in his right hand.

"Now I'm thinking maybe he was tossing me a real salute, you know, like the knights of old saluting someone they'd just knocked off his horse. Am I making any sense, Frank?"

"You are, Ben. I've given this some thought as well, and you may be right. I haven't had any personal experience with captured Luftwaffe pilots, but I've heard from pilots who have that they've been impressed with the code of honor some of them follow, even this late in the war. The Luftwaffe is known for its negative attitude toward the Nazi party and its contempt for Reichmarshal Goering in particular, so it really is incorrect to classify them all as Nazis bastards. Some of 'em may be party zealots but not like in the SS or Gestapo or anything like that."

He paused thoughtfully. "You and I know we should treat them with respect, especially for their skills as airmen, but I don't think those sentiments are shared by many of the new fellows coming into this game. Our propaganda machine has branded all the Germans as Nazi criminals, so I guess it's to be expected that most of our soldiers will continue to think of them as such. Something we'll have to live with." Ben grunted his agreement and finished his beer.

Ben phoned Gwen that night and relayed Reggie's invitation. "Oh, Ben, that sounds like it would be a grand time!" she gushed. "But umm, there might be a problem for me . . ."

"What kinda problem?" Ben interrupted. "Can't you get a Christmas pass? I mean, you've been workin' long shifts, sometimes seven days a week. Surely they can spare you for a coupla days over Christmas, especially with so many of us grounded."

"It's not that, love," Gwen said softly. "It's just that, umm, I . . ."

"What, Gwen? You don't want to go?"

"No, no, Ben. Please don't misunderstand. I do so want to go. It's just that Reggie's family is part of, umm, you know, the aristocracy, and I'm not certain I could fit in."

"Fit in!" Ben sputtered. "What the hell are you, uh, excuse me, Gwen, what are you talking about? 'Course you'd fit in. You're beautiful, you have good manners, and you know how to meet people. I don't understand."

"Ben, dear Ben. I suppose you really don't understand, coming from America where there are fewer class barriers. But look at it from my perspective. Reggie's father is a peer, Lord Percy, and his mum is

Lady Percy. You met my mum, God rest her soul. I loved her dearly, and I'm not complaining, but that's my background. Reggie's family is in another realm."

"But, Gwen, that's utter bull—uh . . . that's nonsense. I promise you that won't make one bit of difference to any of them. If Reggie had any idea it'd be a problem, he wouldn't have insisted that you come with me."

She was silent for a moment. Just as Ben was about to ask if she was still on the line, she spoke softly, "All right, Ben, if you're certain. You know how much I'd love to go with you. Can I think on it a bit?"

"Sorry, no. I want you to commit now and put in for your leave tomorrow."

"All right, love," she said quietly.

They chatted for a little while, said good night, and rang off. Ben sat pondering their conversation. "Class barriers?" he muttered. "Damn, never thought of that. I'll make sure that doesn't come up." He paced the room. "One thing for sure," he snarled, "if that prick cousin of Reggie's, whatshisname Brewster, looks down the long side of his nose at Gwen, I'll bust it right then and there!"

The foul weather continued, and the Giraffes were called upon to take their escape-dog-and-pony show on the road. They briefed flight crews from a range of units on their experiences and assured them there were several clandestine routes home should they be shot down over enemy territory. The dull routines of the briefings were becoming unbearable when the meteorologists forecast a break in the weather. The Giraffes gleefully headed for their home bases.

At Parham, the men of the 509th emerged, blinking in the unfamiliar sunshine like bears waking from hibernation. Silverman toured the base on a last inspection and informed his subordinates of his new assignment and the change in command. He told everyone to prepare for the resumption of operations before the weather closed in again.

Ben sat hunched at his headquarters desk when the phone rang, snapping him out of a daydream featuring Gwen. He snatched up the phone.

"It's 509th, Findlay," he said.

"Ben, this is Bradley at Pine Tree. Got tomorrow's field order. Should be comin' over the teletype as we speak. Uh, thought I'd prepare you. You ain't gonna like it." Colonel Bradley, Eighth Air Force's Division 2 deputy operations officer was one of Ben's closest friends, a regular drinking buddy and fierce handball opponent when they had time to play.

"Yeah?" Ben said warily as he headed for the teletype machine. "What is it, and why ain't I gonna like it?"

"As you'll see, it's that hardened V-2 production site at Nordhausen again, ol' buddy. The top brass has ordered that it be wiped out once an' for all and told General Davis to get the job done, period! Doolittle is back in the back in the States for high-level meetings with General Spaatz, so Davis has been tasked with managing the mission."

Ben groaned. Davis, newly appointed Eighth Air Force Director of Operations, would feel intense pressure to destroy Nordhausen, a key production facility for the V-2 ballistic missiles, and Ben knew the general's reputation for passing that pressure on to his subordinates.

"Not that godforsaken place again," Ben grunted. "We've hit that damn thing twice an' several other groups have attacked it as well. "Hard to hit it from twenty thousand feet and then many of our bombs bounce off the concrete-hardened assembly centers."

"Sorry, ol' buddy, but look closely at the field order," Bradley said. "You'll have an easier time hittin' 'em this time. You're goin' in at ten thousand feet."

"*What!*" Ben shouted as he scanned the field order. "Ten thousand! That's gotta be wrong, Brad. We'd be sittin' ducks. Those sites have some of the best flak defenses in the theater. The 88 mm gunners would pick us off at will!"

"Again, sorry, ol' buddy, but as you see, that's what's in the field order. I just wanted to call and give you a heads up, trying to ease the way, you know?"

"What goddamned fool thought this one up?" Ben shouted. "What the hell's wrong with you idiots up there? At ten thousand feet, this'll be a suicide mission. You gotta be out of your minds!"

"Easy there, pard, don't kill the messenger," Bradley snapped. "The top brass, an' I mean *top brass*, have a blowtorch aimed at Davis's ass. They're really pushing him to get this job done soonest so the Eighth can get back to its main mission of destroyin' the primary heavy industry and oil targets in Germany. The general's under pressure, an' he doesn't like it. So it's two-thousand-pound bombs and ten thousand feet. I know it sounds crazy, but that's what it is."

General Davis, who had a reputation for doing whatever he needed to satisfy his superiors, was known for reacting impulsively to pressure from above. His order specifying the ten-thousand-foot altitude was very much in character.

Ben snorted in disgust. "You better be prepared for some serious blowback from Frank and anyone else ordered to fly this damn fool mission."

"Look, Ben," Bradley implored, "we had one helluva row at the mission planning meeting. I tried my best to convince Davis this was a bad idea, like you say, a suicide mission. He exploded—you know his temper—told me to get the field order cut and transmitted to you and everyone else, or he'd have me arrested and charged with insubordination. Nothing I could do, so I cut the order. Sorry, pard, I had no choice. But I did want to call and warn you . . ."

"But goddamn it, Brad, this is stupid!" Ben yelled. "You can't expect . . ." Realizing he was yelling at his friend who had no choice but to relay the field order, Ben cut short his tirade. "Sorry, Brad. Look, I know it's not your fault. An' thanks for standin' up to Davis. I gotta find Silverman."

Ben worked the phone and caught up with Silverman at base maintenance.

"Uh, Frank, it's Ben. We're about to get the field order for tomorrow's mission. I just got a heads up call from Colonel Bradley at Pine Tree. An', uh, I think you better come up to your office."

"On my way," Silverman said and hung up the phone.

Five minutes later, he strode into the 509th headquarters. "The field order in yet?" he asked as Ben waved him into the office and closed the door.

"Yeah, it came over the teletype. Here it is."

"Why'd Bradley call to give you a heads up?" he asked, scanning the order. "Damn! It's Nordhausen again!"

"Look at the mission profile, Frank," Ben said quietly.

"Ten thousand feet!" Silverman shouted. "That has to be a mistake. Some idiot typed this up wrong!"

"Sorry, Frank. That's why Bradley called," Ben said. "He wanted to soften the shock, said it isn't a mistake. General Davis is being pressed to eliminate this target once and for all so we can get back to our main missions. Said the only way to do it is with two-thousand-pounders at ten thousand feet."

"The hell you say!" Silverman roared. "Damn fool doesn't know what he's talking about. How many missions have you seen him flying with us? *None!* He's nuts if he thinks I'm gonna send my group out on a suicide mission like this! I have to appeal this. If he refuses to change it, I might just have to tell him where he can stuff—"

"Uh, Frank, let's talk this over . . ." Ben started.

"Nothing to discuss, Ben! Get Pine Tree on the blower. I want to talk with Davis! I'll go over his head if I have to. Appeal directly to Doolittle."

"Won't be able to do that Frank. Doolittle's back in the States for meetings with the General Arnold, General Spaatz, and other top brass. Davis is in charge during his absence."

"Should have known that," Silverman snapped. "Doolittle wouldn't have authorized this if Davis had proposed it to him. Get me Pine Tree!"

Ben picked up the phone and asked for Pine Tree and General Davis. Bradley answered. "Ah, Brad, it's Ben. Colonel Silverman wants to talk to General Davis."

"I thought we might be gettin' a call, Ben. Hold on. I'll get the general."

Davis came on the line with his usual barked "General Davis!" Ben handed the phone to Silverman and eased out of the office, shutting the door behind him. Even without trying, he was able to hear both sides of the conversation. Silverman requested that the bombing altitude of ten thousand feet be reconsidered because bombing at the lower altitude courted disaster. Davis's shouted responses echoed through the door.

Frank must be holding the phone a foot away from his ear.

Finally, Ben heard Silverman slam the phone in its cradle. His office door burst open, and he signaled Ben inside.

"Well, that's that," Silverman fumed. "Davis rejected my appeal. Said he wouldn't consider it. We have to knock out this hardened target, and this was the only way to do it. Also told me to get my ass in gear, prepare for this mission, and oh, by the way, to lead it myself. A last honor before I turn over command of the 509th. Then said if I didn't get cracking on this and make it work, he'd court martial my ass right outta the army. The bastard! I should have told him what he can do with his three stars!"

Ben raised both hands in a calming motion. "Frank, please! I'm as pissed off as you are about this. It's crazy. But you're . . . We're under direct orders from Davis to fly this mission at ten thousand feet. A lot of other group commanders are as well. We don't have a choice. Let's try to make the best of it."

"You're right, Ben. Sorry about blowing my stack. Temper's been on a short fuse lately. I'm a little wrung out. Been keeping a tough pace these last six months. Haven't had any real rest."

"Yeah," Ben nodded. "I've seen the stress building in you. What can I do to take on more of the workload?"

"For starters, call Jack at ops and tell him to get going on the mission packages. Then call Harvey at the bomb depot and tell him we want two-thousand-pounders. At this range, we should be able to carry three per bomber. I'll call Murphy and see how many ships he can give me. I hope it's a full twenty-one. Want to show Davis what the 509th can do."

Chapter 34

RALLYING THE TROOPS

The 509th sprang into action. Operations assembled mission packages with maps, charts, and routings. Intelligence drafted the latest estimates on anticipated German fighter deployments and assessed the flak defenses along the route to and around the target. The news wasn't encouraging. The bomb depot began wheeling two-thousand-pound bombs to the B-17s in their dispersed revetments, rumbling past armor crews feeding .50-caliber ammunition into each B-17's arsenal of thirteen machine guns.

Technician crews rushed final service work on the last B-17s in for maintenance. They would have twenty-one available for the 0630 hours takeoff. As they rolled the final aircraft into their revetments, fueling crews snaked hoses around the bombers and pumped over three thousand gallons of high-octane fuel into their various wing and fuselage tanks. Silverman ordered the crews to bed early and set the wakeup call for 0430 hours.

By 0530 hours the next day, all was ready for the mission briefing. Silverman, Ben, and Major Atkins stood on the raised platform and faced the crews. The usual groans wafted from the assembled pilots, navigators, and bombardiers when Ben revealed the target. They were drowned out by shouts of disbelief when Silverman said they'd be bombing from ten thousand feet. One pilot from the rear of the briefing room yelled, "Who's the goddamned fool who ordered that? That's gotta be a mistake."

Silverman chose not to identify or respond directly to the shouter. "We've been ordered to attack at this lower altitude because our bomb dispersion from twenty thousand feet has been too great, and we're not penetrating the concrete-hardened command and assembly centers. That's also why we're carrying two-thousand-pounders.

"This mission will involve special risks, but Eighth Air Force command says we have to assume that and take out this damned target once and for all. I'm not happy about the altitude, but those are our orders. Let's get this job done, so we can shift back to our primary targets of Germany's heavy industry and oil production."

He also chose to ignore the muttered curses and expletives coursing through the assembly. "Let 'em piss and moan for a while, and then we'll get on with it," he whispered to Ben, who stood poised with a long wooden pointer in hand.

"Okay, okay! That's enough!" Silverman commanded. "Save your anger for the enemy. Tell your gunners to be extra sharp. I want every airplane to get through the fighter defenses and reach the target. And, bombardiers, I expect you all to nail those hardened sites. Don't want to have to go back to this target again!

"Now Major Atkins and I have some logistical issues to work out, so we'll let Colonel Findlay spell out details of the mission."

Ben called the group to attention and after Silverman and Atkins had marched out, ordered, "Rest!" The men sat and began muttering among themselves.

"All right, knock it off and listen up!" Ben growled. He listed the takeoff time of 0630 hours, cross-referenced the rendezvous points— they'd be joining an air armada of four hundred B-17s from twenty other heavy bombardment groups—and told them they'd have an escort fleet of two hundred and fifty P-51 fighters. "Yeah, but the 51s won't help us get through the flak," someone yelled.

Ben ignored the comment and gave them the final details of the mission. Stepping to the large map of the site hanging on the wall, Ben tapped a wooden pointer on a section close to the main production site. "This is a concentration camp housing hundreds of slave laborers forced to work in the complex. Your bombardiers are to make every effort to avoid hitting it."

Ben called for any last questions. Hearing none, he called the group to attention again, told the pilots to get their crews to their aircraft as quickly as possible, and dismissed them.

Nobody moved. Ben stared at them for a brief moment. "All right, somebody got questions? If not, you've got your orders. Now get to it!"

"Colonel!" a pilot shouted from the back. "This is nuts! This is a suicide mission!"

"YOU HAVE YOUR ORDERS!" Ben roared. "Silverman isn't any happier with the bombing altitude than you are. But he's been ordered to lead this mission, and by god, you're all gonna fly with him and make it a success! I asked repeatedly to fly this one, but my requests were denied. **So it's up to you! Now get your asses out to your aircraft!"**

They sat in astonished silence for a double beat. This was a Ben they hadn't seen before. Finally, they shuffled out to comply, grumbling and cursing the stupidity of the top brass.

Chapter 35

THE MISSION FROM HELL

The takeoffs, staged at thirty-second intervals, went smoothly, and all twenty-one of the 509ᵗʰ B-17s circled into formation overhead. Ben watched from the control tower balcony as they disappeared eastward.

Okay, well on the way. Let' see, we computed three and a half hours there and a little more back due to headwinds. Should see them back around 1430 hours. Good luck, Frank!

Ben stopped by the mess hall for a cup of coffee and a donut before returning to his office. He riffled through several service records Silverman had recommended he review as part of a search for new squadron and flight leaders. But Ben's mind was on Silverman leading the air armada toward German airspace. He shoved the files aside.

"Can't keep focused on this," he muttered. "They should be approaching the target about now. Wonder how it's goin'? That son of a bitch Davis should be horsewhipped for specifying this low-level attack and insisting that Frank lead it!"

He paced the office and was about to reach for the phone to call the control tower when it rang. He snatched it up.

"Findlay!"

"Ben, Frazer here. Just got a mission report transmitted from Frank. He said, 'target hit . . . looks like max damage . . . badly mauled by flak.'"

"Did you say 'badly mauled'?" Ben asked. "Any details on what the hell that means?"

"Dunno," Frazer said. "Afraid it means they got beat up pretty bad attacking from that low altitude. Jesus, Ben, did the top brass really think they could go in at ten thousand feet and survive?"

Ben sat silently, a feeling of dread overwhelming him. Then he responded, "Ah yeah, Fraz, you know the row we had over the field order. Uh, I got a bad feeling about this one. It was Davis's decision, and I think he's gonna regret it."

Ben hung up the phone and sat staring out the window at the empty flight line. *Another two and a half hours before we find out how bad this really is.*

He paced the office and repeatedly checked his watch. Finally, he grabbed his hat and stormed through to the outer office, calling for Sergeant Sandford, the headquarters driver.

"Let's go, Sandford. Take me down to the tower."

At the tower, he joined a clutch of officers on the balcony, several scanning the horizon with binoculars. After an interminable wait, one of them pointed and yelled, "Here they come!" Ben snatched his binoculars and looked eastward.

"Yeah!" he yelled. Then his voice trailed off. "Oh god, that's Frank leading, and he's smokin'. Number 4 is feathered. Right wing looks beat to hell. How many others do ya see?"

"I count seven, including Frank," someone said quietly.

"Seven!" Ben yelled. "Godalmighty! Can't be just seven! There's gotta be more trailing behind."

But it was seven battered B-17s that finally slipped into the landing pattern. All had obvious battle damage and all were launching flares signaling wounded, or worse, crewmen on board.

"Jesus!" Frazer yelled. "Lookit that hole in the aft fuselage of Frank's ship! You can see right through the airplane!"

Ben sprinted down the stairs to the staff car as the other officers scanned the sky in the desperate hope they'd see more 509th B-17s limping home. The sky remained agonizingly empty.

Ben tumbled out of the staff car as it skidded to a stop at Silverman's parking revetment. His B-17's three remaining engines coughed and backfired to a stop. Firefighters hosed down the Number 4 engine, which continued to smoke and drip oil. The outer portion of the right wing was mangled. The forward belly hatch dropped open, and Silverman slid down to the tarmac. He clung momentarily to the hatch door, steadying himself.

"Get the medics to the back," he croaked. "Got some badly wounded men. Both waist gunners, belly turret, and tail gunner."

Ben stepped to his side. "Lemme give you a hand, Frank," he said trying to steer him toward the waiting staff car.

"Back off!" Frank snapped. "Gotta see to my wounded first." He ducked under the fuselage and walked unsteadily toward the rear fuselage door where the medics were easing the wounded gunners out onto stretchers. Ben trailed along behind.

"Frank, lemme help," Ben said quietly. "Are you okay? Not hit? Godamighty," he breathed, scanning the large holes in the fuselage, "this old bird took some awful hits! Amazed she held together."

"Yeah, we took some big hits, everybody did . . ." Silverman's voice cracked and trailed off as he stifled a snarl. "Sorry, Ben, but goddamn it, what I warned that bastard Davis about is exactly what happened! At ten thousand feet, we were easy targets for the 88s. Made it a turkey shoot."

Silverman looked around wildly. "I didn't have a final count. Tail gunner was outta commission. How many got back?"

"So far, seven, Frank," Ben said quietly.

"Seven!" Silverman shouted. "Oh my god!" He stumbled back against the airplane's horizontal tail. "You sure? Has anybody called in from one of the emergency strips?"

"Not so far, Frank, but we're checking. Look, let me get you back to headquarters."

"No! Base hospital first. Gotta see to the wounded. How about the other, uh, ah, six ships? They got casualties too?"

"Yeah, Frank. I think everybody's got some, uh, wounded," Ben said. He caught himself before saying "dead and wounded."

"Okay!" Silverman snarled. "Hospital first, then debriefing. Then I'm gonna deal with that son of a bitch Davis!"

Silverman seethed with anger as he threaded his way among the doctors and nurses in the hospital's triage center and rapidly filling wards. But he contained his rage until he and Ben reported to the post mission briefing room. The pilots, navigators, and bombardiers who had not been hit or suffered only minor wounds milled about in stunned silence, sipping coffee laced with brandy.

When one of the intelligence officers asked Silverman to take a seat at his desk, Silverman responded with a primordial yell, **"I'll stand! And I'll give you a report that'll curl your goddamned hair! Somebody's gonna pay big time for this screw up!"**

Everyone in the room stood riveted in shocked silence. Ben stepped to Silverman's side. "Frank," he urged, "Frank, get 'hold of yourself. Come on, Frank, take a chair. Have a coffee."

"Back off, Ben!" Silverman shouted and began to pace the room. "I appealed the ten-thousand-foot order. Tried to tell Davis this would happen if he insisted we bomb from that altitude! He rejected my appeal, and that cost us fourteen airplanes, Ben. Fourteen airplanes means 140 good men! Should have gone over his head, appealed directly to Doolittle!"

Ben stepped forward and gripped Silverman's elbow. "That's enough, Frank," he hissed. "I'm taking you to your quarters." Silverman slumped and staggered and would have fallen if Ben hadn't tightened his grip on his arm.

As he led Silverman to the door, Ben turned to the stunned assembly. "Briefing's over. Everybody outta here. The bar is open and drinks are on the house. I'm ordering a base lockdown. Nobody leaves the base. Is that clear?" The flight crews nodded dumbly.

Ben half-carried Silverman to his quarters and shoved him into a chair. Frank hunched forward, holding his head in his hands, mumbling curses. Ben snatched up the phone and told Colonel Samuelson, the flight surgeon, to report immediately to Silverman's quarters. He also phoned the base provost officer and ordered the base lockdown. All gates were to be locked, and the military police were to prevent anyone from leaving the base. Anyone on leave was to be recalled. He then called the base chaplain and told him to get over to the Officer's Club. Finally, he called the noncommissioned Officer's Club and told the sergeant in charge to open the free bar and keep it open as long as anyone could stand erect in front of it.

Ben dropped the phone in the cradle, and it immediately rang. It was Brad from Pine Tree. General Davis wanted to talk to Silverman. "Ah, Brad, this isn't a good time," Ben said. "Colonel Silverman is having a rough time. Could we—"

Silverman lurched forward and snatched the phone from Ben's hand. "This is Silverman," he snarled. "Put the general on."

Davis came on the line with his usual bark, but Silverman cut him off. "Listen to me!" Silverman shouted. "You sent the 509th and all of the other groups on a suicide mission and . . ."

Ben heard Davis shout something about insubordination, relieving him of command, and court martial, but Silverman savagely cut him off. "Don't try to intimidate me!" he roared. "If the other groups took losses like ours, you have hundreds of dead flyers you're gonna have to account for!"

Ben heard Davis scream that he was coming right up to the base to personally fire Silverman. "I'll be here," Silverman snarled and slammed down the phone.

Ben stood dazed, feeling like he was witnessing the buildup to a shoot-out at the O.K. Corral. "Frank, for god's sake! Get 'hold of yourself. Sure, Davis is an incompetent idiot, but he can nail ya on the insubordination charge."

"Let him try. If he presses charges, I'll take his fat ass with me. He's way out on a limb, Ben, and he knows it. If he thinks he can fire me and make me go away quietly, he's bloody wrong!"

Colonel Samuelson, black doctor's bag in hand, rapped at the door and pushed in without waiting for a response from Silverman. "Ah, Frank, I've come over to give you something to help you sleep," he said, reaching into his bag.

"Thanks, but it'll have to wait," Silverman croaked, his voice showing the strain of all his yelling. "Davis is on the way up from Pine Tree, and I need my wits about me when he gets here."

An hour later, the tower called and said Davis's VC-47 had just landed and the general had screamed at a wide-eyed sergeant to drive him to the 509th headquarters. "He'll be there in a couple of minutes." Ben thanked him, hung up the phone, and turned to Silverman. "Davis is here."

"Good! We'll meet the son of a bitch in my office."

When Davis stormed into 509th headquarters, Silverman was sitting erect behind the desk. Ben, hovering in the background, headed for the door.

"Stay where you are, Colonel Findlay!" Davis boomed. "You need to witness this since you're about to become commander of the 509th." Turning to Silverman, he snarled, "And as for you, Colonel Silverman, you're through, you hear me? I'm relieving you here and now. Colonel Findlay is commander effectively immediately. You'll be restricted to your quarters until I can initiate court-martial proceedings"

Silverman rose from his chair and leaned toward Davis. "You listen to me, you sad excuse for a man, much less an officer," he began with a menacing growl, "you're the one who's gonna get fired. I'm taking this to the top, all the way to the top! Do you understand, you pompous little shit? We're getting reports from the other groups who flew this mission, and they suffered losses comparable to ours. You'll have to answer for hundreds of unnecessary causalities . . . General."

Davis, his red face rapidly shading toward deep purple, started to object. Silverman silenced him with a slicing hand motion.

"You aren't going to bluster your way past me and get out of the jam you're in, General," Silverman snarled. "If you press charges against me, it'll be your ass on the line as well. General Doolittle is no fool. If I go, I'm taking you with me!"

Davis waved his arms. He worked his jaw, but the only sound he could utter was something between a snarl and a howl. He spun on his heels and stormed out of the office, slamming the door and shattering the four glass panes.

Ben released his held breath with a whoosh. "Man, oh man, Frank, that was some performance! Whattaya think is gonna happen now?"

"I think Doolittle is going to fire Davis," Silverman said calmly. "Send him back to States and stick him behind a desk in some dark corner where he can't do any more harm."

Ben leaped forward as Silverman slumped back toward his chair. "Tell Colonel Samuelson to come in here!" Ben shouted to the men huddled in the outer office. Samuelson rushed in and helped Ben take Silverman to his quarters. They eased him into the bathroom, peeled off his flight suit, and guided him to his bed.

Samuelson fished a syringe from his bag, checked the contents level, and eased the needle into the primary vein in Silverman's left arm. Silverman sighed deeply and relaxed. "He'll sleep for at least twelve hours," Samuelson whispered. "I'll swing by in a couple of hours to see how he's doing."

Ben returned to the office, told everyone to knock it off for the rest of the day, and headed for the door. The phone rang before he stepped outside.

"Ben, Brad here. Davis is back, and it's really hittin' the fan down here. What the hell happened up there?"

"Oh, not much," Ben said casually. "Davis stormed in here and tried to fire Frank. Promoted me to group commander. Frank ripped his ass pretty good and all but chased him outta his office. You know, pretty much a normal day—"

Brad cut him off. "Ben, this is serious. Doolittle just got back. Wasn't expected until the weekend. He called Davis to his office, and my spies there said it sounds like Doolittle is skinnin' him alive. I'm afraid ol' Davis might go home in a box."

"Swell," Ben gloated. "Couldn't happen to a more deserving prick." He hung up the phone and headed for the Officer's Club.

Chapter 36

RETRIBUTION —

General Davis did go home—not in a box but in full disgrace. Doolittle's aide telephoned and relayed a message for Frank from the general to disregard any orders or threats Davis may have made during his misbegotten visit. He said Doolittle wanted Silverman to come to Pine Tree for a review meeting the following week before he transferred. And he wanted Ben to accompany Frank so they could hold the long-delayed ceremony, awarding Ben his two Distinguished Service Cross medals.

Ben ordered Parham to remain on lockdown for three more days until he determined everyone had recovered from the group's collective hangover. Silverman kept a low profile, sleeping long hours and conferring quietly on the phone with his fellow group commanders. The Eighth Air Force lost ninety airplanes and over nine hundred men on the Nordhausen raid. Post raid reconnaissance photos showed that the V-2 production facility sustained serious damage and probably would be out of commission for several months. No one thought it was worth the cost.

The post-mission report on the Nordhausen raid went into the Eighth Air Force's official records, but the disastrous costs were not detailed.

General W. B. "Andy" Anderson, Davis's replacement at Pine Tree, visited the 509th and ordered Silverman to stand down for as long as it took to rebuild and reinforce the group. Silverman showed exceptional restraint by not pointing out that with nine B-17s remaining, seven of which had been beaten nearly to pieces. The 509th was hardly in an ops-ready condition anyway. Morale at the 509th sank to its lowest level. The flight crews were conditioned to the empty bunk syndrome, but this time, everyone had lost a friend, acquaintance, or close buddy.

Silverman asked the general to join him in a special briefing for the group's remaining pilots and flight crews, to talk about the misbegotten raid, and to attempt to boost their morale by pointing out that despite its heavy cost, the 509th had put the Nordhausen facility out of commission. Anderson promised to expedite the delivery of replacement B-17s and crews but acknowledged it would take time for the 509th to recover.

The next day, Silverman huddled with Ben and the group's other senior officers to map a recovery plan. "My promotion and transfer have been delayed a week while they sort out the aftermath of this mess with Davis," he said. "Getting new airplanes and replacement crews is only the first step. Getting them trained, familiarized with the area, and molded into a team is going to take time. So I suggest you get to it."

As new airplanes and crews arrived, Ben worked with the squadron commanders to fill empty spots in the 509th's crew roster, matching newcomers with experienced crews as much as possible.

At the meeting with Doolittle at Pine Tree, the general spent over an hour chatting with Silverman. They discussed the Davis affair, and Doolittle confirmed that nothing pertaining to the explosive aftermath of the raid would appear on Silverman's record or impede his promotion.

Doolittle said they were looking forward to having him take command the new Boeing B-29 wing being formed in the United States. He said Frank's performance with the Eighth Air Force had earned him the new assignment and promotion to brigadier general. He then ordered his aide to set up the awards ceremony for Ben.

Ben stood rigidly at attention when Doolittle stepped up to him, holding the Distinguished Service Cross medal with bar. As Doolittle's aide read the citation, Ben found it difficult to look the general in the eyes. He had heard so much about Doolittle that he found it hard to believe the living legend was actually pinning the medals on his tunic.

"Colonel Findlay," Doolittle began, "on behalf of the president of the United States, it is truly an honor to present these medals to you in recognition of your courageous duty above and beyond expectations on two missions to Regensburg. Performance such as yours has been a key element in the success of the Eighth Air Force in carrying the war to the German homeland. For years, we were the only American forces attacking Germany, and now we're paving the way for our ground forces to press toward the final defeat of the Third Reich. And hopefully, we'll complete the job early next year."

The general pinned the medals on Ben's uniform, stepped back, and returned Ben's crisp salute. He gripped Ben's hand in a viselike shake and grinned broadly. "And, son, believe me when I say you ought to be damned proud of the part you've played in the U.S. Army Air Forces' success in Europe. Keep up the good work!"

Outside, Frank shook Ben's hand. "Damn fine ceremony, Ben. You richly deserved the medals and the general's comments. I can go on to my new assignment with full confidence I'm leaving the 509th in good hands. Hate to think of leaving the group, but I have no choice." He paused. "Ben, I want you to know I'm really pleased this opened the 509th job for you and put a pair of eagles on your shoulders."

Back at Parham, Silverman recounted the meeting with Doolittle and told his staff he was immediately relinquishing command to Ben. "You still have an air war to fight over Germany, so I'll get out of the way and let you get to it!"

Three days later, all Parham personnel assembled on the airfield's ramp for the change of command ceremony. General Anderson, who flew in that morning on Doolittle's VC-47, called the assemblage to attention. "Due to the pressures of war and the need for newly promoted Brigadier General Silverman to get to his next assignment, we will keep this ceremony brief and to the point," he intoned. "This in no way diminishes the importance of honoring Frank Silverman for his leadership of the 509th or the exceptional combat record this group has achieved under his command."

The men greeted this with thunderous applause and cheers for Silverman.

General Anderson quieted the men and quickly completed the formal declarations in the change of command ritual. Frank handed Ben the 509th standard, and he officially became the new commander of the group. Frank stepped forward to say a few words of farewell but was drowned out by a thunderstorm of sustained applause and cheers. When relative quiet returned, Frank swallowed hard and blinked several times. Regaining his composure, he said, "I have been honored to lead this group of American heroes. I will never forget my service here with all of you. And not to sound too pompous, I firmly believe history will show this to have been a high mark in the evolution of aerial warfare."

He paused and surveyed the assembly. "I leave the 509th with great regret while at the same time I look forward to the new challenge ahead. Good-bye and Godspeed to you all." He turned and marched to the waiting VC-47 with General Anderson and Ben.

At the airplane steps, Silverman turned and gripped Ben's hand. "We've traveled a long trail since our adventure in Spain, Ben. I've marveled at how much you've grown and matured since those early days. And I take some pride in the role I played in that process. I'm tempted to ask that you be assigned to join me in this new undertaking . . . Ah, but I know you have real and compelling reasons for staying with the 509th and seeing this business through to the end."

He gave Ben a wry smile. "And I know that Lady Gwen figures heavily in that decision. I'll get my new address to you as soon as possible. Want you to stay in touch. Don't know how long this war will last, but there may come a time when I'll be compelled to call on you to join me."

They stood looking into each other's eyes. "Until then, good luck and . . ." Silverman's voice cracked. Unable to complete the sentence, he turned and climbed into the airplane.

Ben stood at attention, holding his salute until the VC-47's engines started, and the airplane taxied out for takeoff. He watched it disappear into the distance, turned, and strode back across the ramp. He ordered Major Atkins to dismiss the assembly.

Chapter 37

Back in Business —

The 509th recovery effort progressed smoothly, and Ben notified Pine Tree that the group was ready to return to the operational list. Within days, they were alerted to lead a fleet of B-17s from nineteen other heavy bombardment groups—forming an attack fleet of over four hundred bombers and one hundred and fifty P-51 and P-38 fighter escorts. The target was the Leuna oil and chemical refineries near Merseburg in Eastern Germany.

"Where the hell is Merseburg?" Major Atkins asked as he and Ben studied the huge wall map of Germany in preparation for the mission briefing.

"Over here, south of Halle and west of Leipzig," Ben said, laying a pointer on the map. "The target is the 'Leunawerke,' one of the biggest chemical industrial complexes in Germany. I remember now. You joined us after we took part in earlier raids last year on this target. It's a bitch—not as deep into Germany as Regensburg but it has one of the toughest flak defenses in the Third Reich, and that includes Berlin."

"Great. Real comforting," Atkins muttered. "What's the significance of Leuna? Why throw four hundred bombers at it?"

"Like I said, it's the second biggest refinery in Germany. The damn thing is spread over more than three square miles. They make all kinds of synthetic oil products out of lignite and coal tar, and more importantly, they refine the special fuel used by the Luftwaffe's twin-jet Messerschmitt 262 fighters. Since our escort pilots can't match the 262 in their prop fighters, only thing we can do to counter the jet jobs is cut their fuel supply and bomb their production factories like the one in Regensburg."

Ben stared thoughtfully at the map. "Dunno how many sorties the Eighth Air Force has thrown at this place, but damn it, they seem to get it back in operation almost overnight. The time I went there, it was damn hard to zero in on the aim points. Flak is so heavy it makes its own smoke screen, and the Krauts use huge numbers of smoke pots to further obscure the place. Smoke from fires started when we do hit something combines to make it nearly impossible to see anything on the ground."

"Sounds like the day after tomorrow's gonna be a real picnic," Atkins said. "But since we'll be first over the target, we should have a clearer shot at finding our aim points."

"Don't count on it. And, by the way, it ain't gonna be any picnic," Ben said. "I'll lead, and I want you to shepherd the second section. I'm concerned about the number of green crews we're taking into their first combat on this mission. Have we time to mix up our crews, pairing experienced pilots with new copilots and experienced copilots with new airplane commanders? Same with gunners, team some experienced fellas with the new ones?"

"I think so, but don't we risk breaking up crews that've become well-coordinated teams by doing that?" Atkins asked.

"That's a chance we'll have to take. I think it'd be a bigger risk to throw a totally green crew into a tough mission like this. Can we also shift airplanes with new pilots to inside positions in our defensive formation boxes?"

"That might be pushing it too much, Ben. Lemme talk to the squadron and flight commanders first."

"Good. Now what airplane is available for me? Damn it! I hate to go scrounging around for an airplane each time I lead a mission! But I can't justify a plane and crew of my own. Who am I pushing outta the left seat this time?"

"Lieutenant Bob Gray, skipper of *Tough Lady*," Atkins said. "His copilot is Lieutenant Tony Wallace—good head, senior copilot ready to upgrade to airplane commander. The rest of the crew is a mixed bag. They got shot up pretty badly on that long mission to Brux, Czechoslovakia, early this year and lost three gunners. But Gray has molded the new crew into a close-knit team. They'll serve you well."

"Swell. Tell Gray and Wallace I want to see them tonight and to meet the crew before takeoff. Want to introduce myself and get their first names."

Ben met the two lieutenants at the officer's club bar and informed Gray he'd replace him on the next mission. Gray wasn't happy but had no choice in the matter. "Tony, tell the rest of the crew I'll get out to *Tough Lady* early. Have 'em lined up for introductions." Noting the pilots' puzzled expressions, Ben added, "Humor me, fellas. I like to call my crewmembers by their first names. Think it helps when we're under fire and trying to communicate on the intercom." Gray and Wallace shrugged and nodded.

"And, Bob," Ben said, turning to Gray, "I'll take good care of both your crew and *Tough Lady*."

"Thanks, Colonel." Gray nodded.

Atkins reported to Ben before the briefing that the squadron commanders had agreed to the several crew changes but resisted shifting airplanes in the combat formations because it would break up formation patterns the pilots were familiar with and had practiced.

A nervous current coursed through the assembled aircrews as Atkins opened the briefing. The new arrivals, understandably anxious about their first combat mission, had been talking with veteran pilots who offered blunt assessments of the flak threat at such high priority targets. Leuna! Damn! This wasn't going to be the milk run they had hoped for. Ben scanned the faces of those listening to Atkins. It was easy to identify the new boys, the pale-faced ones sucking their tongues, trying vainly to moisten their cotton-dry mouths. The veterans sat grim-faced, occasionally mouthing curses as Atkins detailed the mission profile. Ben hoped mixing veteran fliers with the new boys would help stabilize all of the crews.

In an attempt to reassure them, Atkins said that two other heavy bombardment fleets from the Fifteenth and Eighth Air Forces would be simultaneously attacking targets in Germany, again to spread the Luftwaffe's fighter forces. Also, he said that mixing inexperienced pilots and other flight crew members with veteran flyers should help lead them through this first mission.

Ben signaled Atkins and stepped forward. "Joe, let me interrupt with a special message for you, navigators and bombardiers. You men heard Colonel Atkins warn about camouflage at the Leuna refinery. I've been there and have seen how much confusion the smoke screens create, combined with smoke and flames from burning oil. It'll be easy to confuse the dummy refinery the Germans have built about a mile west of the target with the real thing. We have excellent photo recon images of the facility under varying light conditions. Study them carefully before takeoff, and coordinate closely with your pilots on the final run to the aim point."

Atkins concluded the briefing with mission timing details—crews to airplanes, engine start, taxi, and takeoff—and called for a time hack to synchronize everyone's watches.

Sandford drove Ben to *Tough Lady*'s revetment thirty minutes early. Lieutenant Wallace had the crew lined up under the bomber's nose. Ben stepped out of the staff car, dropped his flight bag on the tarmac, and faced the men.

"Good morning. I'm Colonel Findlay. Like you to call me Skipper while I'm in command of *Tough Lady*. I know this may seem unorthodox, but I want to get on a first-name basis with you. When we're in the thick of it, it saves time on the intercom. Also builds a closer team spirit. Now each of you give me your call sign, nickname, whatever. Tony . . . ?"

Wallace nodded to their navigator. "Lieutenant Anders Johnson, sir. I'm known as Andy."

Next came their bombardier. "Captain William Franks, Skipper. Call me Willie."

Their radio operator was next. "Sergeant Walt Cumberland, Skipper. Call sign is Sparks."

Their flight engineer was next. "Sergeant Robert Jones, Skipper. Go by Bob."

Next were the two waist gunners. "Left waist, Skipper. Sergeant Alfred Bagnonia. Known as Baggie, but Fred'll do."

"Right waist, sir. Sergeant Louis White. Whitey to my friends."

Ben knew the next man had to be their ball turret gunner. He was barely five feet tall. "Sergeant Jason Kerr, Skipper. Obviously known as Shorty."

And lastly, their tail gunner. "Sergeant Quince McLaughlin. Called a lot of things, Skipper, but I prefer Mac."

"Appreciate you bearing with me," Ben said. "One last thing. No idle chatter on the intercom. If you spot bogies, its heading, number, and type. When you're shooting, keep your heads up. Warnings to other gunners short and to the point."

Glancing at his watch, Ben said, "Time to mount up. Let's go set a Kraut oil refinery on fire." The men scrambled to their stations onboard *Tough Lady*. In the cockpit, Ben turned to Tony. "Complete the preflight checks, while I make a list of everyone's name and clip it on my control yoke." Fastening the list, Ben asked, "Who're the first timers in this mixed crew?"

"Andy Johnson, Bob Jones, Fred Bagnonia, Shorty Kerr, and Sparks," Wallace said.

"We going out with a new navigator on his first combat mission?" Ben asked.

"Yes, Skipper, but Johnson is good, could become one of the best navigators in the group."

"Could he indeed? Okay, as long as you're sure he can get us there. Key, fella, will be Willie on the Norden bombsight. Germans have the refinery well camouflaged, including that dummy setup a mile west of the main facility. And there'll be one hell of a lot of smoke and flames all around the target. Willie will need to keep a sharp eye to find the right aim point."

Once they reached altitude, Ben switched on the autopilot and set the initial course out over the North Sea. He smiled as he surveyed the fighter escort circling over the bomber string. They would swing southeast and head for Northern Germany, hopefully fooling the Luftwaffe into thinking they were headed for Bremen or Hannover. But they would continue on course and head for Halle. There, they would turn south toward Merseburg, the IP. Ben signaled Tony that he was going down to the nose to talk with Willie.

"Dropped down for a chat, Willie," he shouted through his portable oxygen mask. "We're on the northeasterly course en route to our turn over the North Sea. We'll turn toward Germany in about twenty-five minutes. Final course to the target from the Merseburg IP should work out to between 190 and 200 degrees, depending on wind direction."

Willie nodded, scribbling notes.

"Weather over the target is supposed to be clear, so Tony and I should be able to help you acquire the target. Expect a lotta smoke as we approach the aim point. Heaviest probably will be over the dummy refinery, which'll be about ten degrees to the west of the real thing. Don't get suckered in. Real target should be dead ahead. Let's make this one count. We've already scattered too damn many bombs across the countryside around that refinery."

As Ben settled back in the cockpit's left seat, Sergeant Jones sounded the first fighter alert from the top turret. "Bogies two o'clock high . . . Looks like a gaggle of 109s and 190s. Here they come head-on!"

Tough Lady shook and rattled from the recoil of her forward-firing guns. Tracers from the attackers' cannons flashed past on both sides. Shouts from the gunners crackled over the intercom. The acrid smell of cordite fumes swirled through the cockpit, penetrating their oxygen masks.

"Four 262s attackin' from the rear!" McLaughlin yelled from his tail gunner's position. "Looks like they're gonna split an' . . ." His transmission was interrupted by sledgehammer blows of 30 mm shells smashing into *Tough Lady*'s tail section. The bomber twisted and slewed sideways. The left wing dropped. Ben's feet bounced off the rudder pedals. Tony grabbed his control yoke, and he and Ben wrestled the bomber back under control.

"Rudder still working," Ben yelled. "Elevator seems okay. Must be structural damage." He keyed the intercom to call McLaughlin in the tail. "Mac, you all right? Skipper to Mac, report in." The only sound was a hiss of static. "Skipper to Mac, Skipper to Mac . . ." Ben looked at Tony, who shrugged. "Can you hold her, Tony?" He nodded.

"Good. Lemme see what's goin' on back there. He keyed the intercom again. "Skipper to right waist. Whitey, any damage to your station?"

"No, Skipper, but we took some big hits in the tail. Lotta smoke and crap in the air. No fire. I'll slip back and check on Mac." He grabbed a portable oxygen bottle and crawled toward the tail section. Wind whistled through jagged holes in the tail cone. Mac lay crumpled against the ragged fuselage wall. His .50-caliber machine gun was a twisted mess of smoking metal. Whitey ripped off his gloves and grabbed Mac's wrist, searching for a pulse. He felt a weak throbbing and set about pulling Mac out of the twisted wreckage. Blood oozed from rips in the left shoulder of Mac's thermal flight suit, and he moaned loudly.

Curses from various gunner stations punctuated the hammering of *Tough Lady*'s remaining machine guns as the gunners fired at Luftwaffe fighters slashing past with machine guns and cannons blazing. Whitey laid Mac on the floor aft of the waist gun position and slipped a parachute pack under his head. He unzipped Mac's flight suit. Blood ran from two vicious wounds in his left shoulder. "Fred!" Whitey yelled to Bagnonia, who apparently didn't hear him as he hunched, ducked, and twisted to keep the German fighters in his sights.

"Baggie!" Whitey screamed at the top of his voice. Bagnonia stopped firing and gave Whitey a confused look. "What?" he yelled.

"Mac is badly wounded! I gotta hold his head up. Grab the medical kit and toss it back to me."

Fred scrambled forward, snatched the kit from the fuselage wall, and slid it back to Whitey. He then wrestled his gun into position and began hammering away at the swarming fighters.

A pair of 262s pilots seeing that *Tough Lady*'s tail gun was silenced swooped in for the kill. Both pilots throttled back and pitched up their fighters to slow the approach and extend their firing time. It made them easier targets. Jones blazed away with his twin .50-caliber guns from the top turret as Shorty Kerr fired from the ball turret under the fuselage belly. They scored hits on both of the high-speed jet fighters. Pieces blew off the lead fighter, and it snap rolled to the right and exploded. The second rolled left and dived, trailing black smoke.

"*Sonofabitch!*" Shorty yelled. "I got 'em! Both of 'em! Anybody else shootin' at the 262s?"

"Good shootin', Shorty," Jones radioed. "Gave you a little help from the top turret. Let the bastards know they ain't bulletproof."

Whitey continued to work on Mac, stuffing pressure bandages into his wounds. He plugged in his intercom connection and called Ben. "Whitey to Skipper, ah, Mac took a couple of hits. Two wounds in his shoulder. Think I've slowed the bleeding. Tail gun is outta commission. Buncha holes in the aft fuselage, but she's holdin' together."

"Good goin', Whitey. Stay with him. Fred, give him a hand. Fighters are breaking off. Means we're entering the flak zone. Hunker down and concentrate on Mac." Whitey rummaged in the medical kit for more bandages and a morphine syringe. He and Fred reached for their flak jackets and piled them around their wounded comrade.

Up front, Ben and Tony tested the flight control and were relieved to find all control surfaces connected and working. "Skipper to navigator," Ben called on the intercom. "How do we look, Andy?"

"About five minutes to IP, Skipper."

"Bombardier to Skipper. They're laying a smoke screen over the target, but I think I have a good bead on the aim point. Know better when we turn for the final run in."

Exploding 88 mm shells burst along their path, creating black clouds as they spit lethal shrapnel into the bomber string. "Tony, gimme a hand," Ben yelled. "Let's throw in a few evasive maneuvers."

They rolled *Tough Lady* in a weaving pattern, diving and descending to confuse the antiaircraft gunners. Maneuvering may not have done much to reduce the threat, but it felt good to be doing something other than cruising straight and level waiting for a hit.

"IP in less than a minute," Andy called. Then a countdown and the command. "Turn right to heading two zero, zero degrees."

Ben signaled to Tony that he was taking control. "I'll fly the final run to the target," he yelled. "Keep your eyes peeled for the real refinery complex. Alert Whitey. Stand by to help with the turn for home. Do ya see a good path outta the flak?"

"On target, Skipper," Willie called from the nose. "Your airplane, Willie," Ben called back. "Lay it on 'em."

"Bomb bay doors open," Willie called back. "Steady, steady. Got the aim point. Bombs away!" *Tough Lady* lurched upward.

Ben and Tony grabbed their control yokes and rolled the bomber to the right. "Helluva lot of flak everywhere but looks like we have a better path back to the left," Tony yelled. They rolled the airplane left and climbed a thousand feet. The bomber string followed as the antiaircraft gun crews scrambled to adjust for the change in their altitude.

It seemed to take forever to clear the flak ring, but the bombers finally emerged into clear sky and rendezvoused with their fighter escort. Luftwaffe fighters were waiting as they turned west toward the Pas de Calais. Several gaggles of 109 and Fw 190 fighters attacked the retreating bomber string, but no one reported spotting any 262s. The Luftwaffe was concentrating the high-speed jets on the bomber string still approaching the refinery complex.

Aerial battles between Luftwaffe attackers and USAAF escort fighters swirled all around the bomber string, and the P-51s and P-38s scored numerous kills. Several bombers were damaged in the running battles with the German fighters, but no one was knocked down. The attackers broke off as the bomber string swept west north of Kassel and Dusseldorf and headed for Holland and the Channel.

Ben told Tony to "take her down below ten thousand feet," which eliminated the need for oxygen. He keyed the intercom. "Looked good from up here. Anybody able to see the refinery? What'd we hit?" Several responded that thick smoke blanketed the place. Couldn't really tell what they hit.

"I think I put the eggs right on target, Skipper," Willie called out.

Addressing the crew, Ben asked, "How about the group? Did we lose anybody?" Jones in the top turret reported that there were two empty spaces in the 509th's formation.

"Whose ships?" Ben asked.

"Dunno, Skipper. We're pretty badly strung out. Can't tell who is missin'," came the response.

Ben then called Whitey, "How's Mac doing? Need any help?"

"Baggie's here helpin', Skipper. Mac's holding on, but he's lost a lotta blood. We could use another set of hands."

"Comin' up from the ball turret," Shorty broke in. "We can handle it, Skipper."

The two pilots scanned the instruments and checked their fuel status. Sergeant Jones dropped from the top turret and assured himself all four engines were working properly. "Should be able to make it home okay, Skipper. I'll go back and check the rest of the airplane and the crew." He called Ben on the intercom, "The aft fuselage is punched fulla holes from flak and cannon fire, Skipper. But she's structurally sound. Gonna hold together. Mac's the only one wounded."

They crossed the Pas de Calais and made landfall at Harwich on England's southeast coast. The run north to Parham went quickly, and Ben led the 509th into their landing approach pattern. Jones fired a red flare to signal they had a badly wounded crewman onboard.

Ben slid *Tough Lady* in for a smooth landing, turned off on the runway, and taxied quickly to their parking revetment. An ambulance waited, and medics lifted Mac out on a stretcher and sped off to the hospital. Sergeant Sandford pulled up in the staff car, and Ben signaled Tony to join him. The rest of the crew clambered onto a flatbed truck headed to base operations for the post-mission briefing. The maintenance crews gathered to evaluate the damage to *Tough Lady*.

"Tony, thanks for all the help today," Ben said as they sped toward base operations. "Good to see you're up for airplane commander. I've endorsed it, and I'll do my best to speed it up."

"Thanks, Skipper. Glad to help out. Think we did some good work today."

Ben visited the hospital later that afternoon. Mac had survived but had suffered significant damage to his shoulder. The doctors gave him several pints of blood during surgery and now had him in a deep drugged-induced sleep. His war was over. Ben also visited about a dozen other crewmen wounded on the mission. Miraculously, none suffered life-threatening injuries.

Two of the twenty B-17s Ben led on the raid that morning failed to emerge from the smoke clouds roiling over the Leuna refinery—Captain Art Grove and Lieutenant Cal Hutchinson and their crews. No one had seen them go down, so no one saw parachutes. Ben tried not to imagine them plunging into the fiery maelstrom below. "Another twenty good men gone," he muttered. "Damn! Is this really worth the cost?"

Post-mission reconnaissance photos showed their raid was the most effective against the Leuna refinery in many months. For a change, most of the bombs fell within the perimeter of the actual facility and had significantly damaged the main petroleum, cracking towers and storage tank farms. However, many contemplated the cost. The combined fleet lost fifteen B-17s, one hundred and fifty casualties, and the wounded totaled nearly five hundred.

Ben sat shuffling papers on his desk when Tony knocked on the office door and stepped inside. "Lieutenant Richard Davis is here, Ben. Asks to see you about a personal matter."

"Davis?" Ben asked. "Is he the newly promoted airplane commander from A-Squadron?"

"Yeah, sharp kid. Should I show him in?" Ben nodded.

First Lieutenant Richard Davis stepped smartly into the office, snapped to attention, and saluted. "Sir, request permission to discuss a personal matter," he said, remaining rigidly at attention.

"Of course, Davis," Ben said. "At ease. Take a seat. What's on your mind?"

Davis sat upright on the forward edge of the chair. "Ah, sir, I have a personal matter . . ."

"You've already said that, Davis," Ben interrupted, wondering if it was girl trouble. "Sit back, and take a deep breath. Tell me straight out what's bothering you."

"Cal Hutchinson, Colonel. Lieutenant Cal Hutchinson, sir. Ah, he was . . ."

"I know about Lieutenant Hutchinson," Ben interjected. "Was he a friend of yours?"

"He's, ah, was, my best friend, Colonel. We lived on neighboring farms in Iowa. Joined up at the same time and went through flight training together. We couldn't believe our luck when we got assigned to the 509th at the same time. You see, we're, uh, we were like brothers, maybe closer. Now I gotta write his mom and tell her he's missing in action and probably dead. An', uh, an' I don't know what he died for."

Davis slumped forward and ran both hands through his hair. "I mean, seems to me his getting killed, along with his whole crew, and all the others . . . I mean, what the hell? Excuse me, sir. Uh, what are we dying for? We've beat up every real target in Germany. Now I hear we may be going after what's left of the big cities. I just don't understand, Colonel."

"How many missions have you flown?" Ben asked.

"This was my twentieth, sir."

"You're two-thirds there. The way the war's going, you may not even have to fly the full thirty."

"Sir, I don't wanna fly anymore," Davis blurted out, glancing nervously at Ben. "There, you told me to tell it straight out, sir. That's it. I wanna turn in my wings. I'll take any other assignment, take the consequences, court martial if it comes to that. I just don't wanna fly anymore. An', an', it isn't because I'm afraid, sir. I'm not a coward. I just don't believe in what we're doing anymore. All our fellas getting killed, and everyone's talking about how the war'll be over soon."

Ben sat back and pursed his lips. "I see. Have you given this serious thought? I mean, have you been mulling this for some time, or is this a shocked reaction to Lieutenant Hutchinson's, umm, Cal's death? How long have you been on the verge of turning in your wings?"

"I dunno for sure, sir. Our losses have been bothering me for some time. We, uh, my buddies and me, we talk about getting killed a lot I guess. I mean, if you don't talk about it, maybe even joke about it, you'll go nuts, right?" Ben nodded.

"Anyway, Cal's gettin' shot down over that goddamn refinery, spinning into that firestorm. Really hit me hard, and uh, I decided to hell with it. 'Scuse me again, sir. Uh, I, it just seems to be such a waste. And now I gotta, uh, I gotta tell Cal's mom." He stifled a sob and sat quietly, looking at his hands.

"Look, I won't insult your intelligence by telling you that all of us knew this was going to be a dangerous business, Dick. But that's the hard truth. You and Cal, me, all of us knew what our chances were of surviving the full mission requirement."

Ben pushed back in his chair. "I know that doesn't help with your grieving for Cal. I've lost a lot of good friends along the way myself. I know how it feels, and I know how you're hurting. But we still have a job to finish here, and until we do, we have to keep plugging ahead with the belief we're doing something worth doing, something constructive. Kinda hard to think that blowing Germany to smithereens is constructive, but in this crazy war-torn world, I think it is."

He tilted forward and looked hard at Davis. "Dick, you've come a long way since the farm in Iowa. I came from a farm in Michigan, and I know the road you've traveled. You've achieved a great deal. You're one of the youngest airplane commanders in the group. The other younger fellas look at someone like you and think that if you can do it, they damn well can do it too."

Ben waited for him to raise his head. "Am I makin' any sense to you? Does any of this mean anything?"

Davis straightened his shoulders. "Uh yes, sir, I guess it does. You want me to keep flyin', want me to set an example, right?"

"That's right, Dick. I want you to keep flyin'."

They talked for another half an hour. Ben gave him the whole spiel about the importance of daylight bombing, the way they were proving the concept, and the relief they were providing for the ground troops. At one point, he paused and wondered to himself if he believed all of this or was he just parroting the bullshit they had been fed by the top brass.

Finally, Davis sat upright and looked Ben in the eyes. "Okay, Colonel, you've convinced me. I understand what I have to do. Thank you, sir. I gotta live with this. Keep me on the duty roster, sir." He stood, saluted, and strode out of the office.

Ben sat staring out the window for a long moment. "Christ!" he muttered. "Do I really believe in my heart what I just told that kid?"

The 509th flew two more missions in quick succession. On the second, a raid on Nurnberg, Davis's B-17 was bracketed by two 88 mm antiaircraft bursts. It exploded in a fiery ball. No parachutes were seen.

A slow-moving weather front dragged a soggy shroud of rain and fog over England and the Continent, halting all air operations. On the ground, the Allied advance stalled in Belgium when the Germans launched a surprisingly strong counterattack. The battle lines bulged ominously westward under the force of the enemy offensive. U.S. Army troops bore the brunt of the attacks, and several units near the Belgian city of Bastogne remained surrounded.

The Wehrmacht launched the Ardennes Counteroffensive, commonly known as the Battle of the Bulge, on December 16.

Reinforced panzer tank divisions and infantry units thrust through the Ardennes forest region along the borders of Belgium, France, and Luxembourg, one of the weakest points in the Allied offensive line. The attack, which caught the Allies by surprise, was intended to drive a wedge between the British forces along the northern part of the line and the Americans in the southern sector. German Army planners hoped to encircle major American units, recapture the Belgian port city of Antwerp, and force a negotiated peace in Western Europe.

Fighter and bomber commanders throughout the Eighth Air Force watched frustrated from afar, unable to launch relief missions, because of the weather. An opportunity for a quick-reaction attack occurred in late December. Eighth Air Force meteorologists forecast a partial break in the weather along the Ardennes front and in the skies over a number of B-17 and B-24 bases in England, mostly in the south. Parham was not on the list. The stagnant front continued to cover the base in a blanket of oozing rain and fog that kept the 509th grounded.

The Ardennes bombing missions, launched on December 23, dropped more tons of bombs along that front than had been dropped on any other target in a single day in the war. The attacks blunted the Wehrmacht's advance, producing a stalemate as the wintry weather closed in again.

Ben and Joe sat in Ben's office, staring through the fogged windows as cold rain lashed the ramp. "Guess we can use the rest, Joe," Ben muttered. "Damn! Wish we could have been part of this one. Those poor bastards in Belgium. Hope they can hang on."

He turned to Atkins. "Ah, Joe, there's another reason I asked you here." He reached in his desk drawer and pulled out an envelope. "I wanted to present these to you personally." He shook out a set of silver oak leaf clusters. "Congratulations, Colonel. You've earned these. Lemme pin 'em on."

Chapter 38

ANOTHER CHRISTMAS AT
CALVERT HALL —

"Only good thing about being grounded by this lousy weather is I can take Gwen to Calvert Hall for the Christmas weekend," Ben muttered to his reflection in the mirror as he shaved. The 509th remained on alert, but the meteorologists said they doubted there would be another break in the weather for at least four or five days.

"This is gonna be a swell celebration," Ben exulted. "Grab the chance while you can, Benjamin old boy." He reminded himself to swing by the commissary to pick up the crate of oranges and two large hams he had ordered as gifts for the Calvert Hall household.

Ben grinned broadly as he pulled his jeep to the curb in front of Gwen's apartment in Cambridge. She opened the door as he bounded up the stairs. "Hullo, love. I've been watching for you . . ."

Ben swept her into a bear hug and carried her into the hallway, smothering her with passionate kisses. "My word," she gasped, wriggling loose and stepping back. "You fair take my breath away, Colonel." Giggling, she leapt back in his arms and planted a long luscious kiss on his lips.

"You ready, Gwen?" he asked, admiring how her nurse's uniform highlighted her full figure. "Our train leaves in about half an hour." He paused and flashed her a lascivious grin. "'Course, we could take a later train."

"Oh, I hate to sit around waiting . . ."

"Who's talking about sitting around and waiting?"

"Oh, Ben, you're impossible. Umm, I'd love that. Truly, I would. But we have a bit of a journey, and the train connections in London will be complicated."

"Okay, okay. Let's get goin'. Where's your suitcase?"

She paused, stroked his cheek, and kissed him. "It's in the bedroom. No, you stay here. I'll fetch it."

"Where are the tickets?"

"I have them in my purse," she called from the bedroom.

Ben had telephoned Reggie for travel instructions. "Take the train from Cambridge Station to London King's Cross, Sancho," he said. "Normally takes about an hour and a half, but these days, plan on a good bit more. From King's Cross, take the train to Southampton Central Station. Make sure it's Southampton Central, else you'll end up at the harbor. I'll send Watkins in the 'Roller' to fetch you, so give me a shout on the blower before you leave London to confirm what train you're on." Ben hung up and smiled. He'd let Gwen be surprised when they were "fetched" by a uniformed chauffer driving a Rolls-Royce.

The trip turned into more than a "bit of a journey." The train out of Cambridge Station was packed, and people stood in the aisles. Gwen had booked tickets well in advance at Reggie's suggestion, so they had seats, but their compartment was jammed with double its usual occupants.

They were in time to make the connection at London King's Cross Station, so Ben telephoned the confirmation to Reggie. As they chugged toward Southampton, Gwen fiddled nervously with her purse and adjusted her uniform. "Since Reggie's father is a member of the peerage, they must really live in a grand home," she said.

"Well, yeah, I guess you could call it grand," Ben said nonchalantly. Images of Calvert Hall flashed through his mind from his first visit with Reggie in 1939. He had felt like a cat surrounded by a pack of coonhounds, but the family soon made him feel at ease. Calvert Hall is an imposing place with its pillared entry gates, a long driveway leading to the hotel-sized main house, the high-ceilinged entry hall inside, and the large oak-paneled dining room, not to mention the stables and various out buildings. "You'll find it comfortable. I'm sure you'll enjoy the stay."

The train chuffed into Southampton Central Station, and Ben scanned the platform. He spotted Watkins midway along, standing stiffly in his uniform and cap. Brakes squealed as the train jolted to a stop. Ben opened the compartment door and signaled Watkins, who double-timed to meet them and tipped Ben a crisp salute.

"Hullo, sir. Wonderful to see you again. My pleasure to welcome you, umm . . ." He squinted at Ben's shoulder. "My word, umm, Colonel Findlay."

"Hello, Watkins. Nice to see you again. You're looking fit and trim." Watkins smiled and nodded. "Ah, I'd like to introduce my fiancée, Miss Brewster. Gwen, this is Watkins. Calvert Hall's chauffer."

"Honored to meet you, Miss Brewster," Watkins said, doffing his cap and bowing. "My pleasure to drive you and the Colonel to Calvert Hall. Lord and Lady Percy are anxious to greet you and, of course, Wing Commander Percy. I have the motor car waiting without. Would you follow me, please?" He gathered up their suitcases and strode toward the exit. Ben signaled a porter to collect the crate of oranges and the hams.

Gwen flashed Ben a wide-eyed glance and trooped along. "Nice gesture on Lord Percy's part," Ben whispered. "You're gonna like them."

Gwen's eyes popped even wider as Watkins lead them to the Rolls-Royce with the family crest on the door. He held the door open for Gwen and tipped a nod to Ben, who climbed in behind her. Ben suppressed a grin as he settled into the plush upholstery and snuggled against Gwen. "Not a bad lifestyle, is it, m'dear?" he whispered.

"Ben!" she hissed back. "What have you gotten me into? I don't know how to move in *these* circles. What makes you think they'll welcome me? I'm not of their class!"

"I thought we settled that," he said evenly. "First of all, this in 1944, not 1914. And second, there's a war on, remember? Class doesn't mean a damn thing at the moment. These are Reggie's parents. They're wonderful people. They know what you're doing for the war effort, and they'll love you. You'll see. Now no more talk about class. Sit back, Gwen, and enjoy the ride. We're gonna have a swell time."

Anxious to change the subject, Ben raised his voice. "Is everyone well at Calvert Hall, Watkins? How about Miss Elizabeth?" He whispered to Gwen, "Elizabeth is Reggie's little sister."

Watkins nodded. "Thank you for inquiring, sir. Lord and Lady Percy are doing well under the circumstances. His Lordship is looking very tired and worn lately. He's been working so hard on the war effort. Lady Percy is well, although her hip has been giving her a spot of bother of late. And Miss Elizabeth? What can I say, sir? She's very much Miss Elizabeth, umm, perhaps even more so."

"Miss Elizabeth was a rambunctious young lady of thirteen last time I saw her," Ben whispered to Gwen. "Must be at least eighteen now I guess. We'll see . . ."

Ben smiled as he watched Gwen admire the beautiful thatched villages they passed en route to Calvert Hall. He remembered how he had pressed his nose to the window of the local train that took them from Southampton to Romsey when he and Reggie returned from the Spanish Civil War in 1939. Watkins had waited on the platform that time to drive them the short distance to Calvert Hall.

Gwen bolted upright as the Rolls purred through the front gates with the brass plate announcing "Calvert Hall–Romsey Forest." She turned to Ben with a look he couldn't readily interpret. Bates the butler was standing erect in his usual spot when the Rolls crunched to a stop on the gravel drive. "Oh, Ben . . ." was all Gwen could manage.

Watkins stepped out of the car and opened the rear door as Bates moved forward with a curt bow. "Hullo again, mister. Umm, is it Colonel? Yes, of course. Welcome, Colonel Findlay. It is a pleasure to see you again at Calvert Hall, sir."

"Hello, Bates. Really great to be back." Helping Gwen out of the Rolls, he turned. "Ah, Bates, may I present my fiancée, Miss Brewster. Gwen, this is Bates. Been Calvert Hall's butler for many years."

"Pleased to make your acquaintance, Miss Brewster," Bates said bowing. "Welcome to Calvert Hall."

The front door burst open, and Reggie strode toward them with outstretched arms. "Tallyho! The lovely couple has arrived. Good to see you again, Gwen," he said, hugging her and kissing her on both cheeks. "Beautiful as ever." She blushed crimson and murmured a greeting. Turning to Ben, Reggie grabbed his hand and grinned. "And good to see you again, Sancho! Glad the two of you could join us. Come inside. Mother and Elizabeth are waiting. 'Himself' should arrive from London this evening, hopefully in time for Christmas Eve dinner."

Ben pull Reggie aside and whispered, "There's a crate of oranges and two hams in the boot. Maybe Watkins should take them down to the kitchen." Reggie gave him a steady look. "Good show, Ben. They'll be much appreciated."

Gwen clutched Ben's hand as they followed Reggie into the vaulted entry hall. "Trust you had an uneventful trip," Reggie said. "Understand train service can be bloody awful these days."

They stopped as Lady Percy walked slowly to greet them, Elizabeth supporting her by her left arm. "Aha!" Reggie exclaimed. "Here they are. Calvert Hall's two beautiful ladies. Mum, meet Gwen Brewster, Benjamin's fiancée. Gwen, my mother, Lady Percy."

Lady Percy embraced Gwen before she could curtsy. "Welcome, dear," she whispered. "I'm so pleased to meet you. We think so highly of Benjamin and are happy the two of you have found each other." Turning to Elizabeth, she said, "And this is our daughter, Elizabeth. Elizabeth, meet Ben's fiancée, Miss Brewster."

Ben watched as Elizabeth bobbed a quick curtsy and shook Gwen's hand. "I'm very pleased to meet you, Miss Brewster." She smiled. "Welcome to Calvert Hall." Ben thought the smile looked a bit forced.

The initial courtesies completed, they turned their attention to Ben. "Hello, Ben," Lady Percy said, wrapping him in a warm embrace. Her familiar perfume wafted around him. "I am so pleased you're able to celebrate Christmas with us again. Thank you for bringing your lovely lady with you. Is everything well with you? Umm, you seem to have been injured. I mean, the left side of your face . . ."

"Yes, ma'am. Had a bit of a scrape earlier this year. Nothing serious." Ben smiled. "An' thank you again for inviting us."

Elizabeth hung back, watching Ben carefully. Finally, she moved forward. "Hullo, Ben, nice to see you again," she said, extending her right hand. Ben saw her glance at his left cheek, and she blushed crimson when she realized he had noticed. "You're, umm, looking well, Ben," she said quickly. "I'm so glad your wounds have healed."

Ben remembered their first meeting when Elizabeth had flown down the main staircase, screaming a greeting to Reggie and leaping into his arms. When introduced to Ben, she had leapt into his arms and planted a wet kiss on his cheek, thanking him repeatedly for saving Reggie's life while flying with the Republican Air Force in Spain, quite a contrast with the beautiful young lady, who now greeted him so formally.

"Hello, Elizabeth. Wonderful to see you again," Ben said, noting her guarded expression. "Wow, uh, you've really grown up since I saw you last." He immediately regretted how that must have sounded to her. *Dummy! That wasn't very clever.*

"Uh, I mean, it's been several years since I've seen you. An', an, you've changed."

"Thank you, Ben. Do you think I've perhaps become more of a lady than I was when we last met?"

Ouch! I deserved that.

"Uh no, no, that's not what I meant," Ben stuttered. "I, uh, what I meant . . ."

Reggie jumped in and saved Ben yet again. "I say let's not stand here chatting in the draft. Please step into the parlor as the spider said to the fly. This way, Gwen. Ben, take Mum's arm." Elizabeth stepped up and took Lady Percy's other arm. "Dear me, such a fuss over this old lady," Lady Percy said.

They settled in front of the drawing room fireplace, savoring the warmth emanating from the roaring fire. Lady Percy signaled Bates to bring tea. "You have had a long journey, my dear," she said to Gwen. "Were you able to get anything decent to eat along the way? Was there even a dining car on the train? I fear our train service has suffered badly since the war has disrupted our lives so. We'll dine at eight o'clock, so you have a good bit of time to rest and refresh yourself. But you must have something to tide you over until then, must you not?" Gwen smiled and murmured appropriate replies to Lady Percy's inquires.

As Bates passed by, Reggie signaled he and Ben would have whiskey. Bates nodded and strode from the room.

Bates delivered the tea and placed it on a table in front of Lady Percy. He handed the whiskies to Reggie and Ben. As Elizabeth slipped forward to pour tea, she frowned at Reggie, who raised his glass in a mock salute. Ben avoided making eye contact.

The ladies chatted amicably during tea. Gwen settled back in her chair and enjoyed the combined warmth of the hot tea and the roaring fire. Fatigue from the journey and tension over meeting Reggie's family took its toll, and she felt her eyelids droop. Lady Percy quickly noted the signals and leaned forward. "Gwen, my dear, you must be exhausted from your travels. Might I suggest you have a lie-me-down before dressing for dinner? Bates can show you to your room."

Gwen flashed her a grateful smile. "Thank you, Lady Percy. I'm dreadfully sorry. I don't mean to be discourteous or ungrateful, but I really would like to lie down."

Bates stepped forward, but Ben intervened. "Excuse me, Bates. I'm running on the ragged edge myself. If you'll excuse us, Lady Percy, why don't I see Gwen upstairs, and then I can have a 'lie-me-down' as well?" She smiled her agreement. Elizabeth watched without expression.

"And I'll escort the two of you to your rooms," Reggie announced. "Need to have a chat with Ben." He led the two weary travelers upstairs.

Reggie showed Gwen her room. "Your luggage is already in place. Have a bath, if you'd like, and make sure to put your feet up for a bit.

I'm sure Ben has told you we're not expected to dress for dinner. Class A uniform is fine. Rest easy. The gong will sound at seven thirty for dinner at eight. Now I'm going to have a quick chat with Ben.

Reggie led Ben by the arm into the bedroom next door. "Pater is being driven down from London. Expect he'll arrive about 1830 hours. Would like to have a chat with both of us in the drawing room before dinner." Glancing at this watch, Reggie added, "That'll give you a couple of hours to spend with . . ." He nodded his head toward Gwen's room. Ben gave him a sharp look.

"Well, Sancho, here are your digs. Lady Gwen is right next door. Convenient, eh? Now we don't want you slippin' about the hallway in your knickers, right?" Ben shot him another look. "Oh, come on. Don't pretend you don't know what I'm talking about. Can't have you leaving the Lady Gwen all by herself in the room next door. But let's be discreet, okay? There's a connecting door at the end of the bookcase. The key is in this drawer. And stop looking at me like that, okay? See you later."

After Reggie left, Ben retrieved the key and tapped lightly on the connecting door.

Chapter 39

A Muted Celebration
– Christmas 1944

Shortly after six o'clock, Lord Percy, accompanied by his aide Alistair Baxter, arrived from London. Lady Percy was napping, but Elizabeth greeted her father by leaping into his arms and kissing him on both cheeks. "Daddy, it's wonderful to see you again! How're you feeling? Did you have a good trip down from London? Are you so very tired, thirsty? Can we have Bates get you something? Reggie and Ben are here. Ben brought his fiancée. Her name is Gwen. She seems nice, very pretty, and well mannered."

Elizabeth sighed and frowned. "Not sure she's good enough for Ben," she added sadly. "But I guess he knows best. She's a nurse. In fact, she nursed Ben after he was shot down during the Battle of Britain. That's how they met. Can I take your hat and coat . . . ?"

When Elizabeth paused for a breath, Lord Percy interjected, "Slow down, dear child. I'm barely inside the front door. At least let me get into the entry hall." He handed his hat and coat to Bates, who hovered nearby, trying to stay out of Elizabeth's way. "Welcome home, m'Lord," he said, taking Lord Percy's winter garments, "The wing commander and Colonel Findlay are waiting in the drawing room, sir."

"Oh!" Elizabeth exclaimed. "Is this going to be men only? I can't join you?"

"No, dear." Lord Percy smiled, kissing her on the cheek. "Have a few things I need to discuss with Reginald and Benjamin. I'll see you a bit later. We'll sit down and have a nice long chat. I promise."

Releasing a puff of relief and rolling his eyes, Lord Percy turned to Baxter, "This is my daughter, Elizabeth. Dear, this is Mr. Baxter. He'll spend Christmas with us and return to London with me on Boxing Day."

Elizabeth bobbed a quick curtsy and extended her hand to Baxter, who shook it solemnly.

"Father, are you sure I can't join you for conversation in the drawing room?" she asked. Lord Percy gave her a weary smile and shook his head.

She looked crestfallen. "Oh, all right." She pouted. "I suppose you'll drink whiskey and just talk about the war. I'll be so happy when all of this terrible fighting is over, and the world returns to normal."

"There, there, sweetheart," he murmured, patting her on the cheek. "We all will be happy when that day comes. And it may be soon. Now if you'll excuse me. I need to have a few words with Reggie and Ben." Elizabeth stomped upstairs, muttering to herself.

Reggie and Ben rose quickly when Lord Percy and Baxter entered the room. "Hello, Father," Reggie said, extending his right hand. "Good to see you again." Lord Percy grasped Reggie's hand and squeezed his son's shoulder with his left. "And good to see you again, Reginald. You're looking fit. Wounds appear fully healed."

"Yessir," Reggie said and turned to Ben. "You remember Benjamin, Father?"

"Indeed. Indeed!" he boomed, clutching Ben's right hand in a crushing grip. "Good to see you again, m'boy. Ah! See it is colonel now. New promotion, eh? Good show!"

"Pleased to see you again, Lord Percy." Ben grinned, trying to cover his shock at how exhausted his Lordship looked. His gray complexion, sunken cheeks, and bleary eyes reflected the toll the war years had taken on his once-robust body. His stooped posture was even more pronounced, and his stride had been reduced to an uncertain shuffle.

Lord Percy introduced Baxter and looked around for a chair. "Please, sir," Ben said, "take this seat. I still need to stretch my legs after the train trip from Cambridge."

Lord Percy peered at him over his half-glasses. "Harrumph! Thank you. Do need a sit down. Pity your trip wasn't all that comfortable, Benjamin," he rumbled as he settled into the armchair. "Train travel in England is not what it used to be. Bloody war and all that." He paused. "Ah yes, Reginald, I will have a glass of Scotland's finest. How about you, Baxter?" he asked his aide, who nodded his assent. Reggie stepped to the bar.

240

Once they were settled in chairs in front of the fire, Reggie raised his glass. "Welcome to Calvert Hall, Father. Has been, what, six months since you've been able to get down here? How are things going in Whitehall? Winding down a bit, what with the war apparently entering the final phases?"

"Winding down? Bloody hell!" Lord Percy exploded. "Busier than we've ever been, right, Baxter? And the Huns' Ardennes counteroffensive, especially their thrust into Belgium, has knocked our plans into a cocked hat."

"But with the Battle of the Bulge stalled . . .," Reggie began.

"Stalled, maybe, mostly by the filthy winter weather across the front," Lord Percy snapped. "Our ground forces haven't been able to push the Huns back. So there they sit on both sides, up to their arses in snow, and we can't give our lads air support because of the bloody extended overcast."

"The Eighth Air Force was able to get one good attack in when the weather cleared briefly," Ben said. "But the cloud cover moved across the entire area again. We've been on alert to help out since early December but haven't been able to launch effective strikes because of the weather here and over the battle line. Air Transport Command also hasn't even been able to airlift supplies and ammunition to our troops."

"Damn frustrating that we're not able to do a bloody thing to help them, especially the American units surrounded at Bastogne," Lord Percy grumped. "Haven't the foggiest idea how we missed the buildup leading to the counterattack. Too many people were convinced we had the German Army on the run. Terrible mistake. Terrible!"

Reggie refilled everyone's glass and turned to Lord Percy. "Have the feeling you didn't gather us to talk only about the Ardennes mess. What else is on your mind?"

"Right, Reginald. While it may sound presumptuous, I'm convinced the Ardennes mess will be resolved. We'll finally put paid to Herr Hitler and his henchmen, hopefully early next year. So I want to talk about your futures." He paused to quaff his whiskey. "Two possibilities, actually, umm, both of which involve planning and foresight."

Ben leaned forward. "How's that, Lord Percy? I mean, are you talking about the next year or so or long term after the war is over?"

"What I mean, Benjamin, is that it seems certain we're well on the way to defeating Germany, even taking the current counteroffensive into account. I think we can expect to put an end to the Third Reich by midyear. This will lead to considerable instability, if not confusion, in both the British and American military establishments. There will be considerable reductions in force size. I think it is time for the two of you to sort out what you'll want to be doing over the next several years, in or out of the military."

Lord Percy paused to take a long quaff of whiskey, smacked his lips, and set the glass down. He stared at Ben and Reggie from under his bushy eyebrows. "Has either of you given serious thought to this, or are you still totally fixated on fighting the war?"

An uneasy silence settled over room. Ben fidgeted, cleared his throat, and looked at Reggie, who tipped him a slight nod. Ben pressed ahead. "Well, sir, I've been giving this considerable thought. Gwen, ah, she's my fiancée, and ah, well, you'll meet her later. Ah, she's upstairs resting. Will join us later for dinner, and . . ."

"Yes, yes," Lord Percy interrupted. "And I presume the young lady figures in your plans to remain in England a bit longer?"

"Yessir, for sure," Ben said. "We plan to get married as soon as the war in Europe is over, and I want to be sure I can stay in England long enough for that before getting shipped back to the States or being reassigned to the Pacific Theater."

"And how would you arrange to stay in England?"

"Well, sir, I've heard about the USSBS, ah, you know, the United States Strategic Bombing Survey that was formed late last year . . ."

"I'm familiar with the USSBS," Lord Percy interrupted again. "Was part of the original discussions and helped plan how it would be carried out. Do you see yourself playing a part in the survey?"

"Yessir!" Ben responded. "I've spent the last two years flying nearly forty bombing missions, an' I expect I'll be flying a few more before the war is over. Figure I dropped bombs on a lotta the targets they'll be surveying so I can help bring some perspective on what defenses we faced, weather factors, and how that affected our accuracy."

"So what have you done to explore the possibly of joining the USSBS?" Lord Percy asked.

"I passed a letter to the USSBS chairman up through our command chain and asked for details on how I can apply," Ben said. "Got an acknowledgement letter back, saying they'd let me know, but so far, I haven't heard."

"Harrumph!" Lord Percy snorted. "Sounds like you're at least taking some initiative to keep yourself in England for a while after the war ends. But what I'm talking about to you and Reginald is longer term. What are your plans?"

"Sir, I need to finish what we started, helping to defeat Germany by destroying her industrial base, cutting her petroleum supplies, and disrupting her transportation system, mainly railroads."

"Sounds as though you've read too many Air Ministry briefing papers." Lord Percy chuckled.

"Now, Father, I sense you have something in mind for me," Reggie said.

"Of course! Why the hell do you think I've asked you to meet with me?" Lord Percy responded. He turned to Baxter. "Tell him what we've been discussing."

Baxter cleared his throat. "His Lordship has had discussions with Air Marshal Sir Ralph Sorley about the Empire Test Pilots' School, which the air marshal established last year as the Test Pilot's Training Flight at RAF Boscombe Down . . ."

"Yes, I've heard about it and was planning to look into it," Reggie interjected.

"Wonderful," Baxter said. "Then you know a bit about the school. Last year, Air Marshal Sorley became concerned that too many pilots were being killed testing new aircraft that were being rushed into service. He thought a dedicated flight school was needed to train pilots to safely test new high-performance designs, so he ordered formation of the school for test pilots and flight test engineers at Boscombe Down. As far as we know, it is the first training school of its type. I suppose you know its motto is Learn to test. Test to learn."

"Point is, Reginald," Lord Percy interrupted, "this would be a perfect fit for you with your wide range of experience and number of flying hours. Would provide a nice transition to the postwar RAF. We won't always need wartime levels of fighter pilots, but we will need test pilots trained to evaluate and approve new aircraft designs. Worth looking into, eh?"

"Of course, and I'd intended to do just that," Reggie said. "What do you think of the concept, Ben?"

"Sounds like a swell idea," Ben said. "All along I've felt we've taken big risks, rushing new airplanes into service and then putting inexperienced pilots in them and shoving them into combat. I like the idea of a test pilot's school. Wish the USAAF would adopt something like that."

"My primary concern is the range of airplanes I'd have to get current in, including multiengine jobs," Reggie said. "I have bags of single engine time but not any in multiengine types."

"That transition is a big one," Ben said. "It took time, but I managed to transition from the Spitfire to the B-17. If I could do it, you sure can, Reggie."

A soft gong note floated in from the entry hall. "Dinner gong," Lord Percy said. "Better get along. Have half an hour to dress for dinner. We'll take up this topic after dinner or tomorrow."

Ben entered into his room and tapped on the connecting door to Gwen's room. Her sweet "Come in, love" sent shivers down his spine. Gwen stood adjusting her hair in front of a mirror, and Ben swallowed hard as he admired her beauty, accentuated by her white tight-fitting uniform. He slipped up behind her and reached out to embrace her.

"Careful, Colonel." She smiled. "If you mess up my hair, I'll be another half hour getting it right."

Ben stopped short and stepped back. "Okay, pretty lady. You had your chance at a big loving hug. Don't know when you'll have another." Gwen whirled and planted a kiss on his lips, leaving a smear of freshly applied red lipstick across his mouth. "Oh, sir! Are you sure there won't be another chance?" She giggled.

"Sorry, ma'am. I haven't any more time to dally with you." Ben sniffed. "Have to get changed into my formal uniform for dinner."

Ben stepped stiffly down the main staircase with Gwen clutching his arm. All present turned to admire the handsome couple. Elizabeth's expression switched from a steely eyed squint to a mournful puppy stare as she looked first at Gwen and then at Ben.

The party of seven settled into their places at the dinner table. Lord Percy sat at the head of the table with Lady Percy to his right and Elizabeth next to her. Ben sat next to Elizabeth. Gwen was seated on Lord Percy's left with Reggie next to her and Baxter on his left. Elizabeth was thrilled to be sitting next to Ben but shrugged resignedly when she realized he seemed to have eyes only for Gwen across the table.

Lord Percy formally welcomed everyone to the table, which Ben thought was a bit stiff. Lady Percy echoed the welcome and added, "We'll be having a special dessert tonight. Thanks to Benjamin's wonderful gift of a crate of fresh oranges."

The dinner proceeded smoothly. Lord Percy made an effort to chat with Elizabeth, but it was apparent his mind was on other things. Ben focused on minding his manners and wielded his knife and fork in proper British style. As he deftly fixed food on the back of his fork, he thought of his first dinner at Calvert Hall. Reggie's aunt, Lady Bayswater, was seated next to him and had made a point of dismissing him as a peasant bumpkin from the American Outback. Ben decided to fight back. He purposely cut his meat into small pieces, transferred his fork to his right hand American style, and popped the pieces into his mouth. Lady Bayswater sniffed, registering her distain for his boorish table manners, but nearly fainted when he carefully folded his bread, clutched it in his left hand, and used it to push vegetables onto his fork.

But tonight, not wanting to embarrass Gwen, Ben sat up straight and ate like a proper Englishman. Dinner was capped with the special dessert Lady Percy had promised—a sizeable bowl of Scottish trifle, smothered with slices of the oranges Ben had brought.

After dinner, Lord Percy gathered the men in the drawing room for brandy and cigars and continued the conversation about the war and postwar prospects for Reggie and Ben. "As I was saying before dinner," Lord Percy rumbled, "the war clearly is moving into the final stages in Europe, the Ardennes counteroffensive notwithstanding. Don't know how you two see it from your operational perspectives, but at the ministry level, we think it is a matter of time, a short time, before we force Germany into unconditional surrender."

Reggie and Ben nodded. While some raids on targets deep in Germany still encountered strong resistance, both agreed it was apparent the Luftwaffe had suffered huge losses of pilots and airplanes and was slowly being decimated by the relentless Allied attacks.

"So you see, this means thousands of British and American pilots will become redundant once we've achieved total victory in Europe," Lord Percy continued. "Certain that'll be the case in both the RAF and the USAAF. Only so many additional pilots will be needed in the Pacific Theater, which means unless you have a long-term pilot's slot, you'll either be relegated to a desk job or 'demobbed' as our Australian friends put it."

"Understand what you're saying and agree with your assessment," Reggie said. "Can't speak for Ben. I've given it some thought but haven't taken any action. I've been preoccupied with getting back up to form physically after our escape and managing the influx of a new mob of pilots."

"And I've been totally focused on handling my new duties as commander of the 509th," Ben interjected.

"But I think it's time for us to poke our heads up and take the long view. Think of the future," Reggie concluded.

"Right you are," Lord Percy agreed. "Let's leave it there for the moment. Both of you need to give this some serious thought. And I've had a long day. Need sleep. Your mother has a big dinner planned for tomorrow. Invited a crowd of relatives. Think there'll be at least twenty around the table. Damn and blast, there goes my quiet Christmas holiday at home!"

He levered himself out of his chair and called good night over his shoulder as he shuffled out of the room. Baxter trooped along behind him.

Reggie and Ben sat quietly in front of the fire. Ben broke the silence. "Your father's right, Reggie. We need to look to the future. Even my plan to get involved with the USSBS is short term I guess. That probably wouldn't keep me occupied in Europe more'n four to six months, maybe longer. Then what?"

"Then what, indeed, Sancho," Reggie responded. "I've been flying for nearly fifteen years since starting my flight training with the cadets. Flying and a bit of fighting along the way is all I've known. Haven't given much thought to my career path until now. World events have pretty much determined my course so far. Now's the time to start charting my own course."

"Umm, Reggie, speaking of our futures, I've been kinda wrapped up with Gwen and . . ."

"So I've noticed," Reggie interrupted with a sly grin.

"Yeah, okay, okay. But seriously, I've been, uh, whataya call it, self-absorbed, and I haven't asked you about your girl, uh, Lucy. Where are things with her?"

"Thanks for asking, Ben. We'd been on and off for some time. Now, apparently, it's off for good. Can't believe I didn't tell you. She's engaged to a bloke from RAF intelligence."

"No, you hadn't told me. Damn sorry to hear it, Reggie."

Reggie tossed an offhand wave, obviously not wanting to talk about it anymore. "Guess it wouldn't have worked out long term anyway."

The two battle-weary warriors finished their brandies. They stared into the other's eyes as they shook hands and headed upstairs. Once in his room, Ben tapped again on the connecting door to Gwen's room.

Christmas morning dawned clear with a refreshing bite in the rising breeze. They had eaten breakfast in shifts as they had awakened and come downstairs. Ben led Gwen on a stroll around the Calvert Hall grounds, squinted in the pale sunlight, and wondered if the weather also was clearing over central Europe. If it did clear, they could be recalled to quickly launch missions to relieve the besieged Allied troops in the Ardennes. *Face that when it happens.*

Meanwhile, he concentrated on showing Gwen the manicured beauty of the formal gardens and the stables full of sleek thoroughbred horses. "First time I was here, Reggie talked me into riding one of these beautiful beasts," Ben mused. "Forget which one it was, but it was pretty gentle. That is until we headed back to the barn, and Reggie suggested a gallop home. Everything went fine until we came up to a short fence. Reggie and his horse sailed over it without missin' a beat. I'd only ridden work horses back home and never jumped anything with those old plugs, so I wasn't ready for the fence."

Ben chuckled as he remember that frightening moment.

"Unfortunately, my horse was more than ready, so over we went. I dropped the reins and almost flew outta the saddle. Grabbed the horse's mane, and he landed with a thud and skidded to a stop with me dangling under his neck like a cheap necklace. Reggie laughed so hard he nearly fell outta his saddle. Think I threatened to kill him if he told anyone about it."

"Now you've gone and done it yourself, silly," Gwen gasped through her laughter. "I'd have given a tuppence or two to have witnessed that."

"Yeah, okay. Looking back, I guess it is pretty funny, but I could have broken my neck."

"That would have been terrible," Gwen said, stifling her giggles.

That evening, the Christmas dinner guests arrived in a stream of stately chauffeur-driven automobiles. Calvert Hall soon was awash with extravagantly dressed women and their formally attired husbands, companions, and male escorts. Ben fought down a sense of being surrounded by hostiles as Reggie led Gwen and him through a round of introductions. He was amazed at how well Gwen retained her composure.

Ben scanned the room for Reggie's insufferable cousin, Brewster. Ben remembered with disgust how condescending and insulting Brewster had been and how he had sneered when he learned Silverman, Ben's commander, was Jewish.

"Don't see cousin Brewster. He isn't here, is he?" Ben whispered to Reggie.

"No, Ben. He's been sent to some godforsaken outpost in India. Hope to never see him again."

"How about Lady Bayswater? I won't be seated next to her again, will I? An' I hope you can keep her away from Gwen."

Reggie laughed. "Right you are, old bean. Lady Battleax is over there by the fireplace. I'll try not to let her near either you or Gwen."

But that was not to be. Lady Bayswater swooped down on them and demanded that Reggie introduce her to "this lovely young nurse! Such a credit to serve in this important capacity in wartime."

Reggie completed the introductions, and Lady Bayswater gushed over Gwen. She cast a suspicious eye at Ben but seemed not to remember the details of their first meeting at a Christmas dinner years ago.

Nursing a round of predinner drinks, the ladies settled into gossipy clusters around the drawing room. Several cornered Gwen and plied her with questions about her experiences as a wartime nurse. Ben grinned as she handled the queries with style and poise. The male guests surrounded Reggie and Ben and bombarded them with questions about the state of the air war against Germany. This time, they treated Ben with the respect due his rank, the row of ribbons on his tunic, and the importance of his operational assignment.

At dinner, Lady Percy announced they would be "treated to an American specialty, a succulent baked ham compliments of Benjamin, to supplement their traditional roast goose." This earned Ben a round of "hear, hear, and good show."

Ben, again seated across Gwen, ate properly and with care. He tried not to imagine he was under scrutiny, but each time he glanced at Lady Bayswater, seated across the table to his left, she seemed to be peering at him. Finally, she wrinkled her brow, then glared, flaring the nostrils on her hawk-like nose. Ben looked quickly at his plate. *Okay, Benjamin, she's remembered. No more folded bread gambits.* Dinner progressed without incident. All complimented Lady Percy on the succulent ham and thanked Ben for the gift.

As dessert was being served, Bates entered the dining room, stepped to Lord Percy's left shoulder, and whispered into his ear. "Of course! He must take the call," Lord Percy grumbled as he signaled Reggie to follow Bates. Ben watched with interest. *What now? Is this a recall?*

Reggie returned to the table within minutes. "Mother, I'm sorry to disrupt this excellent dinner, but I've just received a call from my deputy wing commander. I've been recalled immediately to Wittering Air Station. Our meteorologists are telling us they expect the weather to clear over central Europe, the Ardennes in particular, within the next twenty-four hours. My wing has been alerted to prepare to escort bombers and aerial supply transports over the battle line, perhaps as early as the day after tomorrow."

This prompted a round of groans around the table, interspersed with "Oh no!" and "Too bad for us but good for our chaps on the line." Lady Percy sighed deeply and reached for Lord Percy's arm. Elizabeth stifled a sob with her napkin.

Turning to Ben, Reggie continued, "Sancho, this is going to be a maximum effort, so I expect you'll be getting an immediate recall as well. As if on cue, Bates reentered to dining room and whispered to Lord Percy that there was a call for Colonel Findlay.

As Ben rose to take the phone call, Reggie signaled him. "I say, Ben, Wittering are flying down an Avro Anson to fetch me back to the station. It's a twin-engine job used mainly for training. This one has a cabin configured as a utility transport. Seats eight to ten, I believe. Anyway, plenty of room for you to join me. Save Eighth Air Force from sending another airplane."

"That'll be swell, Reggie," Ben said. Then eyeing Gwen, he asked, "Need to figure out how to get from Wittering to my base at Parham though, right?"

"Not a problem, old bean. The Anson crew can drop me at Wittering and then pop you over to Parham."

When Ben returned to the dining room, he looked grim. "You're right, Reggie, it is shaping up to a maximum effort. The 509th is alerted for a mission day after tomorrow. And every C-47 in the Eighth Air Force is to be committed to a massive airlift to drop supplies along the battle line. I guess everybody will be needed for this one."

The third phone call was for Gwen. She returned to the dining room and looked at Reggie. "I think you could have two hitchhikers in your Anson. I've just been recalled as well. Can you take me along? I really don't want to face that long train ride."

"Not a problem, Gwen," Reggie said. "Plenty of room. We can get you back to Parham as well, and then Ben can get a staff car to deliver you to your hospital in Cambridge."

"Where do we meet the Anson?" Ben asked.

"There's an emergency recovery field, Hawkestone Station, south of Winchester. 'Bout ten miles from here. Watkins can drive us over in the Roller. Better get changed and packed. The airplane is due in about an hour."

The threesome gathered with the rest of the dinner party on Calvert Hall's front steps. Watkins loaded their luggage in the Rolls and stood by the open rear door. All three embraced Lady Percy and a sobbing Elizabeth and shook hands with Lord Percy. "Godspeed and good luck to the three of you," he rumbled. "If we turn back this counteroffensive, we've got the Hun beaten for certain. Look forward to seeing you back at Calvert Hall soon."

They waved to the assembled guests, climbed into the Rolls, and drove down the long driveway.

Chapter 40

BACK TO WAR —

Watkins eased the Rolls up to the locked gate at the Hawkestone emergency landing station. Twin spotlights flashed on, illuminating the car and enabling the soldiers in the guardhouse to see who was in the car, while they remained in shadow. One of the soldiers stepped out of the guardhouse and ordered all occupants to step out of the car and face the lights. Ben had an uneasy feeling the second soldier in the guardhouse had an automatic weapon aimed at them.

"Wing Commander Reginald Percy, USAAF Colonel Benjamin A. Findlay, and Nurse Gwen Brewster," Reggie called out. "You should have received a signal from RAF Wittering Air Station concerning me. They're sending an Avro Anson down to fetch me back to the station on an emergency recall. Colonel Findlay and Nurse Brewster are accompanying me. They will proceed to Parham Air Station, where Colonel Findlay commands the 509th Heavy Bombardment Group, and Addenbrooke's Hospital in Cambridge, where Nurse Brewster is a member of the triage staff."

"Sir, please step up to the gate and produce your ID," the soldier called out. He signaled the other soldier to douse the searchlights, leaving the gate area illuminated by a bank of overhead lights. He carefully examined Reggie's ID. "Sorry to put you through this, Wing Commander Percy," he said, snapping to attention and saluting. "We're on special alert too. Have been warned enemy infiltrators may be trying to sneak into these emergency bases to meet extraction flights. Umm, we don't have a full personnel complement at these emergency fields."

"Not to worry, Sergeant," Reggie responded. "Good to see you chaps are alert and on the ball. Can't be too careful."

They all got back in the Rolls. The sergeant unlocked the gate and directed Watkins to a parking spot on the airfield ramp. A RAF flight lieutenant trotted over from the mobile airport tower van and saluted. "Welcome to Hawkestone, Wing Commander. I'm Flight Leftenant Smyth. Your Anson pilot radioed they're about twenty miles out. Be on the ground shortly."

The Anson swooped out of the chilly night air, touched down smoothly, and taxied to the ramp. The pilot swung the airplane to a stop with the left side facing the ramp and cut the left engine. He kept the right engine running. An air crewman popped open the rear door and signaled the three aboard. They said quick good-byes to Watkins and Smyth and clambered into the airplane. "Skipper wants to make a fast turnaround," Wing Commander," the crewman shouted. "We were told 'buster, buster' all the way, sir. Apparently, they want you back in a hurry."

Noting Ben and Gwen, he asked, "Are these the other two passengers we're to take on to Parham, sir?"

"Right you are, Sergeant," Reggie said as the crewman slammed and locked the door. "Reckon they're also needed at home soonest, so it'll be 'buster, buster' to Parham as well."

As the Anson lifted into the night, Reggie grinned at his companions and gave them a thumbs up. "Hated to bust up that jolly Christmas celebration, but it'll be worth it if the weather breaks, and we can give our chaps on the Ardennes battle line some help."

They settled back into their own thoughts as the Anson droned northward. Ben pushed the Christmas break to the back of his mind and concentrated on what had to be done to prepare the 509th for the upcoming mission.

Fatigue overtook Ben, and his chin began to drop to his chest when the copilot stepped into the cabin and announced they were beginning a straight in landing approach to Wittering. The Anson touched down smoothly and fast taxied to the ramp. Again, the pilot kept the right engine running as the crewman popped the aft door. Reggie kissed Gwen on both cheeks, shook hands with Ben, and thumped him on the back.

"See you over the Ardennes, Sancho," he yelled as he hopped out onto the ramp."

The Anson was airborne within minutes. The pilots fully understood that "buster, buster" meant to haul their arses with no delay. The short hop to Parham passed quickly, and Ben helped Gwen down onto the 509th's expansive ramp.

Ben's deputy, Lieutenant Colonel Joe Atkins, trotted out from base operations. He greeted Gwen and turned to Ben. "Got a staff car waiting out front to take Gwen to Cambridge," he said. "Also got the mission prep well under way. Looks like the weather is going to break late tomorrow. Should be clear for us to launch the next morning. We expect the field order tomorrow midday."

"That's swell Joe. Knew I could depend on you. I'll see Gwen to the car and meet you in my office. We need to review crew records and find out how many airplane maintenance can give us. You've alerted the bomb depot and armorers?" Joe nodded.

"Oh, by the way, call the motor pool, and tell them to send a second driver in the staff car to fetch my jeep. I left it in the parking lot at the Cambridge train station when Gwen and I left for Calvert Hall. There's no key, but I disabled it by taking the rotor arm out of the distributor. It's lodged inside the left rear wheel." Joe headed for the phone.

Ben took Gwen by the arm and led her to the waiting staff car. The driver hopped out, saluted Ben, and opened the rear door. "Thank you, Sergeant," Ben said. "Swing by the motor pool on your way out and pick up a second driver. He'll retrieve the jeep I left at the Cambridge train station."

Ben turned and embraced Gwen, whispering in her ear, "Take care, love. Sorry our Christmas celebration had to be cut short, but it's beyond our control. Look, uh, I'll be pretty busy for the next few days, but I'll call you as soon as we complete this next mission." Gwen shook with suppressed sobs. "Please be careful, Ben," she murmured. "Call me as soon as you can." He kissed her long and hard and eased her into the car. She blew him a mournful kiss as the car pulled away.

Ben strode back into base operations and signaled Joe and Major Bruce Fielder, newly appointed 509th group operations officer, to follow him. "Let's get over to my office. We need to review all the crew pairings and verify with maintenance how many airplanes they can give us."

Seated around Ben's desk, they ran through the crew list, making a few changes to shift experienced copilots and gunners onto newly formed crews. "I'll lead this mission, Joe," Ben said, noting the look of disappointment that crossed his face. "Don't worry. There'll be more than one mission in this campaign. You'll lead the next one. And we'll swap leading on subsequent missions."

He turned to Major Fielder. "And, Bruce, we'll put you in the rotation. You'll get a chance to lead as well." Fielder nodded and smiled his thanks.

"I'll take Carl Stoddard's airplane, Rolling Thunder," Ben said. "He won't like it, but he'll have to cope. Think he has four more missions to do. He's anxious to get back home, so take someone else's airplane next time, Joe, when you lead."

They worked on the mission planning until 1900 hours and then headed to the officer's club for dinner. "Hit the sack early tonight," Ben said after dinner. "We've got two big days ahead of us. Let's hope the weather fellas are right."

The weather cleared the next afternoon as forecast, and Parham's team shifted into full gear on mission preparations. Maintenance reported all twenty-one of the 509th B-17s were available for the next day's mission. Servicing and arming the bombers continued apace. Ben set the briefing for 0630 hours the next day and take off at 0800 hours. He searched out Rolling Thunder's crew, informed Stoddard he'd sit out this mission, and introduced himself to the crewmembers he hadn't met before.

Chapter 41

BLUNTING THE COUNTEROFFENSIVE —

Ben revved the engines on Rolling Thunder and led the Congo line of twenty-one B-17s to Parham's runway. He taxied into takeoff position, ordered his copilot Walt to lock the tail wheel, and rechecked all instruments and switches. When the green takeoff flare arched from the control tower balcony, Ben advanced the throttles and released the brakes. Rolling Thunder roared down the runway.

Forty-five minutes later, they rendezvoused with ten other B-17 groups over Harwich, England, and maneuvered into the Number 3 position in the string of 220 bombers sweeping across the English Channel. Three other multi-airplane fleets assembled at other rendezvous points and headed for different sections of the Ardennes battle line.

Ben's bomber string made landfall over Oostende, Belgium; overflew Brussels; and headed southeast past Bastogne, where American troops had been surrounded and under siege since mid-December. Their target was the major rail center and marshalling yards near Wiesbaden, Germany, key points for transporting supplies to the German troops along the Ardennes battle line.

They encountered no antiaircraft flak or enemy fighters en route, but Ben called the crew on the intercom. "Approaching Bastogne. Lead groups have already penetrated German airspace. They know we're coming, so watch for fighters."

The first call followed within minutes. "Top turret. Ten, twelve fighters . . . Uh, look like 109s . . . two o'clock high. Rollin' in for frontal attack." Gunners swiveled all forward-firing guns into position. Ben radioed, "Skipper to waist gunners, heads up. Watch for 'em as they swing past. Tail gunner, watch for 262s sneaking in for coordinated attacks from the rear." As it turned out, no 262s rose to engage the bombers.

The Me 109 pilots rolled in to attack in pairs, muzzle flashes winking from their dual machine guns and nose cannons, separated and slashed past on both sides of the B-17. As before, they rolled into vertical turns, exposing the armored bellies of their fighters toward the bomber's gunners, and climbed away to position for another attack run.

"'Nother pair rolling in for attack!" crackled over the intercom. "Heads up. Get 'em in a crossfire!" The second wave of fighters ran into a hail of concentrated fire. They pressed their attacks dangerously close to the bombers, and the left fighter in the second pair bucked under several hits and spiraled smoking earthward. The third wave fared even worse, as the gunners zeroed in on both fighters. The one of the left exploded in a fiery ball. A wing blew off the one wheeling to the right, and it rolled into a violent death spiral.

"Great shootin'!" someone yelled into the intercom. "That's three Krauts who won't be bothering us anymore!"

The fourth wave of fighters rolled in to attack, but the pilots started firing beyond effective range and rolled away before the B-17 gunners could return concentrated fire.

"Looks like they're low-time pilots," Ben shouted to Walt. "The Luftwaffe must be scraping the bottom of the barrel, throwin' inexperienced kids at us."

"Yeah," Walt yelled back. "Could mean there aren't many old hands left in Herr Goering's air force."

The sky suddenly cleared of fighters. "Not much of a show by the Luftwaffe," Ben shouted. Walt signaled a thumbs-up. Ben called their navigator on the intercom. "Bernie, how're we doing?"

"Looking good, Skipper. Expect turn to heading zero nine zero in coupla minutes. IP is Bad Kreuznach then turn to zero one zero degrees for the final run to the rail center."

At the IP, Ben turned Rolling Thunder and followed the two lead bomber groups on the final run to the huge rail center southwest of Wiesbaden. Smoke and flames roiled up from hits scored by the lead groups marking the aim point. There was no antiaircraft fire.

Ben called his bombardier, "Brad, you on the target?"

"Roger, Skipper!"

"You're airplane," Ben responded, relinquishing control. Brad made final course corrections with his Norden bombsight.

"On target. Bomb bay doors open. Steady, steady . . . Bombs away!"

Relieved of its bomb load, Rolling Thunder lurched upward, and Ben signaled Walt to help with a steep turn to the left. As they headed back to England, Davis radioed from the tail gunner's position that the 509th bombs dropped into the center of the target zone and that huge secondary explosions were shooting giant columns of smoke and flame into the sky.

"Skipper to tail. Did everyone make it past the target?"

"Roger that, Skipper. I count twenty following us." Ben nodded, smiling under his oxygen mask. "Swell!" he exulted and signaled Walt to take control and fly them home.

As they passed over Bastogne, Ben called the crew's attention to the columns of smoke along the battle line. "Looks like the close air support fellas are pounding the hell outta the Germans," he said. A chorus of cheers echoed through the intercom.

The 509th post-mission briefing room at Parham reverberated with a cacophony of excited shouts as the aircrews tumbled in to give their reports. They had hit the target squarely, had shot down half a dozen enemy fighters, and had not lost a single B-17. All agreed it had been a good show all around.

Their reports of the half-hearted response from the Luftwaffe confirmed intelligence assessments that the German Air Force was "on its heels." They obviously were unable to replace earlier airplane losses, were resorting to sending inexperienced pilots into combat, and were suffering from diminished fuel supplies. Since no 262s rose to meet any of the attacking bombers, intelligence officers concluded that the combined tactics of destroying the jet fighter's fuel refineries and attacking the few that could get airborne when they returned to their bases to refuel and rearm were greatly reducing the threat from the high-speed fighters.

Ben stood grinning with Colonel Atkins as they watched the flight crews eagerly crowd around the debriefing officers. "Are we on the schedule for tomorrow, Joe?" he asked. "No. High command is rotating us with B-24 groups from the Fifteenth Air Force. We'll be tasked the day after tomorrow and probably will continue some kinda rotation until we've helped the ground pounders break out of the Ardennes."

"Good! Let's let these fellas celebrate a bit," Ben said. "They've been sittin' around too long, waiting for the weather to clear. And they pulled off a textbook mission today. Tell 'em the bars are open tonight, and the drinks are on the house."

Atkins whistled for silence and made the announcement. The response was a crescendo of cheers that threatened to blow the windows out of the briefing hut.

The 509th settled into the mission rotation with the B-24 groups as they took turns pummeling the rail and road systems, supplying the German front lines. These missions, combined with close air support by British and American ground-attack forces, helped open Allied breakouts all along the Ardennes front. By the end of January, the combined British and American armies had pushed the Wehrmacht back to the pre-counteroffensive line. This opened the way for a rush toward the Rhine River, prompting a feverish round of betting as to who would cross the border first to penetrate the Fatherland.

The war in Europe entered the final stages as the British Twenty-First Army Group in the north, the U.S. Twelfth Army in the center, and the Franco-American Southern Group of Armies continued to slug their way eastward.

The 509th had the day off. Ben sat in his office, feet propped on the desk, and stared at the ceiling. Memories of his wartime experiences swirled through his mind. *How had the years passed so quickly since 1938 in Spain and now nearly five years into World War 2?* A knock on the door jolted him back to the present. His clerk stepped in and handed him an envelope. "Official-looking letter, Colonel, from some outfit called the United States Strategic Bombing Survey." Ben reached for the envelope and slit it open. His application to join the USSBS had been approved. He would be contacted by Brigadier General Harold R. Sampson, commander of the Eighth Air Force Detachment tasked with surveying prime targets the 509th and its companion groups had bombed.

The following day, Sampson's adjutant telephoned and asked when it would be convenient to send a C-47 up from High Wycombe to fly Ben down for an interview with the general. Ben agreed the next morning would work fine. Joe would take the 509th out on that day's mission.

General Sampson greeted Ben warmly. "Heard a lot about your career experiences, Colonel," Sampson said, returning Ben's salute and extending his right hand. "I'm especially interested in your time with the 509ᵗʰ. Between you and Colonel Silverman, you bombed all of the targets on our survey list. Think you can bring some real-life experience to this operation, and I'd like you to join me as deputy commander of the detachment."

Ben pursed his lips and nodded. "Uh, when would you want me, General? I'm still very much involved with the 509ᵗʰ. Nobody knows how much longer we're going be pressing strategic attacks against Germany. Not even sure what kinda targets are left. But we still may have missions to complete."

"Been thinking about that," Sampson said. "I know you have unfinished business with the 509ᵗʰ, and I appreciate your desire to continue to lead the group. Actually, we can proceed in a couple of ways. We don't know precisely how long the survey work will take or how long the war will last, so we can have you assigned to us on TDY, temporary duty. We'd effectively have you on call, and when we need your services, you could relinquish day-to-day command to Colonel Atkins as acting commander.

"If we were to take you on a permanent assignment, we'd have to give you some time to wrap up things at the 509ᵗʰ and turn over the command. The way the air war over Europe is progressing, I'm not sure how much longer you'll be conducting your strategic bombing missions."

"I'd prefer to join you TDY on an as-needed basis until we see what develops, sir," Ben interjected. "At the moment, we're rotating missions with the Fifteenth, so we're down to two mission a month."

"I'm monitoring the mission roster," Sampson said. "Looks like they're pretty routine."

"They are, but we're still getting shot at. Germany's fighter command is pretty badly depleted, and their flak defenses are spotty at best. Think the Luftwaffe is running low on fuel, and the antiaircraft units are running outta ammunition. Still I like to retain command of the 509ᵗʰ until our immediate future becomes clearer."

"Agreed," Sampson said. "I can't see Germany hanging on much longer now, so why don't you plan to come over to us in February or the first of March latest?"

"That will be fine, sir!" Ben grinned.

"We'll be equipped with modified Gooney Birds, ones with the double aft cargo doors. They'll also be fitted with tie-downs to hold motorcycles with sidecars and ramps for loading and unloading them. Each crew will include pilot and copilot, a crew chief, three bomb site surveyors, a records specialist, and a German-speaking interpreter.

Combination of the C-47 and motorcycles should let our teams get close to most of the major survey sites."

Sampson leafed through some papers on his desk. "You'll be assigned with RAF Flight Leftenant Richard Crenshaw as your copilot. He flew sixty night bombing missions in Lancasters with RAF Bomber Command and will help assess the effectiveness of their area bombing practices. By the way, Findlay, do you have any time in C-47s?"

"I've only flown one for a few hours on the final leg of our trip home from the German POW camp," Ben said. "But I don't anticipate any problems in getting checked out."

"Great. Let's get on that ASAP. We can send a Gooney up to Parham in the next week or so with a pilot to check you out. I think a day's ground school and several checkout flights should do the trick. And I look forward to hearing details on your escape."

Ben returned to Parham and shared the plans with Atkins. "You'll be acting commander whenever I'm on TDY with the survey group, Joe. Since we don't know how long the survey process will take, I can't say how long this arrangement will last."

Chapter 42

THE END GAME — 1945

On New Year's Day, the Luftwaffe shocked the Allies by launching fierce aerial attacks against American and British airfields across Europe. It was a last-ditch attempt to regain air superiority to protect the Wehrmacht's beleaguered ground troops and to curb the bombing of Germany's major cities. More than 450 Allied airplanes were destroyed, but the Luftwaffe lost over two hundred fighters and bombers and, more critically, nearly two hundred and fifty experienced pilots. This last hurrah left the Luftwaffe badly weakened and actually cleared the skies for unopposed Allied missions deep into Germany. The final aerial assault began on Berlin and other large population centers across the country.

On the ground, Allied pincer movements inexorably pushed the German forces, commanded by Field Marshal Gerd von Rundstedt, toward the Rhine River. Allied commanders mistakenly thought the Ardennes counteroffensive was Von Rundstedt's battle plan, but it came directly from Hitler and, in fact, was opposed by Von Rundstedt. Following the Allied breakout, from the Ardennes, Von Rundstedt sought permission to withdraw east of the Rhine, which was flooded by destroying upstream dam gates, and established his defensive lines there. Hitler rejected his request and ordered him to stand and fight on the west bank of the river. The ensuing series of bloody battles devastated Von Rundstedt's forces, enabling the Allies to capture nearly three hundred thousand German prisoners, and ultimately pushed the Germans into defensive positions across the river.

On January 31, General Carl Spaatz, commander of United States Strategic Air Forces in Europe, ordered Doolittle to begin massive Eighth Air Force bombing attacks on Berlin and other major German cities. Doolittle warned this violated the American principle of bombing only significant military targets and cautioned it could give credence to Germany's accusations that the United States had adopted a policy of terror bombing against civilians. Lieutenant General Ira Eaker echoed Doolittle's warnings, saying it fueled Nazi propaganda charges that the Americans were civilian-killing barbarians. Spaatz ordered the plan to proceed.

The 509th was alerted in early February to participate in the Eighth Air Force's final assault on Berlin. Ben and Joe sat in Ben's office, studying maps to confirm rendezvous points and collating details for the next day's mission briefing.

Joe glanced sideways at Ben. "Uh, Ben, lemme raise some concerns with you," he said. "I'm not sure I see the strategic value of pounding Berlin this way. I mean, are there any credible targets left there? We'll be dropping tons of bombs on a city that's already been blown to hell. Uh, look, I don't want to sound like I'm second-guessing the High Command or anything, but I gotta ask what are we accomplishing by bombing ruins? See, our primary aim point is what's left of the central train station in Berlin! Isn't that place full of refugees?"

Ben started to reply, but Atkins interjected, "Ah, I'm not being insubordinate by raising these questions, am I?"

Ben gave him a long look. "No, Joe, you aren't being insubordinate. You're raising legitimate questions, some I've had myself. Reminds me of the long talk I had with Lieutenant Davis a month or so ago, when I convinced him not to turn in his wings. Said we were playing a critical role in ending the war. He believed me. Kept flying and got shot down and killed two missions later. Damn! I'll carry that guilt forever."

Ben rose from his chair and paced around the room. "And if you believe the rumors, even Doolittle has bucked the top brass about bombing civilian centers. You know, earlier in the war when we hit big cities that had industrial, oil, or rail centers, we also hit populated areas and probably killed one helluva lot of civilians. But they weren't our primary targets. Now I'm not sure. Seems like we're purposely targeting civilians."

He paused and looked out across the airfield ramp. "But orders are orders, Joe, so that's what we're going out to do tomorrow."

The next day, the 509th joined nearly one thousand bombers and more than five hundred escort fighters headed for Berlin. Their targets were government centers and railway stations, the latter serving as air-raid shelters packed with civilian refugees. The Luftwaffe was unable to provide any effective resistance, and Germany's remaining flak defenses were equally ineffective.

Approaching the rendezvous point, Ben stared at the bomber string forming over Southern England. Once en route to Germany, it would stretch over one hundred miles. As he maneuvered the 509th into its Number 2 position, he wondered aloud, "What must this look like from the ground? The fellas in what's left of the Luftwaffe won't be able to believe it."

No German fighters rose to challenge them, even though they were headed for the prime target in Germany. A few flak batteries fired random rounds as the bomber string passed overhead, but the antiaircraft gunners must have felt there was little they could do to deflect such a huge attacking armada.

Flak batteries near central Berlin put up a denser screen of exploding shells, but they were soon blown to smithereens by the carpet bombing. Ben took no satisfaction from hitting their aim point as he watched major sections of the battered city center disappear in billowing clouds of smoke and fire. The intercom was eerily quiet throughout the mission and on the long flight home. His crew avoided making eye contact as they exited the plane and clambered aboard, waiting trucks for the ride to the operations center. They gathered silently around their post-mission briefers, gave desultory reports, and departed.

"Joe, I don't like the looks of this," Ben muttered to Atkins. "I'm sure they're all happy we didn't have to fight our way to the target and back, but Godalmighty, dropping bombs on undefended civilians is like shootin' fish in a barrel! I guess they're thinking about this too."

Post mission intelligence reports showed the raid further leveled large sections of the already-devastated city and killed an estimated twenty-five thousand civilians. Meanwhile, RAF Bomber Command continued to relentlessly pound Berlin at night, ultimately attacking the city with thirty-six consecutive raids.

RAF Avro 638 Lancaster Bomber

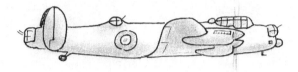

The most destructive raid of the air war in Europe was staged in mid-February. RAF Bomber Command sent successive waves of eight hundred bombers on night raids to drop high-explosive and incendiary bombs on Dresden, southeast of Leipzig. It was the largest city in Germany that had not yet been bombed. The attack ignited a firestorm that consumed most of the city center and estimates of civilian casualties ranged from thirty thousand to over one hundred thousand.

The Eighth Air Force staged daylight follow-up attacks on Dresden over the next two days with more than three hundred B-17s. Smoke from the firestorm created by the RAF nighttime attacks obscured the city on the first raid, so the American bombardiers used their H2X radar bombsights with mixed results. Oil fields near Leipzig were the primary target on the second day, but a solid cloud cover there forced the B-17 groups to attack Dresden as their secondary target. Again, H2X radar bombsights had to be used. Both missions resulted in a wide dispersal of bombs across the city and neighboring towns.

Joe Atkins led the 509th on the Dresden attacks and told Ben the crews returned from the missions subdued and shaken by what appeared to be the total destruction of another population center. Dresden, renowned as a center for culture and the arts, was known as the "Florence on the Elbe." But it was also an industrial area, encompassing over one hundred factories supporting the German war effort. Nonetheless, the Dresden bombing became embroiled in the growing controversy surrounding the Allied policy of shifting its bombing priorities to civilian population centers in the waning months of the war.

Massive attacks against German cities continued. The Eighth Air Force launched a one thousand plane raid against Nurnberg in February, reducing what was left of that city to a smoking heap of churned rubble. Berlin was also attacked repeatedly though early March. On the 13th, a force of nearly one thousand four hundred bombers and over seven hundred escort fighters returned to Berlin. This time, the Luftwaffe launched large numbers of 262s in addition to conventional fighters, and the defenders knocked down thirteen Allied bombers. But again, the Luftwaffe paid a high price in lost fighters and pilots—losses it could not sustain.

Ben's participation in the USSBS began a week later, when a USAAF captain and second lieutenant flew a C-47 into Parham to walk him through a fast-paced ground course and take him on a checkout flight. Ben had little difficulty mastering the docile Gooney Bird, and the captain soon signed him off as fully qualified in the twin-engine transport. "Okay, sir, we'll head back to High Wycombe." The captain chuckled as they dropped Ben at the Parham ramp. "You won't have any problems managing this old girl when you join the survey detachment."

The call came from Sampson's adjutant. He said the general wanted Ben to join the detachment at High Wycombe ASAP to assist in forming the first survey teams. Ben told Atkins to assemble all 509th officers at 0800 hours the next day so he could brief them on his TDY assignment to the USSBS task force. He ordered Atkins to assemble all enlisted personnel at 1300 hours for a similar briefing.

"I want them to understand this is a temporary assignment, and therefore, we won't have a change of command ceremony," Ben said. "That may all change if Germany surrenders before my duty with the survey is completed, but we'll face that when it happens."

"Speaking of that, what do you think will happen to the Eighth when the war in Europe ends?" Atkins asked. "Will we be shifted to the Pacific?"

"Yeah, I expect so. I hear Doolittle's already been tapped for the Pacific, so I guess the Eighth, or at least most of its assets, will be transferred as well. Lot of this is indefinite for the moment. Might even involve transferring back to the States for upgrade training in the B-29 Superfortress. Just gonna have to wait and see. Meanwhile, I expect to be winging off to High Wycombe soon to start planning and flying the survey missions."

Two days later, a C-47 crew picked up Ben at Parham at 0830 hours and flew him to Daws Air Force Station near the Eighth's headquarters at High Wycombe. Ben huddled with Sampson and his staff to begin forming the survey teams, selecting flight crews and choosing the bombed sites they'd be visiting.

Survey teams had been working in liberated Europe since December, following closely behind the advancing Allied armies. Their intent was to quickly collect any records the German occupiers left behind that would provide clues to the effectiveness of the strategic bombing campaign against the rail and road transportation infrastructure, the electrical power grid, and the industrial base.

Sampson said that as soon as the Allied advances allowed, Ben and his crews would be sent in to survey liberated target cities across Northern Germany, starting with Bremerhaven, Bremen, Wilhelmshaven, Hamburg, and Hannover. They would range farther east and south as the Allies overran cities such as Stuttgart, Halle, Nuremburg, Wiesbaden/Frankfurt, Schweinfurt, Munich, Regensburg, and finally Berlin.

Ben smiled grimly at the mention of Regensburg. "I'll make a strong pitch to lead the Regensburg mission. I have some history with that city and especially with the local Gestapo Kommandant if he hasn't been blown to pieces or run away."

"I'll make a note of that," Sampson muttered.

Assembling and training the survey crews proceeded smoothly, and by early February, the task force was ready to fly. Ben and his copilot, RAF Flight Leftenant Crenshaw, clicked from the start and soon had the C-47 crew organized and ready. They spent the next two weeks practicing flying into short rough fields and dispatching the survey teams on sidecar motorcycles.

The Eighth Air Force continued to fly bombing missions, attacking German supply lines throughout February. These concentrated on Luftwaffe airfields, rail centers, major highway intersections, and troop concentrations in support of the final assault to cross the Rhine.

A major breakthrough occurred in early March at Remagen, where advanced units of the U.S. First Army found the Ludendorff Bridge damaged but still intact. This was expanded into a full-scale crossing point that allowed the first U.S. Army units to pour onto German soil. Three other cross-river assaults followed, and by the end of March, major Allied infantry and armor units were slugging their way eastward deep into German territory.

In early April, the Luftwaffe resorted to desperate measures, sending over one hundred student pilots out to attack another Eighth Air Force thousand-plane raid. The students were ordered to ram Allied bombers and parachute to safety, if possible. The suicide operations failed when the young Luftwaffe trainees were unable to collide with many bombers, and all but a few of the young pilots were shot down by Allied escort fighters.

Less than a week later, a massed bomber and escort fighter flotilla attacked Berlin again. The Luftwaffe launched its remaining 262 jet fighters to defend the crippled city. By this time, Eighth Air Force gunners and escort fighter pilots had developed tactics to deal with the 262s, and more than half of the high-speed fighters were shot down. The remaining Luftwaffe units scattered and abandoned Berlin to unopposed Allied bombing attacks. The Allies had won the air war against Germany.

This positive development was overshadowed on April 12, 1945, by the shocking news that President Franklin Delano Roosevelt had died of a massive cerebral hemorrhage at the Little White House in Warm Springs, Georgia. The man, popularly known as FDR, had been the president of the United States for most of the adult lifetimes of many of the soldiers, sailors, and airmen fighting World War 2. He was considered the driving force behind the U.S. war effort. His successor, former Vice President Harry S. Truman, was relatively unknown, leaving most Americans and their Allies wondering what impact FDR's death would have on the outcome of the war.

Ben had the news transmitted to all 509th personnel along with a message of encouragement and ordered the flags lowered to half-staff. He convened a meeting of his headquarters staff to discuss Roosevelt's death and to air any concerns his officers may have.

"We're close to knocking Germany out of the war," one officer said, "but I wonder how much longer it's going to take to defeat Japan? I know the war isn't run out of the White House, but we now have an unknown and untested man at the helm. Does anyone think that poses a threat to our ability to wrap this up here in Europe?"

This prompted a free-wheeling discussion among the officers that Ben let run for thirty minutes before interceding. "I think we all agree we're in the final stages of the war with Germany and that the president's death shouldn't affect either the pace or the outcome. He wasn't involved in the day-to-day running of the war. That was the job of our top commanders. I don't see that changing. And besides, we've got the momentum, and the German war machine is crumbling fast."

He looked at each officer seated around the table. "Everyone agree with that assessment?" All nodded. "Good! So we press on, follow the current plan, and do our best to make each mission a success. We may not be at this too much longer."

"What about the Pacific Theater?" one officer asked. "Our troops are making progress capturing the islands leading to Japan, which'll make it easier for our B-29s to hit targets deep in Japan. But I hear a lot of debate about how tough it's going to be to invade the homeland. War could drag on a long time in the Pacific. Does that mean a lot of us will be shipping out to that Theater?"

"That's the big question," Ben said. "At this point, it looks unlikely. As we know, General Silverman's on his way there to command the new B-29 wing, but I have a feeling we won't be needed, especially not with our B-17s. We just don't have the range or payload capability needed for those long-range, over-water missions. And there are sufficient B-29 units out there to get the job done.

"Meanwhile, we continue doing our job and, as usual, sit and wait for orders. But seriously, I think we're going to be winding down here in the near future. Hell, there just aren't any more targets left in Germany that require massive heavy bombardment attacks."

Ben's prediction came true on April 25, 1945, when the 509th flew its last combat mission. Joe Atkins led the group to join a B-17 fleet that attacked the Skoda armaments factory in Pilsen, Czechoslovakia. They encountered no fighter resistance from the devastated Luftwaffe and only sporadic antiaircraft fire. All twenty-one bombers dispatched returned to Parham unscathed. At the post mission briefing, the crews whooped with joy and danced jigs when they were informed this was their last combat trip. While awaiting word on whether the group would be shifted to the Pacific, they were assigned to humanitarian missions and began dropping food supplies to the recently liberated Dutch during the last weeks of the war.

Ben left Parham on temporary duty with the USSBS and led his first survey mission into Bremerhaven, a major port in Northern Germany. He and his team arrived shortly after British ground forces overran the port city and surrounding terrain. Bremerhaven had been a major base for Germany's Kriegsmarine. Its location at the mouth of the Weser River afforded excellent access to the North Sea. RAF and USAAF commanders had instructed their bomber crews to avoid hitting the extensive harbor facilities to preserve them as a valuable port for supplying Allied occupation troops in Germany after the war. However, the city was declared an open target, and the bombing raids, especially the RAF night attacks, pummeled it into rubble. More than ninety percent of the buildings in Bremerhaven were destroyed.

An overpowering stench of death greeted Ben's team as they stepped out of their C-47 and squinted through the gray pall that hung over the city. They unloaded their motorcycles and drove, coughing and sneezing through a caustic dust cloud into the city to find the British Army brigadier commanding the occupation forces.

He had been notified to expect them and offered to assist in carrying out the survey. "If you're going to be poking about the ruins, which by the way are still smoldering, you need to be aware there is a bloody lot of unexploded munitions lying about, not to mention the odd booby trap," he cautioned. "You'll also want to wear surgical masks to filter out the dust and the smell of decomposing bodies. We're just getting the recovery operations organized, but if you need assistance in getting around, call on us.

"You might want to start your survey along the harbor and work your way into the city center," he added. "Our bomber chaps did a good job of limiting damage to the harbor facilities, but they pulverized the city."

As they drove through the city, Ben and his team gaped at the skeletons of buildings whose remaining scorched walls loomed like prehistoric monsters with blackened claws, gaping mouths, and hollow eyes. Mounds of rubble and bomb craters blocked many streets, and most of the bridges that had spanned the Weser River lay crushed in the water. The railroad station was a smoldering shell surrounded by jagged remnants of walls.

"This is unbelievable," Ben muttered. "Never seen such devastation. The post mission recon photos we've seen didn't come close to showing what really happened here. Godalmighty! How many civilians were killed here and for what . . .?"

"Begging your pardon, Skipper," Crenshaw broke in. "I assume you've visited Coventry in the West Country and maybe toured London's East End. Destruction there is not as extensive as this, but one helluva lot of our citizens were killed in the Blitz, and there are large neighborhoods that look just like this."

"Okay, you've made your point," Ben said. "Can't argue with that. During my years with the RAF, I did my best to help stop the Luftwaffe's bomber attacks on England." He waved a hand at the desolate scene around them. "But this is such a goddamned criminal waste of human lives and property!" He paused to control his emotions. "All right. Need to push past this and get on with the surveying."

The crew set about mapping the destroyed industrial complexes and surrounding infrastructure. They found it nearly impossible to comprehend the devastation surrounding them or ignore the hollow-eyed people shuffling among the debris, shifting bricks and chunks of masonry, and retrieving decomposing bodies.

Chapter 43

VICTORY IN EUROPE! – MAY 1945

The Axis power structure across Europe finally crumbled in a series of mind-bending events. American and Soviet soldiers met and shook hands at the Elbe River, northwest of Berlin, successfully cutting the Fatherland in half. Leaderless and thoroughly defeated, the major units of the Wehrmacht from Finland to Italy and all along the eastern and western battle fronts in Germany surrendered piecemeal. Numerous surrender documents were signed by local Wehrmacht and Allied commanders along both the western and eastern fronts.

In Italy, former dictator Mussolini finally met a gruesome end. He had been imprisoned after he was deposed in 1943, prompting the surrender of all Italian armed forces. On Hitler's orders, he was rescued a few months later by German commandos. He remained in Italy under the protection of the Wehrmacht that continued to occupy the northern part of the country after Italy surrendered and ultimately declared war on Germany. As the Allies began their final assault on the remaining German forces in Italy, Mussolini fled north to seek asylum in Switzerland. He was captured by anti-Fascists partisans on April 27, and executed the next day. The Wehrmacht's campaign in Italy was over.

The final unraveling of the Third Reich occurred on April 30, when Hitler committed suicide in his Berlin bunker as Soviet troops advanced through the smoking rubble of the capital. In his will, he named Admiral Karl Donitz as president of Germany and Joseph Goebbels as chancellor. It was an empty gesture, further diminished when Goebbels committed suicide shortly after Hitler, leaving Donitz the sole leader of a ruined Germany.

The Allies in the west and the Russians in the east captured over two million German prisoners in a period of several days. Because of the sheer numbers, the Allies chose to designate their prisoners disarmed enemy combatants to circumvent provisions of the Geneva Convention covering treatment of prisoners of war. The numbers of enemy soldiers captured exceeded the Americans' ability to properly care for them as POWs, leaving them vulnerable to charges they were violating portions of the convention. Russian commanders along the eastern front, less concerned with the Geneva Convention and seeking vengeance, shipped thousands of German POWs back to Russian labor camps in Siberia.

As the Luftwaffe's command structure disintegrated, individual group leaders took independent control of their units and shifted them to airfields in Southeastern Germany. When Allied forces closed in, the German commanders ordered their pilots to abandon their aircraft and bases and meld back into civilian life.

Nationally, events tumbled into a convoluted series of political maneuverings finally culminating in Donitz ordering General Alfred Jodl, chief of staff of the German Armed Forces High Command, to surrender unconditionally to the Allies in the west. The ceremony was set in Reims, France, site of France's surrender to Germany in the early days of the war. The remaining Wehrmacht forces pushed west to surrender to American and British forces rather than to the Russians.

The Allies, anticipating Germany's ultimate defeat, had prepared an instrument of surrender through the European Advisory Commission in early 1944. A provisional copy of this document of unconditional surrender was compiled for the Reims ceremony and signed on behalf of Germany by General Jodl on May 7, 1945. General Eisenhower declined to attend the surrender ceremony and ordered General Walter Bedell Smith, his chief of staff, to sign for the Allies. General Susloparov signed for the Soviets.

The Soviets then claimed the surrender document was too hastily prepared; did not conform to the original document approved by the Americans, British, and Soviets; and, therefore, was not valid. They insisted the Reims agreement be considered a preliminary protocol and that the original instrument of surrender be signed in Berlin.

The Berlin ceremony was concluded minutes before midnight on May 8, which the Allies designated Victory in Europe Day. The

Soviets designated May 9, since it was after midnight in Moscow when the approved instrument of surrender was signed. Near riotous celebrations erupted throughout the free world as word of the surrender was spread by screaming newspaper headlines, breathless radio announcements, and word of mouth. The war in Europe was over.

Ben and his crew headed back to England following a grueling week-long bomb survey in Hamburg, when the airplane's radio crackled with a terse message, **"All Allied aircraft. All Allied aircraft. Germany has surrendered unconditionally. The war in Europe is over!"** Ben sat momentarily stunned, struggling to process what he had just heard, when the message was repeated. Regaining his senses, he keyed the intercom and relayed the news to his crew. Whoops of joy and laughter rattled the C-47's cabin.

Ben turned to Crenshaw, who grinned as tears streamed down his face. Ben gave him a thumbs-up signal, which his copilot returned with a flourish. "I say, Skipper," Crenshaw croaked, "damn good show all 'round. Seems we've been fighting this bloody war forever, eh?"

Ben's mind flashed back to 1939 in London, when he and Reggie, recently escaped from the Spanish Civil War following the defeat of the Republicans, waited impatiently for orders to join the RAF as fighter pilots. He shook his head. *Been at war for six years, nearly eight if you count the time in Spain.* Not trusting his voice, Ben clenched his jaw and smiled.

As they descended for landing over the villages surrounding Daws Air Station, they saw crowds surging through the streets, waving British and American flags. The pubs were jammed and overflowing. An equally raucous celebration was under way when Ben parked the C-47 on the Daws ramp. The bars in the officers' and enlisted men's clubs were open, and apparently, the drinks were on the house. Ben had to fight his way through the roiling crowd to Sampson's office for his post mission debriefing.

"Welcome back, Ben," Sampson shouted over the din from the celebration outside. "Wonderful news! Been expecting it for some time, but it's still damn exciting to hear it officially. They're letting the troops blow off a bit of steam," he added, jerking his thumb toward the window. "They damn well have earned it. You too."

He rose to shake Ben's hand. "You heavy bombardment boys made a major contribution to this victory. My congratulations. And

I appreciate your bomb survey work so far, Ben. Looks like we'll now get some rest. Survey operations have been put on hold until the brass sorts out details of who's in charge of what parts of Germany. Stand-down shouldn't last more than a week or two. Then we'll get back at it and finish this rotten business."

Ben dropped into a chair, blew a puff of breath, and relaxed. His mouth gaped in a wide yawn that a hippopotamus would envy. He sat up abruptly, covering his mouth. "Sorry, sir. We're all pretty ragged. This last week in Hamburg was a bitch. Destruction is unbelievable. None of us can get rid of the rotten taste and smell of those ruined cities. We all can use some time off."

"I agree. Time to take a break and assess what we've accomplished so far," Sampson said. "Get cleaned up and pack your bag. I'll have a crew fly you up to Parham. You need to celebrate VE-Day with your group. And I guess with your nurse lady friend."

"On my way, General," Ben said, rising and heading for the door. "Many thanks, sir." He turned at the door. "By the way, we only have preliminary data based on a small sample of surveys, but it looks like our precision bombing wasn't so precise."

"How do you mean?"

"Well, sir, I think we're gonna find we put less than 20 percent of our bombs on target. And I think the results will be worse when we get a chance to survey the oil refineries."

"Hmm. Okay, Ben. But for now, we'll let it ride and savor the victory."

Ben headed for a telephone, called Atkins at Parham, and said he'd be arriving that evening. His next call was to Gwen.

"Hello, love," he began. Gwen interrupted with a stream of excited words all run together.

"Hey, slow down." Ben chuckled. "I can't understand a thing you're saying. And what's all that noise in the background?"

"Oh, I'm so sorry, Ben. I guess I'm a bit wound up. Can't believe this terrible war is over. **Over,** Ben! The noise? Oh, that's everyone celebrating, cheering, and singing in the streets. Quite a few are shooting off fireworks. It's bigger than any Guy Fawkes celebration I can remember. Imagine, no more shooting and bombing. Are we truly at peace again, Ben?"

"Yes, Gwen, dear, in Europe at least. An' I don't think the war in the Pacific is going to last much longer either . . ."

"Pacific? Ben, you aren't going to be transferred to the Pacific War with Japan, are you? Please tell me that's not possible! Ben, I couldn't stand that. I really couldn't!"

274

Ben shook his head in frustration. *Damn, why'd I have to bring that up?* "Calm down, Gwen. Calm down! Nobody's going anywhere at the moment. It's too soon to say. Only thing for certain is that I'm flying up to Parham tonight. I have to spend some time with Joe, assessing what's going on at the base. Should be able to get away tomorrow night and drive over to see you. You off duty tomorrow night?"

"Oh, Ben. Wonderful! Yes, I'm off duty. I'm so sorry to be such a nervous ninny. I am so happy the war in Europe is over. It's just that I can't face the prospect of you being shipped off to the Pacific to fight anymore. Please tell me that won't happen. Umm, please, Ben." Her voice trailed off in sobs.

"Gwen, sweetheart, I'll be with you tomorrow night," Ben said, trying to calm her fears. "We'll talk about it then. I still have a lot of work to do here with the bomb survey program—important work. Even if the 509th is transferred to the Pacific Theater, I doubt I'll be going with it. Okay?"

Gwen sniffled, trying to control her emotions. "Okay, love. I hear you. I believe you, and I love you. I'll see you tomorrow night."

Ben rang off and sat, looking at the phone. "Even if the 509th does get transferred to the Pacific, we'd need several months for upgrade training in the B-29 before shipping out," he mused. "The tide certainly has turned in favor of the Allies in the Pacific. Who knows how long Japan can hold out?"

Ben swallowed hard. "Looks like we'll probably be decommissioned," he croaked. "God, that hurts."

Ben arrived at Parham that evening and gathered Atkins and their 509th staff officers in his headquarters office. He grinned as he surveyed the beaming faces around the table, noting that most reflected the blush of several victory celebration drinks. "Greetings, gents," he said. "Looks like you've already started celebrating. Keep it going, and I'll join you once Joe and I sort through what's gonna happen over the next few weeks and months."

Ben folded his hands on the table and looked intently at each officer in turn. He cleared his throat. "Where to begin?" he said. "Been one helluva long haul, hasn't it? We all can be proud of what we've achieved for the 509th, the Eighth Air Force, and our country. There'll be a lot written about what we proved with massed daylight bombing and the role it played in winning the war in Europe. But there's also a downside. I've seen the results of our bombing up close on our survey mission. We weren't as accurate as a lot of people said, but I can tell you the destruction is so complete it's hard to comprehend.

"I don't know what to tell you about our immediate future. Rumors are circulating again about us being transferred to the Pacific Theater. That might be premature," he continued. "We know General Doolittle's going to Okinawa, but I don't think anyone else will be going anywhere soon.

"Meanwhile, we'll continue flying relief drop missions across Europe and taking our ground personnel on recon flights to show them what we accomplished with their support. My bomb survey missions have been temporarily suspended until the top brass can sort out who's in charge of what across liberated Europe and, especially, Germany. So I'll take command here again until I return to duty with the bomb survey detachment. Joe will carry on then as acting commander.

"All we can do now is wait and see what orders come down the line," he concluded. "We're off the duty roster for the time being, so let's join the celebration."

Ben awoke the next morning with a pounding headache and a thick tongue. *Damn, that wasn't very smart, Benjamin old lad. But it was good to cut loose with the fellas. We needed that. Now gotta get my head cleared before I see Gwen tonight.*

He and Joe began culling the 509th records, identifying flight crews that had flown the most missions over Europe. The highest time crews would be the first sent back to the States, probably to an uncertain future.

The official order to begin shifting Eighth Air Force units stateside came two weeks later. This was followed by an announcement that the new Eighth Air Force headquarters would be Kadena Airfield in Okinawa but without transferring men or aircraft. General Doolittle was given the Pacific command and tasked with establishing three B-29 bases on Okinawa, using personnel and equipment already in place.

"Where does this leave us, Ben?" Atkins asked.

"Dunno. Guess we sit tight and wait for orders to ferry our birds back to the States. Doesn't sound like we'll be making the shift with the Eighth."

That evening, Ben drove to Cambridge to see Gwen. "Know she's gonna press me for answers about the future. Gotta convince her to be patient," he muttered. She met him at the door and welcomed him with a fierce embrace and a lingering kiss. Questions about the future didn't come up for the rest of the evening.

Chapter 44

SORTING THROUGH THE DEBRIS – SUMMER 1945

The euphoria that followed the Allied victory in Europe soon faded into despair. Nations on both sides of the war began the herculean tasks of picking through the postwar debris and starting the process of rebuilding. It soon became evident that the enormous cost in human lives, resources, and destroyed cities and infrastructure meant no one had really won the war. Even the moderate summer weather, with temperatures hovering in the low 70s, did little to lift the spirits of those poking in the ruins.

Ben waited impatiently for orders to restart the bomb survey missions, while the Western Allies and the Soviet Union wrangled over details of the postwar occupation of Germany and control of liberated Eastern Europe. He and Joe turned to the task of drafting a plan for fitting extra fuel tanks into the 509th's twenty-one serviceable B-17s for the ferry flight back to the States.

The only bright spot in the dismal situation was the extra time Ben had to spend with Gwen. As their bond grew stronger and the threat of being separated again by war diminished, they talked seriously about their wedding. They would set the date as soon as Ben could get the paperwork processed.

"Where should we have the ceremony, love?" Gwen asked as they snuggled one afternoon on the sofa in her flat.

Ben pondered a moment. "Dunno . . . Say, what about asking Reggie if we can be married in the chapel at Calvert Hall?"

"Oh, Ben, that would be ever so lovely! It's a beautiful location. Do you suppose Lord and Lady Percy would agree? I mean, would we be imposing too much?"

"I doubt they'd feel that way. Look, why don't I call Reggie? He'll give me a straight answer."

Reggie had recently been appointed chief of operations for the Empire Test Pilots' Center at RAF Boscombe Down near Amesbury in Wiltshire. His aide signaled he had a phone call. "Wing Commander Percy here."

"Hello, Reggie. It's Ben, and . . ."

"I say, Sancho!" Reggie interrupted. "What superb timing! Was just about to ring you. Have a brilliant proposal that'll provide you some badly needed diversion."

"Ah swell, but can I tell you first what I'm calling about?"

"Of course, of course. Do tell, dear chap."

"Well, Gwen and I have had a serious talk, an' now that the war's over, uh, at least here in Europe, we want to get married as soon as possible."

"Good show! And none too soon. How can I help? Be your best man or give the bride away? At your service, Benjamin."

"Thanks, Reggie. We can get to those details later. First, I, uh, we, were talking about where we'd like to get married, and uh, I said I'd ask you about the chapel . . ."

"At Calvert Hall, of course!" Reggie broke in. "Wonderful idea! Perfect place."

"Uh, do you think you folks would agree?" Ben asked.

"Not a worry, old man. They'd be delighted. When is this to be? Should we 'book' a date?"

"Reggie, that's fantastic. Gwen is right here, and she's squirming with excitement. We can't set the date quite yet. I have to file a request and probably fill out a pile of forms. Have no idea how long that's gonna take. Let us get that ball rolling, and I'll call you when we know more."

"Right ho, Sancho, let me know, and we'll get it laid on."

Gwen, listening in on the phone, squealed with delight and hugged Ben. "Oh, Reggie," she shouted into the phone, "thank you, thank you! This is so exciting."

"Now then, back to the role I'm to play in this ceremony," Reggie said. "Am I to be best man or giver away of the bride?"

"Best man, best man," Gwen whispered in Ben's ear.

"The lady says best man," Ben said. "We'll find someone to give her away."

"How about His Lordship?" Reggie asked. "Would 'Himself' be acceptable to your lady?"

Gwen rocked back wide-eyed. "Would that be possible?" she gasped.

"Did I hear Gwen ask if that would be possible?" Reggie asked.

"Uh yeah. I mean, would it?"

"I think I can speak for the old boy," Reggie said. "And if his schedule will work with yours, I'd say he'd be delighted."

Gwen grabbed Ben in a fierce hug as tears streamed down her cheeks.

"Uh, Reggie, this, uh, this is fantastic," Ben stammered. "We'll need some time to work the details, you know, the paperwork and all. I'll let you know soonest."

"Capital! Okay, let me tell why I was going to ring you," Reggie said. "Now that I'm chief of operations here at Boscombe, what say you come down for a visit? Want to show you around, brief you on our operation, and get you back in the cockpit of a Spitfire. 'Bout time we got you out of that multi-motored turd dropper and back into a real airplane. Have two beautiful Mark IXs sitting here on the ramp, just waiting to be flung about the sky. I can send an Anson to collect you any time. Interested?"

Ben gripped the phone. "Interested? You bet! I'm just sitting around at Parham with Joe waitin' for word on what happens to the 509th. An' the bomb survey missions probably won't start for another coupla weeks. I'm free almost any time. What day looks good?"

"Next Tuesday. Anson crew will meet you at 0730 hours. Come prepared to be humiliated by a real fighter pilot. 'Til then, cheerio."

Ben rang off and turned beaming to Gwen. She smiled bravely but failed to conceal her concern that he could be exposing himself to danger flying some silly aerial competition with Reggie. Ben spent the rest of the afternoon and evening convincing her it was going to be just fine.

Back at Parham, Ben looked gloomily at the pile of paperwork he had been avoiding. "Better get this cleared out before I turn over command to Joe," he muttered. "Wouldn't be right to hare off to play fighter pilot with Reggie leavin' this mess behind."

Three hours later, Ben pushed back his chair and stretched. "Not my favorite thing by a long shot," he grunted. "Now I gotta get a letter off to Mom and tell them about Gwen and me setting the date. Hope she won't be too disappointed about missing the wedding."

Boscombe Down buzzed with activity when the Anson crew dropped Ben in front of the operations center. He spotted an array of aircraft that appeared to be assigned to the school. Two gleaming Mark IX Spitfires caught his eye and quickened his pulse.

The school had gone through several iterations since its formation in early 1943 as the Test Pilots' Training Flight. RAF Air Marshal Sir Ralph Sorley organized the school after he saw too many pilots killed flying new advanced combat aircraft. In mid-1943, the unit was renamed the Test Pilots' School and attached to the Aeroplane and Armament Experimental Establishment at Boscombe Down with a mission to train professional test pilots. The first class included pilots from the RAF, the Royal Fleet Air Arm, the Royal Navy, and three pilots from the Bristol Aeroplane Company. It was renamed the Empire Test Pilots' School in mid-1944.

Reggie waved a greeting when Ben walked into the operations center. "What ho, Sancho," he yelled, striding over to grab him by the shoulders. "Welcome to Boscombe. Let's step into my office and chat about our test pilot operation here and then discuss flight plans. We'll do a quick tour of our station, and then we'll get you kitted up and introduce you to our mounts."

Ben grinned as Reggie led him on a walk-around of the two Spitfires on the ramp. "These are Mark IX variants," Reggie said. "Look essentially the same as the birds we flew in the Battle of Britain, but there are differences. Let me see, we started back in '39 with the original Mark 1, but I think we'd moved up to the Mark 1A when the war started, right? Had the bigger Merlin engine and the three-bladed air screw."

"Right," Ben said. "This version looks pretty much the same, except for the four-bladed prop and the different radiator layout."

"Ah yes, but these birds have the Merlin 60/70 series engines, me lad. These babies develop 1,720 horsepower at altitude, which gives a tremendous increase in rate of climb and top speed. And they're fitted with the Bendix-Stromberg anti-G carburetor so you can push over into a dive to pursue an escaping enemy fighter without worrying about fuel floating in negative G and starving the engine. Remember how we had to do a half-roll and pull into a dive to keep positive G on the old carburetors?"

He slapped the side of the fuselage. "There are also changes in the fuselage contours that affect the handling characteristics and wing changes that affect the pitch and roll rates. These variants also weigh more, so the control forces are heavier. And that big four-bladed fan up front generates one helluva lot of torque, so you'll need both rudder and aileron to compensate on the takeoff roll."

Reggie smiled as Ben puckered his lips in concentration. "Even with that, Sancho, they're still the most beautiful flying machines ever built."

"Yeah, as you say, 'piece of cake,'" Ben said. "Jump in, light the fire, and away we go."

"Well, hardly. I did warn you about the changes in control forces and handling characteristics," Reggie said. "But you've had enough time in Spits to easily adapt to those. Even so, I'll have you spend a bit of time reviewing the cockpit layout, placement of all the knobs, and so on. In the air, I'll give you a bit of time to feel her out before I, umm, what do you Yanks call it? Ah yes, 'wax your ass,' in a little mock aerial combat."

"We'll see about that." Ben grinned.

"Now a bit more about the Mark IX. It was developed to counter the Luftwaffe's the then-new Focke-Wulf 190. They were beating us so badly we had to stop daytime operations over Europe. Remember how we had to stand down in mid-'42 until we were ready to take on the 190s?"

"That was about the time I was transferring to the USAAF," Ben said.

"Righto. But by late '42, we had these in service and were able to match the 190s. We had a top speed of 410 mph, an increase of 40 mph, and our service ceiling bumped up from thirty-six thousand feet to forty-three thousand. Climb rate was four thousand feet per minute. Made one helluva great fighter. The 401 squadron bagged the first Luftwaffe Me 262 jet fighters with Mark IXs in '44."

"Okay, okay," Ben said, raising his hands in mock surrender. "You've convinced me. I'll buy a dozen. Now can we go fly?"

"Of course, old man." Reggie sniffed. "Just wanted you to know a bit more about what you're taking on when you strapped your arse into one of these."

Ben greeted his two-man ground crew, who helped him into the cockpit and adjusted his parachute and Sutton safety harness. He was momentarily overcome by the familiar smell—a mixture of high octane fuel, oil, leather, and sweat. His mind flashed back to 1939 and the first time he settled into a Spitfire cockpit and looked out along its long pointed nose. He flew Spitfires with the RAF for three years before transferring to the USAAF's Eighth Air Force and trained in B-17 bombers. "Last time I flew one of these sleek babies was in '42," he muttered to the crew chief. "Guess I still know how."

He spent twenty minutes familiarizing himself with the cockpit as the crew chief pointed out the switches, controls, and instruments and reviewed the critical airspeeds in the pilot's operating manual. "Thanks for the review," Ben said. "It's all come back pretty quickly. Let's get this lovely lady into the air."

"She is a beaut, sir," the sergeant said. "Lovely to watch. Must be a thrill to fly."

As the ground crewmen hopped off the wings, Ben started the pre-start checklist. He scanned the switches and noted the position of the controls. He donned his oxygen mask, plugged in the radio connection, and checked the oxygen level. He set the elevator trim for takeoff, cycled the flight controls, and opened the radiator shutter.

"Okay, let's crack the throttle a bit and prime her," he muttered. He then signaled for engine start and shouted "All clear?" to the ground crew, who responded with thumbs-up, calling, "Contact!" Ben flipped on the magneto switches and simultaneously pressed buttons for the starter and booster coils. The mighty Merlin engine roared to life, sending a familiar tingle up his spine. The feeling was almost sexual.

Pre-taxi checks completed, he signaled Reggie he was ready to roll. Reggie called the tower for takeoff clearance and pumped his right fist to Ben in the old Spanish Republican salute before taxiing to the runway. Ben trailed behind him and, as briefed, lined up off Reggie's right wing for a formation takeoff. As he added power, the initial propeller torque caused him to veer, but he quickly compensated with rudder and aileron. He held his positioned on Reggie's wingtip for a smooth formation takeoff.

Reggie's voice crackled in his earphones. "Everything under control, Sancho?" Ben double-clicked his transmitter with an affirmative. "Excellent. Let's climb straight out as briefed and level at angels fifteen over the Down's practice area." Ben glanced at the rate-of-climb indicator and marveled how quickly they soared toward an altitude of fifteen thousand feet.

"Okay, me lad," Reggie radioed. "I'll stand off a bit and orbit overhead, while you work out the rust with a few aerial maneuvers. Try not to break anything."

"Just watch me, old man," Ben mocked. "There's less 'rust' than you think. I'll show you a couple of maneuvers. Maybe you'll learn something about aviating."

He wracked his Spit into a series of tight turns, grunting heavily as he wound them up to just under four Gs. The nose dropped during his first turn, but he quickly compensated with a slight rollout and back pressure on the control stick."

"Begging your pardon, sir," Reggie chided over the radio. "But I did mention that the Merlin powering your machine is not only more powerful than in the early variants you flew but it's also a bit heavier. Needs a little more back pressure on the stick."

Ben didn't reply as he grunted through two more high-G turns without losing a foot of altitude. Sweat formed on his face, allowing his oxygen mask to slip down, pinching his nose. "Forgot to tighten the straps," he snarled at himself. "Haven't pulled Gs like this in quite a while."

"Okay, Reggie, clear the area. Gonna try a few aerobatics," Ben radioed. Emboldened by how quickly he felt comfortable in the cockpit, he launched into an abbreviated version of the air show routine Brice had taught him years ago. He flew a fairly smooth routine until he entered a loop and nearly ran out of airspeed as he pulled over the top. "Don't stall," he yelled at himself as he rammed the throttle full forward and pulled the Spit onto the downside of the loop.

"I say," Reggie radioed, "stall inverted and you're likely to fall into a spin. Wouldn't like that, would we?"

"Forgot how much heavier this beast is than the old Mark 1As," Ben snapped. Puffing with relief, he rolled out straight and level. "Okay, Reggie, let's try a little mock aerial combat."

"Thought you'd never ask, dear fellow. Let's do just that. I'll fly out to the northwest about five miles and then turn in for a head-on attack. Usual rules, to break off from a head-on pass both parties break right. Once beyond each other, it's free for all. Prepare to have your ass waxed, sir!"

Ben flew to the southeast and turned for the head-on pass. The two Spitfires screamed at each other with a closing speed of nearly seven hundred miles an hour and sliced past each other in a flash. Both pilots rolled their aircraft into high-G left turns in an attempt to gain a firing position on the other's "six o'clock" position. They ended up on opposite sides of a great circle, chasing each other's tails.

"Coming after you, you miserable cur," Reggie grunted under the high G-load. Concerned about pulling his Spit into a high-speed stall, Ben glanced down to check his airspeed. When he looked back up, Reggie was gone.

"What the hell!" he exclaimed. "Where'd he go?" He checked his rearview mirror just as Reggie dropped down behind him into perfect firing position.

"Pop, pop, pop. Fight's over. Score one for Reggie," crackled in his headset. Both pilots rolled out to reposition for another fight.

"How the hell did you do that?" Ben demanded.

"Trade secret, old cock. Let's have another go and see if you can figure it out."

On the second go, Ben did not take his eyes off Reggie's airplane. When they rolled into their turns, Ben held his Spitfire level, pulling to tighten the turn. Reggie pulled his Spit into a near-vertical climb that started as a chandelle turn to the left and progressed into a modified loop that allowed him to slice across the circle and position his aircraft on Ben's tail. Ben saw him coming this time and duplicated the vertical maneuver, causing Reggie to undershoot and slide outside Ben's turn radius. Ignoring the wing buffeting and stall warnings, Ben gritted his teeth and pulled through the loop, ending up in firing position on Reggie's tail.

"Pop, pop, pop yourself, you cocky Brit," Ben radioed. "Score's even."

"Damn! You're a quick study for a dumb farm boy from the colonies," Reggie retorted. "Enough piss and vinegar left for another go?" Ben double-clicked his radio.

They flew two more combat maneuvers. Reggie won the first, and the final mock fight ended in a stalemate. Ben noted that Reggie's tactics involved considerable vertical maneuvering.

"You spent a lotta time goin' vertical, climbing turns, wingovers, and loops," Ben radioed as they flew back to Boscombe.

"Righto. We learned that the hard way. That and preserving airspeed in close combat. Call it energy management. Get above the other bloke. That's the secret," Reggie said. "Helped us outmaneuver Jerry's best fighters, including the 109 and the 190. Didn't help us against the 262s. They could hit-and-run, blast past us at speeds we couldn't match. Bloody good thing the Luftwaffe wasn't able to field a big number of them. Would have played havoc with our heavy bombers."

They rejoined in close formation, and Reggie grinned and waved. "What say we head back home?"

Ben eased back in his seat for the return flight and savored the feel of the Spitfire's snug cockpit. He scanned the lush Wiltshire countryside, watching the shadows lengthen across the Salisbury Plain as the sun set behind him. "That's Stonehenge," he radioed as they descended toward the airfield.

"Indeed, Sancho. Been standing there since about 3,000 BC and still puzzles the archeologists," Reggie replied. "Don't know to this day how the ancients maneuvered those huge stones into place or why. By the way, Romsey is just off to the southeast there beyond Salisbury. Might you have time to pop down to Calvert Hall for a quick hello?"

"Reggie, I'd love to. But I won't have time. Need to get back to Parham. Let's talk about it after we land."

"Speaking of which, let me lead you into a fighter pilot's overhead approach." Reggie chuckled. "That is, if you think you can still do it. See you on the ramp."

They lined up with the runway, and the two Spitfires roared inbound in trail formation. Over the runway numbers, Reggie wracked his airplane into a tight 360-degree left turn, popped the landing gear, and spiraled down to a smooth wheel landing. Ben followed closely behind, grunting under the high-G forces and was delighted to see his airplane perfectly lined up with the runway centerline as he rolled out of the turn. He closed the throttle and held his Spitfire nose high as it dropped smoothly onto the runway.

"Piece of cake." He grinned behind his oxygen mask. "Some skills a fella never loses like ridin' a bike."

He taxied behind Reggie to the ramp, swung his airplane into its parking position, and shut down the Merlin engine. Ben sat reminiscing about his experiences with the Spitfire, while the cooling engine pinged and crackled, and the instrument gyros whined to a stop. *Hard to believe we fought off the Luftwaffe with our small band of fighters. Major turning point that. Bought enough time to get America involved in the war.*

His ground crewmen hopped up on each wing to assist him as a sharp banging on the side of the fuselage roused him from his reverie. "I say," Reggie yelled, "are you going to sit there daydreaming, or will you join me at the Mess bar? I need to wet the old whistle."

Ben cleared his throat. "Uh yeah, Reggie. Be right out. Just thinking about the old days. We sure had some wild times."

"Had our innings, Sancho, but what say we get maudlin about the 'old days' over a pint? Kindly get a move on."

Comfortably seated in the Mess's overstuffed leather chairs, the two pilots drew heavy drafts from their pints of bitter. "Ahh," Reggie sighed, smacking his lips. "Elixir of the gods. Nothing like quaffing a pint with one's best friend."

Ben gave Reggie a long look. "Am I really? I mean, am I really your best friend?"

Reggie pursed his lips and returned Ben's look. "You know, Benjamin, giving it some serious thought, I have to say that's the truth. Can't think of anyone I have a closer bond with. We've known each other going on nine years. Saved each other's arses a few times. What else could we be but best friends?"

Ben sat quietly for a moment. "Yeah, I guess you're right. Can't say I look forward to the two of us going our separate ways, but that's gonna happen sometime, eh?"

"It will, but that doesn't mean we can't stay in touch, see each other along the way. Look, I'm really happy with this test pilot assignment. Intend to make it my career with the RAF. How about you? Are you thinking of staying in the peacetime USAAF? You're a colonel at a very young age. Think you can hold that rank?"

"Dunno. Not sure how the system works. Nobody told me the promotions were temporary combat upgrades. Wonder if anyone has figured this out? We could have a whole bunch of young field-grade officers after the war. Would I just stay a colonel for the next twenty years? Too many unknowns right now to make me comfortable with staying in the air force."

Ben sipped his pint and rubbed his chin. "You probably remember that back in Spain, Ted and I talked about how swell it would be to buy a private airfield somewhere in the Midwest after the war. Thought we'd run a flight school, do some crop dusting, and maybe operate a small charter service. One or both of us might sign on with an airline and run the airport on the side."

He chuckled. "Sounds kinda naive today, but back then, it seemed like it'd be a wonderful life. Not sure anymore."

"Could be a very nice life, I suppose," Reggie mused. "But after your wartime experiences, I suspect it would be a bit dull, don'tcha think?"

"Yeah, s'pose it would."

"Meantime, you said on the radio you mightn't have time to make a quick stop at Calvert Hall," Reggie said. "You under a tight schedule to get back to Parham?"

"Yeah, unfortunately. I told Joe I'd only take the day and would be back late this evening. We're making final arrangements to ferry our airplanes back to the States, probably next week. I have to hold final commander's calls with the troops and say good-bye, since my work with the bomb survey group will keep me in England for at least another four or five months. I'll turn over command of the 509th to Joe, who'll lead the flights back home. I'll stick around to oversee the final deactivation of the 509th."

"What about reassignment to the Pacific?"

"Apparently, that isn't gonna happen. Eighth Air Force headquarters already have been transferred to Okinawa, under General Doolittle, but they're absorbing B-29 groups already in Theater. From what I hear about the progress of the war out there, I'd say there's a good chance our B-17 pilots won't have time to retrain in the B-29 and get to the Pacific. Anyway, we hear there's not that big a need anyway for replacement crews. Still all indefinite at this point. But I do need to get back to Parham."

"Well, you'll see the family at Calvert Hall for the wedding, which reminds me, where are you in the nuptial planning?"

"We've completed all the paperwork—what a bunch of bureaucratic crap—and are waiting for the final approval. I'd say another coupla weeks before we have it all wrapped up. Then we'll make definite arrangements with your folks. How much lead time do they need?"

"As much as you can give," Reggie said. "Looks like a late July or early August wedding. Weather could be beautiful that time of year. Mother will be over the moon. Excellent excuse for a grand end-of-the-war celebration."

"How can I help?" Ben asked.

"You could supply a few specialties from your commissary, something like you did at Christmas," Reggie replied with a grin.

"Can do and will do." Ben grinned back then frowned. "Look, I don't know anything about planning a wedding, you know, stuff like how do we arrange for the preacher, what the bridegroom is supposed to wear, and do we have a big wedding party? What about dinner? Can you help?"

"I haven't a clue, Sancho. I'll turn that over to Mother and, I guess, Elizabeth. Tell them to coordinate with Gwen. Think we'd better stay out of the planning. 'Himself' has agreed to give the bride away, with the caveat that duties might call him away at the last minute. Face that when the time comes."

"Reggie, I can't thank you enough," Ben said softly. "This is a wonderful gift to Gwen and me. We'll be forever in your debt."

"Happy to do it, Ben. Wouldn't have it any other way. I'll go back to my test piloting, and you continue counting bomb craters for the top brass. Let's let the ladies sort out what they're best equipped to handle. I'm still in line as best man, right?" Ben nodded.

They drained their pints and levered themselves out of the overstuffed chairs. "Now let's find that Anson crew and get you back to Parham."

"I could always take one of your extra Spits and save you the trouble of rounding up a crew," Ben said with a sly grin. "You know, drive myself home."

"Would love to, old cock. Know you wouldn't mistreat it. But my signature is on the paperwork, and I wouldn't want to have to explain if some RAF inspection bloke came looking for that Spit before you could get it back to me."

"Not like the good ol' days," Ben chided. "The RAF has gotten stuffy and hidebound since winning the war."

Chapter 45

THE 509ᵀᴴ GOES HOME – JULY 1945

Back at Parham, Ben called a staff meeting with Joe, his squadron commanders, and administrative officers. "Joe, schedule two commander's calls day after tomorrow," Ben said. "I'll meet with the officers and flight crews at 0730 and the enlisted personnel at 1430. We'll be getting orders soon to fly our birds back to the States and begin moving all other personnel to Southampton for a boat ride home. Want to get the men ready."

"What about our support equipment and stores, bombs, and ammunition?" Joe asked.

"First elements of a base deactivation team will arrive here tomorrow to take on that task. We'll leave it to them."

They spent another hour reviewing what needed to be done to ensure the group's planes and personnel were ready for the departure. "Okay, think we've covered everything," Ben said. "Any questions? Seeing none, this meeting's over. You all have your lists, let's make this as smooth an operation as possible.

"Finally, Joe, organize a change of command ceremony following the enlisted commander's call. Tell Sergeant Benson to get the group band tuned up and ready. We'll have everybody corralled anyway, so we can just march 'em out to the ramp, and I'll officially turn over the command to you. You'll lead the 509ᵗʰ home." Joe nodded his thanks.

"Might sound like I'm shoving a lot of the grunt work off on you, but I've been alerted to expect a recall next week to restart bomb survey operations. The detachment has been upgraded to a group, and I'm to be named its commander. Been ordered to organize the operation along group lines, with squadrons and flights, and double the number of survey teams. Seems the brass wants us to cover as many sites as possible, while the Americans, Brits, and French negotiate with the Russians over who controls what in occupied Germany. I understand they're forming four occupation zones, with the Russians taking control of Eastern Germany. Berlin's going to be divided four ways as well. Seems the bickering over Germany is just starting. Not sure how all of that's going to play out."

At 0715 hours, Joe paced across the briefing room stage as the 509th's officers and flight crews settled into their chairs, gossiping and swapping joke. One called out, "What's the word, Joe? More food drops on our liberated friends in Holland?" Another yelled, "Naw. We got leftover bombs, so we're gonna drop 'em on a couple more German cities, stir up the rubble one last time."

Joe smiled and waved off the questions. "Hold your horses. Colonel Findlay will be here in a couple of minutes. Think you're gonna like what he has to say."

Ben strode into the briefing hall, followed by his administrative officers. Joe called all assembled to attention. Ben stepped up on the stage and stared out at the group. He ordered them "at ease" and waited as they settled in their chairs and stared expectantly at him.

"We've been tasked with another important mission," he began. A collective groan swirled through the flight crews. "What now?" someone muttered loudly.

"This is one you're gonna like," Ben said with a grin. "Men, the day after tomorrow, the 509th is flying home!"

The room erupted in a roar of cheers, applause, and whistles. "Hot damn!" someone hollered. "Goin' home to momma!"

Ben let them celebrate for a couple of minutes then raised his hand for silence. "That's right. Home to momma or whomever. Takeoff is scheduled for Thursday at 0800 hours. First stop will be Prestwick, Scotland, for refueling. Your ships have been fitted with extra tanks, and you're going to be lightly loaded, so we expect you'll be able to make Keflavik Air Base in Iceland on the next leg with plenty of reserves. Of course, that'll depend on the winds, but we've provided for that with extra fuel. The group will overnight at Keflavik and get an early start for the major ocean crossing. If prevailing winds allow, it could be nonstop to Floyd Bennett Field in Brooklyn, but be prepared for a fuel stop and possibly an overnight in Gander,

Newfoundland. Next day, Floyd Bennett in Brooklyn for sure." This prompted another riotous outbreak of cheering and whistles.

Ben signaled again for quiet. "Couple more announcements. Colonel Joe Atkins has been named the new commander of the 509th." Another cheer erupted. "I've been assigned command of the new group that's been formed to complete the bomb survey work I started when I was temporarily assigned to the USSBS detachment at High Wycombe. That detachment has been expanded to a group in an effort to get the surveying mission completed as quickly as possible."

He paused and surveyed the assembly. "So I'll pass responsibility for the group to Joe at a change of command ceremony at 1600 hours." Ben paused again, to organize his thoughts and control his emotions. "We've completed a tough job here with the Eighth Air Force, and we paid a heavy price for our success. You've all made big sacrifices, and you should be damn proud of what you've achieved and also damn happy you've survived. We must never forget our comrades, who made the supreme sacrifice, paid the ultimate price, to win this war. Carry their memory with you for the rest of your lives. I can assure you that I will, and that I'll always remember what an honor it has been to lead such a group of heroes." The group responded with a spontaneous standing ovation.

After they regained their seats, Ben turned to Joe. "Now I'll let Colonel Atkins complete the briefing with details of the flight back home."

As he turned to leave, Ben stopped and grinned at the assembly. "Oh, I almost forgot. One more announcement. Members of a base deactivation team will begin arriving tomorrow. Their task will be to inventory everything left on the base and prepare it for shipping back to the States. That includes what liquor stocks remain in the bars in the officers' and enlisted men's clubs. I think we should lessen their burden by not leaving a lot of heavy bottles behind. To that end, the bars will open on completion of the change of command ceremony. Drinks will be on the house."

Another standing ovation rattled the Quonset hut as Ben tossed Joe a crisp salute. "Just make sure nobody's too badly hungover for the trip home," he yelled.

Joe called the group to attention as Ben strode out of the hall. As he reached the door, someone started singing "For He's a Jolly Good Fellow," and everyone in the room joined in the refrain that echoed across the Parham base.

The afternoon briefing for the enlisted personnel also was greeted with enthusiasm, albeit at first a bit more restrained. But the news that they'd soon be boarding trains to Southampton where ships waited to take them home brought them cheering and shouting to their feet. The final announcement that the club bar would be opened after the change of command ceremony and drinks would be on the house generated a roar of approval.

All the 509th officers and enlisted personnel stood fidgeting in ranks on the Parham ramp at 1630 hours. The 509th group band played several patriotic songs until Joe called the group to attention. He joined Ben on a makeshift stage on the tarmac, and all presented arms as the band played the "Star-Spangled Banner." Ben ordered the men to parade rest and welcomed them to the ceremony. He said many complimentary things about Joe, thanked the men again for their service, and called for the 509th colors standard. He handed the flag to Joe and formally turned over command of the group. Acknowledging a round of applause and cheers, Joe pledged his full support to the 509th and said he was honored to be leading them home.

Joe closed the ceremony, thanking Ben for his leadership, and commended all personnel for their loyal service. He then added, "I know we're standing between you and free drinks, so I declare this ceremony completed."

He dismissed them and watched amused as they scrambled to their respective clubs.

The predawn calm at Parham was shattered as ground crews started the four Wright Cyclone engines on each of the twenty-one B-17s they were preparing for the transatlantic flight back to the States. The combined roar rattled the far corners of the base and woke everyone, whether or not they were scheduled to fly with the group. In the operations center, Ben and Joe studied the latest weather forecasts for the North Atlantic.

"Looks like you'll have good weather to Keflavik and probably beyond, Joe," Ben said. "Westerly winds are surprisingly light for this time of year. You can thank the weather gods because it looks like you'll be able to overfly Bluie West One in Greenland."

"Hmm, yeah. That's the rough base near Narsarsuaq, right? I've heard about it. Has some wild-ass final approach up a fjord, right?"

"Yeah, wild ass doesn't do justice to that approach. I flew in there as a pickup copilot with a B-17 crew that flew me home for transition training after I transferred from the RAF to the USAAF. Final approach fix is a wrecked ship in the fjord, and then you make a tight turn around a mountain and flop onto a temporary runway. Don't complain about missing that experience."

Ben stood on the control tower balcony and watched as Joe led the B-17 fleet to the runway. A captain staying behind to wrap up the operations center stepped to his side. "Care to do the honors, Colonel?" he asked, handing Ben the large-bore pistol that would fire the green flare signaling takeoff.

"Uh yes, of course. Thank you." Ben raised the flare gun, pulled the trigger, and with a loud chuff, the green flare arched into the sky. The four engines on Joe's airplane roared, and his B-17 accelerated down the runway. He was followed at thirty-second intervals by the remainder of the 509th bombers.

Joe circled over Parham, forming the 509th into a tight formation and then led the group on a low-level flyby along the runway. All crewmen onboard waved and pumped their fists in the air as they roared past. The captain took the flare pistol from Ben and fired volley after volley of green flares as the formation swept past, climbed, and headed northwest to Prestwick. The assembled ground crews yelled and waved good-bye, flinging their caps in the air.

Ben walked down to the ramp, paced around kicking at chunks of loose tarmac, and headed for the operations center. He riffled through a few discarded maps and weather reports and walked back to his former headquarters office. It was in an orderly condition. All files had been packed for shipment back home. A single battered typewriter was left for collection by the base deactivation team. He stepped into his former inner office and sank into his chair that squawked as if to protest being awakened. Leaning back, he stared out at the empty ramp. The silence rang in his ears.

Feels like I spent a lifetime in this place. Hard to believe it's over. Faces paraded before his unfocused eyes—lots of faces. *Where was Frank Silverman? In the Pacific yet? Ted, ah god, Ted! Never see him again. The Giraffes and their wild escape through Poland. Did any of the other fellas make it? And Sandy Saunders. Did the Polish underground fighters get him out? What about all the young 509th flight crews whose names he'd forgotten but whose faces would plague his dreams?*

The telephone jangled, and Ben tipped forward to lift the receiver. "Tower, Colonel. C-47 from Daws Air Station just called in. On the ground in about fifteen minutes."

Ben muttered thanks, replaced the receiver, and scanned the office with a long thoughtful look. "Almost hate to leave this place," he mused. "Had a lot of great times here, along with a helluva lot of bad ones too. Memories for a lifetime." He phoned Gwen and told her he was returning to Daws to resume the survey flights. Said he'd be back in about two weeks to check on the base deactivation, and then they'd have a long weekend.

"Meanwhile, I hope you're makin' progress with the wedding plans," he said. Gwen said she was coordinating plans with Lady Percy and Elizabeth and had everything in hand. "Safe flights with the survey, Ben. Get that nasty job done and come see me soon." She sent him a juicy smooching sound before ringing off.

Ben walked to the door, his footsteps echoing throughout the vacant headquarters building. He paused for a last look around, stepped through the door, and quietly closed it behind him. He strode toward the operations center without looking back.

After takeoff, Ben asked the captain piloting the C-47 to request a low-level flyby along the Parham runway.

Chapter 46

THE SURVEY CONTINUES

Ben pushed the expanded bomb survey group to quickly conduct the remaining missions, some of which ranged deep into Germany. When they received orders to survey the Regensburg area, he took the mission.

"Have a personal reason to lead this one," he told his crew. "I bombed the Messerschmitt factory there three times. Got shot down on the second trip and spent some time as a guest of the local Gestapo commander. It wasn't a nice visit. Escaped from a POW train wreck and got home after a long trek north through Poland and rode on a Polish fishing boat and a Swedish freighter.

"First mission I got after returning to operational duty was Regensburg again. Got beaten to hell again, but we made it home. It'll be a treat to go back a final time with nobody shootin' at me. I want a close look at how much damage we did to the factory and hopefully the Gestapo headquarters. I hope we blew that rotten bunch to hell."

The now familiar brownish-gray pall cloaked Regensburg as Ben circled the city to give the surveyors an overall view. He guided the C-47 to a landing on the patched runway next to the Messerschmitt factory. Crews from the USAAF technology branch were poking through the tangled wreckage of the main assembly hall, retrieving records, machinery, and airplane and engine parts. Amazingly, they found several intact and flyable 262 twin-jet fighters in camouflaged revetments in the forest behind the factory. These were being prepared for shipment to the States.

Messerschmitt Me-16 3 Komet Rocket Powered Fighter

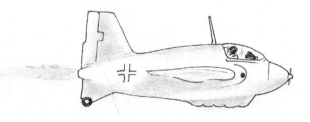

As the survey crew measured and photographed the charred ruins, Ben clambered around piles of shattered glass, bricks, and twisted steel girders. "Looks like we did a pretty good job of putting this place outta business," he remarked. "What I find incredible is how they salvaged enough stuff to continue hand-building those damn jets out there in that other building. Our reconnaissance photos showed we had destroyed it too. We wondered where the hell their replacement jets were coming from."

After plotting the spread of the bomb craters around the factory, they headed in to Regensburg. They found familiar scenes, overlaid with the stench of death still hanging heavily in the air. Blackened shells of buildings lined every street. Hollow-eyed people shuffled about, some darting like frightened rats into dark cellars when the survey crews approached. "Never get used to this," Ben said. His crewmen agreed, their replies muffled by their surgical masks.

Ben consulted a map. "Figure we're about here," he said, "which means the city center is a short distance north and to the left. Should find Gestapo headquarters somewhere nearby."

Following a circuitous route detouring around streets clogged with debris, they found a columned facade standing resolutely in front of the crumpled remains of a burned-out building. The brass plate identifying it as Gestapo headquarters reflected the thin sunlight penetrating the haze.

"Well, I'll be damned!" Ben exclaimed, staring at the heavy oak doors that somehow had remained intact and firmly locked. "We did manage to put a bomb or two down ol' 'Oberwhatsit's chimney. I sure hope he was here with my pal 'Schultz' at the time. Like to think of those bastards roasting in hell." He resisted the temptation to call for a bulldozer to push the front wall into the blackened hole behind it. "Standin' there like that reminds me of the Nazi salute," he snarled.

It took three days to complete the Regensburg survey, and the crew boarded their C-47 for the flight back to Daws. They completed their post-mission briefing and headed for the officer's club for a drink. "How much longer do you think these missions will take?" Crenshaw asked. "We've covered most of the major sites in the eastern part of Germany. What do we concentrate on next?"

"High Command asked us to survey Dresden, but I told Sampson I wanted to pass on that one, let the RAF handle it," Ben said. "Don't think I could face what we'd find there. Understand the city and most of the people in it have either been blown to bits or burned to a crisp. I don't think Dresden will go into the history books as one of the best examples of effective strategic bombing."

Ben paused and sipped his beer. "Besides, we have primary targets left in the southwest, Stuttgart and Munich among them. And I want to get back to the Leunawerke refineries near Merseburg. Hopefully, we can wrap this up in the next couple of months."

The next day, Ben told Sampson he had to fly back to Parham to check on the base deactivation process and requested a three-day pass to cover the weekend. Sampson grinned as he signed a pass and handed it to Ben. "Greet the Lady Gwen from me." He chuckled. "See you Monday morning. Stuttgart will be the next stop for you and your crew."

Crenshaw and a pickup crew consisting of another survey pilot and a crew chief flew Ben to Parham, dropping him at flight operations. Crenshaw wished him luck and said they'd be back to pick him up at 0730 hours on Monday. Ben avoided the operations center and his former headquarters office and headed for the maintenance hangar where the deactivation team had set up their operations. The lieutenant colonel who headed the team briefed Ben on their progress and showed him manifests of the equipment and supplies that had been shipped out.

"The place already looks pretty bare," Ben said. "You fellas don't waste any time."

"That's our job, Colonel. And the quicker we wrap all this up, the sooner we get to go home too. Last thing we'll do is decommission the tower, pull out the equipment, and paint a big white X in the middle of the runway, signaling that the base is closed."

"I see," Ben muttered. "Ah, what other bases are close to Cambridge that might stay open for a while?"

"The RAF has several bases around Cambridge. Closest one is Station 415 Cambridge. I dunno for sure how long the RAF will keep it operational. And there's Station 133, the Eighth Air Force base at Bassingbourne, southwest of Cambridge. Far as I know, it isn't scheduled for deactivation yet."

"Thanks. Uh, coupla favors. I need to use a phone, and I need to purchase some supplies from what's left in the commissary. Finally, do you have a jeep I can requisition for the weekend?"

"Phone's right here, Colonel. You know where the commissary is, sign for whatever you want. And the motor pool still has several jeeps. Help yourself to one. Just sign it out with the sergeant on duty."

As Ben turned to leave, the colonel called out, "Colonel Findlay, almost forgot there's some official-looking mail for you that came in yesterday. I was going to forward it to you at Daws, but here you are. Much quicker."

Ben thanked him and slit open the envelope. It was from the adjutant running the Eighth Air Force deactivation detachment at Pine Tree. It was addressed to Colonel Findlay, Benjamin A., from the commander of the Eighth Air Force deactivation detachment. *Why the hell did they mail it to me here? Guess they don't know I'm based next door at Daws?*

"Sir," the letter began, "It is my pleasure to inform you that your application to marry British citizen, Miss Gwendolen M. Brewster, has been approved . . ."

Ben skidded to a stop in front of Gwen's Cambridge apartment and bounded up the stairs to her front door. She answered his knock and flung her arms around his neck as he grabbed her in a passionate embrace. "Got some great news, but it can wait," he gasped. He awoke an hour or so later in bed, still clutching her naked body to his equally naked body.

"Uh, did I actually say hello?" he mumbled. "All I remember is a mad dash to your bedroom." Gwen giggled and lightly bit his ear. "I think you said something endearing like, 'First, sweetheart, let me carry you to your boudoir.'"

"Good. Glad I remembered to make my manners." He grinned.

"Okay, Colonel, now what's the great news?" Gwen asked.

Ben fished the letter out of the inside pocket of his uniform jacket. "This, my love. This document here says we can get married!" Gwen squealed with delight and grabbed him, smothering him with kisses.

The long weekend passed all too quickly. A persistent and unseasonably cold rain provided an excuse to spent the time inside, much of it snuggled under the covers. In between times, they worked on wedding and honeymoon plans.

"We better choose a date for the wedding, maybe a couple of possibilities, so I can have Reggie check with his family at Calvert Hall," Ben said. "Any particular date suit you best?"

"Umm, how about July 18? It's Mum's and Dad's wedding anniversary," Gwen said with tears welling in her eyes. "It's, umm, it's a Saturday. That's only four weeks away. Do you think it will allow enough time to make final arrangements? We already have most of the details taken care of."

"Sounds fine to me. I'm sure I can get a ten-day leave with no problem. Let me call Reggie tomorrow, and if it works for them, we'll announce it. Uh, by the way, I bought some stuff still left in the commissary—half a dozen canned hams, canned fruit, coffee, condensed milk, sugar, and so on," Ben said. "Also put aside a few cases of liquor and some champagne. Amazed there was any left behind. Anyway, I've stored it at Parham and will take it down to Daws when I fly back on Monday. Reggie and I can get it on down to Calvert Hall. How's everything else coming together?"

"I think we're doing quite well. Lady Percy has been such a dear," Gwen said. "She insists that she and Elizabeth can make all the arrangements with the help of her household staff. And Elizabeth, bless her heart, she has agreed to be my maid of honor."

"Has she?" Ben said, raising his eyebrows in surprise.

"Yes, she has, and don't look so surprised. We both know she's in love with you. But she knows it isn't to be, so she's making the best of it. She's a very brave and decent young lady."

"Aw, Gwen, she's still a kid," Ben protested. "It's puppy love. She'll find some bright young fella her own age, and they'll have a great life together."

Gwen punched him on the chest. "Benjamin Findlay, you know so little about women. It's maddening!"

"What about your wedding dress?" Ben asked, anxious to change the subject.

"We're still on active duty, Ben. I don't think a wedding dress would be appropriate. Besides, there's the expense, and I'm not even certain we can find one already made or the material to have one made. I'd like us to be married in our dress uniforms. You can buy me an expensive dress when we renew our vows in ten years."

"See, you've got it all worked out." Ben shrugged. "Dress uniform is fine with me. Don't get a chance to wear mine much. It isn't going to be a big wedding. You'll have Elizabeth as maid of honor, and I'll have Reggie as best man. Other than that, all my close buddies from the Eighth Air Force and the 509th group have already gone home."

He grabbed her face and kissed her tenderly. "Is that gonna bother you? I mean, having just a small wedding? Uh, you don't have much family, do you?"

"No," she said quietly. "Auntie in Bristol is all, and she's in a nursing home, so . . . But I'd like to invite several of my nurse friends from Cambridge." Ben smiled and nodded.

Satisfied the wedding plans were well in hand, Ben asked about her desires for a honeymoon. "Can't fly off to any place exotic, but there are some nice places in England and, ah, maybe Scotland?"

"Ben, I'd like to rent a cottage in the Cotswold and spend a quiet week just getting used to being Mrs. Benjamin Findlay. I hear Castle Combe is a lovely spot. Perhaps we could find a nice little cottage there."

Ben hugged her tightly. "I'll find out and book us a place, love."

The next morning, Ben phoned Reggie and told him he was on his way back to Daws to resume the survey flights. He shared the good news about their wedding and asked if Saturday, July 18, would work for the Calvert Hall family.

"Of course, of course!" Reggie shouted. "I'll confirm it with Mother, but I see no difficulty. Shall we book the rector from Romsey Forest to preside, or do you want to find a USAAF chaplain?"

"Ah, let's go with the Romsey Forest rector."

"Capital! I'll phone Mum and ask her to set things in motion for July 18. I think it'll work best to let her book the padre. Now how many guests should we plan on?"

"Ah, not sure, Reggie. I'll ask Gwen to work up a list of friends and fellow nurses she wants to invite and send it to your mother. All of the fellas I served with in the 509th have returned to the States. There's only a deactivation detachment left at the old Eight Air Force headquarter, and I don't know any of the fellas involved in that. I'd like to invite General Sampson, my survey copilot Crenshaw, and maybe some other members of the survey team. Not more than six or seven. Are any of the Giraffes left around?"

"I'll check and let you know, Ben. Any idea how many will be overnight guests?"

"Hey, Reggie, we can't impose like that. We'll find . . ."

"Not a problem. You won't be imposing. Calvert Hall can accommodate a goodly number of overnight guests. Have Gwen tell Mum how many she expects."

"Okay, Reggie. Thanks. Ah, one more thing. Gwen wants to spend our honeymoon in a place called Castle Combe in the Cotswold. Is there some kind of a directory where I can find a nice little cottage to rent for a week?"

"I'll put Bates on to it. He'll find something suitable."

"Godalmighty, Reggie, you've got an answer for everything! What would I do without you?"

"Muddle through, I s'pose, Sancho. Muddle through. Now get on with your bomb crater counting."

"Oh, by the way, Reggie, I've bought some stuff left over in the commissary—canned hams, liquor, and other stuff. I'll haul it down to Daws on the C-47 tomorrow, and we can figure out how to get it on to Calvert Hall."

"Wonderful! That'll be appreciated. Umm, how much stuff? Do we need a lorry, or will a van do?"

"Van'll do fine. Call you after we arrive."

That night, Ben wrote a long letter home, bringing his mother and father up-to-date on his bomb survey work and announcing the wedding date.

Ben waited on the Parham ramp as Crenshaw landed and taxied the C-47 up to the operations center. He swung right so the left side door faced the building, shut down the left engine, and kept the right one idling. The crew chief opened the door. Ben wheeled the food and liquor forward, and they loaded it onboard. He hopped onboard, and the flight engineer slammed the door as Crenshaw started the left engine and taxied back to the runway.

"Mornin'," Ben said as he strapped into the cockpit jump seat. "Anything on the ops schedule for this week?"

"Top o' the morning, Chief." Crenshaw grinned. "Trust your weekend was successful. Yes, we've two missions set—Stuttgart and

Munich. And the Leuna oil refineries are on the docket. Probably get assigned that in the following week or so."

"Okay," Ben grunted. "In Stuttgart, we'll want to look closely at the Porsche and Daimler factories. We've been raiding the city, alternating with RAF Bomber Command, for nearly five years with mixed results. Those deep valleys that split the city into sections have made it damn near impossible to hit all our targets cleanly. It'll be interesting to see up close what we did."

At Daws, Ben asked the flight engineer to help shift the food and liquor to the commissary for safekeeping. Ben reported to General Sampson and shared the news of the impending wedding. "Like to apply for a ten-day leave starting on the sixteenth, General. That'll give me a couple of days before the wedding on the eighteenth and seven days for a honeymoon in the Cotswold."

"Congratulations, Ben. No problem on the leave. You're ahead of schedule on the surveys. Think we can spare you for ten days with your new bride. Are all the arrangements made?"

"Yessir, we're going to be married in the chapel at Calvert Hall. That's near Romsey Forest, southeast of Salisbury. It's the family home of my good friend Wing Commander Percy. His family has been really swell, offering the chapel and opening up their home. Reggie's father is Lord Percy, a bigwig in the Air Ministry. Wonderful people. They're making it into quite a family affair. His Lordship has agreed to give Gwen away, and Reggie will be my best man. Ah, and his younger sister will be Gwen's maid of honor."

"Impressive. Percy is the pilot you flew with in Spain and the Battle of Britain, isn't he?" Ben nodded.

"And, General, we'd be honored if you could join us for the celebration and reception, maybe spend an overnight at Calvert Hall," Ben said. "I can get you the coordinates later."

"Glad to join you, Ben. Is there an airfield nearby? I could fly down with one of our Goonies and bring along anyone else you might be inviting." Ben told him about Hawkestone and gave him the tower frequencies.

Circling low over Stuttgart two days later, Ben yelled to Crenshaw, "First time I've flown over this place without having battled Luftwaffe fighters on the way in and dodging flak over the target. Damn tough challenge. But take a look from this altitude. I guess we did more than a little damage."

He continued to circle as the survey team snapped photographs of the bomb crater patterns in and around the city center and the major industrial complexes. Ben landed, and they rolled out the motorcycles to begin the detailed inspection.

The last raid on the city had been in mid-April, and many of the streets were already cleared of debris. But the partial walls of bombed-out buildings lined them like giant scorched stalagmites reaching into the leaden sky. "Christ!" Crenshaw exclaimed. "The center of the city's been totally destroyed." He shuddered. "Looks like the bloody backside of the moon."

"Yeah, we did one helluva job on the city," Ben muttered. "The intel fellas said something about the people hiding in shelters dug into the hills. Guess that helped limit the civilian casualties. Let's take a close look at the factories, see what we accomplished there."

Both the Porsche and Daimler main factories were badly damaged. Some replacement facilities had been cleverly camouflaged in the wreckage, and supporting machine shops had been dispersed from the main buildings. The factories had continued to produce until the end of the war.

"I dunno," Ben grumbled. "When you add up the number of bombers and crews we lost attacking this place, it makes you wonder if the top brass knew what the hell they were doing. I mean, look at this, we bombed the shit outta these factories at a high cost of men and airplanes, and they were still producing aircraft engines, tanks, and all kinds of stuff right up to the end of the war!"

"I say, what's the answer?" Crenshaw asked. "Next time, and I hope to God there isn't a next time, what do we do, develop some super bomb that'd flatten everything in a place like this, put it out of commission forever?"

"I don't see that happening, but what the hell? I don't have the answer," Ben said, shaking his head. "Do know, though, there's gotta be a better way than this to solve the world's problems."

Their trip to Munich followed what had become a routine for the survey missions. Ben circled the city for aerial photography, and they landed to make a detailed inspection. As they toured the city on the ground, it was evident that at least half of the buildings in the center city were burned-out ruins, and the transportation and utility infrastructures had been destroyed. Ironically, the famous Hofbrauhaus beer hall where Hitler held early Nazi planning sessions and his Braune Haus headquarters survived with limited damage.

"Looks like we all had our priorities right," Crenshaw joked. "Destroyed most of the city and the factories around it but spared the beer hall."

"Now comes the hard part," Ben said. "Dachau, one of the Nazi's most notorious concentration death camp, is about ten miles northeast of here. We never targeted it, so there's no survey work to be done there, but I wanna tour it. Stories circulating about what went on there are almost unbelievable, so I want to see for myself. You interested?"

"Yes, although I've a feeling I may regret it," Crenshaw said.

Their first impression as they drove up to the main gate was that Dachau was a typical Wehrmacht military base. The heavy stone wall supporting massive oaken double doors was topped with a huge eagle, perched with wings spread on a large wreathed swastika. It appeared neat and well maintained. Inside they found scenes of unimaginable horror. The camp had been liberated three months earlier by a detachment of the U.S. Amy's Forty-Second (Rainbow) Infantry Division, so it had been "cleansed," and hundreds of bodies had been removed for proper burial. But the rough barracks remained, some still occupied by prisoners who had not yet been repatriated and others housing SS troops and officers being held for prosecution as war criminals. And the cells, torture rooms, gas chambers disguised as showers, and crematory ovens stood as stark reminders of the barbarity perpetrated on hundreds of thousands of prisoners since the camp opened in early 1933.

"What does that say?" Crenshaw asked their U.S. Army guide, pointing to iron scroll wording over the prisoner's gate.

"Arbeit Macht Frei," he said. "In English, 'Work will make you free.' That's part of the Nazi's attempt to disguise this as a work camp. You can't imagine what we found here when we first entered. It's going to haunt my dreams for the rest of my life."

"So this is Heinrich Himmler's legacy," Ben snarled. "As head of Hitler's police, including the Gestapo and SS, he was the mastermind of this rotten place and a whole string of similar camps across Germany and occupied Europe. Wish we could have gotten to him and the rest of Hitler's sub humans without having to destroy half the damn world along the way."

"You know, Ben, we've been agonizing over the destruction and civilian casualties we've encountered during our bomb surveys in Germany, but look what was happening in this bloody twisted country!" Crenshaw said. "Can't say everybody in Germany was responsible for this kind of obscenity but one hell of a lot of them were, even by passively letting it happen."

He gazed stunned at the scene around them. "We paid a bloody high price to end this, but I have to believe it was a price that had to be paid to put an end to this kind of horror. Can you imagine what would have happened if we hadn't beaten the Luftwaffe to a standstill and the Germans had successfully invaded England? What would America have done? Trying to invade Europe from across the Atlantic would have been a dead loss."

"Yeah." Ben sighed. "Damn hard to balance this all out. Have to leave that to the historians."

That evening, Ben received a call ordering them to add a quick visit to Nurnberg after leaving Munich the next day. They were to make a brief stopover en route north to the Leunawerke oil refineries near Merseburg, located west of Leipzig.

"I remember on one of our missions to Nurnberg we targeted the Nazi's party rally grounds," Ben said en route to the city. "What a monstrosity. Wasn't hard to hit, but the damn thing was so spread out we couldn't confirm how much damage we did. Left a lotta holes in the parade grounds, though."

"It was one of the main aim points during our night raids," Crenshaw said. "Bloody hard to find in the dark, so most of the time, we just stooged about, and if we didn't find it, we dropped our bombs on the city center and buggered off home."

"A bit different than our obsession with daylight pinpoint bombing that wasn't so pinpoint after all," Ben said.

Following a low-level aerial survey of Nurnberg, Ben landed, and the crews spread out for a ground inspection. They found the now familiar depressing scene, row upon row of scorched building skeletons and groups of confused, desperate-looking people, picking among mountains of rubble.

"Where the hell do they start in clearing out all of this debris and rebuilding?" Crenshaw exclaimed. "I mean, cleaning up is one thing, but where will they dump these millions of bits and pieces?"

"Guess they'll build mountains outside of town," Ben said. "Now let's see if we can find some of the main buildings. This was Hitler's showpiece, called it the most German of German cities."

Hitler selected Nurnberg as the central site for the Nazi Party's rallies, which prompted the Allies to target it for propaganda purposes, to show the German people that the Third Reich's showcase city was vulnerable to attack. The Deutscher Hof Hotel that served as Hitler's headquarters when he attended the massive party celebrations was a particular aim point. As they drove past the battered building, Ben pointed out the Hitler balcony on the second floor. "That's where he stood when he reviewed the thousands of troops who paraded past during the rallies. Doesn't look like much now, does it?"

"Wish he'd bloody well been there when we blasted this place," Crenshaw grunted.

The Nurnberg Haupbahnhof, the city's main train station, and the central city square flanked by the Frauenkirche stately cathedral also sustained severe damage, as did the Saint Katharine's Church, where the Nazis had stored the Imperial Regalia of the Holy Roman Empire they had confiscated from Vienna. The relics from what the Nazi's considered the "First Reich" were venerated and used as patterns for much of their insignia and massed demonstrations of military pomp and power. The Second Reich, which by their reasoning began with the formation of the German Empire in the late 1800s, lasted until the end of World War 1 in 1918. Germany's defeat in that war was used by Hitler and the National Socialist Party, commonly known as the Nazis, as justification for organizing the Third Reich and launching what became World War 2.

"So much for the thousand year Reich," Ben snarled. "Still can't understand how one crazy son of a bitch could gather a buncha madmen around him and highjack a whole country. I mean, look at all this pain and suffering those bastards caused here and all across Europe!"

"This is payback for what the Huns did to the East End of London and Coventry, not to mention other cities," Crenshaw snapped. "Need to keep that in mind when we agonize over what happened here. We didn't start this bloody war. Hitler and his goons did."

Their next stop at the Nazi's rally grounds on the Nurnberg outskirts showed the Allied bombing attacks had severely damaged the Luitpold Arena, in which 150,000 soldiers and party officials regularly gathered to hear Hitler's infamous speeches. Even greater damage was visited on the adjoining Zeppelin Field with its Roman-columned Zeppelin Tribune that was dominated by a massive concrete wreathed swastika. During night rallies, banks of vertically pointed antiaircraft searchlights formed columns of light along the tribune that projected thousands of feet into the sky.

"That's where the huge swastika was set," Ben said, pointing to a scorched area on top of the tribune. "We could see the damn thing from altitude and tried to put bombs on it, but the flak was so heavy we didn't want to risk anymore crews just to knock it down. U.S. Army engineers finally blew it to bits with high-explosive charges in April."

After completing the Nurnberg survey, Ben loaded the crews and headed for Merseburg and the Leunawerke refineries. "I expect we're gonna find some really awful bombing results at these rotten refineries," Ben said to Crenshaw. "We were fooled several times by the camouflage and smoke screens the Germans used to disguise the main refinery buildings. They also built a fake refinery complex off to the side of the real one, which made it damn hard for our bombardiers to find the right aim points. That and the heavy flak made it one of our toughest targets."

Ben's concerns were well founded. The most dramatic survey results were gathered during repeated low-level flights over the expanse of the refinery complex. Significant bomb crater patterns were found in and around the dummy complex, indicating many of the crews, including pathfinder bombers using radar bombsights to pinpoint the real refineries, were fooled into dropping tons of bombs on fake buildings. Even when the bombardiers were able to identify the real site, the smoke screens and intense flak often caused them to miss their aim points.

Bloody hell!" Crenshaw exclaimed. "Look at those bomb crater patterns to the west. That one grouping over there looks to be at least a mile, maybe more, outside the perimeter of the refinery border. Were some of these missions flown in bad weather?"

"Some were," Ben said. "I remember leading an attack on this damn target once with solid cloud cover. The Pathfinders used their H2X radar bombsights to find the target, or so we thought, and we dropped on their command. Everybody else dropped in sequence on us. This shows that wasn't a good way to do it."

Ben and his crew bunked in for the night with the army detachment that had taken control of the Leunawerke facility. The next morning, he sent the surveyors on their rounds, and he and Crenshaw drove along the extensive network of road and pipelines crisscrossing the site. They noted how few of the cracking towers and other refinery elements had been destroyed. The pipelines interconnecting them had been cut in many places, but the Germans had included cutoff valves and a network of bypass pipes that enabled them to keep the facility producing vital fuel and oil products.

"Gotta be one of the hardest targets to destroy spread out like this," Ben mused. "With airfields, factories, and even rail centers, we had concentrated aim points. Didn't have that here. Hell, we'd hit one part, blow that up, and they'd shift production to another section and use other parts of the pipeline system."

He shook his head. "Even incendiaries didn't help. See how far they had their storage tanks dispersed? We'd set fire to one tank farm, and they'd shut it down and switch to another one."

The crew spent another day logging details of the damage to Leunawerke before flying back to Daws.

"I'll be taking a ten-day leave next week," Ben said to Crenshaw on the flight back. "As you know, Gwen and I are getting married on the eighteenth. Guess you'll be flying down to Romsey Forest with General Sampson and the others. Then we'll spend a week in the Cotswold."

"I say, looking forward to the big celebration," Crenshaw said. "Imagine having a lord of the realm giving away the bride. Are we really invited to stay overnight at Calvert Hall?"

"You are, indeed." Ben grinned.

"Times has changed, eh?" Crenshaw joked. "Wait'll I tell my lot I'll be spending the weekend as the guest of Lord and Lady Percy. That'll make 'em sit up and take notice. Have to be on my best behavior."

"Reggie has a wonderful family," Ben said. "They'll go out of their way to make you feel comfortable."

308

Chapter 47

THE IMPENDING WEDDING – JULY 1945

Three days later, Crenshaw eased the C-47 onto the runway at Hawkestone emergency landing station and taxied to the makeshift operations center. Ben and the crew chief shifted the commissary goods out of the back door and stacked them on the tarmac. The crew chief saluted and slammed the door. Ben strode beyond the left wingtip and saluted Crenshaw, who revved the engines and taxied back out for takeoff on the return flight to Daws. Flight Leftenant Smyth stepped forward and saluted Ben. "Welcome back, Colonel. Understand you've returned for your wedding. Congratulations, sir."

"Thank you, Smyth. Glad to be back. Surprised to see you still here. How much longer will Hawkestone be kept open?"

"No plans to close us down, Colonel. We still have a lot of flights going to the Continent, and RAF High Command think we need to keep several of these emergency strips open. I've been looking forward to getting posted to an operational squadron, but now with the war over, I'm not sure that'll happen."

"Hard to tell at this point," Ben said. "A lot of us pilots will be looking for cockpit jobs soon, I reckon. Ah, have you been informed there'll be another C-47 in here tomorrow? General Sampson'll be flying down from Daws Air Station at High Wycombe in late afternoon with a group of wedding guests."

"We're on to it, sir. We'll have the welcome mat out. Your chauffer is waiting over there with the, umm, with the Rolls-Royce. And another chap is standing by with the van behind it."

"Can I have them drive out here so we can load this stuff into the van?" Ben asked.

"Certainly, sir," Smyth said, beckoning the Rolls and van out onto the ramp.

Watkins snapped Ben a crisp salute. "Welcome back, Colonel. The wedding party is waiting your arrival at Calvert Hall. Evans will load these into the van and follow us to Calvert Hall."

Ben smiled as the Rolls purred through the ornate front gate and stopped before Bates, who stood rigidly at attention by the front entrance. Reggie led Lady Percy, Gwen, and Elizabeth out to greet him.

"Welcome, Colonel Findlay," he said, saluting with mock seriousness. "We're so pleased you could join us."

"Pleased to be here," Ben said, returning the salute with equally mock seriousness. "I understand there's to be some sort of festivities at Calvert Hall."

"Oh, please do stop this silliness," Lady Percy huffed as she pushed Gwen forward. "Embrace this lovely young lady, and let us go inside."

Ben wrapped Gwen in a tight embrace, held her out at arm's length, and kissed her. He then stepped to Lady Percy and gave her a warm hug. He turned to Elizabeth, ignored her extended right hand, and hugged her tightly. Elizabeth stiffened then relaxed into his embrace. "Thank you, Ben. I enjoyed that," she whispered. "You and Gwen make such a beautiful couple . . ." She suppressed a sob as Ben released her.

"That was ever so lovely," Reggie mocked. "Now Mother has invited us all inside. Step lively, ladies and gents."

Inside, Ben paused to scan the large entry hall, noting again the beauty of the high-beamed ceiling, paneled walls, marble floor, and glittering chandeliers. A combined scent of wood wax, freshly cut flowers, and cooking smells from the below-stairs kitchen enveloped Ben like a soft embrace.

"Thank you for again inviting us into your beautiful home, Lady Percy," he said. "You're really making our wedding a very special event."

They gathered in the parlor for tea, and Gwen sat next to Ben, clutching his hand. She clearly was enjoying herself immensely. Bates supervised the arrival of the formal tea service and, with a hint of a smile, placed a glass of scotch in front of Reggie and Ben. They both avoided eye contact with Elizabeth.

"Benjamin, let me tell you how delightful it has been to become better acquainted with Gwendolen and to help her plan the wedding ceremony," Lady Percy said. "She is such a dear, and I do believe we have everything ready for the day after tomorrow. Vicar Wadsworthy has graciously agreed to preside, and Elizabeth will make a perfectly beautiful bridesmaid.

"And," she added with emphasis, "His Lordship has informed us he can join us for the weekend and is delighted to give away the bride."

Gwen beamed and squeezed Ben's hand. "Ma'am, I'm overwhelmed at the way you and your family have adopted us," Ben said. "This will be something we'll treasure for the rest of our lives."

He hesitated to control his emotions and continued quietly, "Now what am I supposed to do to help out?"

"Absolutely nothing," Reggie interrupted, "except stay out of the way. You and Gwen can have some time together tonight, and then I'm to get you out from underfoot and let the ladies get on with it. Of course, you will not be allowed to see the bride-to-be on you wedding day until she arrives at the chapel on His Lordship's arm.

"And tomorrow night, I've planned an intimate bachelor's party at the Bell Ringers' Pub in Romsey Forest. General Sampson and the rest of the male guests will join us as we toast you on your way into married life. Why even 'Himself' has said he'll attend if he can get down here from London soon enough. It promises to be quite a jolly affair."

Ben grinned and looked quickly at Gwen, who smiled and nodded. *Better watch yourself, Benjamin. Remember the last party Reggie and ol' Stitch Threadwell laid on for you. Gotta be sober and on my toes for Saturday.*

After tea, Ben and Gwen sat in the Calvert Hall conservatory, holding hands and discussing their future. "Lady Percy said Bates had booked us a lovely little cottage in Castle Combe for our honeymoon," Gwen said. "Apparently, it's situated near the Market Cross, overlooking the By Brook. It sounds beautiful."

"Great. I'm looking forward to a relaxing week of just being with you," Ben said. "And I think you need a long rest too. Did Lady Percy say how much it'll cost to rent the cottage?"

"No, Ben. She said I mustn't inquire. She said it was to be a wedding gift from Lord Percy and her and a small thank you for the service we've given England during the war. Isn't that ever so sweet?"

Ben sat mulling this then said quietly, "They've all been wonderful, treating us like family. Imagine that, all this for a lowly farm boy from 'Michigan'." Gwen giggled and kissed him on the cheek.

The dinner that evening was a festive affair, enhanced with some of the edible treats Ben had brought with him. Lady Percy presided at the head of the table, but Reggie dominated the evening, proposing toasts and ordering the soon-to-be-married couple to kiss on demand. Elizabeth joined in the fun, laughing gaily at Reggie's antics. But in unguarded moments, her smile faded as she gazed wistfully at Ben.

That evening, Ben escorted Gwen to her room, kissed her, and whispered, "Should I knock on the connecting door in a little while?"

"Ben, I'd love that, but let's wait until the day after tomorrow. I want to concentrate entirely on the wedding, make it a wonderful experience I'll never forget. We'll have a full week in Castle Cove . . ."

He silenced her with a tender kiss. "See you in the morning, love."

Ben wandered back downstairs and found Reggie in the drawing room, sipping a brandy. "Mind if I join you?" he asked.

"Not at all, old bean. Have a seat. Want one of these? I can ring Bates." Ben nodded. "Thanks. That'll be swell."

They sat quietly savoring their drinks. Ben broke the silence. "Reggie, I consider myself one of the luckiest men in the world. When I look back to our first meeting in Spain and all the adventures we had along the way, surviving two wars, it's hard to believe how fate has smiled on me. And now I'm about to marry the love of my life in this beautiful place, supported by you, your wonderful parents, and Elizabeth. Don't know how I deserve all this good fortune."

"Could say something smarmy like it's because you're such a 'swell' bloke, but that wouldn't be appropriate to the occasion," Reggie said. "I've been mulling the same thing, as it turns out, and wondering why I'm here alive and well when so many of my comrades are not. Count your blessings, they say. I do, although I haven't spent much time considering who the source of those blessings is. Maybe it's time I gave that some serious thought."

"Interesting," Ben said. "I said something like 'thank God' some time ago to Gwen, and she looked surprised. Said that was the first time she had heard me mention God. I shrugged it off, said up till then, God had been the first part of one of my overused curse words. I don't come from a religious family mainly because the old man rejected my mother's efforts to get us boys involved in church. Maybe that'll change with Gwen."

"Let's leave it at that for the time being. Otherwise, you'll have me on my knees with my hands steepled under my chin," Reggie said, hoping to lighten the moment. "Besides, I have something to share with you. Was going to make it a surprise for you and Gwen day after tomorrow."

Ben sat forward with interest.

"One of the special guests arriving in the morning will be a lady by the name of Simpson, Beatrice Simpson. She and I are old friends from Oxford days. Lost touch when I went to Spain to fight the Fascists. Met her recently at a party and discovered there was still a spark there. Been seeing her regularly. She's been working in the RAF intelligence sector."

"You rascal," Ben said. "Why've you been keeping this from us? I mean, is it serious?"

"Dunno yet. Might be. Thought it a bit premature to mention I guess. But I'm anxious for you and Gwen to meet her. Think you'll like her."

They chatted on about Beatrice and other items of interest until Ben felt his eyelids drooping. "Woof! This brandy on top of the wine and champagne at dinner is beginning to get to me. Think I'll hit the hay."

"Before you go, Sancho, how about a ride tomorrow morning? Not too early, say around 1000 hours?"

Ben gave him a long look. "Ah okay, I guess. Help clear my mind and all. But no hurtling over hedges! Don't wanna break my neck on the day before my wedding."

"Agreed. That would be a bad show, eh? We'll take it very easy. So breakfast at 0830 hours, followed by a ride of an hour or so?"

"Agreed," Ben said. "G'nite." He did not tap on the connecting door.

Next morning after a hearty English breakfast, Ben and Reggie mounted their horses and trotted out of the stable yard. It had rained earlier, but now the sun drew the sweetness from the damp flowering bushes. Ben breathed in the soothing scent and settled back for a relaxing ride. They cantered along the periphery of the Calvert Hall estate, flushing out a flock of pheasants and startling a small herd of deer munching on the succulent grass.

"What a beautiful place!" Ben exclaimed. "You're lucky, Reggie, to be the heir to of all of this."

"Umm, s'pose I am, Ben. It has been my home all of my life, so I don't see it with fresh eyes like you do. I do love it here, though.

Frightens me to think how close we came to losing this and everything else that stands for England. It's a minor miracle we were able to hold out alone against Germany during those dark days of '40 and '41."

"I'll never forget that whirlwind tour of London you took me on just before the war," Ben said, shaking his head. "I thought you were nuts showing me what you said I'd be fighting for. Soon learned you weren't. Now looking back at the war, I see what an awful threat Hitler and his henchmen were to the world." Ben paused. "I haven't shared details of what we saw in the Dachau concentration camp during our survey mission to Munich, uh, I mean, I couldn't believe what I was seeing. The gas chambers, the torture rooms and experimental clinics, and the ovens, my god, the ovens! And we saw the camp after it had been cleaned up. What would the world be like if Germany had won the war? They'd have brought all that horrible stuff to England. That had to be stopped at all costs.

"And now when I look at this beautiful place and think about the Castle Combe village where Gwen and I'll be spending our honeymoon, it puts all the sacrifices we made in perspective. You're damn right, Reggie, this all was worth fighting for."

Their tour of the Calvert Hall estate completed, they walked the horses back to the stable.

Gwen huddled with Lady Percy and Elizabeth in the library, reviewing lists of preparations for the wedding when they walked in. Gwen beamed at Ben, the high color on her cheeks evidence that she was enjoying herself immensely.

"Pleasure to see you both," Lady Percy said, arching her eyebrows. "But your assistance is not needed at the moment. We ladies have a good many details to resolve yet. We will require your presence in the chapel at four o'clock for the rehearsal, but in the meantime, you're free to occupy yourselves elsewhere."

"Will 'Himself' arrive in time for the rehearsal?" Reggie asked.

"Reginald, I do wish you wouldn't refer to your father as 'Himself.' It sounds so disrespectful," Lady Percy scolded.

"Sorry, how's about I call him 'Da' or something more informal?" Reggie replied with a grin. This earned him a glare and a "tisk."

"No, your father will not be here in time. Bates has agreed to stand in for him and escort Gwen down the aisle for the rehearsal. Now we do have some urgent and important business to attend to."

"Well, Sancho, it's quite clear we're not welcome here." Reggie sniffed. "Let's find somewhere else to get into mischief." He turned to march out the door. Ben grinned, blew a kiss to Gwen, and turned to follow him.

Settled in the drawing room, Reggie turned to Ben. "Bit early in the day I s'pose, but this is a very special day, or at least the day before a very special day, so I think a wee dram of Scotland's finest is in order. Agreed?"

Ben hesitated. "Humm, I guess so. Might help relax me from all the pressure I'm feeling," he added with a smirk.

Bates responded to Reggie's call and soon reappeared with a tray and two crystal glasses containing generous dollops of Springbank Scotch. Reggie raised his glass. "Here's to us, Benjamin, and to all of our departed comrades. Hope they're resting in peace." They sipped in silence.

They were finishing their second scotch when Elizabeth entered the room and announced that the wedding rehearsal would begin in the chapel in fifteen minutes. And she added with emphasis that, "Mother and Gwen would appreciate your serious participation."

The rehearsal went smoothly, with Bates performing the duties of giving Gwen away, since Lord Percy had not yet arrived from London. After two run-throughs, Vicar Wadsworthy announced he was satisfied they had the procedure down pat. He said he looked forward with pleasure to meeting with them again at 3:30 p.m. the next day to prepare for the actual ceremony.

"Sure you still want to go through with this, Sancho?" Reggie whispered in an aside to Ben. Looking lovingly and longingly at Gwen, Ben whispered back, "You betcha!"

"Then that is that." Reggie grinned. "Now then, we need to switch into our party mode and prepare ourselves for an evening of food, drink, and hilarity at the Bell Ringer's."

Ben cast Reggie a doubtful look. "Reggie, I appreciate all you've done for Gwen and me and for planning tonight's bachelor party. But . . ."

"But what, old bean?" Reggie interrupted. "We're just going to have a bit of fun to ease you on into married life."

"I know, Reggie, 'a bit of fun,' and I appreciate it very much, really I do. But I remember the going-away party you and Stitch threw for me when I transferred from the RAF to the USAAF . . . Ah, at least I remember part of it, especially the hangover the next day. I gotta be upstanding and sober when I meet Gwen in the chapel tomorrow afternoon."

"Not to worry, old chap," Reggie said smoothly. "Just a bit of innocent fun. Ben, you have my solemn promise. We will not deliver you back here in a stiff or catatonic stage. Loose and a bit intoxicated but not smashed."

"Wish I could say that reassures me," Ben muttered. *However, old friend, I intend to police myself, show some restraint, and stay in control.*

Ben joined Gwen in the solarium and spent the next hour and a half holding her hand as they quietly chatted about their future after tomorrow's ceremony. "We've never talked about children," Gwen said.

"With good reason!" Ben joked. "I didn't want to press our luck until, uh, you know, until we were married."

"Benjamin, you're impossible!" Gwen responded, tweaking his cheek. "I'm serious. How do you feel about having children?"

"Great, fine, swell. I'd like to have a big family, if I could afford it. How about two to start with? You know, a little girl for you and a little boy for me."

"That's wonderful, Ben. Once we get settled in America, I want to have children early in our marriage, when we're young enough to really enjoy them, to grow up with them."

That settled, they moved on to other topics. Ben said how he'd been thinking about his future in the army, whether he'd want to make it a career. "Of course, that decision may be made by the army once someone figures out how many pilots they're gonna need once the war is really over. That is after we defeat the Japs in the Pacific."

"Do you think that will happen soon, Ben? Are we close to defeating Japan?"

"Good question. Fact is nobody knows. There's a lotta talk about how we may need a long-term bombing campaign, which is why the army and Marines are capturing all those islands leading up to Japan's main island. Those islands are serving as forward air bases, cutting the over-water flying time for our bomber fleets. Even the new B-29 Superfortress is operating at the limits of its range to reach Tokyo and beyond."

Gwen clutched his hand and fought back tears. "Oh, Ben, Ben, Ben, you aren't going to have to go over there and fly more missions, are you?"

"Love, I have no way of knowing," Ben whispered. "I still have an important job here with the bomb survey group, so I don't think I'll be going anywhere soon. But I guess a lotta fellas can do this job, so I could be transferred to the Pacific. But for the moment, it looks like they have all the pilots they need. Wish I could tell you for sure, but I don't think anybody knows."

They sat quietly, each lost in their own thoughts, until Ben broke the silence. "Makes me wonder about Frank Silverman. They had a specific assignment for him, commander of a newly formed B-29 group. He could already be over there." Gwen stifled a sob and pulled Ben into a tight embrace.

"Meantime, I'm concentrating on what I do when I return to the States, stay in the army if they'll have me or go on to some civilian job, hopefully one involving flying," Ben said. "If I do stay in, I'm thinking I'd like to join the Flight Test Training Unit at Wright-Patterson Air Force Base in Dayton, Ohio. The army has patterned it after the RAF Empire Test Pilot's School Reggie's part of. It'd offer a lotta interesting flying with nobody shootin' at you. Could be a great job."

"But that could be dangerous, couldn't it?" Gwen pressed. "I mean, flying a lot of new untested airplanes. Wouldn't there be a great deal of risk involved?"

"Some risk, I suppose, but all flying involves risk up to a point. The object of the test pilot's school is to teach you how to safely fly test flights. You know, how to deal with situations. Anyway, there's no guarantee I can even get an assignment there, so it's probably too early to talk about it," Ben added, trying to calm Gwen's concerns.

Ben drew Gwen into his arms and kissed her. "Now if you'll excuse me, miss, I have to change for my party. Reggie'll be knocking on my door in a little while. Are you going to be all right tonight?" he asked with concern.

"Lady Percy and Elizabeth and I have planned an intimate dinner party tonight, something light and full of girl talk. And I'm not certain I want to know about your evening," she teased.

Ben was right. Reggie was banging on his door within the hour.

Chapter 48

BEN'S BACHELOR PARTY
– JULY 17, 1945

The bachelor party at the Bell Ringer's started off as a quiet gathering of hale fellows well met. Ben was delighted when General Sampson arrived with Crenshaw and several other pilots from the bomb survey group. He introduced them to Reggie, who directed them to the bar. Ben whooped a special greeting when Reggie returned with RAF Flight Leftenant Duncan Whitford, one of the five Giraffes who made the escape trek across Poland.

"Duncan, what a pleasure! Great to see ya," Ben exclaimed. "Damn! If only we had Archie and Art here, we'd have a swell Giraffe reunion."

"Hullo, Ben, wouldn't have missed this party for anything." Duncan grinned. "Umm, be even better if Sandy could join us as well, wouldn't it?"

"You betcha! Have you heard anything from him? Did our Polish partisan friends keep him safe and get him out?"

"Only have second-hand information so far, but it appears he's all right and is about to be repatriated. Dunno when or where."

"That's fantastic! I heard one of the other two escape groups got to the Swedish freighter connection, but the ship was intercepted by a German patrol boat and had to run back to port in Malmo. Those fellas were interred for the duration, but they could be repatriated soon as well."

"No news from the third group," Reggie said. "If they were captured en route to the coast, I doubt they or their escorts survived."

He clapped Ben and Duncan on the back. "But look, we're here to celebrate the impending wedding of this 'ere bloke," he shouted. "See him into his own form of imprisonment," he added with a grin.

As the party gained momentum, the noise level soared to an uncomfortable decibel level. Rutherford, the Bell Ringer's landlord, rang the pub bell for silence and announced, "Quiet, gents, if yer please. It gives me great pleasure to welcome a special guest what's graced this 'umble histablishment to satisfy his thirst during many a fox hunt. His Grace, Lord Percy of Calvert Hall!"

Reggie stepped forward to greet his father as all assembled applauded. "Welcome, Father. Really pleased you could make it. As you can see, we're having a bit of a party. Umm, they may seem a bit rowdy at first glance, but this is a collection of fine blokes who've gathered to honor Ben on the eve of his wedding."

"Ah well, they seem harmless enough." Lord Percy smiled, waving to the group. "Evening, gentlemen. Pleased to have been included in the guest list. Carry on with your celebration. Ah hello, Benjamin," he continued, gripping Ben's hand. "Congratulations. Gwen is a lovely young lady. You're very fortunate."

Ben nodded eagerly. "Thanks, Lord Percy, and thank you, sir, for agreeing to give away the bride. Gwen and I are greatly honored."

"My pleasure, Benjamin. My pleasure. Thank you for asking me."

The pace of the party quickly shifted back into high gear, and Lord Percy turned to plow his way to the bar. "Make way for His Lordship!" Rutherford bellowed. "Plain to see 'ere's a gentleman with good taste what's got a thirst. Umm, you're usual, sir?" Lord Percy nodded and accepted a generous portion of Springbank, the Bell Ringer's finest scotch.

"Like to offer a toast," he said to Rutherford.

The landlord vigorously rang the bar bell again to silence the revelers. "Attention all. His Lordship means to offer a toast to our honored guest."

They all turned toward Lord Percy, who raised his glass. "We owe a great debt of gratitude to all of you who rallied to us when we stood alone against the Nazis. They had conquered the nations of the Continent up to the very shores of the English Channel, and it was up to us to hold the line. Bolstered by our stalwart allies from America and throughout the Commonwealth and, harrumph, our Russian friends from the east, we together prevailed and defeated the Nazis and the Italian Fascists. And this is not an exaggeration, in the process saved the free world.

"We are here tonight to honor one who played a heroic role in that honorable fight. He joined our Royal Air Force on the eve of the war in 1939 as an individual, who understood what we were fighting for and against whom we were fighting. Before that, at the tender age of eighteen, he had volunteered for the Republican Air Force in Spain to fight the Fascist-backed Nationalists in what was a preview of the greater struggle we would face all across Europe. A true hero in the eyes of us all!

"So I ask you to raise your glasses to toast this young man, whom we honor tonight." Then holding up his hand to quell the building cheer, Lord Percy added with a sly smile, "I offer this toast with one caveat. We normally do not appreciate men from foreign climes coming among us and stealing our women, Benjamin, but you are such a bloody fine bloke we'll allow it this one time. To Benjamin!"

The crowd erupted with raucous laughter and shouts of "To Benjamin! Hear, hear! Speech, speech!"

Ben grinned sheepishly blushing like a schoolboy at his first dance, his face red and his ears burning. Following several more prompts to make a speech, he stammered, "Uh, thank you, Lord Percy. Those were kind words, 'an, uh . . . I very much appreciate them, even though you make me out to be more of a hero than I am. A lot of us saw a duty that needed to be done here, and we answered the call. Sad to say, a lot of us didn't survive to see victory in this fight. But I appreciate your kind words, sir, and, I'd like to dedicate them to all of our fallen comrades who are the true heroes."

He paused to control his emotions. "Uh, thank you all for honoring me tonight. Gwen and I will cherish this memory for the rest of our lives. Now let's get on with the party!" The crowd cheered.

Not needing a second invitation, the airmen then surged to the bar. Ben was surrounded throughout the evening by well-wishers, jostling to keep his glass filled and ignoring his protests that he had to stay sober for tomorrow's big event. Lord Percy escorted General Sampson to the snuggery for a quiet word about the progress of the bomb survey and asked if the results might prompt an upgrade in Allied heavy bombardment aircraft and operational procedures. They huddled for over an hour before Lord Percy said he was going to slip out and head for Calvert Hall. He asked Sampson to come up to London and brief the Air Ministry as soon as he could prepare a preliminary report.

Signaling Reggie, Lord Percy eased past the rollicking crowd and out the exit. "Tell Watkins I'm ready to go home," he said to Reggie, who had slipped out behind him. "Wonderful party. Great group of young men, Reginald. Good show honoring Benjamin like this. Now try to keep yourself and Benjamin somewhat sober for tomorrow. Wouldn't want to escort Gwen down the aisle and present her to a pair of bedraggled and hungover airmen."

Reggie grinned and nodded. "See you in the morning, Father. And thank you again for this wonderful gesture to Ben."

There were varying reports as to how long the party continued and how many of the stalwarts remained standing at the end. Reggie had led the group in several irreverent skits that poked good-natured fun at Ben, who accepted them in good humor. For the rest of the evening, Ben desperately tried his subterfuge of sipping drinks and leaving mostly full glasses behind as he moved through the party. He was partially successful, since he could still walk when Reggie escorted him to the Rolls-Royce and directed Watkins to return them to Calvert Hall. He instructed Watkins to return to the Bell Ringer's later to fetch General Sampson and the guests who were staying overnight in Calvert Hall and to help Rutherford herd the remaining partygoers upstairs to their rooms.

At Calvert Hall, they clattered into the entry hall where Reggie shushed Ben with exaggerated gestures. "Mustn't wake the household, Sancho. Remove your shoes, sir, and creep as quietly as possible to your chamber," Reggie hissed. "And one more thing, old boy. No knocking on the connecting door tonight, ya hear?"

It was a solemn group that straggled in for the breakfast buffet next morning. Reggie bustled about as normal. However, Ben noted the dark circles around his eyes that showed more than a hint of redness. In fact, mostly everyone in the room looked a bit red-eyed.

"Umm, morning, Ben," Reggie rasped. Then clearing his throat, he continued, "Sorry, bit of a morning throat. Sleep all right, did you? Think I'll have a Bloody Mary to get things going. Join me?"

"No, thanks. I'll stick with coffee and orange juice." Ben grinned. "Yes, I slept soundly. Woke up feeling great. Did you go back to the party after delivering me home?"

"Umm, yes. Went back to help Rutherford and Watkins get all the boys tucked in. Also had to escort General Sampson and our other overnight guest home."

"I didn't hear you come in," Ben said. "Must have been a bit later." "A bit."

General Sampson and Lord Percy strode into the breakfast room together. They had been conferring again in the library. Both looked surprisingly fit, even though they had enjoyed last night's party to the fullest.

"Morning, gentlemen," Reggie said, raising his Bloody Mary glass. "Anyone care to join me in a little 'hair of the dog' that obviously bit most of us last night?" Several sheepishly raised their hands, and Bates stepped out to prepare a tray.

"Umm, the ladies are having breakfast in the solarium," Reggie announced. "And they have left word they are not to be disturbed," he added, looking directly at Ben. "Meanwhile, enjoy this typical English breakfast repast. The rest of the day is open until the ceremony in the chapel at 1600 hours. Dress is formal uniform. 'Til then, feel free to wander the halls, inspect the gardens and grounds, and take a horseback ride, if you're so inclined. Scottie, the head groom, is at your service in the stables."

Lord Percy stepped forward. "Let me add my welcome to Reginald's. It is a pleasure and honor to have you as guests in our home. I very much enjoyed 'hoisting a few' with you last night and am pleased to be able to show our gratitude for what you've done for King, country, and the free world. I'd be interested in chatting with you about your war experiences, if you'd like. You'll find General Sampson and me in the library after breakfast. Now let's 'dig in.'"

Reggie signaled Ben to follow him into the outer hall. "Umm, Ben, Beatrice will be arriving in less than an hour. Watkins will drive me to the station to meet her train, and I want you to be the first to meet her when we return. Okay?"

"Of course, Reggie. I'm anxious to meet this new lady in your life. Uh, Gwen is dying to meet her as well, but I can't see her before the wedding."

"Taken care of, Sancho. After you've met Beatrice, I'll escort her over to where Mother, Elizabeth, and Gwen are hiding out and make the introduction there. Mother and Elizabeth met Beatrice briefly about a month ago, but she's anxious to spend some time getting to know them better. What better way than to help with the fussing over Gwen?"

Ben heard the Rolls-Royce purr up to the front door and stepped outside as Reggie was helping Beatrice from the rear seat. Ben was struck by her tall slim figure highlighted by a trim tailored RAF uniform. He remembered Reggie telling him she was assigned to a RAF intelligence unit. Reggie stepped forward with a broad smile.

"Ben, may I present Miss Beatrice Simpson. Beatrice, this is Colonel Benjamin Findlay, fellow warrior and best friend. Ben stared unabashedly into her bright hazel eyes as they shook hands and exchanged greetings. Her smile dazzled him.

"I'm pleased to finally meet you, Colonel Findlay. Reggie has told me so much about you."

Ben blinked and raised his eyebrows. *Oh, oh. Here we go again. What kinda tails has Reggie been spinning now?* Regaining his composure, Ben stammered, "An' I'm happy to meet you, uh, Miss Simpson. I hope Reggie hasn't raised your expectations too much. And by the way, I prefer Ben to Colonel Findlay, if you don't mind. Colonel Findlay sounds awfully formal."

"Not at all, Ben," she responded with an amused smile. "As long as you'll agree to call me Beatrice. Miss Simpson sounds terribly formal as well." Ben nodded agreement.

"Now that we've sorted that out, let's find a quiet corner where we can chat, umm, informally of course," Reggie said, steering them to a sunlit anteroom.

Ben studied Beatrice as she took Reggie's arm and proceeded to the anteroom. She was nearly as tall as Reggie, even in regulation RAF low-heeled shoes, and walked with an easy natural grace. Her gleaming auburn hair was cut in a regulation bob that framed her face and accentuated her bronzed skin, high cheekbones, full lips, and strong chin. She cut a striking figure in a uniform that made most servicewomen border on frumpy.

He grinned. *Ah yes, Reggie, she's a beauty. And it looks like she's quite capable of keeping you in line, old man.*

Reggie asked Bates to bring tea and shook his head when Bates inquired with a surreptitious wink and a nod if he wanted his usual scotch instead of tea. They settled into overstuffed chairs, and Beatrice turned to Ben. "Reggie tells me you two first met during the civil war in Spain in 1938, flying Russian pursuit planes for the Republican Army," she said. "According to his account, you had some exciting times."

"Well, yes, we did," Ben said, settling back in his chair and trying not to stare at the beautiful lady seated across him. "Can't, uh, vouch for the accuracy of his account, but it wasn't dull."

"Come now, Sancho, not sure it's cricket for you to question the accuracy of 'my account' of our exploits," Reggie huffed. "Stayed quite close to the facts with few of my usual exaggerations, if I say so myself."

Beatrice laughed brightly. "Oh, come now yourself, Reginald. Your tendency toward exaggeration is legendary. And by the way, who is Sancho?"

"That was my code name, uh, you know, 'Nom de Guerre' in Spain," Ben said. "Our squadron was code named 'La Mancha.' Reggie was Quixote, so naturally, they called me Sancho. Reggie still calls me that. Dunno if it's a compliment or not."

"Of course, it's a term of endearment," Reggie interjected with a sly grin. "Sancho was Quixote's loyal companion through the best and worst of times. Saved the ancient knight warrior's ars . . ., umm, that is to say, saved him from harm numerous times."

"Well, I think it's a wonderful Nom de Guerre." Beatrice chuckled. "Sums up your relationship nicely."

"Yeah, I guess it does," Ben said. "All in all, we did have a swell time in Spain, even if the war didn't turn out quite like we hoped."

"And then you escaped to England and joined the RAF and fought in the Battle of Britain," Beatrice said. "That was two years before America became involved in the war. What prompted you to do that?"

"Lotta things I guess. Truthfully, I'm not sure what prompted me to volunteer for Spain. Adventure, love of flying, escape from home, and following a man I greatly admired, Frank Silverman, our squadron commander. Once there, I was sickened by what I saw the Nationalists and their German and Italian supporters doing. Reggie and I flew mostly against the German Condor Legion pilots, and it became evident after the civil war ended that Germany had bigger designs on Europe."

Ben cleared his throat and sipped his tea before continuing. "Reggie had a lot to do with it at that point. We'd developed quite a bond in Spain, and once back here, he spent a lot of time showing me what England stood for and what a threat Germany was to that way of life. Showed me we had no choice but to fight to preserve it."

Ben sat back and shook his head. "How'd I get up on my soapbox like this? That's enough about me. Tell me how you and Reggie met and where you're going from here."

The directness of Ben's question prompted Beatrice to sip her tea, while she collected her thoughts. "Umm, I suppose Reginald has told you we first met at Oxford. He left school for Spain, and then the war intervened, and we lost touch. Now we've reconnected and enjoy each other's company. We'll see what transpires."

"Meantime, we're taking it day by day," Reggie said. "Right now, of course, we're focused on your wedding."

They chatted and sipped tea for another forty-five minutes, Ben plying Beatrice about her family background, and she asking him about his early life on the farm in Michigan.

"I say, careful about asking Ben about life 'down on the farm,' Beatrice," Reggie cautioned. "He can quickly get maudlin and end up teaching you some ditty about crowing roosters and carrying a milk pail on his arm."

Ben stiffened then relaxed and smiled, remembering a long liquid evening in Spain when he had taught that song to Reggie and two lovely flamenco dancers and, in the process, most everyone else in the café.

"Hate to break this up," Reggie said. "We'll have plenty of other times to chat about old times. Meanwhile, I need to get Beatrice over to the solarium to spend some time with Mum, Elizabeth, and Gwen. Anxious for Gwen to meet you, love," he said to Beatrice.

They rose, and Beatrice offered her hand to Ben. "I've had such a lovely chat, Ben." She smiled. "I look forward to the next time. Congratulations, and best wishes on your wedding. I'll see you in the chapel."

Ben watched with a bemused smile as Reggie led her from the room.

Chapter 49

THEY WED – JULY 18, 1945

Reggie returned shortly. "Four more hours of freedom, Sancho. S'pose you have something to occupy your time? How about polishing the brass on your uniform or maybe add a lick of polish to your shoes? I have a few tasks to complete, and then I'm going to put my feet up for a short nap. Why don't you do the same? We can then have a spot of lunch before the ceremony, okay? You aren't getting nervous, are you? Think maybe I am. You do have the rings, right? Shall I take them for safekeeping?"

Ben held up his hands. "Slow down. I'm already six questions behind. Everything is going to work out all right. Lunch is fine. Meanwhile, I have plenty to occupy myself. Think I'll take a short nap as well.

Reggie prattled on about final arrangements for the wedding all through lunch, and Ben headed for his room to change into his formal uniform. "Don't think I'm nervous," he muttered, "at least I wasn't until Reggie got going. I'll take my time getting dressed and report as ordered to the chapel. Piece of cake."

Reggie paced like a caged lion as he and Ben waited in the chapel's sacristy. "Trust everything is in order," Reggie muttered as he opened the door a crack and peeked out into the chapel. The soothing tones of the hymn *Oh, Promise Me* wafted through the door from the chapel organ. "Looks like everyone's in place," Reggie whispered. "Expect Vicar Wadsworthy will be signaling us soon. Ah! There he is. Let's go Benjamin. Courage, me lad, into the breach."

They stood facing the congregation as the organist played *Oh, Perfect Love,* and the ushers, Flight Leftenants Whitford and Crenshaw, escorted Lady Percy and General Sampson to their respective front-row seats. Ben grinned as Elizabeth, looking beautifully mature in her bridesmaid's dress, glided elegantly down the aisle and took her place on the altar.

The organ switched to the *"Wedding March,"* and all rose and turned to face the rear of the chapel as Lord Percy, erect and dignified, led Gwen on his arm down the aisle. Ben's spine tingled as he stared at Gwen's beaming face aglow with her most dazzling smile. Lord Percy announced to Vicar Wadsworthy that he was presenting the lady for marriage, and Ben stepped to her side and faced the vicar.

Wadsworthy welcomed all in attendance with, "The grace of our Lord Jesus Christ, the love of God, and the fellowship of the Holy Spirit be with you" and waited for the "and also with you" response.

The vicar continued with several readings from scripture, which were new to Ben, and a hymn was sung. Ben glanced sideways at Gwen and lost the thread of the continuing service. He refocused on the proceedings and tensed when the vicar asked that, "Anyone present who knows a reason why these persons may not lawfully marry, to declare it now." He relaxed when no one spoke up.

The vicar then led them through their marriage declarations, and Ben's loud "I will!" prompted a ripple of laughter in the chapel. Gwen answered "I will" in an equally definite, but much softer, tone. Ben's mind wandered again until the vicar asked them to join hands and repeat their wedding vows. As distracted as he was staring into Gwen's beautiful eyes, Ben concentrated on the wording of the vows, especially "to love and cherish till death do us part."

The Vicar then led them through the exchange of rings, waiting patiently while Reggie fumbled through all of his pockets before producing the gold bands.

Ben was fully focused now and took particular notice when the vicar concluded, "In the presence of God and before this congregation, Benjamin and Gwendolen have given their consent and made their marriage vows to each other. They have declared their marriage by joining hands and by giving and receiving rings. I therefore proclaim that they are husband and wife."

Ben eagerly accepted the vicar's invitation to "kiss the bride" and then joined hands with Gwen as the vicar declared, "Those whom God has joined together let no one put asunder." They knelt as the vicar blessed them and offered the closing prayers.

The beaming couple held tightly to each other as they strode as husband and wife back down the aisle.

The wedding reception in Calvert Hall's large dining room featured a bounteous buffet augmented by the food Ben had purchased from the Parham commissary. The hall's crystal chandeliers and an array of lighted candelabra made it a glittering affair. Gwen was surrounded by a laughing gaggle of her nurse colleagues who had traveled by train from Cambridge, while Ben accepted congratulations and a few good-natured condolences from the male guests. Reggie called for the group's attention.

"I have a few letters and congratulatory telegrams I'd like to read aloud," he announced, "including a letter from Benjamin's Mum and Dad and a telegram from General Frank Silverman, who by this time has probably arrived at his new post as commander of a B-29 wing in the Pacific Theater of operations.

"I'll let Ben have a private read of the one from his family," Reggie said, handing him the letter from his mother. "But I think Ben will approve of my reading the telegram from General Silverman. It reads, 'Heartiest congratulations, Ben and Gwen, stop. Best wishes to a beautiful couple, stop. New assignment off to good start, stop. Have a wonderful life together, stop. Hasta Luego, stop.' This gent has a lot of class," Reggie added, passing the telegram to Ben, who struggled to control the lump in his throat.

Reggie read a number of other communications from Ben's friends and colleagues and then called for everyone to "charge their glasses for a round of champagne toasts." That completed, he ordered the newlyweds to perform the first of many crowd-pleasing kisses.

Elizabeth joined in the laughter and cheering for the couple, but a look of melancholy lurked in her eyes.

The buffet was savored by all, especially those who had endured strict-food rationing throughout the war and faced continued rationing in the postwar years. Following dinner, all were directed to the ballroom for dancing. The ten-piece orchestra began with a sentimental waltz for the bride and groom. Ben shuffled Gwen around the floor, muttering he was sorry, but he'd never learned to dance. That ordeal completed, the band switched to the latest Glenn Miller tunes, and the ballroom sprang to life as the young people threw themselves into the latest dance routines. Even "Himself" took Lady Percy for a twirl on the dance floor.

An hour later, Ben whispered in Gwen's ear that it was "time to beat it outta here" so Watkins could drive them to their Cotswold honeymoon cottage before dark. He signaled to Reggie, who was in the middle of a grotesque rendition of the jitter bug, that they were leaving and received what appeared to be a nod of agreement. Upstairs they changed quickly into their regular uniforms and descended, carrying two suitcases. Bates intercepted them at the bottom of the stairs and hustled the bags out to Watkins who waited next to the Rolls, which was festooned with white satin ribbons.

Reggie spotted them heading for the door and shouted for silence. "The newlyweds are bailing out on us," he yelled. "Everyone outside! Collect a bit of rice, and we'll send 'em off fittin' and proper." Ben and Gwen ran a gauntlet of hugs, kisses, and pats on the back as they ducked through a shower of rice into the Rolls.

It purred out the gravel driveway into a bright and sunny afternoon. Ben waved and saluted, and Gwen blew kisses.

Chapter 50

CASTLE COMBE, THE HONEYMOON –

A red-cheeked rotund lady, who had been alerted that they were en route, greeted them at the front door of the vine-covered cottage. Her eyes widened as she spotted the Rolls parked at the front gate and Watkins waiting patiently with their bags. "Good evening. We're Colonel and Mrs. Findlay," Ben said. "We've booked the cottage for a week."

"My lor', my lor', so ye 'ave, my dears. Do come in and be welcome to Castle Combe," she beamed, peaking past them for another look at the Rolls. "I'm Mrs. Pengraves, 'ere to do for ye as needs be. Just put the cases there," she said to Watkins. "I'll see to 'em in a moment."

Ben thanked Watkins for a smooth ride and reminded him to return for them next Sunday morning. Watkins touched the bill of his cap, wished them "all the best, sir and madam," and departed.

Mrs. Pengraves bustled about, giving the newlyweds an instructional tour of the cottage and helping them get settled. "Cottage is named Maplewoods on account of them rare maple trees in the rear garden," she said. "Cottage were built more'n a century ago an' now is owned by Captain Stevens. He bought it jus' a'fore the war, umm, this past one, not the Great War," she added, smiling. "Many of these 'ere cottages be two hundred years old. Built in Cotswold style, they are. Thick stone walls an' slate roofs of split natural stone tiles. Some are listed as ancient monuments and mustn't be changed to preserve their beauty an' character."

Ben smiled at her tourist brochure description of the place.

Looking about, Mrs. Pengraves pursed her lips. "Now I do believe I've showed you ever'thin' ye need to know about cottage, so I'll be goin'. If you 'ave any questions or need anythin', you rap on the door of 'Journey's End' cottage there at bottom of the hill." She regarded them with a broad smile. "Such a lovely couple," she murmured and bustled out the door.

Gwen puffed a long sigh of relief as Ben wrapped her in a hug. He held her tightly, savoring the feel of her body next to his. "Thanks ever so much, love," she whispered. "I really needed this."

"Me too."

They carried their suitcases upstairs, unpacked, and shed their uniforms. Ben rolled her onto the bed. "Been longing to do this for the last forty-eight hours," he said. "Being that close to you and not being able to grab hold of you was torture. Now I gotcha!"

It was dark when they awoke still entwined. "Should we think about a bit of supper?" Gwen asked. "We could go down to one the pubs, or I could fix us some scrambled eggs. Mrs. Pengraves said there were eggs and bacon, milk, and other food in the kitchen."

"I'd be satisfied with just you," Ben leered.

"That's quite enough for now, Colonel," Gwen said with a smile, pushing him off the bed.

They decided on a supper of scrambled eggs, bacon, toast, and coffee. Gwen felt quite domesticated preparing the meal, while Ben admired her from his seat at the table.

"Listen to this," he said, holding up a printed page he found on the breakfront. "Castle Combe is known as the Prettiest Village in England. It has charmed visitors for over a century with its beautiful cottages, narrow winding streets, and the picturesque Market Cross down by the By Brook River. It originally was an ancient Briton hill fort that was taken by the Roman Legions and ultimately conquered by the Normans who built a castle on the site. Only the outlines of the castle remain."

Ben looked up and grinned. "Ol' Bates really picked a beautiful spot for us, didn't he?" Gwen smiled and nodded.

"In the Middle Ages, Castle Combe was a center of the wool industry, and these cottages were built for the weavers and spinsters," Ben continued. "Water from the By Brook was diverted to power the mills. In modern times, the village, which is located on the southern edge of the Cotswold, was declared a conservation area and a wildlife sanctuary."

He continued reading, "There are many hiking trails nearby as well as such historical sites as Amesbury, the Neolithic monument of three stone circles thought to have been built around the village about 2,600 BC. Stonehenge, perhaps the better known prehistoric monument consisting of a ring of huge standing stones, is located two miles west of Amesbury. And the huge Wiltshire White Horse carved in the late eighteenth century into the chalk on a hillside on Cherhill Down also is nearby."

Ben tossed the paper back on to the breakfront. "So you see, m'dear, we have enough places of historical importance to keep us fully occupied for the week."

"Really," Gwen mocked. "That certainly gives me a great deal to look forward to." She sidestepped quickly to elude Ben's grasp.

After supper, they moved into the sitting room and cuddled on a small sofa. "What's on that small plaque on the fireplace mantle?" Gwen asked.

Ben retrieved it and read,

"And Castle Combe presents this charming scene

Of hills, woods, and meadows cloth'd in green.

Here grand terrestrial scenes, almost celestial nice,

Make Castle Combe, sweet vale, an earthy Paradise.

Edward Dowling—Nineteenth Century.

"How sweet!" Gwen gushed. "This is such a beautiful place. I feel as though I could live here all my life, far away from war and all the stress of modern life."

"Yeah, it looks beautiful and inviting now, but you'd soon get bored with it and wanna get back to the real world," Ben said. Gwen punched him on the chest. "That's for pretending to be such a cynic," she huffed. "Ben Findlay, you are just as much a romantic as I am. You just think it isn't manly to admit it."

"Hey, I can be very romantic, and you seem to enjoy it."

"I don't mean that kind of 'romantic.' Now stop teasing me. I just want to relax and enjoy the serenity of this beautiful place. Don't you too?"

Ben, realizing his heavy-handed humor was misplaced, if not ill-timed, swept her into an embrace and whispered, "Of course I do, love. Just putting on my macho boor act, which I'm not very good at."

He planted a long kiss on her lips. "Now let's plan what we're gonna see and do for the rest of the week. We could pop over to Boscombe Down Air Station to see what Reggie's up to. It's just over the hill at Amesbury," he added with a sly smile. The smile faded quickly when she shot him a stern look.

They took long hikes into the lush rolling hills around Castle Combe, stopping at out-of-the-way pubs for modest lunches that unfortunately reflected the continued food rationing. One afternoon, Ben counted his savings from his USAAF pay and told Gwen to get into her formal uniform for a special dinner at the Manor House Hotel. The meal was not all that memorable, but the wine was excellent, and the setting in the fourteenth-century manor house made it an extra special evening out.

They rented bicycles and extended their excursions farther into the Wiltshire countryside surrounding Castle Combe, stopping on hilltops to enjoy beautiful vistas and savor picnic lunches Gwen had prepared. Closer to home, they explored the winding streets of Castle Combe, marveling at the wide array of charming cottages and the bustle of activity in Market Cross.

"Ben, I'll carry memories of this time here with you for the rest of my life," Gwen said, resting her head on his chest. "It would be ever so lovely someday to bring our children to this enchanted place and show them where it all began."

Ben started to point out that "it all began" a bit before this but thought better of it and settled for "yeah, it sure will."

The days flew by as is often the case when two people very much in love were having such fun. Suddenly, it was late Saturday afternoon, and Gwen busied herself straightening up the cottage and preparing to pack. A tap at the door interrupted her. She opened the door and found Mrs. Pengraves holding two wrapped pasty meat pies still warm from her oven and smelling mouth-wateringly delicious.

"Don't want to be a bother, love, but I thought these might do for a bit of supper." She beamed. "Been seeing you and the colonel about the village an' bicycling off on excursions. Dear me, you've been out and about quite a bit, obviously enjoying our little village and its surroundings."

"What a wonderful surprise," Gwen exclaimed. "Do come in. Would you like a cup of tea?"

Saying she hadn't meant to intrude, Mrs. Pengraves stepped inside. Gwen called to Ben upstairs and asked him to join them for tea.

Settled at the table, Mrs. Pengraves smiled and looked inquisitively at Ben. "So, Colonel Findlay, you're from America, come all this way to help us fight the Germans. Where is your home in America?"

"Michigan. I lived on a farm in the state of Michigan. That's in what we call the Midwest."

She peered closely at him. "My lor, you musta been a mere boy when you come here to fight in the war!" she exclaimed.

"I also flew as a volunteer pursuit pilot for the Republicans in the Spanish Civil War before coming here," Ben said.

Mrs. Pengraves' hand flew to her mouth. "But you couldn't been more'n a schoolboy then," she said in amazement. "Did your mother know ye were doin' that?"

"She sorta did but didn't know exactly what I was doin' in Spain." Ben smiled. "Anyway, that's all in the past now. What's important is my future with this lovely young lady," he added, taking Gwen's hand.

Mrs. Pengraves plied Gwen with questions about her family, where they lived, and what she did in the nursing corps, finally asking, "An' you'll be goin' to America to live now, dear?"

"Yes, perhaps sometime soon, when the war is totally over. We don't know where we'll be living. That'll depend on whether Ben stays in the army or returns to civilian life."

"My lord." Mrs. Pengraves sighed. "What an interesting life you've lived. And so young still. An' what a grand adventure ye 'ave ahead of you. God bless you both!"

Noting the time, Mrs. Pengraves quickly excused herself and thanked Gwen for the tea. "I best be getting on 'ome, or Mr. Pengraves will think I've run off with some handsome young man." She giggled.

"Oh, by the way, no need to spend a lot of time straightening up, dear. That's my job an' I'll see to it Monday mornin'. Jus' leave the key on shelf by the door." She gave the newlyweds a last long look and left.

Ben cocked an eyebrow at Gwen. "What a charming little lady." She giggled.

That night, their last in Castle Combe, Gwen snuggled against Ben in bed. "I haven't wanted to spoil our honeymoon by asking, love, but you said you'd tell me about the Regensburg mission and how you got that scar on your face."

Ben sighed. "Okay, Gwen. 'Bout time I told you the full story." He pulled her against him and began with a description of the Regensburg mission, how *Round Trip* was hit, and he was thrown clear. He detailed his capture, where he was held prisoner, and how they escaped through Poland. By the time he finished an hour later, Gwen was clutching him tightly and sobbing uncontrollably.

"Hey, hey, Gwen, it's all in the past. It's okay now. I made it, see?"

"Oh, Ben, when I realize how close I came to losing you, I'm frightened all over again. Please, please, tell me you won't have to go on to the Pacific for more fighting!"

"Chances are pretty good I won't have to, love."

They rolled into a passionate embrace and eventually fell into deep sleep.

Watkins arrived at ten o'clock, helped them into the Rolls, and drove down the hill on the way to Calvert Hall. Mrs. Pengraves stood in the doorway of "Journey's End," smiling and waving good-bye with a tea towel.

Chapter 51

BACK TO WORK

Watkins wheeled the Rolls up to Calvert Hall's main entrance, and Bates stepped out to greet them. "Hello, Bates, we're only going to make a quick stop to pay our respects and thank Lady Percy again for everything she's done for us," Ben said. "Watkins has our things packed in the car and will drive us on to Hawkestone Station to meet a C-47 coming in to pick us up."

"Right you are, sir. A Flight Leftenant Crenshaw has rung to say he'll arrive at Hawkestone at 1500 hours," Bates said. "Umm, that would be three o'clock this afternoon, would it not?"

"Yes. Great. That'll work fine," Ben said.

"Lady Percy and Elizabeth are waiting inside, sir. Lord Percy is back in London at the Air Ministry, and Wing Commander Percy has returned to his duties at Boscombe Down. But Lady Percy would like you to join them for a light lunch before you depart."

Ben turned to Gwen, who smiled and nodded. "I'd love to if we have the time, dear."

They lunched in the solarium, and Ben thanked Lady Percy for making their wedding such a special celebration. "Entirely our pleasure, dear boy," she responded. "We enjoyed every minute of it and are so happy to get better acquainted with this lovely lady," she added, reaching out to pat Gwen's hand. "We hope to welcome you back to Calvert Hall again soon. Will you be staying in England for some time, Benjamin, or will they be sending you back to America?"

"Not certain at this point, Lady Percy. I still have some bomb survey missions to complete, then we'll see what happens. We will be going back to the States eventually. I just don't know when."

"When you do go to America, I'd very much like to visit you," Elizabeth chimed in. "Remember you promised some time ago that you'd love to show me around your country."

Gwen cast Ben an amused look.

"Ah, Elizabeth, that's not exactly what I meant," Ben said, remembering his first meeting years ago with Elizabeth and how she had bombarded him with questions about the United States like an inquisitive schoolgirl. He had described the parts he had seen and said he'd like to explore the whole country. Elizabeth had taken this as an invitation to escort her on a grand tour of America.

"You mean, you wouldn't like me to visit you in America?" Elizabeth asked, crestfallen.

"We'd love to have you visit us, Elizabeth," Gwen cut in, flashing Ben a stern look. "Trouble is, we don't know when we're moving there or where we'll settle. Look, you've done me a great honor serving as my bridesmaid, and I'm so grateful to you for that. You'll always be welcome in our home. We'll certainly stay in touch with you and let you know where we settle."

Ben looked on impassively, not wanting to dig himself in any deeper. He was saved by the clock, which showed they had to leave if Watkins was to get them to Hawkestone in time to meet Crenshaw. They thanked Lady Percy again and apologized that they had to be going to make the rendezvous. Lady Percy and Elizabeth escorted them to the car. They paused for a round of hugs before stepping into the Rolls.

"Safe journey," Lady Percy said. "Do know you're welcome here at Calvert Hall at any time. "God bless you both." Elizabeth smiled bravely through her tears.

Ben helped Gwen settled into one of the C-47's less-than-comfortable bucket seats, strapped her in, and said he'd go to the cockpit for the takeoff. "Appreciate you picking us up," he shouted to Crenshaw. "Guess we're stretching the rules with Gwen, but she is still on active duty, so we're legal, right?"

"Of course, we're legal." Crenshaw grinned. "As long as no one in authority knows about it, we needn't worry about explaining ourselves."

"Yeah. Look, since we're already stretching things a bit, how about making a short diversion up to Station 415 at Cambridge? We could drop Gwen there, and she can get a taxi into town. Be a lot better than taking her to Daws and putting her on a train in High Wycombe for a long journey through London and up to Cambridge."

"Much more civilized." Crenshaw winked. "How do I explain this to operations at Daws?"

"Tell 'em I need to drop something off at Station 415 that has to be delivered to Parham. I think the runways are closed now, so we can't land there," Ben said.

"Done, and maybe we better do a quick fly past of Parham on the way back to Daws, just to confirm the runways are closed."

Crenshaw eased the C-47 onto the runway at Station 415 and taxied up to base operations. "I'll get Gwen through ops and arrange a taxi," Ben said. "Stand by, shouldn't take too long."

Ben held Gwen closely while they waited for the taxi. "Sorry we can't go home together, love. Have to wait to carry you over the threshold. Anyway, this is a lot better than saying good-bye for a long separation. I hope to wrap up the bomb survey work in the next month or so, and then we'll be able to figure out what we do."

He turned her face to his. "Are you comfortable about moving to the States when I get my new posting?"

"I'll go happily wherever you go, love," she said, kissing him. "Come see me as soon as you can."

The taxi arrived, and Ben helped her get in. He leaned in and gave her a long kiss. "Take care, beautiful lady. I'll be dreaming of you tonight." As the taxi moved away, she waved out the back window and blew him a kiss.

On their return flight to Daws, Crenshaw circled over Parham where, indeed, large white crosses had been painted on the runways. Ben sat deep in thought as they circled the base and headed southwest to Daws.

Ben huddled with General Sampson scanning the list of sites left to survey. These included a concentration of heavy industry sites in the Ruhr valley around Dortmund, Duisburg, Essen, Hagen, and Herne that Allied bombers had attacked repeatedly throughout the war.

"We need to wrap up these survey missions as soon as possible," Sampson said. "The Russians are becoming increasingly difficult to deal with, and the wrangling over who controls what parts of Germany is really heating up. We also need to complete our survey of

Berlin. Since it's inside the Russian sector, they might make it difficult for us to operate there."

"How accurate can any bomb survey of Berlin be?" Ben asked. "The city has been pulverized by artillery as well as bombing. And I understand the final battle for the city was fought hand to hand with machine guns, rifles, and grenades. I've even heard German troops fought the invading Russians with knives. I mean, how the hell are we supposed to tell who or what caused the damage we're documenting?"

"You have a point, Ben, but there are some sites that were specifically targeted from the air, and we need to determine how effective we were in hitting them."

"I suppose, but we faced some of the most intense flak defenses over and around Berlin, so I think a lotta groups fought their way in, dropped their loads wherever, and bugged the hell out for home," Ben said. "I remember how hard it was to find the aim points, so I'm not sure we put many bombs on target. Add to that the RAF's nighttime carpet bombing of the city and the Russians final massed artillery attacks, and we have a problem determining who did the most damage."

"True, but we still need a close-up look to try to determine what results we achieved. You flew a number of missions to Berlin, so I want you to concentrate your activities there. Assign the other teams to the Ruhr targets. Take at least three other teams into Berlin, assign them specific sectors of the city, and get some results as quickly as possible. Tempelhof Airport has been reopened, so base your operations there."

Ben pushed his survey crews to complete their assignments while he concentrated on Berlin. On their first visit, they found the central sections of the city pulverized into rubble, much like in the other major cities and industrial centers they had surveyed. But the city was not totally destroyed, and the outlying neighborhoods sustained less damage. Prominent landmarks like the Brandenburg Gate still stood, pockmarked and damaged, but largely intact.

The Reichstag on the large curve of the Spree River was a hallow shell, while the Olympic Stadium built for the 1936 summer games was relatively untouched. The shattered bell tower of the Kaiser Wilhelm Memorial Church loomed above the blackened remains of the cathedral, and all that remained of the Berlin Cathedral was a scorched shell. The Alexander Platz shopping center and nearby central train station were destroyed. The area around Hitler's underground bunker behind the Reich Chancellery was a moonscape of rubble—concrete and masonry mounds covering twisted beams and girders. Ben pushed his crews to complete their survey in three days.

"Hardly had time to phone Gwen, much less get up to Cambridge to see her," Ben grumbled to Crenshaw as they took off on the return flight to England. "Helluva way to start married life, but I guess it could be worse." Crenshaw grunted in reply.

They ran into a line of violent thunderstorms west of Berlin, causing them to continually shift their flight path to avoid the worst of the towering lightning-filled thunderheads. Saint Elmo's fire, the spectacular blue-violet plasma generated when a high-energy electrical charge ionizes air molecules around a structure moving through the field, formed a glowing ball on the aircraft's nose, hissing and buzzing like a hive of giant bees. Ben watched in fascination as what appeared to be tiny flames danced up the aircraft's nose, flicked around the windshield, and flashed to the leading edges of the wings. The static generated by the phenomenon temporarily cut out the radios.

Suddenly, a lethal bolt of lightning slashed across the windshield, temporarily blinding both pilots. Ben blinked and ducked as the brilliant flash triggered memories of his last mission over Regensburg in *Round Trip*. "Damn, that's too much like having a German 88 explode in your face," he yelled at Crenshaw. "Lucky this stuff is not as dangerous."

"Godalmighty!" Crenshaw yelled. "That was a bloody great smack. Everything looks back to normal, though. Lightning protectors seemed to have worked." These functioned like lightning rods on buildings, capturing the energy from the bolt and conducting it to metal wicks on the trailing edges of wings and the tail to be safely discharged.

The bolt obviously struck something on the aircraft, possibly the radio antenna atop the cockpit. The instrument panel lights blinked, and several instruments dropped off line then returned.

They penetrated a heavy rain squall, and Ben switched to flying on instruments. "Looks okay for the moment, but we're getting strange readings on the engine instruments," he said. "S'pose it might have damaged the engine ignition systems?" Crenshaw shrugged.

As if in reply, the mighty Pratt & Whitney R-1830 radial engine on the C-47's port wing surged, and began to run raggedly. Engine RPMs dropped, and the oil pressure fluctuated. Hansen, the crew chief, hunched over the throttle quadrant. "Can't figure out what's happening," he yelled.

"Hope we don't have to feather the damn thing," Ben shouted. "Don't want to wallow through this crap on one engine."

"May not have that luxury, Skipper," Crenshaw yelled, tapping the engine instruments. "Number 2 looks a bit sick too. Could be getting ready to pack it in as well."

Ben concentrated on flying the transport and maintaining their course, while Crenshaw and the flight engineer struggled with the fuel mixture to get the engines running smoothly. It was a losing battle. Both engines seemed well on the way to failing.

"We're at ten thousand feet," Ben yelled. "That gives us some time before we have to decide to bail out. Don't want to put the crew overboard in the blind at this altitude. What's the ground elevation at this point?"

"We're just west of the Elbe River. Pretty flat terrain down there, nearly sea level," Crenshaw said. "Can afford to trade some altitude to maintain airspeed. Suggest we press on and hope we break through this squall line. If we don't and can't keep the engines running, we'll still have time to bail out."

"I'll buy that," Ben said. "Appreciate it if you can keep the fans turning, though. I'll continue to concentrate on flying."

Despite their best efforts, the C-47's engines continued to lose RPMs. "Gotta descend to maintain airspeed," Ben yelled. "Watch the altimeter. Give me a heads up as we get close to five thousand feet. We'll decide then whether we jump."

"Getting lighter up ahead," Crenshaw yelled. "Might be getting through this muck. That'll open some other options."

They popped out of the squall line at six thousand feet, and Ben looked out across a broad flat plain of open fields. "Help me pick a field," he yelled. "We're still losing power on both engines. Maybe we got a bad bunch of gas at Tempelhof. Could it be water contamination? Whatever, now's the time for everybody to decide to jump or ride out a forced landing."

Crenshaw polled the crew on the intercom. All voted to stay with the airplane. "Everyone wants to stay onboard, Ben," he yelled. "Are we near any emergency strips?"

"Don't see any. Doesn't matter now. We're losing power on both engines. Need a place to put her down quickly before they both quit."

The words were barely out of his mouth when Number 1 engine coughed, sputtered, and stopped dead. "Feather Number 1!" Ben yelled. "Help me on the rudder pedals to keep her straight."

Scanning the terrain ahead, Ben spotted a fairly long field that looked level, covered with what appeared to be marsh grass. "Goin' for that field out there at one o'clock! Need to bleed off some altitude. Everybody brace for an emergency landing!"

With that, the Number 2 engine backfired and quit without warning. Crenshaw quickly feathered the second prop, and Ben was left flying a heavy glider with a lousy glide ratio. "Need that altitude now," he snarled, pushing forward on the control yoke to maintain airspeed.

They swooped silently toward the field. "Gonna be close," Ben grunted. "Leave the gear up. I'll put her in on her belly. Get ready to cut all switches. See any ditches or other obstacles?"

"Looks clear. No trees," Crenshaw said.

The powerless C-47 dropped at a high rate, and Ben eased back on the yoke to stretch the glide. The Gooney Bird shuddered on the verge of a stall but kept flying. They swept over a small road and a ditch, and Ben pulled back on the yoke to stall the aircraft and land. They slammed down in a nose-high attitude, and the shriek of the aluminum underbelly slashing through the tall course grass was earsplitting.

"Good show!" Crenshaw yelled. "Nicely done . . . Oh shit! Look out! Bloody great rock!"

They were still traveling fast when the right wing smashed into the rock, shearing off the outer section and spinning the airplane's nose violently to the right. The airplane pitched up and rolled sideways as the left wing dug into the ground, spewing up clods of dirt and grass. Ben clung to the control column as the airplane skidded another one hundred yards in this cocked angle. Finally, it lost momentum and slammed back onto its belly. Shock waves shot up his spine as he slammed back into his seat.

They sat momentarily stunned in the silence. "Everyone okay?" Ben yelled. "Get out before we catch on fire."

Hansen popped the aft cargo door, and they tumbled out. A strong odor of aviation fuel wafted across the field as they ran away from the wreck. The engines apparently were not hot enough to ignite the gas fumes, and Crenshaw had turned off all the switches, so there was no electrical ignition source.

They surveyed the wreck from a respectable distance as steam rose from the crushed grass along the crash path. "Everybody okay?" Ben asked. Assured no one was injured, Ben added, "Let's give it some more time before we get close. She's still leaking a lot of gas, an' it could still light off."

"Bloody good flying, Skipper," Crenshaw said. "If it hadn't been for that damn rock, we'd have slid to a nice smooth stop."

"Thanks," Ben grunted then sagged and dropped to his knees.

"You hurt?" Crenshaw asked, dropping to his knees next to Ben. "Don't see any blood. Any broken bones?"

"Nothing serious," Ben mumbled as pain lanced through his left shoulder, nearly causing him to vomit. "Jammed, uh, jammed my left shoulder. Same one I broke bailing out over Regensburg. Don't think it's broken again but feels like it could be dislocated. Shit!"

"Here, let's get you lying down," Crenshaw said, spreading his flight jacket on the grass. "Take some pressure off that shoulder." Ben groaned as the crew helped him lie flat. "Can I check out the shoulder, or will it hurt too much?" Crenshaw asked.

"Check it out, but go easy," Ben said. "Don't try to move it."

Crenshaw probed the shoulder carefully and checked the socket. "Feels like the socket is in place, Ben," he said. "You may have popped the joint, but I think it has slipped back in place now. Can you move the arm?"

"Lemme try," Ben grunted. "Yeah, you're right. I think it is back in place. "Hurts like hell, but I can move it."

"Do you need morphine?" Crenshaw asked. "We've got a full emergency medical kit on the airplane."

"Naw, I don't want anybody going back on the airplane until we're sure there's no more fire risk," Ben said. "Anyone got an aspirin?"

"Happen to have a packet in my pocket," Crenshaw said. "Have to shift you to get at it. Better take two."

They helped Ben sit up, and he took two tablets, working up saliva to help swallow them. He leaned against Crenshaw's legs. "Lemme rest here a while. The shoulder is feeling better already. Think I better fashion some kinda sling to support it, though." Crenshaw rigged a web belt around Ben's neck and looped it under his left elbow.

"Ah, much better. Thanks," Ben said. "Okay, let's figure out where we are and how we get the hell outta here."

"I say, the cavalry arrives!" Crenshaw shouted, pointing to a large British Army Bedford truck rumbling across the field toward them. "Must be a Brit Army unit bivouacked near here."

The driver honked the truck's horn and leaned out of the window. "Hallo," he called as he eased the truck to a stop and hopped out. "Saw you blokes prang from our camp a few miles back. Thought I'd better come over for a look-see. Bloody dicey emergency landing. Anyone injured?"

He saluted. "Corporal Simmons here. Part of an engineering battalion working on locks on a canal over there. Trying to get them functioning again."

"Couldn't have arrived at a better time, Corporal Simmons," Ben said, returning his salute. "I'm Colonel Findlay, commander of the U.S. Army Air Force's bomb survey group. We were en route back to England after surveying bomb damage in Berlin. Didn't get very far."

"No, sir, Colonel. You're only about seventy miles from Berlin. Nearest village is Osterburg, about ten miles north of here. We have several large engineering units working in the area. How about I run you and your crew over to headquarters? Umm, anything you want to retrieve from your airplane?"

"Yeah, there are charts and preliminary survey reports I want to take with us," Ben said, turning to Crenshaw. "Won't try to shift the motorcycles and survey gear. Whattaya think, Dick, is it safe to go back into the airplane?"

"I expect it should be as long as we don't turn on any switches. I'll fetch the reports. Just have to leave the rest of the stuff for the recovery crew."

Corporal Simmons radioed his unit, reported the crash, and asked them to relay a message to USSBS headquarters that Ben's crew had made a crash landing west of Berlin. No one was injured. He added the map coordinates of the crash site.

"Now, gentlemen, let me give you a lift to some place where a rescue crew can come and fetch you back to Berlin."

Chapter 52

JAPAN SURRENDERS! – AUGUST 14, 1945

Three days later, Ben checked in with General Sampson at Daws Air Station, having been picked up in Berlin by another USSBS crew. His shoulder still ached, but he had dispensed with the sling.

Ben had telephoned Sampson from Tempelhof where he and his crew had been taken for medical checkups. He gave Sampson details of the accident, including a preliminary report that the crash recovery team found significant amounts of water and contamination in the C-47's fuel tanks. No one could explain where the water had come from, but it had been found in the tanks of three other airplanes refueled at Tempelhof at about the same time as Ben's.

"Good to have you back, Ben," Sampson said as Ben walked into his office and saluted. "Take a seat. How's the shoulder?" Ben flexed his left arm. "Coming along. Fortunately, didn't break anything."

"Great! You've seen the flight surgeon here, right?"

Ben nodded. "He gave me some strengthening exercises and said to take it easy for a week or two. Guess I'll be off flight status until he clears me."

"Not a big problem, Ben. You and your crew had pretty much wrapped up the Berlin survey. And the other crews are well along with their surveys of the Ruhr sites. There's plenty of paperwork, report writing and such, to keep you busy without any flying."

Ben screwed up his face. "Yessir, I know. Can't say I look forward to that."

Sampson leaned back in his chair and smiled thinly. "Still, it has to be done." He picked up a folder. "Preliminary accident report says you did one helluva fine job of dead sticking your airplane into that field. Damn shame about the rock. Maintenance says the Gooney's a total write-off.

"Meanwhile, how about a three-day pass for you and your crew? Crenshaw can go home for a visit. The rest of the crew can spend some time in London. And you'd probably like a lift up to Cambridge."

"Right on, General. Many thank, sir. I'll give Gwen a call."

Ben hopped off the C-47 at RAF Station 415 and trotted into base operations. Gwen was waiting inside, beaming her beautiful smile through tears. She rushed into his arms.

"Ben, Ben, Ben," she whispered between kisses. "Are you all right? You said you hurt your shoulder. Is it better? Do you need to see a doctor? Does this mean you won't be flying any more survey missions?"

Ben cupped her face in his hands and kissed her into silence. "Slowdown, love, I'm okay. I'll be off flight status until the shoulder fully heals. Doc said a week or two. Meanwhile, we have three days. Let's go home." She led him outside to the waiting taxi she had taken from Cambridge.

At the door of her flat, Ben hefted her in his arms and, ignoring her protests and the pain in his left shoulder, carried her over the threshold. "Now, Mrs. Findlay," he said with a grin, "what's for supper?"

They spent three idyllic days being husband and wife, loving each other passionately, and going for long walks around Cambridge.

"I've decided to apply to the Flight Test Training Unit at Wright-Patterson air base," Ben said during one of their outings. "If they'll have me, I think it'd be a great job. I'll get a lot of professional pilot training and a chance to fly a range of airplanes. I'm really excited about the possibilities, and I hope you'll approve. I've heard some good things about Dayton, Ohio. Think you'll like it there."

"Ben, I still have reservations about the kind of flying you'll be doing," she said softly. "It might be dangerous, might'nt it? But if that's what you want, what will make you happy, then I'm fine with it." He wrapped her in a crushing bear hug.

Their long weekend passed all too quickly, and Gwen stood on her front steps waving good-bye as Ben rolled away in a taxi. He grinned and blew her multiple kisses.

Back at Daws, he and Crenshaw sat at his desk, completing reports on their latest surveys. The door burst open, and his sergeant clerk rushed in. "Sorry for the interruption, Colonel. Report just came in over Armed Forces Radio. Our fellas have dropped some kinda super bomb on a Jap city called Hiroshima. Apparently, this thing destroyed the whole city. One bomb, and Hiroshima is gone!"

"Thank you, Sergeant," Ben said, reaching to turn on the radio on his desk. "One bomb, eh?" he said, giving Crenshaw a long look.

Crenshaw stared back, openmouthed. "You thinking the same thing I am, Ben, of our conversation when we were surveying Stuttgart?"

"Yeah, don't I remember you saying if there was a 'next time,' maybe we'd have a super bomb that'd flatten everything, destroy cities and other major targets in one fell swoop so we wouldn't have to go back again and again to finish the job? Looks like we're at 'next time,' doesn't it?"

"I say, good god almighty," Crenshaw whispered. "What's the world come to?"

It was August 6, 1945, and the world had just come to the Atomic Age. An awesome genie had been let out of the bottle and would never be put back in again.

Updated reports of the Hiroshima bombing were mind-numbing. A single "silver plated" B-29, accompanied by two supporting B-29s, had carried a single bomb from Tinian in the Mariana Islands to the major Japanese port city. After dropping the weapon at an altitude of thirty one thousand feet, the B-29 pilot had dived and turned away to escape the shock wave from the blast. The bomb had detonated at an altitude of about two thousand feet, instantaneously obliterating over four square miles of the city and setting much of the rest on fire. It was estimated as many as one hundred thousand people were killed by the blast. These casualty estimates would be revised upward many times.

Ben and his fellow officers expected the Japanese government to sue for peace as soon as they realized the awesome power of America's atomic bomb arsenal. But nothing happened for two days, and on August 9, a second atomic bomb was dropped on Nagasaki, another important port city. Kokura, a nearby major industrial city with a huge munitions plant, had been the primary target, but heavy clouds and smoke obscured the city, forcing the B-29 crew to proceed to the secondary target, Nagasaki.

"Anybody know for sure where Hiroshima and Nagasaki are?" Ben asked. "Get the USAAF atlas outta the files. Let's locate 'em and see what we're talking about."

They found Hiroshima on the southwestern coast of Japan's main island of Honshu and Nagasaki on the southwestern tip of a peninsula off Japan's Kyushu Island. Both were major sea ports and munitions and military equipment manufacturing centers.

"How many of these super bombs do you suppose America has, Ben?" Crenshaw asked. "Can't have stockpiled large numbers, can they?"

"Dunno. This program has been so secret we don't know anything about it. Don't even know what an 'atomic' bomb is, some kind of really high-powered explosive compound I guess."

He paused. "Wonder if Frank Silverman had anything to do with this? All we know is they gave him command of some new B-29 wing that organized somewhere in Oklahoma and then apparently deployed to the Pacific. Interesting . . ."

Details of the atomic bomb attacks filtered out over the next several days as the Allies waited for Japan to respond to their demand for unconditional surrender. The Hiroshima mission was led by Colonel Paul Tibbets, commander of the recently formed 509 Composite Group that was given the responsibility of carrying out the atomic bomb attacks. His B-29 was named *Enola Gay*, honoring his mother Enola Gay Tibbets. The Nagasaki raid was led by Major Charles W. Sweeny, commander of the 393rd Bombardment Squadron from the 509th Composite Group. His B-29 was named *Bockscar*, named after the original pilot of the bomber.

America's President Harry S. Truman had ordered the bombs used in the belief they would bring a quick end to the war and eliminate the need for a costly and deadly invasion of the Japanese mainland. Meanwhile, the Soviet Union declared war on Japan as part of an earlier agreement to shift its military forces eastward following Germany's defeat in Europe, putting further pressure on Japan's military leaders.

Finally, on August 15, 1945, after protracted negotiations over the postwar status of Japan's emperor, Imperial Japan surrendered unconditionally, ending World War 2. The formal instrument of surrender was signed on September 2, 1945, in a ceremony, on the battleship USS *Missouri* in Tokyo Bay. General Douglas MacArthur, recently named Supreme Allied Commander in the Pacific, chaired the ceremony and signed the surrender agreement for the United States.

Ben had a long emotional telephone conversation with Gwen, who could not control her emotions. She laughed, sobbed, even screamed with joy when Ben said, "Yes, love, this means the war is over—totally over. There's no chance I'll be reassigned to a combat assignment in the Pacific."

After she settled down, Ben said, "Look, we have a lot of things to do here at Daws. This abrupt end of the war leaves us all with more questions than answers. Give me some time to help sort out where we are and more importantly where we're going, and I'll call you soon. Now get some sleep."

"Ben, I'm too excited and happy to sleep. I'm going to laugh, cry, and sing all night."

As news of Japan's surrender flashed around the world, a stunned public was shocked at how abruptly the war in the Pacific had ended. But the enormity of the atomic bomb attacks did not detract from the joyous celebrations that heralded the end of a global war that had engulfed Europe for nearly six awful years and the Pacific region even longer. The double edge of the atomic sword was yet to be felt.

Chapter 53

WRAPPING IT UP —

General Solomon called Ben and the other officers of the USSBS group to a staff meeting. "The news from the Pacific leaves us all a little stunned," he said. "We were following the progress of the fire-bombing missions in Japan and marveling at the amount of damage and casualties they inflicted on Tokyo and other major Japanese cities. But we thought there'd still be one helluva fight to invade and conquer the Japanese homeland."

He paused and looked around the table. "All that changed with two big blasts over Hiroshima and Nagasaki. And that's not all that changed. We suddenly live in a new age, the Atomic Age, and all bets are off concerning heavy aerial bombardment. I'm sure the USSBS will be airlifting special crews into Japan to assess the damage inflicted on those two cities by single A-bombs. Makes our work here look pretty insignificant by comparison."

He rose and paced the room. "I haven't heard formally, but my guess is High Command will order us to cease our bomb survey work in Europe. I think we've gathered enough data to satisfy the final report writers. And at this point, everybody will be focusing on assessing what happened in Japan. So for the moment, we will stand down until we get further orders.

"You've all worked very hard on the survey missions, and I appreciate your efforts. Now I want all of you to take a breather. Colonel Findlay will work up a leave roster that'll give all of you some time off. We'll do it on a rotating basis so we can keep a minimum number of crews on alert.

"Thank you again for your excellent work," he concluded. "Ben, please take charge."

"Okay, sir. Flight Leftenant Crenshaw and I'll get to work immediately on the leave roster," Ben said. "If anyone has special requests or needs that have to be addressed, let us know soonest. Otherwise, we'll work it out on a seniority basis. If we keep a minimum of three crews available while the rest are on leave, that should be enough."

They completed the roster by the end of the day and began releasing pilots and crews on leave the next morning. "How about you, Ben?" Crenshaw asked. "You want to get up to Cambridge I suppose?"

"Yeah, but I just had a long weekend with Gwen. You take next week, Dick, and I'll mind the store. The following week works fine for me. Got a lot of paperwork to catch up on." That paperwork included submitting a formal request that he be assigned to the USAAF Test Training Unit.

When his turn came, Ben spent a blissful week with Gwen in Cambridge and returned to Daws refreshed and anxious to receive word on his next assignment. Two weeks passed at a desultory pace. All bomb survey missions were put on hold, while they waited for expected orders to disband the group. Ben watched each day's mail for word on his test pilot's school application.

Finally, an envelope arrived from USAAF headquarters. Ben opened it with shaking hands. "Eyowee!" he yelled, pumping his fist in the air as he read the words "accepted for assignment to the USAAF Flight Test Training Unit at Wright-Patterson Air Base, Dayton, Ohio." Reassignment and travel orders would be issued in about thirty days.

He quickly telephoned Gwen. "This means we'll be heading to the States by November at the latest, m'love. Maybe home in time for Thanksgiving!"

Gwen brushed aside her concerns about his new flying job and joined Ben in the excitement of the moment. "Oh, Ben, this is wonderful! I'm so looking forward to seeing America. I'll miss England, of course, but there's so much to look forward to with our new life in America. Where exactly is Dayton, Ohio? What's the climate like? Is Ohio a big province, umm, I mean, state? I'm going to find an encyclopedia and read all about it."

"I've never lived in Ohio, so I don't know much about it," Ben said. "Probably not much different from Michigan, except there won't be as many lakes. I think you'll like it."

They chatted on for another twenty minutes, discussing among other things how and when she would give notice at the hospital and resign from the nursing corps. Ben finally said he had a big to-do list, including phoning Reggie with the news. "I'll try to get up to see you week after next, Gwen. Until then, keep well and know how much I love you." She sent him a smacking kiss.

Ben telephoned Reggie.

"I say, good show, Sancho!" Reggie shouted. "Won't be as good as our Empire school of course, but they might be able to make you into a test pilot anyhow," he teased. "Thinking ahead, we might have some joint exercises in the future, maybe even a pilot exchange program. All sorts of exciting possibilities, eh? When do you leave?"

Ben said he wouldn't have his formal orders for another thirty days or so, which left time for them to get together for proper good-byes. He added he wasn't sure how he and Gwen would travel, but he'd request going by ship rather than flying. "I'd like a leisurely boat ride of five days or so. Give us both time to really relax and make a gradual transition for Gwen. Might be able to get a ship out of Southampton, which would be great. We could swing by Calvert Hall for a final visit."

"Capital! That'd be wonderful," Reggie said. "My folks and Elizabeth would really enjoy that. I'll arrange to be there as well, umm, perhaps with Beatrice."

They hung up and Ben stepped down the hall to General Sampson's office. "Come in, Ben. Take a seat," he boomed. "Got some news to share. My next assignment has come through. Going to Offutt Field outside Omaha, Nebraska, as chief USAAF liaison officer with the Glenn L. Martin Company there. They were one of the primary producers of the Boeing B-29. In fact, they built the two bombers that dropped the atomic bombs on Hiroshima and Nagasaki. Should be an interesting and challenging job."

"Congratulations, General. That sounds great. I have a bit of news myself. My assignment to the USAAF Flight Test Training Unit at Wright-Patterson came through." Ben grinned. "Gonna learn how to be a professional test pilot."

"Damn fine! I'm hearing good things about the school. That'll be a great assignment. And by the way, good timing for both of us," he said, reaching for a telex on his desk. "I've just been informed that our USSBS unit is to be deactivated as early as next month. So we'd all be looking for new jobs."

"I see. What's the schedule for deactivation?" Ben asked. "I expect to have my new assignment and travel orders confirmed in thirty days or so."

"That might work out just right," Sampson said. "It'll probably take us a month to get all the paperwork completed, get all personnel transferred, and dispose of the C-47s, motorcycles, and survey equipment. Not sure about the airplanes and equipment, but I'll find someone to take that on."

He leaned back in his chair. "Now then, how about your new wife? Can you arrange concurrent travel back to the States for Gwen as well?"

"I haven't asked yet," Ben said. "Wonder if I need my formal orders first or if I can start that ball rolling with this early notification letter?"

"Take it to Colonel Perkins in personnel. He'll help you with the red tape," Sampson said. "Man's a whiz at working with the regulations."

Ben gathered his group staff and passed on the word about the deactivation. All took it as great news that they would be heading home soon. Ben turned to Crenshaw. "Dick, I've enjoyed working with you on these surveys. You've been a big help. I don't know how the RAF works, so can't say where this leaves you. Will you go back to some kind of a pilot pool?"

"Reckon I'll be put on extended administrative leave pending a decision on whether I will stay on active duty or be demobbed with a lot of other blokes," he said. "At any rate, I'm going to be available to help with the deactivation to the very end."

The next few weeks passed in a blur as Ben waded through the paperwork swamp to get the unit deactivated and oversee disposition of its airplanes and equipment. Colonel Perkins helped him file an application for concurrent travel for Gwen and request ship transportation back to the States. While waiting for a response, Ben fussed over what seemed like an inordinate amount of time for the requests to be processed.

"Need patience, Ben," Perkins said when Ben had called him for the fourth time in so many days. "Military bureaucratic wheels grind slowly in normal times. Now with a lot of work piling up because of the number of units being deactivated and troops being sent back to the States, things are going to move even more slowly. You may not hear until the last minute."

"Okay, okay, I'll try not to get so antsy," Ben said. "But Gwen has to wrap up her duties at the Cambridge hospital and resign from the WAAF nursing corps as well and get ready for the move. Really appreciate your efforts so far and grateful for any help you can offer in expediting things."

Finally, official word arrived, and it was all good news. The army granted Ben and Gwen concurrent travel, citing Ben's willingness to remain behind in England to conduct the bomb survey missions. They were booked on RMS *Queen Mary* for the trip to the States, departing from Southampton on Monday, November 15. Ben was issued a thirty-day transit pass to get to Wright-Patterson and awarded an additional two-week home leave en route. This meant they could spend Christmas with his family in Michigan before checking in at the Flight Test Training Unit on December 29. The full package of reassignment orders, travel vouchers, and related documents would be delivered to Ben within fifteen days.

"That gives us six weeks to wrap up everything here before heading home," Ben mumbled. "Damn tight, but I think we can do it."

He reached for the phone to call Gwen. "Good news, m'love. We got our orders. We sail on RMS *Queen Mary* from Southampton on Monday, November 15." This prompted a moment of stunned silence from Gwen. She soon regained her composure and squealed with delight.

"We'll have a two-week home leave en route to Ohio, so we can spend Christmas and meet the whole family. I think my brother will be home on leave pending his next assignment. Can't wait to see him again and introduce you."

Ben dug into the administrative tasks related to deactivating the USSBS group, determined to wrap them up within the next two weeks. Sampson called him into his office and said he had one more mission for Ben to fly.

"Headquarters wants our Gooney Birds flown up to USAAF Station 102 at RAF Alconbury near Huntingdon. Apparently, long-range plans call for keeping Alconbury open as a USAAF air base for an extended period, so they're gathering airplanes that aren't going back to the States. We have nine left after your one-way trip to Berlin. I'm told the one you pranged has been written off."

"Not surprised," Ben said. "The right wing was pretty badly damaged and the props and probably a lotta belly panels as well. Uh, okay on the ferry flight. When are we talking about, in a couple of days?"

"Don't think there's any rush, but getting them off our books here is one more thing we can scratch from the to-do list. They're all airworthy, aren't they? No reason we can't fly 'em all off together, is there?"

Ben thought for a moment. "No, in fact, I'd like to take them up there together. Might use them for a little air show here and along the way," Ben said.

"Oh? What's you plan?"

"How about I form a nine-ship diamond formation, buzz the field here after takeoff, and then buzz Alconbury in formation before landing. In fact, we could do a formation flyby over Cambridge, since it's on the way. Give the folks there a little air show," Ben added with a grin.

"Hmm, see your plan, Ben. There's a certain young lady who's still a nurse in the Cambridge hospital, right?" Ben nodded. "Okay, no harm in that. You comfortable with the formation flying skills of all the pilots?"

Ben nodded. "Yeah. Besides, it'll be a simple formation, and we won't do any fancy maneuvering. It'll be a treat for our fellas, better than flying a boring ferry flight in string up there."

"Okay, Ben, sounds harmless enough. Just don't break anything."

Ben gathered the pilots and told them of the plan. All agreed it would be fun. He briefed them on the takeoff sequence and how they would join the formation, drawing the diamond grouping on a blackboard. "I'll take the lead in ship one, and you, Scotty and Stan, in ships two and three, tuck in tight off the outer trailing edges of my horizontal tail. Al, you, George, and Sammy position ships 4, 5, and 6 here, off the tails of Scotty's and Stan's airplanes. Frank and Jess, you position ships 7 and 8 here, and finally, Norm, you position ship 9 here in the slot position. Bingo, we have a neat diamond formation that'll look swell. Any questions so far?" All shook their heads.

"Good, piece of cake as our Brit friends would say. "We'll have a practice run tomorrow morning. Takeoff at 0700, form up west of here over Watlington, see how tight we can hold the formation and then do some gentle maneuvering. Then I'll lead us into a wide left turn, and we'll shift into a string formation in numerical order. On our return to Daws, we'll land with minimum separation.

"'Couple more things," Ben said, pointing to a map of England on the ops room wall. "After we leave Daws, we'll hold the diamond formation en route to Alconbury. We can loosen it up a bit for the cross-country leg to reduce the strain of close formation flying. Everybody comfortable with that? Good. We'll fly a northeast track direct to Cambridge, tighten the formation, and circle the city twice. Give 'em a little air show."

"And show off to a certain nurse there," Crenshaw joked.

"Well, yeah. Is that okay?" No one objected. "Right. Then we'll proceed northwest to Alconbury."

The practice run went smoothly, and Norm in the trailing positions said the formation looked very good. After landing back at Daws, Ben called the tower and briefed them on the plan for the next day's ferry flight. "We'll takeoff, join the formation, and come back for two low-level passes along the runway," he said. "On the final pass, we'll give everybody a group wing-waggle and head north for Alconbury via Cambridge." He then phoned Alconbury and briefed them on their arrival and the two low-level formation flybys. Said he'd radio the tower when they leave Cambridge with a more precise arrival time.

Ben called Gwen that evening. "I'm gonna be flying overhead tomorrow, love, leading nine of our C-47s up to Alconbury. We'll do a couple of circles over Cambridge en route to show off our formation flying skills. Takeoff will be 0700 hours, and we'll do two formation flybys here at Daws before heading north. Expect us overhead between 0830 and 0900."

"Oh, that'll be such fun, Ben! Will you be able to stop by and see me and not just fly overhead? Be ever so nice to see you . . ."

"Sorry, not this time, Gwen. Got a thousand things to finish at Daws. Say, what's the word on your requests to resign from the hospital and the WAAF nursing corps?"

"Both sets of paperwork are circulating in the system. I've been told unofficially there'll be no problem with either. Soon I'll be just plain old Mrs. Gwen Findlay, war bride."

"Poor thing," Ben chided. "I'll do my best to make it up to you." They chatted a while longer before ringing off.

The departure airshow went smoothly. Ben grinned when he saw a large contingent of the Daws personnel out on the ramp, waving as they swept past on their last flyby. He radioed the other pilots, "Okay, now we hold the formation to Cambridge and Alconbury. Loosen it up a bit en route and then shift in good and tight for the flybys. Everyone comfortable with that?" The eight other pilots responded "Roger that" in sequence.

They arrived over Cambridge, and as they descended to 1,500 feet, Ben searched for Addenbrooke's Hospital. Spotting it, he rolled his C-47 into a gentle left turn, and the formation swept past it. He laughed when he spotted Gwen and what seemed to be most of the hospital staff gathered on the roof, waving what looked like tea towels.

At Alconbury, a crowd gathered on the ramp to watch the C-47 formation roar past at an altitude of 750 feet. As they completed the second run, Ben radioed, "Okay, great show all. Follow me another couple of miles out, and I'll lead us into a wide left turn so we can shift into string formation for the landing."

Ben slid his C-47 onto the runway, touched the throttles to keep the tail elevated, and rolled to the taxiway turnoff at the far end of the runway. As he turned, he glanced back and saw the tight string formation of C-47s on final approach. Two already were on the runway and rolling out behind him.

"Last time I'll fly anything in Merry Ol' England," he said to Crenshaw. "Got enough memories to last me a lifetime." Crenshaw grinned and gave him a thumbs-up.

Ben met with Alconbury's deputy commander, signed over the C-47s, and joined the other pilots in the officer's club for lunch. The nine flight engineers headed for the enlisted men's club. After lunch, they boarded an Alconbury C-47 for the trip back to Daws.

Chapter 54

HOMEWARD BOUND – NOVEMBER 1945

The next weeks passed quickly as Ben completed his to-do list. Gwen's paperwork came through, and she completed her duties at Addenbrooke's Hospital and resigned from the WAAF nursing corps. Ben was unable to join her going-away party at the hospital, which she reported was a wonderful affair.

"I'm going to really miss all my good friends here," she told Ben on the phone. "We've been through so much together. And now I may never see them again." She choked back a sob and added quickly, "But I'm soon off on a grand adventure in America, and that makes up for a lot."

She said she had found a renter for her flat who also bought her furniture and kitchen appliances. "So I'm reduced to a steamer trunk and two suitcases. Not sure yet where I'll stay until we board the ship in Southampton."

"Yes, I've been pondering that as well," Ben muttered. "Haven't worked out the details yet."

As usual, Reggie provided a solution. During a phone chat with Ben, he asked about Gwen's situation. "She's rented her flat, sold everything she's not taking with her, and now is looking for a place to stay until we board the *Queen Mary*," Ben said. "She has a steamer trunk and two suitcases."

"That's easily solved. We'll get Gwen, bag and baggage, on a train to Southampton where Watkins will meet her with the Roller and take her to Calvert Hall. Mother and Elizabeth will be thrilled to have her as a houseguest until you can join her. It'll be a short trip from there to Southampton the day of your departure."

Ben gulped. "Reggie, this is too much! Are you sure it'll be all right with your mother?"

"Of course, of course. I'll confirm it with her, but I see no problem, really. When do you wrap things up at Daws? Can you get away to spend a few days at Calvert Hall as well? 'Himself' ought to be able come down from London, and Beatrice and I can join the party. It'll be a grand send-off."

Ben clutched the phone. "Reggie, I'm at a loss for words. We can never thank you enough for everything you've already done for us. And now this. Gwen will be 'over the moon' as she likes to say."

"Not at all, old bean. We go back quite a ways, eh? Glad to help. You can repay me when I come to America for a visit."

"It'll be a privilege and honor, Reggie."

"Umm, Ben, a passing thought. I'm wondering if I can justify running an Anson up to Cambridge on some sort of errand? Could bring Gwen back down here to Boscombe Down, and it'd be a short run for Watkins to come and fetch her . . ."

"No! No, Reggie, thank you for the thought. I really appreciate it, but that would be pushing the system too much. You must know that it could end up being a career limiting caper. Thanks all the same. I'll arrange train tickets for Gwen. When should she come down?"

"Sooner the better. Now what about you? What kind of baggage will you be dragging along?"

"I'll have a footlocker, a B-4 bag, and one suitcase. Since this is an official transfer for me, I'll have transportation ship the locker and B-4 bag to the dock, and I'll collect it before we board the ship."

"Excellent! Now your departure is only ten days from now. How soon can you wrap things up at Daws? Can you hitch a ride to Hawkestone Station? The RAF are keeping it open a bit longer to support a lot of transportation flights still coming out of Germany."

"I'll see what I can arrange, Reggie. Shouldn't be too difficult. We still have a lot of logistics flights wandering around England. Meanwhile, our USSBS group is planning a going-away party for me day after tomorrow."

It was a rousing party, hosted by General Sampson, who had announced earlier that he, too, was leaving soon for his new assignment at Offutt Air Force Base. The attendees toasted and roasted the two officers for successfully leading the group, now known by their self-proclaimed title as the "Whole Counters." Ben dropped all restraints and participated fully in the festivities. It was, after all, his last hurrah in England. His hangover the next morning was intense but tolerable.

The next day, Ben hitched a ride on a High Wycombe C-47 bound for Portsmouth. He had called Reggie with the travel arrangements, and Watkins was waiting at Hawkestone Station when the C-47 crew dropped him off before proceeding to Portsmouth.

The Rolls pulled up at Calvert Hall, and Gwen rushed into his arms before he had completely stepped out of the car. She kissed him, laughed, and cried all at the same time as he struggled to stand upright. "Well, hello, Mrs. Findlay, nice to see you too," he mumbled as she covered his face with kisses. "Mmm, you look delicious in that pretty dress." He had never seen her in civilian clothes.

Stepping inside, Ben was treated to a round of warm embraces from Lady Percy, Elizabeth, and Beatrice. "Okay! Wouldn't mind doing another round of that," he joked. Gwen grinned and pinched him.

"Umm, I happen to be here too, old man," Reggie quipped. "But don't expect a hug from me." Ben shook hands vigorously and gave him a backslapping bear hug anyway.

After dinner, Ben sat in the Calvert Hall conservatory sipping scotch with Reggie, while Lady Percy, Gwen, Beatrice, and Elizabeth gathered for coffee in the sitting room.

Ben swirled his drink and contemplated everything that had transpired since he received his transfer orders. "I guess Gwen and I accomplished everything needed to wrap up our lives in England," he said. "If anyone calls and says there's something else I need to do, tell 'em I ain't home."

Reggie chuckled. "Do believe you've done enough, Sancho. And you're taking home a real prize. Gwen looks radiant. Stunning lady."

"As is Beatrice, my friend. How's your relationship progressing?"

"Proceeding smoothly. Might even say heating up, Ben. We're both seriously considering making it a lifetime contract."

"Hey, that's great! No wedding plans yet I guess?" Reggie shrugged. "Not quite yet but could be sooner than you think."

"What a damn shame we're leaving in two days," Ben said. "I could return the favor of serving as your best man. Any chance you could finalize things before we leave?"

"Hardly, but thanks for the thought."

When they finally retired to bed, Ben was amused to find he and Gwen were no longer assigned adjoining rooms. They crawled into bed and spent a long and loving night in each other's arms.

Lord Percy arrived late Saturday afternoon, and Ben and Reggie sat with him in the library. Bates entered with a tray of drinks. "I say, thank you, Bates," Lord Percy rumbled. "Good of you to anticipate my needs." He turned to Reggie and Ben. "As for you two. You both look pleased as punch. War's over, thank God, and you have interesting assignments in the flight testing world. Add to that you're beautiful women, and what more can you ask for?"

"Not much, Father," Reggie replied. "So far, my new assignment is super. Still have a lot work to develop professional test pilot skills, but it's coming along nicely."

"And you, Ben," Lord Percy said, "you'll be doing essentially the same thing in your new assignment?"

"Yessir. The USAAF has taken the lead from Reggie's outfit at Boscombe Down, but I think we'll also develop a testing regime that specifically addresses our needs. Hopefully, we can have cooperative programs along the way."

"Fine, fine. We're going to have to cooperate closely with the American militarily. Don't trust the bloody Bolsheviks one bit. Stalin's already proving to be a questionable ally, if I can even call him that anymore. Russians already have most of Eastern Europe under their thumb. Not much hope of relief for them following the war. Our next adversary is Mother Russia and her block of captive countries. Democracy versus Communism. Hope to God it doesn't degenerate into another shooting war."

They gathered for a formal dinner to honor Ben and Gwen and send them on their way to a new life in America. Ben sniggered when he remembered some past memorable dinners at Calvert Hall. He resolved to behave himself and not distress anyone with his pretend Bohemian table manners. Two sets of eyes gazed at Ben throughout the meal—Gwen's eyes gleaming with love, excitement, and happiness, and Elizabeth's, which resembled a mournful beagle's eyes about to spill tears.

Sunday started with a brief service in the Calvert Hall chapel and was capped with a sumptuous midafternoon lunch. Lord Percy left that evening, wishing the newlyweds Godspeed on their journey to America.

"I say, what's the schedule for tomorrow's departure?" Reggie asked.

"We sail at 1730 hours, but they want us checked in by 1530 and be onboard by 1700," Ben said. "What time should we leave here?"

"Probably take an hour plus for Watkins to get you to the wharf. I should think leaving here at 1400 hours would suffice. We'll send you off with Watkins in the Roller, and then I'll drive the Rover down with Mother, Beatrice, and Elizabeth."

"Reggie, you don't have to . . ."

"Nonsense. We'll see you off from the wharf with flags waving."

They said their final good-byes while being jostled by the crowd on the wharf. All four women embraced with tears streaming down their cheeks. Ben and Reggie quietly chatted about their new assignments. Finally, it was time to board. Ben did another round of hugs and turned to Reggie.

"This is 'so long,' old friend, not good-bye," he said, struggling to control the lump forming in his throat. "Look forward to seeing you in the States. Have a lot more to say, but I'm not sure I'm up to it right now."

"Smile, Sancho. Got some exciting times ahead of us. At the moment, I really don't have the words to say a proper good-bye, excuse me, I mean 'so long' as you say. They'll come to me as I lie awake some dark night. Have to write them down and send you a maudlin letter, eh?"

He took Ben by the shoulders. "Now take this beautiful lady onboard. We'll find some place to have a cuppa tea and come back for the actual departure. Need to be sure you actually leave."

Ben stood on the aft deck of the ship as the tug boats nudged the *Queen Mary* out of her berth and into the main channel. Gwen, dressed in her new going-away outfit nestled against him. As they cleared the docks, Ben gripped the railing, watching four figures standing at the end of the quay. Reggie snapped to attention, raised his right hand in salute, and held it. Ben returned the salute as the ship moved away. Then as if they both heard the same command, they clenched their right fists and gave each other the arm-raised salute of the Spanish Republican Army.

Tears blurred Ben's vision as the lights of Southampton faded into the mist. He swallowed repeatedly, trying unsuccessfully to clear the lump in his throat. He clutched Gwen, who held his arm and peered up at his anguished face.

"What's wrong, love?" she whispered. "We're going home, and we're together." Home! That she would call it "home" made Ben's heart skip a beat.

"I know, I know," he choked. "Just remembering my first boat trip with Ted and the other fellas, on our way to Spain on the ol' rust bucket 'Escobar.' What a miserable tub that was. After we got through that awful storm in the middle of the ocean, an' knew we weren't going to die, Ted and I spent a lot of time talking about our lives. You know, what we were going to do after we finished that business in Spain.

"Oh god!" he choked, pounding his fist on the railing. "How dumb and naive we were! We thought we'd sashay into Spain, help whip the Nationalists, and go home heroes." Sobs welled up in his throat.

"There, there, love," Gwen whispered, wiping his wet cheeks. She kissed him softly. "You had no idea what you were getting into, how it was going to turn out."

"Oh, I guess so, but that doesn't make it any easier. Gwen, I still miss Ted somethin' awful. Feel guilty, I guess, about his getting killed. And then all those great fellas I flew with and later commanded. I can't begin to remember all their names. But a lotta their faces are still fresh in my mind, and, uh, and I dream about them. And now I'm leaving that crazy bloke back there on the quay. Owe him more than I can ever repay."

"Of course, you're sad about parting with Reggie, dear. And you probably miss Ted the most because you bonded at such a young age. But you can't blame yourself for his death. You had no control over that or all of your other comrades who've been killed or gone missing. You have to let go of it, love. Besides, we have each other, and so much to live for."

"You're right, of course, Gwen," he added, giving her a sad smile.

After a pause, he turned and clasped her face in his hands. "You, sweet thing, I can't tell you how much I love you! Look, I don't know how much longer I'll stay in the army. I'm excited about joining the Experimental Test Pilots' School, but I don't know that I want to make the army a career. Too many awful experiences, too many bad memories. I first thought they'd want me to step up to Boeing's B-29 bomber—man what a machine that must be—but not much sense to it now that the war's over. Much better future as a test pilot I guess."

"Ben, I know how important staying in some sort of flying job is to you. If the test pilot's job doesn't work out, you'll find some other way to stay in aviation."

He turned back to the rail. Southampton had dissolved into a bright glow in the mist. "If it doesn't work out with the test pilot's school, I'll be part of a big surplus of pilots, and the army might just want to me get out right away."

"Ben, whatever you decide to do, I'll be at your side."

He grabbed her shoulders and kissed her long and hard. She gasped when he released her. "Dear me, that was enough to take one's breath away."

"Look, Gwen, you know how Ted and I talked a lot about our airport idea, how we'd like to open our own airport after the war. That won't happen with Ted, of course, but maybe I could find another partner who wants to join with me if we're both released from active duty. I dunno. My thoughts are all mixed up right now."

Ben swallowed and bent to peer into Gwen's face. "Umm, whataya think, will you be happy in the Midwest? If I don't stay in the army and we leave Ohio, maybe in Michigan or Minnesota? There are lots of beautiful spots out there. An', an' if it comes to that, we could find a little airport or maybe buy a farm and build our own airstrip. Gwen, it could be a swell life!"

She pressed herself to him, hugged him fiercely. "Oh, Ben, that would be ever so lovely!"

He grinned and kissed her again. *Ever so lovely. Wonder how that's gonna play back home?*

The End

Author's biography for Don Fink—*Return from the Abyss*

Donald E. Fink, Jr., a native of Michigan, attended high school in Minnesota and earned a bachelor's degree in journalism from the University of Minnesota. He learned to fly at the age of fifteen and, after receiving a commission through the university's AFROTC program, served four years in the U.S. Air Force, including three years with NATO in France.

After completing his Air Force active duty commitment, he joined the McGraw-Hill Companies in New York City and started a thirty-five-year career with *Aviation Week & Space Technology Magazine*. He had assignments in *Aviation Week* bureaus in Washington DC; Geneva, Switzerland; Paris, France; Los Angeles; and finally New York. He was named assistant managing editor and managing editor and served the last ten years as the magazine's editor in chief, with additional duties as editorial director for *Aviation Week*'s group of magazines, newsletters, and television productions.

Fink holds commercial single and multiengine ratings in fixed wing aircraft and helicopters. His assignments with *Aviation Week* involved flying civilian and military aircraft and helicopters for pilot reports published in the magazine. The highlight of these activities involved flying the USAF/*Lockheed U-2* high-altitude reconnaissance aircraft on a long-endurance mission with a *U-2* instructor. He lives in Virginia with his wife Carolyn. They have three married sons and five grandchildren.

Synopsis of

RETURN FROM THE ABYSS
BY DON FINK

Ben Findlay, a young Michigan farm boy, is thrust early into manhood while flying as a volunteer fighter pilot for the Republican Air Force in the Spanish Civil War. When the Republic falls in 1939, he escapes to England and flies Spitfires as a volunteer pilot with the Royal Air Force during the Battle of Britain and the early years of World War 2. When the United States enters the war, Ben transfers to the U.S. Army Air Forces and opts to fly B-17 bombers with the U.S. Eighth Air Forces, then the only American military units carrying the war directly to the German homeland.

While flying his thirtieth bombing mission, the one that would qualify his crew to return to the United States, Ben's bomber, *Round Trip*, is ripped apart by a direct hit from a German 88 mm antiaircraft shell, fired from a flak emplacement, defending Regensburg, Germany. Ben is knocked unconscious and ejected from the disintegrating airplane. He falls thousands of feet before coming to and deploying his parachute. He lands near the flak nest that shot him down.

Return from the Abyss, a sequel to the author's earlier novel, *Escape to the Sky*, traces Ben's odyssey as he is captured with a broken shoulder by German Wehrmacht soldiers. After recovering in a German hospital, Ben is questioned and tortured by the Gestapo and sent to the Luft III prisoner of war camp. Thus begins a wild adventure that includes a bizarre escape from captivity, a trek to freedom across occupied Poland, and a clandestine ship ride back to England.

Ben returns to duty, and the reader rides with him on several harrowing bombing missions deep into Germany as the war in Europe winds down. Ben is reunited with Gwen, the British nurse he met while hospitalized, recovering from wounds suffered when he bailed out of a flaming Spitfire earlier in the war. World War 2 ends, first in Europe and then in the Pacific Theater, when the United States drops atomic bombs on Hiroshima and Nagasaki. Ben remains in England after hostilities end in Europe to lead a group conducting bomb damage assessments for the U.S. Strategic Bomb Survey before returning to the States.

Edwards Brothers Malloy
Thorofare, NJ USA
June 15, 2015